BROTHER'S KEEPER

A Novel by

Edgar Hulse

© 1998, 2001 by Edgar Hulse. All rights reserved.

No part of this book may be reproduced, stored in a retrieval system, or transmitted by any means, electronic, mechanical, photocopying, recording, or otherwise, without written permission from the author.

ISBN: 0-7596-7954-1

This book is printed on acid free paper.

BROTHER'S KEEPER

And the Lord said unto Cain, "Where is Able thy brother?"
And he said, "I know not: Am I my brother's keeper?"

Genesis 4:9

For Phyllis, loving wife, reluctant editor

PROLOGUE

Wednesday October 30, 1929

Jonathan Freeman stood at the third floor brokerage office window looking out over downtown Scranton. The morning sun tinting the eastern sky shed little warmth on his miserable day. Behind him ticker tape machines click-clicked, spelling in precise digits the calamity of yesterday's, Black Tuesday 's, sell off. A theater marquee across the street and two stories below advertised a gangster movie, "Gunned Down." He tugged at his ear, *that sums up how I feel.*

He turned and surveyed the office. More than half the desks were empty, and the balance occupied by hollow-eyed automatons and in the air the smell of dust and despair. On the desks were telephones, perched like ravens, morbidly silent. The usual office banter was suppressed as stunned people tried to assess the situation and pull themselves together after the fourteen million-dollar careening market drop of the day before. If they hadn't experienced it themselves, they would have been informed by the morning headlines of any newspaper in the land reporting the collapse with I-told-you-so glee.

Standing, homberg in hand, he stroked the variegated beard that partially covered the breast of his funereally dark suit, a suit that he deemed appropriate for the day. Jonathan Freeman would be 70 years old on the day before Thanksgiving, and thought the calamity a singularly ironic birthday present.

He was in the brokerage office to obtain a more precise appraisal of his losses; losses that he estimated at one quarter million dollars. The general communications breakdown over the previous twenty-four hours had convinced him of the need for a personal visit. The funds with which he had speculated represented the entire cash reserve of his business and his personal savings. He squinted, *a seventy-year-old fool.*

Lost. Everything he had earned since stepping off the boat from Liverpool in 1890. Almost everything. He still retained a few unmortgaged properties. "Enough to support me until they plant me," he muttered.

He thought of his grandchildren who had been enjoying life, cruising along at half speed in the anticipation of the largess inherent in his passing. Especially Samuel, the oldest and his favorite; the one with the most promise. Sam, who had been bare knuckle boxing against his wishes. Who, like most favored young men in prep school, thought he had all the time in the world and approached each day with unhurried ease.

Eyes closed, his weary head nodding, and with Sam's dark eyed image sharp in his mind, Jonathan said, "Ah, Sam my boy, now that your world has turned cruel, we'll see of what stuff you are made."

CHAPTER 1

December 1931

    The night the security guards blinded Wilbur, Sam was crouched low on a railroad embankment in a clump of winter-thin sumac, the cold crawling up his spine one vertebra at a time. Twenty feet away stood a line of rail cars with gondolas full of coal. Hard coal was selling for six dollars a ton and he had buyers waiting. Besides the money, Sam knew hard-pressed families with empty coal shuttles that would take the coal at prices or promises they could afford. Promises didn't worry him. Raised in the village, a dark-haired, bright-eyed, snot-nosed kid always into mischief—everyone knew him and he knew them.

    Sam hated the times. Everyone that he knew in the Pennsylvania mining villages and surrounds was unemployed and desperate: miners, mill and rail workers, everyone, and no government aid. People were driven to living off the land and each other. It was a challenge just to stay alive. Sam was twenty-one and determined to meet that challenge. He had no choice; the family money was gone, and with it the carefree days lolling around thinking about college.

    Using his stepfathers truck, Sam was keeping his four half-brothers busy moving merchandise in Scranton and neighboring counties under the guise of a wholesale supply business. It was a continuation, a remnant, of his grandfather Jonathan Freeman's construction and freight hauling enterprises—what Sam had salvaged after the Crash. They were moving goods according to season and opportunity, everything from huckleberries off the local mountain slopes to bootleg whiskey. The whiskey trade was the heart of it, and Sam's biggest worry was the impending repeal of prohibition. That night, it was coal they were after: anthracite coal, black gold.

    Sam was nearly invisible on the cinders wearing a hip-length dark coat, his black hair under a knit watch cap. Still, he felt exposed as the moon played striptease with the uncertain cloud cover scudding before the biting wind. An owl sounded nearby. Hearing the predator, all living things fell motionless.

    The looming shapes around him—coal cars, a towering colliery, and hills ominous and foreboding—coaxed old childhood fears to the surface, and Sam shuddered. Some old horrors, we never outgrow. Sam settled himself and listened, sucking up shadows and sounds, a sensory sponge shivering with the cold and accumulated fears. He could hear his brothers Wilbur and Josh on a nearby gondola filling burlap bags with coal. Ernie and Alfred, his twin brothers, were on an adjoining string of cars cramming their bags full and throwing them to the ground. When they dropped the full bags, Sam would begin to move them to their hidden truck. He prayed no one was watching. Both rail and mine owners employed security guards, but Sam thought it unlikely they'd be out in the remote staging area in the middle of the night. He knew if any were to venture out, it would be Hunky Walters with his crew. Hunky was a big bastard, built like a steam engine and he didn't mind the cold.

Hunky was a merciless hireling of the mining companies. The previous week, he'd dragged a sobbing woman, recently widowed, from company housing. Her husband killed in a mine cave-in and her credit on the company's ledger exhausted, she was a liability to be shed. Witnesses claimed Hunky suggested, with an appraising eye, that the sobbing woman get herself to a brothel.

Sam didn't like any of it—being a thief, living off others, exposing the boys to danger and the family to disgrace. He knew there had to be a way out of the goddamn valley, the poverty and degradation. Cowering there, cold and fearful, Sam knew that it was up to him to get the family out. They depended on him, Sam Freeman. He had to find the way.

A sound of brief scurrying a few yards along the slope snapped Sam out of his brooding. It was the sound a rabbit makes scratching for gravel trying to stay ahead of the dogs. He held his breath and listened; then released his breath slowly and sniffed the air. Nothing—except the vapors from burning waste dumps, smoldering coal dumped with the rocks and slate, the unmistakable stink of acrid smoke, a stench dragged from the seething depths of the earth.

Then, Sam did catch something, a whiff of something strongly foreign. He flared his nostrils and there it was—garlic. Somebody reeked of garlic, somebody close.

Railroad dicks! They'd planned for it, knowing there was always a chance the bastards would show. It was Sam's responsibility to get to the truck and, if it hadn't been discovered, get it out of there. They couldn't lose the truck! The boys knew to scatter and disappear through the area swamp where pursuit would be difficult and capture unlikely. If you got caught the dicks would rough you up. You'd have to spend the night shivering in a cell, hoping to be bailed out in the morning, praying there was money for bail.

Sam whistled the alert, turned and leaped down the slope he knew was loose gravel and cinder. He hit and rolled hoping the garlicky intruder had lost his direction. Sam's heart was pounding; he could hear shouts and movement up near the rail cars.

Then there was a loud shout, "Now," and one, two, three...five lantern beams probed the darkness.

Sam loped along a path across the rocky moonscape thinking *they mean business tonight.* When he reached the section of dirt road where he'd hidden the truck, Sam slipped up beside a gnarled old willow tree. His pulse was thumping in his ears. He couldn't think straight for worrying. All kinds of what-if cluttered his mind: *What if the boys were caught or injured? What if the truck had been discovered and this was a trap? What if?*

Jesus, they had him talking to himself! His bowels felt loose. He was worried about Wilbur, only fourteen, spending the night in a cell. But Wilbur was with Josh; he'd take care of the boy.

Sam decided to stick with the plan. He calmed himself and, concentrating, searched the landscape. They hadn't found the truck. Sam could barely see it, and he knew where it was. Sam ran to it, parked on a rise, and opened a door, quiet on greased hinges. He slid into the driver's seat, released the hand brake, and pressed the clutch pedal to the floor. The gravel crunched breaking the heavy silence. Sam furtively scanned the passing shadows as he rolled away.

Back on a coal car, Josh heard Sam's whistled warning. He dropped a half-filled bag of coal. "Wilbur," he called softly, "let's go." Bending over the rusty metal rim of the gondola, Josh saw a lantern come on. It was only two dark cars down the track.

Wilbur's hand brushed his shoulder. Josh heard him whisper, "I'll go down the other end."

Before Josh could answer, Wilbur was gone. Josh shook his head, *Damn kid, thinks this is a game.* Josh threw his leg over the rim and started down the ladder. He jumped to the embankment from the middle rungs, no time for climbing. A narrow light beam danced behind him as he bounded down the slope. At the bottom of the embankment, Josh entered the shallow water at the marsh edge. He parted the tall swamp grass, pushed aside the thick reeds and rushes, as bottom ooze sucked at his boots. The stink of decay, of flora and fauna long dead, entered his nostrils as Josh disappeared in the morass.

Alfred and Ernie, atop an adjacent line of cars not covered by the security guards, watched Josh's escape beyond the lights. Moving as silently as the loose coal would permit, they reached the dark edge of the car, eased over the rim and followed.

After leaving Josh, Wilbur crunched across the coal to the far end of the gondola and started down the ladder. Halfway down, he was suddenly illuminated; his shadow falling long and thin on the railroad car. Wilbur released his gloved grip instantly and dropped to the ground. But before he could begin his dash into the night, a strong hand clutched his coat at the shoulder. Halted, he turned to see the broad grinning face of Hunky Walters and his raised nightstick. Before Wilbur could react, the stick slammed across his temple. Numb, he fell to his knees. Another blow cracked his skull and Wilbur slid into a dark abyss.

A thin scar in Sam's left eyebrow, a reminder of an overhand right, lent emphasis to any expression of his concern or puzzlement. And he was both concerned and puzzled over the events of the night. *How did the dicks know they were there?* Sam was chewing on the question when he made it home that night. He knew the boys had to slosh through the treacherous marshy hollow while looking over their shoulders, then hike five miles with wet feet. It wasn't likely the dicks would brave the swamp. Apprehensive, Sam couldn't shake the nagging guilty feeling that he should have gone back for Wilbur. He rolled it over and over in his mind. Wilbur was a game kid, but a kid; he'd be scared witless out there. *Damn.*

Sam closely inspected the shadows and familiar shapes of nearby houses and fenced yards, and the winter-curled grasses eerily silver in the moonlight. He tested the subtle scent of smoldering household fires. Chained neighborhood curs growled and snapped their tentative territorial challenges. A feral wind gnawed at Sam's bones as he approached the rear of their clapboard house and crossed the open stoop. A mop leaning frozen in a corner, it's handle and stiff strands giving the appearance of an emaciated waif, startled him. Shivering, Sam admonished himself, *Get a grip!* Hinges creaked as the door opened and Sam entered the warmth of the kitchen.

Pop, Sam's stepfather, a soft-spoken plodding man, held a supervisory position at the silk mill before it closed, and the house was larger than those occupied by mill workers and miners. Built by Jonathan Freeman's construction company, the home was two stories tall. A kitchen and living room were on the first level; four bedrooms filled the second. The kitchen was expansive and the heart of most daily activity. It contained a coal stove, a sink with a pump to draw well water, and a large rectangular wooden table. The living room was used only on Sunday after church for tea and bible readings.

In the rock-walled cellar was a round coal furnace that heated only the first floor, a root cellar, coal bin, and laundry tubs. The cellar was where matriarch Elizabeth Freeman, Lizzy, could be found, if she wasn't in the kitchen, doing laundry or making large bars of yellow soap from lye and reclaimed animal fat. In the backyard against a weathered board fence stood a proud two-holer.

When Sam entered, the only sounds were of the frame house creaking in the wind, and an occasional glowing ember dropping in the bowels of the black cast-iron stove. Lingering was a warm, heavy odor of pillow-like bread loaves. Arranged in a comforting row under bleached white dish towels, they were evidence of Lizzy's afternoon efforts. Sam pulled a cord lighting a single swaying bulb and filled the room with waltzing shadows. He murmured silent encouragement for his brothers running in the dangerous night.

Bone weary, Sam eased onto a chair. After a moment, too tense to sit, he rose and pumped water into an enameled teakettle and set it on the stove. Bending, he adjusted the bottom vent to hurry the kettle and add some heat to the room. He tossed his knit cap on the table and ran the fingers of both hands through his thick hair.

Watching droplets fall from the spout onto the hot surface, Sam was suddenly soured by the bitter taint of recollection. He drifted back a short two years before to worry-free times, steering his grandfather's touring car, his mother in the front seat smiling under a wide-brimmed hat, his brothers in Sunday coats and knickers bickering in the rear seat. And the girls...ah, the girls—wasp-waisted maidens, parasols twirling in the seductive summer sun, pretending to be unaware of the sons of affluence in the ostentatious touring car.

Those days were gone, like his grandfather's wealth. Sam wiped his forehead, *A short time ago, we had the world by the ass and now we're stealing coal!* He recalled the defeat in his grandfather's eyes, and words, lips twisted by stroke, "Well, Sam my boy, the world has turned cruel. Now you are your brothers' keeper."

Jaw set, and choked with emotion, Sam had vowed, "I will, Grandfather, I will."

Steam was rising from the kettle, but it had yet to whistle when Alfred and Ernie came pushing through the doorway. Alfred looked around the kitchen, poked Ernie and said, "I told you we'd be the first home after Sam." Ernie, his usual taciturn self, only grunted as he removed his heavy cloth coat and threw it over a chair before turning his palms to the stove.

Inseparable, the twins had few similarities physically or temperamentally. Alfred was lean and whip-agile with a quick wit. He had a high forehead and thinning hair. A long thin nose set between darting eyes gave a fox-like quality to his appearance. When fatigued, his left foot slapped slightly as he walked, reminder of a childhood injury. Ernie stood over six feet tall and was described by old Doc Pankow, the only physician in town, as "muscular obese." His thick arms were the size of Alfred's legs. His eyes, set back in a beefy face, missed little. He was intelligent, but of a slow and calculating nature. Once decided on a course of action, he was as determined and unstoppable as a rhino.

Jarred from his reverie, Sam asked, "Did you see Josh or Wilbur?"

Ernie looked to Alfred then shook his head of unruly blond hair. Alfred shrugged and moved a loaf of bread to the table and removed a disc of paraffin from a jar of fruit preserve. Half the weight of his twin, Alfred was always hungry. "Make the tea," he said to Ernie. He was half Ernie's size, but in charge.

Alfred was pouring tea into thick mugs, the steamy aroma filling the room, when Josh came in. Josh, often taken to be Alfred's twin, had a similar agile body and quick demeanor. Differing facial features, a broader nose, prominent cheekbones and square chin, gave him a handsome chiseled look. His face was flushed red by cold and exertion. He was breathing heavily, covered with muck, and smelled like swamp ooze.

"Jesus," Alfred said, "did you crawl across the bottom?"

Ignoring the comment, Josh began to peel the wet coat from his back.

Sam said, "Don't hang that in here. Lizzy will skin you. You better go out and come in through the cellar. Leave your coat and boots by the wash tub."

Josh turned to the door.

Sam asked, "Wilbur with you?"

Biting his lower lip, Josh shook his head. "No, but he'll he along."

Sam took this as a bad sign. He felt something was wrong.

Before his brother could ask, Josh blurted, "I told you to leave the kid out of this."

Rebuked, Sam wondered what was bothering Josh? Speechless, he fixed his gaze on Josh's retreating back. *There was something Josh wasn't saying.*

Sam's earliest memory of his half-brother Josh had been captured and printed. The picture taker caught him as a young boy hand-in-hand with Josh, a runny-nose toddler, walking down the worn tracks of a dirt road in a bleak mining village. Behind them, the bleak timbers of a colliery standing like a giant omnivorous praying mantis framed small tired houses and leaning picket fences. They were two stick figures in drab ill-fitting clothes wandering a ghost town in the making. It was how Sam thought of himself—at the lead saying, "Take my hand. Follow me."

The four by six-inch photograph was stuck under the frame of Lizzy's bedroom mirror. It was one of the first things she saw each morning. When Sam last saw it, it had faded to a weak sepia print of dull images and muted background. Faded though it was, it represented Sam's idea of his duty and obligation to his brothers.

Sam pondered. *When did I accept the notion that the responsibility for my brothers was mine?* Had Lizzy placed the load on his shoulders because he was born of her first husband, her only true love? Perhaps, but Sam didn't think so. No, he had assumed the role of protector on his own, had drawn it on like a coat tailor made. Though they—Josh, the twins Alfred and Ernie, and Wilbur—were his half brothers, born of Lizzy though of different seed, they were family, brothers as tight as any, devoted to their mother and each other. Sam was certain of this with all but Josh—with Josh, he was never sure.

Sam recalled a bloody nose received defending Josh, accused of taking a boy's wagon. Later, when Sam found Josh was at fault and confronted him, Josh shrugged it off asking, 'Who asked you to butt in?" As protective as Sam was of Josh, he had to acknowledge that Josh was out of step with everyone else. With Josh there was a wrong way, and his way. His way or the highway, and he had no time for anyone who thought otherwise. That wasn't the first time Josh had let him down, and it sure as hell wasn't the last.

Worry had Sam fully in its grip by the time false dawn tinted the filmy curtains. He was feeling the assumed burden of oldest brother. He looked at Josh who had settled his lanky frame on a chair, his arms resting on the spindled back, and at Ernie slouched half asleep beside the hot stove. Sam turned to Alfred and asked the question hanging heavily in the room, "You think they grabbed him?"

Alfred, staring at the linoleum floor, said without conviction, "Nah, he'll be okay."

Ernie uttered an oath.

Josh raised his head and looked out the window at the promise of sunlight. He said, "It's getting light out. We better have a look around."

Sam bounded upright, sending his chair clattering across the floor. Sam's cheek was twitching; he needed to punch somebody. "If those bastards have hurt that boy, I'll have their guts." His fingers tightened around imaginary innards.

His brothers jumped when the chair dropped. They looked at each other uneasily, struck by the venom in his words.

Alfred started to speak but stopped when floorboards creaked overhead. Lizzy was up. If the mines and mills were working, she would have been up in the black of earliest morning, filling carbide lamps, stirring a pot of thick oatmeal, and stuffing lunch buckets. But the whistles had sounded weeks ago halting work for the duration. Ernie turned to Alfred, Josh smoothed his damp hair. They all looked at Sam. An unspoken question charged the atmosphere—What will we tell Lizzy?

In mounting unease, they waited, listening to her slow descent, one complaining stair at a time, until their mother, Elizabeth Freeman-Cordy, Lizzy, stood framed in the doorway. Her thick arms folded under her formidable bosom. A flowered robe cascaded over her broad hips and fell to hover around the tops of her black low-heeled shoes. Her graying black hair, combed straight back, was secured by a pair of silver clasps. Bright azure eyes lit her handsome face.

She coughed and her brow furrowed. She appeared perplexed by her sons arrayed in the kitchen with Wilbur, her youngest, missing. "Where's Wilbur?" she asked in a coarse morning voice.

Any response they might have made was interrupted by the loud invasive sound of someone clattering up the wooden front porch stairs. Whoever it was stomped across the porch and banged with exuberance on the front door.

To be first at the door, Sam jumped across the kitchen and without a word strode through the shadowed living room. He jerked the door open and was surprised to see little Billy Burns, a lad he recognized from church. A wool hat pulled down over the boy's ears framed wide eyes and a button nose. Billy stood trying to harness escaping breath, billowing before him in the frosty air. Looking up at Sam, Billy forced his message, "Wilbur's hurt. Doc Pankow wants you at the hospital, as soon as you can"

Sam's worst fear was realized, and he was acutely aware of Lizzy, a thundercloud looming behind him. Acid rose in his throat.

CHAPTER 2

December 1931

When something dreaded happens, when fearful anticipation surrenders to awful realization, when a child is injured or a lover lost, there is a prolonged moment of defensive rejection before gasping despair overcomes. Knowing this intuitively, Sam turned to face his mother expecting a furious assault, but her eyes were empty and upon her face a cloudy bewilderment.

"What happened?" she asked.

Sam said, "Wilbur is in the hospital."

"What happened!"

Sam saw her brief confusion was ebbing, dissipating; Lizzy stood stiff as starch, her gritty strength quickly returning. He knew he'd be interrogated.

Sam leaned against the front door, closing it. Behind Lizzy, Josh, Alfred and Ernie stood, all awaiting his explanation. With a dry throat, he began, "We were after coal. The dicks came and we scattered like we planned. We all got back here except Wilbur." Sam's hands fell to his sides. "I don't know what happened. Maybe he fell. Wilbur was with Josh." As he spoke, they all moved slowly instinctively toward the kitchen, drawn like sentinels to a campfire. It was where all serious family discourse occurred.

The boys stood uneasily around the table, awaiting Lizzy's pleasure. "Sit down," she said. She moved to the hissing kettle blowing vapor on the black stovepipe. "We'll have tea."

Sam shook his head; it was like something out of Kipling. *Bloody English, surrounded by Zulus, they have tea.*

Sam watched with a mixture of admiration and foreboding as she reverted to routine while organizing her thoughts. Her flat shoes slapped on the linoleum and their nerves as she marched around the room pouring tea and considering her assault. "Well?" she demanded, glaring at Josh. "I'll know what went on before we go."

Josh froze, his hot brew held in both hands inches off the table. His eyes widened in why-me surprise. He lowered the cup to the table with steady hands and looked at Sam. "We heard Sam's whistle, but it didn't give us any time. The dicks were there with their lanterns before we could move. Wilbur went for the ladder at the far end of the car before I could stop him. I went over the side on my end and looked for him on the embankment."

Josh was sitting on the edge of his chair and had both hands in the air. He raised his voice; "I looked for him. I did…but the lights were all around, and I had to get out of there." He shook his head; his hands began to tremble. "I didn't see him. I don't know where the hell he went."

Alfred spoke up, "Josh is right, the alarm and the lights hit us all at the same time."

Ernie nodded in agreement, as all eyes turned to Sam.

"I whistled as soon as I knew they were there. I don't know where the bastards came from." It was a weak explanation but it was all Sam had to say.

Josh said flatly, looking at Sam, "Wilbur shouldn't have been with us."

"Josh is right," Lizzy stood with her arms akimbo, her voice stem, "I told you to keep him out of any dangerous business." She glared at Sam.

"You know Wilbur," Sam said, "He wouldn't take me seriously, wouldn't listen. Life's all a summer afternoon baseball game to him; he's on the mound with bases loaded. The count's three and two and he's in control."

Sam was right, but it was no consolation. An uneasy quiet permeated the room.

Alfred broke the silence, "It's getting light out, you better get to the hospital."

Sam went for his mother's coat. He said, "Josh, you come with us. You two," he pointed at the twins, "get Pop off to work." He used the term 'work' loosely. Pop, once a supervisor, now reported as a watchman where he roamed the deserted silk mill and grounds for thirty dollars a month—a bone tossed by the owners.

Sam went out and chased a pair of lean mongrels from their sheltered spot beneath the truck. Josh, snarling at the frost, cranked the chilled engine while Sam adjusted the choke and stroked the accelerator pedal. Cold and voiceless, they both moved slowly. When Lizzy appeared, Sam helped her onto the chilly front seat where she sat hunched between him and Josh. Wrapped in a black cloth coat with a false fur collar, her hat low over her eyes, Sam thought her a churning volcano. He knew she feared for Wilbur, was full of unspoken blame and anger waiting to explode. The tension appeared to have Josh on his end of the seat ready to meld with the door.

The sky was unseen overhead as fog, created by the frigid air settling over burning dumps, dispersed in the valley. The dumps—impurities, slate, rock, bits of coal and coal dust cast up out of the earth and accumulated in long mounds, miniature mountains—compressed and yielded to spontaneous combustion. Resulting harsh ubiquitous vapors spread into every depression and lung in the valley. Residents, long exposed, became used to the acrid air and with grim resignation, went on about their threatened lives.

Pop, always the spectator, in wool shirt and coveralls stood on the porch and watched their departure. Sam carefully followed the probing headlamps into the mist. He pressed the flat black horn button, but it was too cold to respond.

Sam thought Mid-Valley Hospital was appropriately named, being situated halfway up the eastern slope of the broad valley midway between the city of Scranton to the south and the mining villages to the north. Originally the pillared mansion of Ira Cooper, a prominent physician, it had, at his bequest been converted to a community clinic. Sam remembered old Ira, a bald man with outrageous mutton-chop sideburns and endless compassion. Ira was remembered as a local hero mostly for his gallant efforts during the killer pandemic, the Spanish Flu of 1918. The virus killed one half million people in the United States that year, and twenty million worldwide, exceeding the number slaughtered during the Great War.

Memories of frozen corpses stacked, waiting to be buried, still reoccurred for Sam with the passing of a hearse or a black-shrouded widow. He shivered with the recollection and privately gave guilty thanks for his own survival.

Dreading arrival, Sam slowed the truck as it moved through the diminishing mists, ostensibly trying to decide whether to enter through the front or rear entrance. The front first floor entrance faced west and the valley's meandering Lackawanna River. The river, an old bawd, her bosom exposed to those who would use her; dirty and swollen by moisture off the mountains, wended her way down to Scranton and the steel mills.

The rear entrance opened at the second floor level due to the sloping terrain, a feature common to the area. Sam parked in front of the chalk-white hospital. Brightly pristine, the building was maintained largely by bartered service offered in lieu of cash. Sam knew that in spite of its bright appearance, it was a place to be avoided.

Holding the wide front door for Lizzy and Josh, Sam was filled with trepidation fueled by nostalgia. The odor of antiseptic and thinly masked putrefaction churned old memories - visions of wet black-streaked miners strapped to backboards and brought to these halls to die. The hollow-eyed face of his cousin John, only sixteen, killed while 'robbing pillars', a hazardous practice designed to remove every last ton of coal remaining in an otherwise exhausted vein, was among them. The ghostly pale face of his father, dead of an infected mastoid years before antibiotics, was there as well. It was a recalled procession of horrors, of loved ones lost, and now Sam was afraid Wilbur might join them.

Sam turned to his mother, and saw fear in her eyes but strength in the set of her jaw. Her gaze was fixed on an approaching young nurse wearing a white cap, uniform, and shoes that clacked on the hardwood floor. The nurse appeared stiffly serious as she surveyed their small group. Curls of auburn hair bounced lightly above her green eyes and pert nose.

"Hello," she said, a slight catch in her voice. "I'm Emma Cooper. I believe we've met in church." She gazed at Sam and Josh briefly before she turned to take their mother's hand. "Wilbur is just down the hall...this way."

Sam had seen her in church and knew she was old Ira's granddaughter. Motioning for Josh to follow, Sam squeezed his cap in both hands and followed her.

She seemed hesitant when she opened a door and said, "Wilbur asked for you."

The small room was austere. Containing a high narrow metal-framed bed, bedside stand with a pitcher of ice water, and two chairs of light oak, it was scrubbed military-clean. Except for a small-framed print of Jesus, the white painted walls were bare. It was dust free, ready for inspection.

At the sight of Wilbur, his head swathed in gauze bandage, Lizzy groaned. Fearing she might faint, Sam took her elbow. He walked her to the bedside where she placed both hands on the taut white sheet. She walked her fingers forward until they gently touched her youngest son slumped motionless on his pillows. The bandages circling Wilbur's head left only his mouth and lower jaw exposed. There was a speck of dried blood on his swollen lower lip, and his voice was slow and thick when he spoke, "That you, Mom?"

"Yes," she said, "I'm here." Glancing at Josh, then turning to Sam, she said, "I want you to leave us alone."

Sam was stung, feeling rejected. Laboring to understand what she was feeling, he turned and walked from the room.

Out in the hall, Josh began to speak, then held his hands aloft in a gesture of futility. Shoulders rounded, he fumed and slouched toward the exit door.

"What did the doctor say? Will Wilbur be all right?"

She lowered her eyes and was silent for an uncomfortably long time.

Sam felt like screaming at her silence.

Finally, in a whisper, Emma said, "You should ask the doctor."

Sam placed his hands on her shoulders. "Look at me," he insisted. Then aware that his manner was threatening, he released her. He exhaled heavily.

She closed her eyes. "He took several blows to the head. His skull is fractured."

Sam hissed, "Goddamn."

"Wilbur is blind," Emma said, gently placing her hand over Sam's.

"Blind? You mean permanently?"

"I'm sorry."

Sam stood in the lonely corridor, dazed, his eyes closed. Wilbur's pain was his pain, but the numbing guilt was his alone. For Wilbur, the summer sun had set and long lonely night begun. Arms crossed, trembling fingers splayed over his rigid belly, Sam tore at himself, dreading the stained dawns to come. He moaned in anguish and slumped against the wall. He was damned, frustrated, powerless—no act of vengeance could make Wilbur see. But, he had to do something.

Sam clenched his teeth, then out of a mounting sense of guilt and frustration he bellowed and punched the wall.

CHAPTER 3

June 1929

The Cooper cottage was one of only two built on the pine sheltered shores of Lake Sheridan, a secluded twenty acres of spring-fed frigid black water. Doctor Ira Cooper gave angling as the reason for the cottage on the remote mountain lake, but Emma, his granddaughter, knew it was his retreat from the tribulations of life and the great mystery of inevitable death. But, it was true the bass grew to boasting size in the serene depths.

It was for the solitude alone that Emma came to its shores. She had discovered that she could sit for hours contemplating the placid surface, puzzling over random ripples, and feel absolutely certain that her God was present.

Emma denied, when accused by her sisters, that she was the least bit interested in the young boxers from a distant training camp as they ran on the forest trail that circumvented the lake. But the trail did pass near the cottage, and Emma would follow the young men with her eyes until they were out of sight beyond the trail bend.

Wild flowers: columbine, tall daisies, black-eyed Susans, blankets of buttercups, pale violets, and their cousins flanked the woodland trail, and Emma, enjoying their mixed fragrance, was gathering them on a clear summer morning. Droplets of dew remained in the long morning shadows and her feet were damp.

Emma was contemplating a return to the cottage when she heard throaty male voices and the fall of determined feet. Instinctively, she faded into the trailside shadows, and stood like a forest nymph to watch the intruders pass.

She saw, as they approached, that it was the dark-haired athlete and his bulky companion, Emma had seen them before; they passed each morning like clockwork. She felt that there was something special about the dark one, something besides his good looks that defined him. As they neared, she decided it was his intensity, and imagined she could see and feel his grinding purpose. Watching them measure the trail with rhythmic strides, Emma could hear that they were engaged in conversation.

In the alternate sun and shade of the trail, and in the strained syllables of the distance runner, Sam Freeman asked his partner, "Feeling any better, Lenny?"

Lenny, thicker with heavy dense muscle not designed for running, breathed laboriously, "Yeah."

Sam laughed, "Me too. I always hurt the first couple of miles until I get loose. Then I settle into the rhythm and feel great."

"I hurt all the time," Lenny admitted.

Glancing at Lenny running beside him, Sam said, "This is my last run. I'm through fighting."

Lenny came to a halt, surprise on his face, 'Wadda you mean? You joking?"

Sam stopped beside him. "Nope. My grandfather gave me an ultimatum. I knew it was coming." Sam kicked a pebble off the path. "If I continue fighting, I'm out of his will. He swears he'll cut me off—that brawling is not Christian and that I'll come to no good." Sam shrugged broad shoulders and said, "I thought about it, and I'm quitting." Compromising, he offered, "Maybe I'll box in college."

"Shit," Lenny turned and looked at the water's edge near the trail. "You know, I'm not really surprised. Knowing your grandfather, I wondered what you were doing in the boxing stable."

Sam listened, bouncing in place.

Lenny's arms hung at his sides. He scuffed his shoes on the path. He asked, "How do you feel about it?"

Sam grinned, "To tell the truth, I hate getting hit on the nose."

Lenny's roar at Sam's admission echoed out over the placid surface of the lake disturbing birds along the shore and in the pines. Lenny asked, "Will you stick around? Be my second? Stand in my corner?"

Sam gripped Lenny's massive shoulders, "Damn right…you're a more promising heavyweight than I am anyway."

"Bull," Lenny replied. Lenny looked out over the surface of the lake smooth as sheet steel in the mists. Impulsively, he said, "Hey, you don't have to train anymore and I'm damned tired of running, let's take a dip."

Emma watched as both athletes pulled their sweatshirts over their heads and shuffled erratically to the water shedding shoes and clothing as they went. She stood amazed as the two jumped off the bank and hit the water wearing only white socks. Both men bellowed immediately, expressing shock as the frigid water enveloped their heated bodies.

She smothered a laugh as Sam sprang from the lake, his wet hair a shining black helmet fit tightly on his brow. On the grass beside the water, wonderfully naked, Sam jumped and flailed his arms, shouting. "Hoo, hoo, hoo!" Goose flesh covering his body caught the light giving his quivering muscles an eloquent sheen.

Emma trembled, viewing the perfect naked male bounding in the morning light. Peripherally, she noted Lenny's struggle up the bank, but it was Sam's image that filled her senses and was to reoccur in her dreams.

CHAPTER 4

December 1931

There was a ditty scrawny village children sang skipping down alleys taunting whomever. They were indiscriminate in their discrimination. The tune went something like—"The Irish hate the English, The Germans, the Dutch—And we don't like anybody very much." That's the way it was in the Pennsylvania mining villages. Immigrants brought their preachers and priests, keepers of their myths, with them. They built their churches and temples and clustered around them, like iron filings around a magnet. The established inhabitants resented and feared them. Shrouded by their esoteric beliefs, they huddled viewing the world outside as a fearful place. Their prejudices multiplied. Weakened by their sparse desperate existence, husbands and wives laid in coffin-dark rooms pelvis to pelvis in comfortless couplings. Driven from the hungry belly of Europe and various other shores by famine and persecution, they gathered in this strange new world daunted by their surroundings. Assembled in their meeting places they—Hunkies, Polacks, Limies, Krauts, Wops, and Micks—felt sheltered from the greatest threat of all: their neighbors.

The men were trapped. If there was no work, they failed as providers. If there was work, they were forced to descend into the hostile earth, down deep dank shafts, listening to the soul-tearing creak of the support timbers, the incessant dripping water, and scuttling rats while threatened by seeping gases, watching and fearing their canaries would die. Afraid when there was work, afraid when there wasn't, many sought oblivion in alcohol.

The women, those that survived numerous pregnancies, used, empty and gaunt, cowered in the clapboard shacks, bent to their menial labors, prayed in the priest-dark nights, clung to the children that survived, feared, and too often received, the worst from their men.

It was an unusual man that flourished, avoiding the exhaustion of the mines. Stanley Walentynowicz, Hunky, was one. As a young man, fresh off the boat from war impoverished Europe, he joined relatives in a coal-mining village. One trip into a mine where dog size rats kept cats at bay, and Hunky knew there was something better for him. He changed his name to Walters and went to work for the mining company's security force. It was not an easy decision. The pay was lower, and the men working with the oppressive owners were despised. But, Hunky persisted.

He ignored the working stiffs, considering them dull men with no vision, and ingratiated himself with those in power.

Hunky had an asset—he was a sadist. There was not a miner in the anthracite fields that didn't know of the time Hunky forced Luigi Venezia's hand into a conveyor gear box, that didn't hear him scream, that didn't experience Luigi's pain when with seven fingers he reported for work, that didn't swear defiance. By age thirty, Hunky was established as the company's chief of security.

Hunky was who Sam waited for standing on the frozen ground beside Hunky's favorite haunt, a local speakeasy frequented by miners. Since Wilbur had breathed, "Hunky," through bandages and puffed lips, Sam's initial rage had tempered and become cold hard purpose. Wilbur's blindness ate at him. Feeling both guilty and outraged, Sam was determined to give Hunky a thorough debilitating beating. He was aware Hunky could swing a nightstick, but Sam had been fighting bare knuckle on the river. They were both hardened men.

Hidden, waiting back off the lonely road, watching a few barren trees sway in the wind, Sam twitched his nose against the ammonic odor of the drinker's favorite outside urinal. He shuffled his cold feet and flexed his hands in anticipation of the night's brutal work.

Most of the miners frequenting the speakeasy were there to escape. Hunky went to listen and watch the frustrated brawling men. He would sip a pint of brew, draw on his pipe, absorb gossip and leave cold sober. That was how Sam wanted him—conscious of who he was as Hunky felt his terrible wrath.

When finally Hunky stepped through the door out onto the board walk and into the circle of light offered by a carriage lamp, Sam knew him immediately. The memory of his large head, barrel chest, thick legs and arrogant stride had been turning in his thoughts. Hunky paused and surveyed the barren night before turning toward the dark space where Sam stood waiting. The boardwalk ended abruptly and he stepped off onto the frozen wheel-rutted surface of the narrow road.

"Hunky!" Sam spat the name offensive to his tongue, and stepped from his dark hiding place.

Hunky stopped, tilted his head slightly, and squinted. His eyes narrowed and his mouth spread into a cruel slash, a serpentine leer. Hunky growled viscerally, then said, "Ah, it's one of the Freeman trash. Why are you here? There's nothing to steal."

"You know what I'm doing here, Shitface," Sam said, stepping closer. "I'm here to teach you to pick on men not boys."

There was nothing slow about Hunky. His massive arm, swinging in a wide arc, had the speed and power of a great bear's. Sam anticipated the move and shifted his stance so that Hunky's closed fist caught only his black woolen watch cap, spinning it off into the night. With as much strength and fury as he could gather, Sam boomed a right cross that caught Hunky just below the heart. The bulk of Hunky's coat absorbed the blow and he grunted. Sam's follow-up punch, a left hook, cut Hunky's brow. In return, Hunky's open hand struck Sam on the side of the head. Dazed, Sam faltered, lost his balance, and dropped down on one knee. Unable to quickly move, Sam expected a kick, but Hunky swung again.

Hunky, his sight hindered by blood running off his brow and into his eye, misjudged Sam's height and missed him by inches. Hunky's momentum carried him past Sam, he regained his footing, turned and charged with a roar. Pivoting and slipping aside, Sam evaded his charge. He kicked Hunky's knee as he hurtled past. It was a strong kick well placed. The knee gave way. Hunky collapsed and fell on his side, his knee awkwardly bent. Hunky screamed a curse that contained no fear, only disdain and hatred. He struggled to stand, one eye closed, the other flashed fire, and his lip curled. He spit at Sam. Sam, in his seething unreasoning hatred, kicked again and his heavy boot smashed Hunky's face. Sam fell away, emotionally drained and physically spent, his ears ringing, his chest heaving, sucking air.

Sam stared at Hunky sprawled on the ground. A silent hulk, he seemed not to be breathing. Sam thought that he had killed him, and didn't care. He edged closer to Hunky and bent over his bulky form. Close in, Sam could hear the blood bubbling in Hunky's broken mouth. He wasn't dead, but looked it. Sam straightened painfully and looked around. The road was empty—no witnesses. Sam could hear voices within the tavern, and chairs scraping the plank floor. Another night of drinking ended, men were shouting farewells, and would soon be emptying into the night.

Sam took another look at Hunky, motionless on the unforgiving ground. "Die, you bastard." he snarled before slipping away in the enveloping darkness..

"You look like shit. You feel all right?"

It was the next morning. The brothers were delivering pilfered coal in Carbondale, a few miles north of Scranton. Josh was staring at Sam slouched behind the steering wheel of the truck. His words caused Sam to turn and stare back. "Yeah, I'm okay."

Josh curled his collar against the brisk wind. He motioned the twins up onto the tailgate, jumped up onto the running board and took a handhold. "Well, then," he waved his free arm at the road ahead, "let's roll."

Sam eased off the clutch and the truck jerked ahead. He didn't feel okay. He was preoccupied and distraught as he considered the previous night's assault. He tortured himself, *I shouldn't have left him alive.* Hunky would be ruthless in his vengeance. The whole family would suffer, being excluded from any work in the goddamn valley. He shouldn't have left him, the sole witness, alive. Thoughts twisted like worry beads in his mind. Missing his favorite cap, Sam unconsciously ran his fingers through his blowing hair. *What good did it do? Wilbur was still blind.* By midmorning, unable to concentrate he quit work leaving the boys to finish.

At home, Lizzy considered Sam as he brooded over a bowl of vegetable soup, sopping it up slowly with thick slices of bread.

She wiped her wet hands on her apron and asked, "What's wrong?"

Sam knew he owed her a truthful answer, but he lied, "Nothing...just thinking about that little red-haired nurse at the hospital."

"Is that it?" His mother leaned against the sink and stared into cold greasy water.

Sam knew she knew that wasn't it. He knew he should tell her about his fight with Hunky. She had to know, but he couldn't find the words. Hunky was going to be more dangerous than ever. Sam knew he'd made a mess of things. He needed to think, needed fresh air. He grabbed his jacket and left the house.

Sam was in the back yard walking in circles, deep in circuitous thought, when he got the news.

Little Jimmy Alberto, a neighbor's boy, stood on the bottom fence rail, his knickers against the rabbit wire, his face flushed with the news, and cried, "Did you hear what happened?"

In no mood for trivia, Sam waved his hand in disinterest.

His voice elevated, his eyes dancing, Jimmy blurted, "Hunky is dead. They found him in the ravine off Charles Street. Say he broke his neck."

Sam jerked to attention, Could it be true?

The next day, a Saturday, Sam was outside furiously chopping wood, his ax ringing in the bitter cold air. He couldn't work hard enough to assuage his rumor-fueled agitation. Out of the house, away from the heavy silence and questions smoldering unasked, he was working up a steamy sweat. *Who should I talk to? Somebody must know something.* His mind had begun to clear when a small man entered the yard by the rear gate. Sam recognized him by his stature and bantam rooster walk. He was the Welshman, Dan Owen.

"Sam," he greeted, his slow manner and shallow voice hinting of black lung disease. Dan was an intense man with haunted eyes. Sam knew him to be fearless, having endured many trips down hellishly long slopes in mining cars they called 'gunboats'. He was dressed in a brown water-proof-stiff hunting coat with bulging game pockets, dark dew-wet pants and boots. Burdock burrs clung to the wool socks exposed at his boot tops. He carried a Fox double-barreled twelve-gauge shotgun.

"Dan, looks like you had some good hunting." Sam planted his ax in a section of apple tree stump.

"Yes, I was up on West Mountain with Homer's dog, Blackie. That mongrel can hunt."

Dan reached into a blood stained game pocket and withdrew a pair of limp cottontail rabbits. He thrust them at Sam saying, "Here's some stew."

"Thanks." Sam accepted the rag-like rabbits, thinking Dan a little too heavy with the twelve gauge. "Will you have a home brew?"

"I'd like one, but I can't linger, the wife will be wantin' me home." Dan searched the surrounds with hooded eyes, and Sam realized he had something to say. "Sam," Dan paused choosing his words, "that business with Hunky…I heard some fellas found him passed out and was helpin' him down Charles street when he slipped and fell into a ravine." Dan's eyes were as steady as death. "And," the boys agree, "that's the true end of it as far as all is concerned." His eyes never wavered from Sam's.

Grasping the message, Sam stood slack-jawed not knowing what to say. Dan slung his shotgun in the crook of his arm and started to leave. Before opening the gate, he stopped and turned to Sam. Reaching inside the open front of his coat, Dan withdrew something. He tossed Sam's lost watch cap to him, saying, "You'll be needing this these awful nights."

CHAPTER 5

March 1932

Wilbur's hospital stay dragged on. The family was worried; it appeared old Doc Pankow didn't know what to do with him. His superficial wounds had healed, lumps receded, and abrasions disappeared; on the outside he looked fine, but he couldn't see much more than shadows. The doctor, treating him like a cracked egg, was afraid to release him; afraid that like Humpty Dumpty he might fall.

Lizzy had established an informal but effective visitation routine so that Wilbur was seldom alone. Josh would read to him: Theodore Dreiser, William Faulkner, Eugene O'Neill, and Robert Frost's "Collected Poems." Alfred and Ernie would appear in tandem, and keep Wilbur informed about local happenings and prospects for the coming baseball season—discussing whether the Philadelphia Athletics would repeat as pennant winners. When alone, Wilbur would listen to a radio that had appeared mysteriously in his room. He memorized the words to popular songs including, ironically, "Time on My Hands."

Sam was usually the last one to visit him each day; "To tuck him in," he would say. One evening, Sam stepped into the hospital out of a soft rain, feeling its' gentle kiss an assurance of winter's passing. He shook the few raindrops off his gray porkpie hat and headed for Wilbur's room.

He passed Emma in the hall, and said softly, "Good evening." He never said much to her; she was so pretty, she made him nervous.

"Evening, Sam. How are you?"

The way she looked at him made him feel like a bug on a pin. He was uncomfortably aware that he hadn't shaved for two days and his face was shaded by a dark stubble. "Fine," he said, and managed to ask, "are you leaving for the day?"

"Shortly," she said, "after I change out of this uniform."

"Well," he said, "have a nice night."

She removed the pin securing the nurse's cap perched in her hair.

Sam believed he could feel her eyes on his back as he walked down the hall.

Wilbur, sitting in bed and staring at the window, heard his brother enter. He said "I can see light and shadow, Sam."

Sam nodded, unseen. "That's great, Will." Doctor Pankow told him that Wilbur might gradually regain a portion of his sight, but that the damage was to frustratingly slow healing nerve tissue, and that it would be some time. "Take it slow," Sam said, "and you'll be back on the pitcher's mound next summer." The doctor didn't think so.

"You think?" Wilbur turned his head and rubbed his hands, one clenched inside the other, like he was holding a man on base. Life for Wilbur was a game in progress. He would rather play than eat. For him, the bases were loaded and he was about to baffle the clean-up batter with his curve ball.

"Sure," Sam said, sounding positive.

"Will you still catch for me?"

"You know I will. I'm the only one that can handle your fast ball."

Wilbur grinned and shifted his weight against the pillows. "I bet Babe Ruth couldn't hit sixty homers off me."

Sam changed the subject. "You are looking good. The food must be agreeing with you."

Mom's will be better. I miss her Yorkshire pudding. Sam," he lowered his voice. "How about getting me out here?"

Sam moved and stood by the bed. He took Wilbur's hand. "Pretty soon. Buddy. The Doc wants you stable, no jumping around." Sam ventured, "I think we'll be taking you home Saturday...three days."

"Good." Wilbur seemed to relax.

Placing his fingers on Wilbur's face, Sam said, "You're going to be okay."

"I know," Wilbur said. "it's just so slow."

Sam patted his cheek, "Think Saturday," he said.

It was velvet-black outside Wilbur's window when Sam left the room. He turned slowly toward the hospital exit, his thoughts on Wilbur's progress. Sam had trouble believing Wilbur would be permanently sightless. He prayed often that it wasn't so.

There was a small hooded light at the nurse's desk; the corridor ceiling lights were off. Shadows in the long hall were broken only by an occasional dim wall sconce. The passage to the outside seemed a long eerie tunnel. Voices fluttered like disturbed bats, squeaking pain and loneliness in the night.

Something moved in Sam's peripheral vision, and he turned to look. Off the hall in a small cubical, a consultation room, a table lamp lent a subtle glow. Most of the room's far wall consisted of two French doors, the glass reflecting the room's interior. A gowned woman, standing before the doors, seemed an apparition suspended in air. She was turning as if rotating on a pedestal while appraising her image. It was that slight motion that had caught Sam's eye. After a moment, he realized it was Emma Cooper reflected in the glass. Entranced, he stood as motionless as a stag in a beam of light.

Emma stood statue-perfect, dressed in a shimmering satin gown. Her short reddish hair complemented a sculptured-ivory neck. The gown, cut low in back, exposed flawless skin.

Sam watched as her hands left their perch at her hips and began to descend the pleated fabric caressing her body. Her chin dipped as she watched her hands glide lower. Twisting fluidly, so that the gown defined her waist, she presented her profile to the glass. Her left foot raised and fell almost imperceptibly before settling on the rose carpet. Then she stood immobile, a slender Venus smiling at the reflection of Sam fixed in the dusk outside the room. Tantalizingly, she slid her hands gently forward and down her thighs.

Breathless, Sam stood mesmerized by the vision. Emma stood motionless. Finally, Sam withdrew and eased down the hallway, his heart imitating a bass drum. He realized he'd never really seen her before. He thought, at first, he should feel guilty, a voyeur, but instead felt privileged. He hoped she hadn't seen him standing there in the dim light.

That night, for the first time in his memory, Sam's thoughts weren't of Wilbur, or Hunky, or work, but of himself. Somehow the vision of Emma brought him an acute self-awareness, a painful realization that he was incomplete. Lying in bed, he twisted and turned, kicking the tangled sheets and covers. He endured a fitful night—full of dreams, disturbing dreams he'd never reveal to anyone. And, lying awake, he tortured himself wondering if Emma was waiting for someone: a friend, a lover, who? He asked himself, *would she don that gown for me?*

Saturday, Sam borrowed a roomy four-door Ford to transport Wilbur. He was afraid Pop's truck would offer too stiff and jarring a ride, and hoped the boxy sedan would be more comfortable. It was a perfect balmy day full of warming sun. Green lush grasses, nature's benediction, covered the hillsides. Sam had Wilbur by the elbow as he inhaled the perfume carried in the air, and moved with hesitant steps to the automobile. Wilbur, in a new shirt and long trousers volunteered by Alfred for the occasion, took a back seat beside Josh. Josh poked one finger in Wilbur's ribs, and Wilbur gave a hoot. Sam swallowed a notion to chastise Josh, guessing they were all feeling a bit giddy.

"Let's get home," Sam said, "Mom's waiting for us."

Members of the hospital staff, which Sam was pleased to see included Emma, watched and waved as they drew away. The Doctor's last words were, "No running, no jumping, no baseball," but he didn't dampen their spirits. Sam wasn't paying attention as he anticipated every ripple in the rutted roads. He doubted the truck ride would have been much rougher, and was relieved when they arrived home without incident.

Lizzy, in a flowered dress, her hair upswept and cheeks flushed hearth-warm, bit her lower lip as she stood and watched Sam and Josh help Wilbur climb from the Ford. Wilbur's hair, shampooed and brushed for the trip home, glinted in the sun. Alfred and Ernie, also washed and combed for the occasion, relieved Josh and Sam. They escorted Wilbur, one on each arm, as they started for the porch stairs. Sam and Josh trailed behind.

"Hey, let go, you guys," Wilbur said, trying to twist his arms free, "I've walked this path a thousand times."

Ernie looked to Alfred. Alfred shrugged and they released him. Wilbur stepped hesitantly forward, his hand searching for the end of the stair rail. His toe caught an irregularity in the walk and he tripped, his shoe slapping the stone, but he didn't fall. Nervously watching, everyone jumped involuntarily. Wilbur grinned for his unseen audience, and grabbed the handrail. Head up, he climbed the wooden stairs.

On the porch, Lizzy embraced him. Nestled on her bosom, Wilbur clung to her, his head turning, nuzzling side to side. He said, "It sure smells good around here, like beef and pudding. What is this…a special occasion?"

"Inside everybody," Alfred said, holding the open door.

Once inside, they all passed the offered stuffed furniture comfort of the living room and gravitated to the warmth of the kitchen. After a gathering and shuffling of chairs, they all settled in around the familiar table with Wilbur at the head.

Wilbur asked, "Where's Pop?"

Lizzy said, "He'll be here shortly. There was a bit of trouble at the mill." She placed a shallow pan of warm corn bread on a trivet and proceeded to pour tea.

The noshing and joshing began slowly, almost solemnly, but soon the volume of conversation increased as they tried to talk over each other. In the buzz of table talk, someone mentioned Hunky. Hearing the name, Wilbur asked, "What did happen to him?"

All eyes turned to Sam, who sat mute not knowing what to say. Wilbur sat, apparently puzzled by the sudden silence, until Lizzy spoke filling the void. "Yes," she said, "a strange accident that. But, as the good book says—bread cast upon the water."

A moment passed, then Ernie spoke, "It's good to have you home, Will."

Above a general murmuring of agreement, Alfred said, "Amen."

Monday, Sam returned to the hospital. His thoughts of Emma, reverberant as the tones of a summoning church bell, pulled him there. There comes a vulnerable time to each man when struck by a woman. When this happens she can lead him around by the nose. This is especially true if it is the woman's design. Women, Mother Nature and Cupid know what they are doing.

It was one of those warm breezy teasing days that make you ache for summer. Budding trees feathered the brow of surrounding hills, a prelude to a lush verdant crown. The hum of insects, a faint chorus sensed rather than heard, supported the trill of sparrows, robins and jays. Below the rolling slope, in the broad valley bottom, the river swollen with spring melt and rain, pushed along its' banks swirling with the effort of spring cleaning.

Rolling to a halt on the crunching gravel, Sam, his black hair parted and combed flat and cheeks closely shaved, eased the truck in beside the rear entrance. Looking up he saw many draperies, stirred by fresh fingering breezes, flapping out open windows.

"Forget something?"

Startled, Sam turned at the sound of Emma's crisp voice. A flowered babushka covered all but the front of her hair; an idle auburn wisp swept her brow. She wore a long blue skirt and patterned blouse with sleeves rolled to her elbows. Her cheeks were flushed and her green eyes glistened. Balancing an armload of white linens, she was far lovelier than Sam remembered.

"No," he replied, then, hurried for something to say, asked, "n-n-new uniforms?" He could have amputated his stuttering tongue. Flustered, he opened the door and stepped out of the truck.

"No, just a spring thing," she seemed amused by Sam's obvious discomfort. "We are taking advantage of the day and airing some linen." She placed her load of sheets on a utility cart beside the hospital door. Turning to Sam, she asked, a hint of a tease in her voice, "And how, Sir, may I help you?"

Smitten, Sam considered the question as though the fate of the world rested on his answer. "Well," he decided to take the risk, "Greta Garbo is in Scranton...er, I mean she's not here personally, but, ah, her latest talkie is at the theater, and I wondered," he took a deep breath, "would you like to go and see it with me?" He shut up, knowing he'd risked it all.

Emma stood appraising him, her arms folded.

Not good, I've made a mess of it. Sam felt a nervous tic under his left eye, a tic he'd only rarely felt before—anticipating a bare-knuckle bout, or in a mine lighting the fuse of a dynamite charge. And, now in the presence of this slip of a woman.

After an agonizing silence, Emma asked, her face expressionless and her voice deadly serious, "Sam Freeman, are you asking me for a date?"

Sam felt the tic again, knowing he'd gambled and lost.

"Well," she grinned, "the answer is...I'd love to."

CHAPTER 6

April 1932

Josh was eighteen months younger than Sam who, at age 21, was out in the world fighting a man's battles, accepting offered kudos. Josh, held out of school one year due to 'growing pains', undiagnosed rheumatic fever, was tolerating his last year, his senior year, in Olympic High School. Josh knew that it was due to his mother's insistence that they all complete high school, and Sam's willingness to support them that allowed him and his brothers to remain in school. For this opportunity, Josh was begrudgingly grateful, though he itched to escape the boredom of the classroom. Still, he resented Sam's attitude, his willingness to accept long hours in a mine or colliery, when they were working, or moving contraband over dark roads at night resented Sam's way of wearing the dust and danger with pride. It grated on Josh being hidden in Sam's shadow, a boy overshadowed by a man, feeling insignificant as a sapling undernourished and unrecognized in the shade of a taller tree. He felt deprived.

Partly because of Sam's sacrifices, Josh would be the second member of the family to graduate from Olympic High. Josh considered the school a great joke on the populace. His own curiosity and desire to understand the complexities of people and life led him to read and ponder works far beyond those offered in the Olympic classrooms. He had most recently absorbed Milton's Paradise Lost and had no trouble envisioning himself in the role of Satan.

Josh thought the principal, Ezra Grimes, a clown, and the teachers a covey of frustrated old maids. His remembrance of Grimes—parading stiffly along a village lane with hurried steps, his dark trousers high-water short, his fist full of buttercups, and beside him a good head taller, Elsa Gooding, pedagogue, all elbows and knees, kissing her diminutive Bible with lemon-puckered lips—tripped Josh into private hysteria.

Josh often ridiculed the school song—"Here's to Olympic High School; the Tan, Maroon and Gray." Tan, Maroon and Gray! Josh snorted, "No wonder the area is depressed. Tan, Maroon and Gray...Jesus." Josh considered himself above it all. Smart enough to stay ahead of the class, though rarely opening an assigned book, he appeared disinterested. Yet, when a teacher questioned him, he had the answers.

Josh was interested, but not in writing or arithmetic. His interest was in the swarm of young bodies around him. His quick eyes captured impressions of those most innocently demure, images to be revisited in his late-night fantasies. Unknown to them, they were prisoners in his mind, submissive, begging, yielding to his every tortured whim. Contemplating them, he considered other studies distracting.

Handsome, tall and sinewy, Josh moved with an insolence that bespoke his attitude. His high forehead and prominent cheekbones often bordered a sardonic smile. Considering the girls around him, he felt he knew their innermost secrets. His interest in them was no secret. A girl walking past his desk, avoiding his sprawled feet, would be scrutinized, her reality remolded in his fantasy. In his imagination, mounds of curvaceous flesh would swell and undulate under the drab draping ankle-length dresses. Flaring his nostrils as they passed, he would capture their essence, their odors, musky traces of perspiration, anxiety and desire. Distracted by his interest, they would blush and giggle, causing great consternation amongst the myopic teachers.

Josh was often the topic of conversation when the girls gathered. They could be overheard on dewy damp foot shuffling mornings huddled near the Girl's entrance.

"Sue Ellen loves Josh."
Eyes widened, "Really?"
Softer, "She says they did it."
Eyebrows arched, "Do you believe her?"
"I don't know, but wouldn't you?"
"No. He scares me. He looks at me funny…gives me the creeps."
Young heads nodded in unison.

Still, strangely attracted but uncertain, the girl's skirted Josh, dancing, approaching, retreating, maidens lured to the dance, glowing in the mysteries of men and menses. Josh imagined he could have them, that they would pretend offense, but yield. He viewed all females young and old as unstable. He observed his married cousin and others—married women who left steady hardworking men and returned to former lovers who had used and deserted them. Josh perceived this as a basic trait of women upon which he could trade.

Elizabeth Freeman - Cordy, Lizzy, Josh's mother, was responding to a summons requesting her presence in the school principal's office. She strode toward the two-story red brick school, her steps heavy on the hard packed ground. A flock of wooly clouds, their shadows sliding across the landscape, promised a rainy May day. Lizzy growled, "What's this nonsense? Doesn't Grimes know it's laundry day?" Children at play heard her pass and stood silently watching her flailing arms, hearing echoes of their own mothers. Someone was in trouble.

Olympic was a relatively small school, accommodating only grades eight through twelve and was sparsely staffed. Inside, Mister Grimes, a wiry scurrying busy little man supervised the teachers, one for each grade level. He was pacing back and forth the length of his office. He had summoned Elizabeth Freeman-Cordy. Such was the hardship, burden, and duty imposed by his position. Grimes had dealt with the large volatile strong-willed protective woman in the past. He appeared to be considering ways to minimize the upcoming confrontation.

In his outer office, on a lineup of dark walnut-stained wooden chairs, sat the players- to-be in the impending drama. Mildred Conners, a late blooming slip of a girl with doe-like eyes sat beside her mother. Mrs. Conners, a fat woman breathing laboriously, shifted restlessly with nervous anticipation. She was there with her daughter's troubles while her husband, damn him, lay at home in a drunken stupor.

Sitting three chairs removed, Josh sat casually appraising a bronze-framed print of an eighteenth century sea duel, and two wide-beamed wooden ships locked in mortal combat. Familiar with the reproduction, Josh was able to relax and lose himself totally in the billowing white clouds, white sails, and gray-white cannon smoke. In his imagination, shattered men, their limbs torn by cannon fire, fell to the decks awash with blood and saltwater. Josh noted cobwebs on the ceiling above the print and incorporated them as drifting battle haze.

Grimes' secretary, tall and stork-like with dark-rimmed spectacles and black hair in a bun, was the first to sight Lizzy striding down the hall toward the office. She abandoned her desk and, without a knock, entered the principal's inner office.

Josh inhaled sharply and bolted upright when his mother burst through the office doorway. His time of reckoning had come.

Lizzy glowered at him before nodding curtly to the flustered Mrs. Conners. Turning to the abandoned desk, she asked of no one in particular, "Where's the secretary?" Her voice seemed to fill the high-ceilinged room.

Lizzy was obviously in no mood for small talk, and Josh pointed to the inner office door just as it swung open. The secretary appeared and stood rigidly beside the door. Eyes averted, she said, "Mister Grimes will see you now." Her involvement in the proceedings ended, she scurried to her desk.

Josh started for the door. His mother's meaty hand grabbed his collar halting him in his tracks. "Ladies first," she scolded, shaking him.

Mrs. Conners rose arduously and waddled through the doorway, her busy hands ushering her diminutive daughter before her, a mother duck with her only surviving duckling. Josh watched with inner amusement as Grimes straightened and stretched his spine in an effort to make the most of his five feet five inches. The big women dwarfed him. He waved one arm in an all-encompassing gesture directing them to the chairs set in a semicircle in front of his huge oak desk. "Ladies," he said, "Thank you for coming."

Replying, Mrs. Conners murmured, "You're welcome."

Principal Grimes, protected behind his fortress of a desk, pushed a large ledger to the side and placed a glass weight on a stack of papers. He placed his pen in the ink well, suspending temporarily his less trying task of bookkeeping. He cleared his throat. "I, ah," he began tentatively, "have called you here," he looked quickly as a ferret from woman to woman while pointing at the center of his universe, his desk, "to discuss a delicate matter." He exhaled.

Josh noticed Grimes was beginning to perspire. Covering his mouth, he smiled thinly, thinking—I'm the one who should be sweating.

Grimes clasped his hands and stretched taller. "I may as well come right to the crux of the matter," he said. He looked directly into the stormy eyes of Elizabeth Freeman-Cordy, and blurted, "Your son," he nodded at Josh, "has taken vulgar advantage of this child." He turned, his hand pointed at Mildred.

Josh felt his mother stiffen beside him. "How do you know this?" she asked.

"Miss Jenson the eighth grade teacher, found them together in an empty classroom. He," Grimes jabbed a trembling finger at Josh, "was exposed. She," he revealed, "was caressing his manhood."

Mrs. Conners gasped.

Lizzy remained ominously quiet.

Mister Grimes rose slowly, one hand stroking his chin. He said, "I believe that a matter such as this should be handled by the parents. I believe it spares everyone…involved," he tripped over the words., "embarrassment." He moved from behind his desk. "I feel I can rely on you mothers, ladies, to assure there will be no further problems of this nature." Grimes bowed stiffly to each of the women. "I consider the matter closed."

Mildred was sobbing, her face buried in her mother's skirts.

Josh sat with shoulders slumped. He knew what awaited him; Lizzy was not one to spare the rod. He looked over at the trembling girl. *Silly bitch*, he thought.

That night, Josh was sprawled naked across his bed. Ernie and Alfred stood examining the numerous welts that laced his back in a crisscross pattern from shoulder blades to hamstrings. Each welt was flame red and appeared ready to burst, but there was no blood or oozing fluid. Alfred waved his head from side to side, "No doubt about it," he said, "Mom's an artist." Looking at Sam seated on the bed beside Josh, gently applying a thick black salve to the wounds, Ernie nodded his agreement.

The thick pungent odor of the ointment hung in the air. With each of Sam's strokes, Josh shivered in reaction. Sam assured him, "I'm being as easy as I can." With two fingers, Sam scooped another dollop from the wide-mouthed jar. Sam added, "You don't deserve any sympathy. What the hell's wrong with you, messing with a girl that young?"

Trembling, Josh turned his head and replied with a sneer, "I like to be the one to break em in."

Sam looked at the twins standing in curious disbelief. They all knew the embellished story of Josh's transgression would find its way to the ladies' socials and quilting bees as titillating gossip, casting aspersions on the family. Privately concerned about Emma's reaction, Sam spat, "Damn it, Josh," and jabbed him in the ribs.

Josh jerked in response.

"You can't go around acting like a randy goat."

Alfred said, "Yeah, the family black sheep."

Ernie added, "Black goat."

Josh closed his eyes, moaned and sighed. His lips parted. Sam felt his muscles go lax.

Incredulous, Sam said, "Jesus, Josh…I swear you're enjoying this."

Josh smiled, a languorous dreamy smile.

CHAPTER 7

May 1932

Sam's arrival at day's end soon became a constant in Emma's life. As surely and solemnly as dusk, he would pull onto the gravel drive behind the hospital, the pickup's engine gasping with the last hill climb of the day. Sam's smile, his joy at the sight of her, gave Emma a welcome lift.

It was midweek, and so far Emma had given no indication that word of Josh's deviant behavior had reached her. Sam was uneasy, wondering if he should tell her himself and put the incident behind. He was trying to work up the nerve, not knowing, fearing how she might react. He didn't want to scare her off.

Sam stepped from the truck and looked for her. Emma stood, a sad shadow against the background of the stark white building. Slumped alongside a pillar, a raincoat draped over her shoulders, her eyes downcast, she looked the epitome of dejection. After considering her for a moment, assessing her mood, Sam decided it was not the time for divulging depressing secrets. He asked, "Want to ride?"

With a weak smile, she said, "We can walk."

Sam asked jokingly, "Afraid to ride with strange men."

"You're not so strange," she smiled. She dismissed the notion with a wave of her hand and confided, "I just need to walk at the end of the day…leave behind the frustrations and ills of this place." Her eyes begged for understanding.

Sam took her elbow, and they walked. He could feel the weariness in her step. The smell of antiseptic lingered on her.

The Cooper home was located a mile from the hospital at the end of a curving lane that rose gradually caressing the hillside. Appropriately somber in his navy blue jacket and porkpie cap, Sam strolled alongside Emma as they started up the gentle rise. They took care not to hold hands or give any appearance of intimacy until out of sight of the hospital and puritanical eyes. Overhead, scattered clouds, relieved of their moisture, slid eastward away from the sinking sun. A warm ground level breeze carrying the lingering fragrance of fading lilac edged them on.

As they rounded a curve, Sam took Emma's hand. Warm, slight and uneasy, it felt like a newborn kitten in his. They moved easily and without conversation, bathed in the magic of early evening.

Emma broke the spell, "I told everybody about the motion picture. Wasn't Garbo amazing?"

Sam recalled the movie. More than a week had passed, and they had been in the company of Emma's older sister Ruth. Sitting beside Emma, he'd held her hand in the dark Cinema. His freehand flexed in memory.

"Sure, but there are better shows coming." He took the opportunity to ask, "How about this Saturday?"

Emma stopped and turned until they faced each other in the remaining soft light, "I can't," she said, "I have to work."

"All day?"

She caught the disappointment in his question and asked, "Don't you have to work Saturday?"

Sam shrugged, pushing his hands deep into his pockets, "I could make it a short day."

"Well." Emma said, resuming the walk, "my father doesn't like me out late."

"Unless you're with Ruth." Sam could see the Cooper home. The silhouette of the imposing Queen Anne with distinctive gables and surrounding porch was unmistakable on the crest of the hill. Sam thought the walk seemed shorter each time they made it. He was desperately uneasy. He took her hand and asked, "Em, when can I see you? We never have any real time together."

She laid her other hand lightly on his arm, "What about Sunday?"

"You mean church?"

"You're a Methodist aren't you?" Emma smiled, "I was thinking about after church." She hesitated, her eyes brightening, "You could come and meet my father."

Sam swallowed hard and thought about that.

"Just my father. Mom and Ruth are in Philadelphia visiting my married sister Ellie."

Sam chewed on his lip, *Why does a guy never consider a woman's family?—never get past the hormones, never think long term, never consider the responsibilities, never consider that before too long the daughter is going to look like the mother.*

"Since Ruth told Daddy about you, he's been wanting to meet you." Emma's words and dancing green eyes brought Sam out of his musings. He saw that she was amused by his squirming.

Sam grasped her shoulders and pulled her to him. Embracing her, he kissed her fully on the mouth. Her moist lips pressed on his; she felt warm and yielding against him.

When he released her, she exclaimed, "Sam, what got into you?"

Sam pushed his cap to the back of his head, *What did get into me?* he wondered.

Emma laughed and started toward the house. Over her shoulder, she said. "I'll tell Daddy to expect you Sunday."

Sam watched her ascend the front stairs, then started back down the hill. He was in turmoil, feeling like a frantic ant in a sand trap slipping inexorably down into the maw of an ant lion. He considered his dilemma: no money, a tentative existence in a terribly depressed economy. Wilbur's hospital and doctor bills, his mother and his brothers depending on him—he'd promised to take care of them. *Jesus, he'd promised!* And now Emma. *Damn the lust in me.* He began to run in the dark, hurtling down the slope.

Breathing heavily, leaning against the truck, he knew it wasn't just his aching loins—he loved her. He also knew that if Harry Cooper were any kind of a father, he'd laugh at him. "What the hell am I going to do?" he asked the face in the side view mirror.

That night, Sam counted sheep. He stared at the ceiling and tried to imagine lazy streams and placid waters. He counted backwards from five hundred. He closed his eyes and talked to himself, *My toes are asleep, my legs are asleep, my body feels heavy, I'm sleepy.* Nothing worked.

When, finally, he dropped into a turning, troubled darkness, he dreamed. He was walking with Emma. She was naked and her body was as lush as he thought it might be. Her auburn hair was long and fell in luxurious sheaves around and between her perfect breasts. He was fully clothed in a denim shirt and long trousers. Emma's arm was in his. She looked lovingly up into his eyes as they strolled along a vague lane. Hordes of people gathered in a swirling mist. Some had fallen, others were crouched, exhausted. Dressed in rags, they were emaciated, taut dry skin covered their skulls, their faces. Like serpents, they squirmed and crawled around and over each other. Their thin arms and boney claw-like hands extended, they begged. Writhing and moaning, their eyes hot red coals fixed on him, they, cried, "You promised, you promised." Horrified, he recognized them—they were his brothers. Emma, her flesh on his flesh, said, "Let's get some ice cream."

Sam woke with a start. He was, disoriented, in a sweat. He sat up in bed.

From across the bedroom, propped up on one arm, Josh stared at him through the vague light. He asked. "What are you moanin' about?"

The next evening, Sam got a reprieve. He breathed a silent sigh of inner relief when Emma gave him the news as they strolled.

"I won't see you for a few days," she said softly, apologetically, searching Sam's face for a reaction. "Father and I are going to Philadelphia over the weekend for a visit and to escort mother home."

Sam nodded solemnly. He hesitated to comment, afraid Emma would misinterpret how he felt about gaining a few days to breathe, to think, to get his act together. Sam pulled her to him and they stood in a calm embrace. His head filled with her perfume, his eyes closed, Sam remembered his dream of the night before. He remembered too, that he had yet to explain about Josh.

"Sam, you're trembling."

He held her at arms length, both hands on her shoulders. "I'll miss you," Sam said, managing a thin smile. "But I'll find something to do."

CHAPTER 8

May 1932

Flanagan's was a good place to hide. It was a speakeasy in a nondescript vertical-plank building on a corner in the small mining village of Throop. Everybody knew where it was unless asked; then with a puzzled expression it was, "Flanagans?" It was where Tom Donavan the village constable got his weekly stipend for having such poor eyesight. Inside, Flanagan's was as sparse as its parsimonious owner could make it. It was as lean as Flanagan himself. The bar was constructed of boards and hardware confiscated from abandoned hay wagons. There were three rough wooden tables located strategically in the dim corners. Kerosene lanterns provided dubious illumination in the windowless den, and kept Flanagan outside the reach of the hated utility company. There was a pervasive odor, a combination of coal oil, tobacco, beer and mildew. Each time a body entered or departed, the rusty strap hinges on the door sounded a horrendous screech notifying those inside of the event, and saving Flanagan the expense of a doorbell.

It was the screech of the hinges that caused Clarence the bartender to look up and welcome his second early afternoon customer. "Sam. Is it you?"

"It's me." Sam removed his cap and tossed it on the bar.

Clarence set a limp newspaper aside. "Isn't it early in the day for business?"

"It is. I'm here for a pint or two." Sam sat on a hard three-legged stool. Looking around. he asked, "Where is the old miser?"

Clarence smiled, "In the back with his nose in the inkwell, workin' on both sets of books."

"Well, don't disturb him. He must be in great pain."

Nodding agreement, Clarence placed a jar of beer in front of Sam.

Sam looked down the length of the bar at a bent one-arm man who appeared to be asleep. He put two nickels beside the beer and said, "Give Joe a pint." The bent man turned his head, and peered out from under a slouch hat; his canvas cheek bulged with a chew. He spit into a brass spittoon. "Sam Freeman is it?"

It was Joe Turner that Sam had come to find. Joe had left an arm buried under a mountain of coal and was curved by osteoporosis. He looked ancient, but Sam knew Joe, a symbol of everything wrong with their existence, was only fifty. He also knew that Joe was all eyes and memory. It was a rare word dropped in the valley that missed Joe's ear.

"It is," Sam said and left his stool to sit next to the little man. "How's Joe?" he asked.

"Not spry enough to be chasing Harry Cooper's daughter."

"Jesus, Joe, you don't miss a thing do you?"

Joe took a swallow of beer. A wisp of foam remained above his lip, giving emphasis to his crooked smile. "You know me," he said, "information's me only trade."

"I suppose you think I'm not in this grand place for the company."

"I know your grandfather, and I knew your father…rest his soul. You're just like them. Not one to be hangin' around gin mills in the middle of the day without reason. What is it you need to know?"

"Christ. No 'How do you do'. No 'Thanks for the pint'. Right to the guts of it."

Sam feigned irritation.

Joe Turner pushed the shapeless hat back on his head, 'Well?"

Sam looked around. Clarence had left the bar. They were alone. He leaned closer to Joe, "I need to make some cash. Who's running the whiskey in from the Jersey coast?"

Joe sighed. He looked away from Sam, and took a long pull on his beer. He pressed a thumb and index finger to his closed eyes.

Sam waited. He caught the musty smell of the bent man. He wondered where he lived, where he slept, if he bathed.

Finally, Joe said, "You need money this bad?"

Sam didn't answer.

"They still hold bare-knuckle bouts on the river," Joe grabbed Sam's biceps, "fifty bucks, if you're the winner."

Sam had a fleeting vision of Hunky's broken and bloody face. "And scrambled brains if you're the loser." Placing his hand over Joe's, he said, "No, I need some real money."

"It's an awful risky business."

"I know."

Joe shook his head, "You think you know…you could end up dead."

"We're all going to end up dead; it's just a matter of when."

Joe studied Sam for a long moment. "You're a Freeman all right." He looked around. They were still alone. He whispered, "Here's who you want to see…"

The only time Sam had been on the Atlantic shore was during a family excursion to Atlantic City. This was nothing like that. Standing uneasily in a salt marsh he could see the light at Barnagat Inlet across the bay as it sliced the night like a saber. His nostrils filled with the odor of sea and shore creatures dead and alive. He moved his boots in the giving sand and wondered what it smelled like at low tide. He wished he could see the ocean's lip as it slobbered on the shore instead of just the ripple of the bay.

Sam wasn't sure he was in the right spot. He'd pulled off route 9 onto a dirt road as instructed, and had driven to the shore and parked. The lighthouse was east northeast as described. He must be there—where the whaleboat laden with cases of whiskey would beach.

He felt naked, exposed, in a foreign environment. Sam wished, selfishly, that his brothers were with him. But they weren't. It was Sam's decision. If the shit hit the fan, he would be the only one sprayed. He rubbed his coarse two-day growth of beard, *Where's the goddamn boat?* He needed to see the three flashes of light and know it was there. If it came soon, he could make it to Scranton with his truckload of hangovers before daylight. If the Coast Guard hadn't intercepted the launch. If he was in the right place. If the cops didn't show. If highjackers didn't blow him away. Jesus, they can't call this easy money! Sam tried to spit in disgust, but his mouth was dry.

There they were: three flashes. Sam squinted at them as he struck a match. As he returned the signal, he saw the silhouette of the craft sliding in on the greasy waters of the bay. He ran to get the hidden truck.

Like worker ants, Sam and the boat crew carried the cases of contraband through the ankle-deep brackish water and across the slipping sand. They were soaked by sea and sweat by the time the rear leaf springs were bent flat by the whiskey weight.

"Damn good thing we didn't have one more case," the stocky seaman said.

Sam looked at the two boatmen as he stretched a brown canvas over his cargo. There were two of them, one dark, stocky and talkative, and a pock-faced redhead, quiet and thin as a blade.

Sam was surprised how well the redhead, now lighting a cigarette, had pulled his weight. Straining on a rope, carefully keeping both men in sight, Sam grunted as the canvas drew taut over the stacked cases covering them completely.

The dark man said, "Well, you got the stuff and we got the envelope. Good luck." He offered his hand to Sam.

Sam shook the man's hand and watched as they both turned and trudged to the empty boat now riding high in the water, swaying at the line. He watched as they pushed off, and felt relieved when they were gone. It didn't pay to trust anybody. Sam took a last walk around the truck checking the tires. As he put his foot on the running board and reached to pull himself into the driver's seat, he saw a glint of light over the water. "Shit, a signal."

He started the engine and eased the transmission into low gear. The wheels turned slowly moving the loaded truck over the packed sand. He wondered where the hijackers would be waiting. Sam shifted gears when the truck lifted out of the sandy lane and onto a graded dirt road. It would be before he reached the paved highway. Sam pressed the accelerator to the floor and reached across the seat feeling for the sawed off shotgun.

Running without lights, he was almost at the roadblock before he saw the black hulks—two sedans parked bumper-to-bumper across the road. Sam couldn't see the speedometer, but figured he was hitting about forty miles an hour. Sam clenched his teeth and pointed the radiator cap at the slight space between the two cars. *Four tons at forty miles an hour should do it.* He thought he saw shadows scurrying for the roadside.

One of the sedans jerked back from the center of the road just before the truck reached the makeshift barricade. Sam quickly turned to careen through the slight opening. There was the scream of tearing metal and the popping sound of gunfire as Sam, thrown against the steering column, fought to control the swerving truck. He was having trouble breathing; it felt like someone had kicked him in the chest. In the mirror, a single headlight appeared in the darkness. Sam checked and saw that he still had both headlights. He'd need them; the moon had disappeared and the night was as dark and deadly as deceit.

Recalling a curve in the road ahead, Sam eased up on the gas. He planned to coast to the side of the road beyond the curve without flashing any taillights. The disabled vehicle was far enough behind for his ruse to work. In the curve, Sam turned the lights off, and double clutched into low gear. The hum of tires on asphalt diminished as the truck rolled to a stop on the soft shoulder. Grabbing the shotgun, he scrambled out of the cab.

Sam crouched in front of the truck when the one-eyed pursuit car rolled by. He pointed the stubby shotgun in the general direction of the car's rear wheel and discharged both barrels. With a blast that left his ears ringing, a double load of number four shot tore rubber from the rear wheel. The sedan swerved out of control and lumbered into a ditch.

Sam had the truck rolling before his pursuers had jerked to a halt. As he passed them, he could see the driver struggling to open his door. Sam shifted into high gear, and shouted, for his own satisfaction, "So long, fellas."

Adrenaline kept Sam alert for fifty miles, but as he rolled down Lackawanna Avenue in Scranton at the end of his hundred and eighty mile drive, he was struggling to remain awake. He might have fallen asleep if it were not for the sharp pain in his chest. Probing gingerly, Sam thought, *bet I broke a couple of ribs.* Long fingers of dawn were parting the darkness, and he had to find a place to hide the truckload of trouble. Turning through the streets, he finally located an alley that ran behind a junkyard surrounded by a high board fence. The truck could remain safely hidden there for an hour or two.

Sam steered the truck in until it was scraping the fence. *This will have to do,* he smiled seeing the gas gauge registered empty. He surveyed his surroundings in the half-light. A brown rat crossing the alley was the only living thing in sight. There was room for a vehicle to pass between the truck and a windowless brick building across the alley. Sam slumped against the seat feeling numb except for the pain prodding his chest. He wrapped the shotgun in his black jacket and opened the truck door. "Time to collect," he said.

Wincing with each step, Sam found the back door of the building where he'd first met his partners in crime. It was a wooden door that opened outward, and the hinge pins were exposed. He smiled, *Assholes.* Removing the pins, he entered the building. Leaning against a dingy wall, Sam sniffed the musty air and listened for any movement. Nothing—too early for low-lifes.

He was seated in a cramped cluttered office when he heard the key in the outer door. A doorknob bumped a wall. There was the sound of men shuffling as they moved inside.

"Close the door. Gus, you make some coffee. You, come with me." It was the voice of the fat man, a voice of someone used to being obeyed.

Sam judged there were three: Fat Man, Gus, and one other. Sam positioned the shotgun on his lap. He guessed he looked threatening enough with the heavy beard, and pain putting the 'no bullshit' look in his eyes. He felt calm, maybe it was exhaustion, a sheen of sweat covered his palms.

Fat Man, *what is his name?* didn't blink seeing Sam seated there. As he moved slowly to a small metal desk, swaying flesh beneath his chin revealed his irritation. A sturdy wooden chair groaned as he lowered his bulk onto it with some effort.

The other man, Sam guessed, was a light heavyweight, thick through the arms and shoulders, maybe slow but strong. He was wearing a gray fedora and vest, handsome, a ladies man, probably a smooth talker, but silent, thinking, now. There was a pistol in a shoulder holster under his left arm. Right handed, a counter puncher, Sam bet.

"Put the gun on the floor," Sam said, standing, the shotgun pointed at the man's patent leather shoes.

Counter Puncher looked to Fat Man.

Fat Man nodded. Counter Puncher lifted the pistol grip by two fingers and placed it on the worn carpet. He kicked it to Sam; he'd done this before.

"Stand in the corner," Sam said, pointing at the corner behind the fat man's desk. Counter Puncher walked calmly into the corner and stood glaring at Sam. The look on his face said, *I'll kill you for this.*

Sam said, "Turn around and drop your pants, I don't want any quick moves" Counter Puncher, disbelieving, looked to Fat Man who said, "Do it."

Fat Man was starting to sweat. His face was red above his tight shirt collar by the time his henchman stood facing into the corner with his trousers bunched at his feet.

"Where's the coffee?" Gus yelled from the other room Fat Man raised his hand to steady Sam, and shouted, "In the cabinet by the window, where it always is." By the tone of his voice, Sam knew he had control.

"Got it, Boss." Gus banged a distant cabinet door.

Fat Man turned to Sam. "Well, Delivery Man, what do you want?" He placed his fleshy hands palms down on the desk. He wore a white shirt with vertical stripes and a blue necktie pressed between his belly and the desk. Through heavy-lidded dreamy eyes, he viewed Sam with disdain.

"My money."

The fat man grinned, "No merchandise, no money." He turned his palms up as if to say—it's that simple.

"Look," Sam said, "the truck is hidden here in the city. When I'm holding the money, I'll tell you where it is."

The fat man said, "That ain't the way it works."

Sam raised the shotgun until the barrels were within a foot of the fat man's nose. "I'm not going to piss with you. And you don't have all day. I can't guarantee your competition or the cops won't find the stuff. So, give me the goddamn money."

Beads of sweat covered Fat Man's forehead, and Sam imagined the wheels turning in his head. Faced with the dilemma, he was chewing on Sam's words. Finally, he said, "Okay, but if the stuff ain't there, we'll come looking for you."

"It's there," Sam said, allowing the shotgun to swing down to his side.

Fat Man pulled an envelope from a desk drawer. He laid it on the desk.

Sam said, "Open it. Spread the bills so I can count them." The fat man shrugged and opened the envelope. He spread the contents, ten one hundred dollar bills, on the desk.

Sam nodded and Fat Man put the bills back in the envelope. Sam said, "In the alley behind Valley Salvage." Pulling the truck key from his pocket, he threw it on the desk and took the fat envelope. With the money heavy in his hand, Sam eased out the door.

CHAPTER 9

May 1932

Reverend Christer, of the First Methodist Church, was able to sustain the souls of his family members, but he depended on the benevolence of the congregation to feed their bodies. Sunday collections were sparse to be generous, lean to be accurate. The collection plates returned to the center aisle with few coins and only an occasional dollar bill. Cash was rare in most households; many of the townsfolk got by on the barter system, giving what they had: fresh vegetables, eggs, preserves, baked goods, a rabbit or a chicken. Those that had some cash were understandably reluctant to part with it. But, he was a popular preacher and goods appeared on his doorstep with adequate regularity.

Elizabeth Freeman-Cordy gave routinely. Each Thursday, she sent Ernie to the parish house with a donation, usually loaves of bread but sometimes a potpie or preserves. Ernie was her errand boy of choice. Quiet and dependable, he could be relied upon to conduct himself in a respectful manner. Yielding to direction when in the presence of his twin Alfred, he was independent and confident in his actions when Alfred wasn't around. Lizzy knew that his size and demeanor assured that few rascals would be apt to challenge him in the course of his duties.

Ernie would never tell his mother, but he looked forward to his weekly chore. The reverend had three very attractive daughters. Early on a spring morning, with the sky full of woolly altocumulus clouds grazing like sheep across a pale blue meadow, pollen and nature's purpose in the air, Ernie arrived at the reverend's gate. He closed the white picket gate behind him and inched cautiously up the dew-wet flat stone walk toward the Christer front porch. His eyes flicked nervously inspecting the limbs of the two Oak trees flanking his path. He was anticipating the aggressively raucous blue jay that had circled and dived to harass him the week before.

"He's gone."

Surprised by the voice, Ernie tensed. Turning, he saw Lisa the reverend's youngest daughter seated on a porch swing partially obscured by a trellis and a rampant trumpet vine. She was smiling, obviously amused by his cautious approach.

He returned her smile. "I hope you're right, but I believe it was a she." Ernie enjoyed Lisa's company. At age twelve, she was considerably younger than him and their relationship was platonic, innocent and unassuming. Their frequent discussions concerned the natural world around them and little of themselves. With Lisa, Ernie was at ease. Her two older sisters were budding young women one and two years older than Ernie and took great satisfaction in making him uncomfortable.

"You got your hair cut," Lisa observed, tossing her own curls.

Ernie rolled his brown eyes upward as if trying to see the results of his mother's handiwork. Lizzy had worked quickly while he sat resolutely wrapped in a bed sheet. The results were subject to opinion. Ernie thought the disappearance of his sideburns and the tuft of brown hair remaining on top made his full face look like a fuzzy pumpkin. His mother thought he looked fine. He shrugged, "It'll look okay in a week."

Lisa leaned forward in her seat, "What have you got?" she asked pointing at the basket swinging at Ernie's side.

"Bread and a jar of preserves. Berry, I think." He set the basket on the porch. "And, something for you." Ernie reached under the cloth covering the basket and withdrew a small wooden carving of a woman in full skirt and bonnet. He gave it to Lisa.

"Oh," she said, her eyes widening, "she's beautiful."

"I whittled it," he said, "from a piece of pine." He shuffled one of his ankle-high shoes, and fiddled self consciously with his hands. "It's your Sunday skirt and bonnet."

Pleasure lit her fine features. "Well, so it is. Thank you, Ernie. Thanks for not carving the likes of my daily drabs." Her hand flicked the hem of her gray dress as she studied the delicate figure. She pushed off the porch surface with one foot, setting the swing in motion. "She looks so real; her skirt folds so naturally, you'd think it was cloth."

For something to say, Ernie asked, "What are you doing?"

"Waiting for humming birds," Lisa turned her blue eyes upward and tossed her halo of blond curls. "It's quiet and cool here in the mornings before the sun comes around." She laid the carving in her lap.

"Do you see a lot of hummingbirds?" Ernie glanced around.

"Sure. There's one now. See him high by the trumpet vine?...They love the orange blossoms. They collect nectar and aphids."

Lisa's enthusiasm was contagious and he allowed his eyes to follow the vine wound through the trellis. "There's one now," he pointed at a hovering mite. "He looks more like a carpenter bee than a bird. Whoa—there he goes." The hummingbird flashed blue and white out of sight.

"Sometimes," Lisa said, her open expression urging belief, "they bathe in the puddles of dew trapped in the broad coleus leaves." She moved on the swing, patting the white slats beside her, "Sit here and watch with me."

Ernie looked at the eyebolts and chain suspending the swing.

"Oh, sit down, you're not that heavy" He shrugged and eased his two hundred pounds onto the swing fearing its collapse. To his relief, it creaked but held.

"See," Lisa laughed, looking up at him bunched on his end of the swing. "You're not as big as you think."

He swung uneasily, one white-knuckled hand gripping a chain.

Beside him, Lisa smelled like store-bought soap and rose petals. "Now, take your shoes off. It's more fun with them off," she said, stiffening her knees and wiggling her toes. The swing moved easily. "I think toes are funny, don't you? Mine look like asparagus," she giggled.

Ernie's shoes thudded on the porch deck. He moved tighter to his end of the swing leaving an inch or two of white slats between him and beaming Lisa. They sat swaying gently, quiet except for the creak of the wooden swing.

"You can be my best friend." Lisa brushed the light hair on his wrist with her fingertips. She considered Ernie, her thin lips slightly parted. "If you want. Do you?"

Ernie succumbed to the motion of the swing and Lisa's soft inviting words. He closed his eyes and floated peacefully, smiling inwardly, not wanting to lose the moment. His hands folded in his lap, Ernie resisted an urge to twiddle his thumbs.

The sun had inched further onto the end of the porch when he opened his eyes and said, "They migrate, you know."

"Who?"

"Hummingbirds...to Central America."

"I wish I could," she stated matter-of-factly.

"Migrate?" he asked turning to search her face.

"I would leave this town and never look back." She caught his eye. "Would you miss me?"

"Very much," he said, "You always miss your friends."

Josh knew of Ernie's weekly deliveries. Better you than me, he thought. He considered Reverend Christer a phony and a weakling. *If you can't do it, teach it; if you can't teach it, preach it.* In Josh's opinion, the preacher was a leech at the bottom of the food chain. *Feed him? Bullshit, let the asshole get a job.*

Sitting in the family pew on Sundays—Josh called *Sindays*—with the unyielding hardwood bench under him, the dry odor of hymnals in his nose, and his mother behind, Josh took pleasure in allowing his eyes to wander over the females of the congregation. This Sunday it seemed every woman had a youngster in tow. From rosy cheek to innocent cheek, his glance drifted. His perverse thoughts were delicious, divorced from the senseless pulpit prattle, as he stored images for his fantasies. *I'm Lucifer fallen here amongst the lambs,* Josh smiled. Anyone observing him would think him happy in the Lord's house. Indeed he was, before the fleshy display.

Josh noted the reverend's daughters seated several rows in front and to his left - three plums ripe for picking. Their mother was with them; used goods, he wasn't interested. His eyes settled on the youngest daughter Lisa. All done up in ribbons, her hair was a splash of sunlight in the dimness of the cavernous church. She tuned her head and beamed a smile. He shuddered with delight. Josh felt his brother Ernie stir at his side, raise his hand and discreetly wave his fingers. Lisa returned the gesture.

Shit. Chagrined, Josh flushed. Lisa wasn't smiling at him; she was smiling at Ernie.

He looked at his brother's face, a clown in repose. *Sweet innocence, disgusting.* Josh looked at Lisa who had turned away. He felt the lust stir in him, the heat rising in his groin. Josh felt himself. He was as hard as the bench. He placed his hand palm-down over the bulge—*where there's a need, there's a way.*

After the service Josh and his brothers milled about in front of the church waiting for their parents to end a conversation with a garrulous older couple. Josh stood in the shade of an old maple, picking at the thick bark and looking at the church building. *How drab. Why don't they dress it up like the Catholics? Methodists are so tight-ass. As much fun as a wheelbarrow full of dead babies. No card playing. They think God gives a shit if they play cards or go to the Nickelodeon.* Josh chuckled, thinking maybe a bored Methodist girl could use a little fun, a little touching diversion.

Someone tapped his shoulder. Josh turned to his brother Alfred. "You headed home?" Alfred asked.

Alfred looked as relaxed as usual. He had removed his necktie and stuffed it in the breast pocket of his coat. His stiff winged collar was open at the throat, and both hands were buried in his trouser pockets.

Josh said, "Maybe after I get a little more religion." He nodded.

Alfred followed his gaze. Ann Christer and her daughters were exiting the church.

"They are something, aren't they?" Alfred appraised the two older sisters standing beside their mother in their Sunday best.

"How old are they?"

Alfred turned his hands easily, "Sarah and Beth are seventeen and nineteen and, according to Ernie, the youngest will be thirteen next Saturday."

"Hmm," Josh tugged at his tie, *I'll see that she gets something nice, something warm to hold.*

The warm summer day had started torturously slow, the hours sliding like warm honey on a sticky bun. Everything was in bloom, Mother Nature at her gentlest. Offered a reprieve, people allowed the sharp hardship of winter to slip into forgetfulness. Josh strolled with relaxed stride along the picket fences of

Martin Street. He amused himself watching the bees in the random wild flowers and intentional hollyhocks and day lilies. "You guys," he said speaking to the laboring bees, "get as enthused about fresh blossoms as I do." He shifted a small package wrapped in bright blue paper from his right to his left hand. Looking ahead, he saw he was nearing the Christer house. He considered the likelihood of Lisa being home alone. *Well, if she isn't like a bee I'll have to make one more pass.*

The front of the house was a blaze of color. Mounds of red Impatiens splashed with daisies billowed under the mature trumpet vine. Josh couldn't see the preacher getting his hands dirty, and wondered who tended the blooms. There was no one on the porch, Josh squared his shoulders and knocked on the screen door. He stepped back a respectful distance, hearing the tap of heels on hardwood. Ann Christer appeared. Though the mother of three, she had a freshness and poise that belied her age. There were creases at the corners of her eyes, and her brow was wrinkled above drawn and tired eyes.

She opened the door with one hand, a damp cloth swayed in the other. "Yes?"

"Good day, Ma'am, I'm Josh, Ernie's brother."

"Oh, of course," she brushed a wisp of gray hair from her forehead, "what can I do for you?" Adjusting her soiled apron, she added apologetically, "I'm washing the woodwork."

Josh presented the gift-wrapped package. "Sorry to interrupt you. Ernie forgot to leave this. It's for Lisa."

"How nice," she said, raising her hand to accept it.

"Uh, he asked that I give it to her in person."

"Oh, surely," she stepped aside, "won't you come in? I'll call her."

"I'll wait here," Josh stepped quickly back as the door closed.

Minutes later, Lisa and her mother were at the door. Lisa pushed the door open. Her mother asked, "Would you like some lemonade?"

"Please."

Lisa studied Josh as she crossed the porch and sat on the swing.

Josh, lean and handsome, half closed his dreamy eyes and considered her secrets.

"You're Ernie's brother."

"Yes," Josh answered as Lisa gave the swing a push setting it in motion. The movement of the swing and a puff of warm breeze lifted her light summer frock. Josh enjoyed a quick slash of pink panties between alabaster thighs.

Lisa followed his glance. "You're not like Ernest, are you?"

"No, not at all." Josh eased himself onto the swing.

CHAPTER 10

June 1932

Saturday, a week later, Sam stood on the Cooper front porch waiting to see Emma. If not for the wide bands of tape circling his torso, he would be totally relaxed, having heard Harry Cooper had gone on to New York City on business. Sam knew that before the crash Emma's father had diverse holdings. He assumed Harry's trip to the big city concerned whatever remained.

Minutes before, Emma's sister Ruth assured Sam, "She'll be right down." He didn't notice any change in Ruth's demeanor; perhaps word of Josh's peccadillo had not reached the family's ears. Maybe, Sam thought, *I'm making too much of it.* He dropped his shoulders and rolled his head trying to stay loose in spite of doctor Pankow's tape job. The tape bothered Sam more than the cracked ribs did.

He walked to the porch rail and gazed across the valley. Overhead, the limitless sky was a clear pale blue. Sunshine filled the afternoon. An intoxicating fragrance drifted in the air. Sam surveyed the surrounding bushes and blossoms looking for the source. There was beauty in the harsh world, he decided—it was what made life bearable.

The screen door creaked and Sam turned to see Emma coming toward him. Dressed in a white blouse with puffed sleeves and a full lavender skirt, she glowed with a natural radiance. She took Sam's hand and kissed him on the cheek. "I missed you," she said.

Sam blinked his eyes to stifle a fleeting image of her naked in his dream.

Emma stood searching his eyes. "Are you all right? You seem a little stiff and your eyes look like you could use some aspirin."

Sam smiled, "Yes, nurse, I'm all right." He placed his hands on his rib cage. "Just a cracked rib. Fell down…clumsy of me. But I'm okay outside of an occasional hurt to remind me of it."

"Oh," she said, "I'll bet they're sore." She shook her head and appraised him. He was wearing a white short-sleeved shirt, revealing his muscular arms, and black slimming trousers. The shirt, bright, creased and obviously new, provided a sharp contrast to Sam's hair, parted and slick as patent leather. She sighed, "Well, you look perfectly splendid on the outside."

Sam glowed in response. He said, "I thought we could take a ride."

Locals, lovers, and stargazers referred to the spot, a jog off the road following a ridge beneath the summit of West Mountain, as the 'Overlook'. It offered a panoramic view of the Lackawanna valley—the beauty and the scars. A verdant carpet stretched in all directions, its rolling serenity broken by random slashes of defiled earth and obnoxious ungainly structures. A canopy of majestic trees pierced by intrusive belching-black stacks and giant spider-like collieries.

Emma scanned the expanse as Sam stopped the truck in a stand of towering hemlock. The spreading boughs of the conifers framed her view and their scent overwhelmed her. "Oh," she said, "it's beautiful from up here."

Sam asked, "You don't think it's beautiful down there?"

"You can't see the dirt and trauma from here. It looks like the Bible's promised land from this height. Down there, it looks like the quarries of Egypt."

"The quarries of Egypt?"

She huffed, "You know; hot, dusty, slaves struggling with their burdens. Men straining to raise blocks of stone up a pyramid, weighted by tasks that won't be completed in their lifetime."

Sam smiled, "Wow, a woman goes away, a philosopher returns."

Emma blushed.

Sam kissed her, his lips brushing her velvet cheek; he caught the pleasantly insidious lure of nubile woman and perfume.

She returned his kiss and, aware of Sam's injury, embraced him gently.

Sam said, "Let's get out of here. There's a blanket behind the seat." He climbed out of the cab and circled to open the passenger door. Emma had the door open and one foot on the running board. Sam grabbed the blanket, took her hand and led her to a shaded patch of lush grass. From the highway, an odor of recently mowed grass drifted in to grace the air. Sam commented, "Smell the grass. The state crew must have mowed today."

She said, "It's good somebody is working."

Sam spread the blanket and they sat looking out over their portion of the world. Sam took Emma's hand and said, "I have to talk to you."

Emma sensed his apprehension. She teased him, "About your brother or my father?"

"Not your father," he said.

"Josh?"

"Yes. I don't know what to say. It's really embarrassing. We're all disappointed in him." Sam looked out over the valley. *What could he say?*

"Sam, it's all right." She placed a hand on his shoulder. After a long silence, she asked, "What did he do actually?"

Sam plucked a long blade of grass and tied it in a knot while searching for words to explain and minimize Josh's action. "A school boy's foolishness, that's all it was." He avoided her eyes and spoke in a matter-of-fact tone trying to hide the depth of his concern. "Josh was romancing some young girl...they were touching."

"Touching?"

"Josh had his pants open and she was holding him."

Emma hesitated a moment before she said, "Sam, I appreciate your family's concern and embarrassment, but they are adolescents. If that's all it was, a one-time thing, not behavior born of his fantasies, if it was just a clash of hormones and opportunity..." her words dropped off as she studied the set of Sam's jaw. "How was she touching him, Sam? Like this?" Emma slid her hand over his lap and between his legs.

Sam's lips parted as he drew a quick shallow breath. Surprised, he considered her, feeling her hand moving on him.

"Just touching is not a sin," she said in a husky voice.

He felt himself swelling with her caress.

"Especially not if you plan to be married."

Yielding to her, Sam closed his eyes. Later, whenever he recalled the moment, he marveled at Emma in the role of salesperson, master of the assumptive close.

Sunday, a week later, Sam was sitting on a large overstuffed sofa, one you could get lost in, in the Cooper living room. Emma had finally dragged him in to meet her father and he was nervous about it, expecting the worse. He blinked, *Daddy, I want you to meet Sam, he's a self-employed bandit*. Looking out across a marbled foyer, Sam considered his escape. It seemed women, Emma at least, want formal commitment so she had insisted he come in and ask for her hand. He understood how she felt. He was going along with her desires but feeling damned uncomfortable and not a little foolish about it.

He slid his fingers over the arm of the sofa feeling the rich fabric, wondering what it was called. It looked like velvet with elaborate brocade. Looking around the room, Sam counted six electric lamps, each with enormous ruffled shade over an embossed glazed ceramic base. Each with a different equestrian scene: mounted huntsmen, Roman cavalry, Day at the races, their complimentary styles creating a sense of intentionally overstated luxury. They would be feature items at any estate sale.

A wide fireplace of polished marble dominated the wall furthest from Sam. Miners know marble; this was imported from Italy. A hint of damp ashes mingled with the scent of furniture polish told of evenings when light cast by the fire danced in the room. Framed photographs of various sizes, full of dark sepia images, were spread across the mantle. Their disorganized placement indicated that they were removed, viewed, and replaced with some casual frequency and were not just dust collectors. On the broad white plaster wall above, dominating them, hung an imposing portrait of a bald man with outrageous sideburns and handlebar mustache. He was dressed in a fitted double-breasted frock coat and wore haughty pince-nez with filigreed silver frames. Sam recognized Doctor Ira Cooper, the family patriarch, Emma's grandfather.

Sam was tolerating Josh's new black dress shoes, one half size too small for him. He looked down at them, pinching, protruding from under the cuffs of his Sunday trousers. They appeared funereal against the Persian carpet. Sam tried to flex his toes with no success. His only suit coat, of shiny blue-black fabric, stretched snugly across his broad imprisoned shoulders. The sleeves were too short. His shirt collar, stiff as an English saddle, was choking him. He anguished over the absurd silk handkerchief Lizzy had placed in his breast pocket with a flourish.

Before abandoning him, leaving the room in search of her father, Emma had cooed, "You look dashing."

Sam sighed thinking, *I'm a fool.*

"Ah, there you are."

Startled, Sam jumped to stand stiffly in front of the sofa. A tall heavy-set man with disciplined red hair and a ruddy complexion was striding robustly into the room. Sam took immediate notice of his energetic eyes; they seemed never to be still, as if he had to observe everything at once. Sam could envision him as a general officer brandishing a sword, issuing orders, trailed by his aide-de-camp, Emma, smiling impishly at his elbow.

Harry Cooper offered Sam his large hand. Sam took it, and they stood mutually gleaning first impressions. Sam regretted his damp palm.

"Yes, Sir, here I am," Sam said, noting the strength of the grip, Sam thought, *not a man to toy with.* Sam smiled to himself, Harry didn't appear to be the No-fun-on-Sunday Methodist he'd envisioned.

Emma, sparkling in pale yellow frock and patent leather shoes shiny as oil, bounced to a seat on the far end of the sofa. Her eyes never left Sam.

Harry watched as Sam's eyes followed her. He chuckled, "Yellow is her color."

Embarrassed that his enchantment was so obvious, Sam folded onto the sofa when Harry waved his hand. Sam noticed that Harry had removed his Sunday coat and moved with ease as he took a standing position behind a wing back chair.

"Sam Freeman," Harry Cooper reflected pensively, two fingers supporting his chin, "I knew your father. We had many of the same friends. A shame, his passing on so young; we all miss him."

Harry's manner was so sincere, his sentiment so introspective, Sam felt no response beyond a nod of his head was needed.

"And, your mother, a gracious woman, has remarried. Or, so I've heard."

"Yes," Sam said, "a good temperate man, Robert Cordy. He's a supervisor at the silk mill when it's running."

"Your grandfather, Jonathan Freeman, how's his health?"

Sam was beginning to think he should have brought the family album. He shifted uneasily and thought about his grandfather before answering.

"Physically," he said softly, "he's recovering from a stroke. I visit him often." Prolonged sorrow was evident in Sam's voice as he continued. "He sits on his porch on temperate days watching the world go by. He's not the same man he was before his losses. I think he feels that his life's work amounted to nothing—like he's been trampled by three of the Four Horsemen, and sits waiting for the final pale horse of death."

"Who handles his affairs?"

Sam hesitated before continuing with a slight shrug, "Well, all he's got left are those houses along Old Quarry road. Those and the double he lives in. Before his stroke, the first business day of every month he would hitch a mare to his surrey and collect rents." Sam ran his fingers along the back of the sofa. "He enjoyed the monthly round. Most tenants had been there for years, and they invited him in. Regardless of their ability to pay, he accepted what they gave, and granted them grace without complaint or criticism."

"They offered him tea or their latest distillation," Sam explained wryly, "he never drank tea. Moss Williams lives in the last bungalow on the lane, so he was the last stop. By the time he reached Moss's place, it was usually the twilight of the day and grandfather's senses. Moss, a burly supervisor at the colliery, would slip an envelope into his pocket, make him comfortable, and turn the mare for home. He always made it through the village and home undisturbed. That was then, now half the places are empty and Moss shows up religiously with whatever he can."

Harry and Emma listened to Sam relate his tale, his fondness for the old man evident in the telling. Harry said, "I believe circumstances would have killed a lesser man."

They sat quietly, each with separate thoughts, until Harry waved, and said, "Emma, get us some tea."

Emma rose from her seat and, seemingly without effort or sound, exited the room. Sam watched Harry watching her and wondered what a man who had raised four daughters was thinking about a guy lusting after his youngest. Considering his face, Sam decided he'd make a good poker player...wondered if he'd raise on a bluff, and decided he would.

A motor car passed the house laboring up the hill, and there was the tinny sound of a horn. It echoed behind Harry as he said, "You know, Sam, Solomon maintained a peaceful household, by never comparing one wife to another, by treating them equally. Likewise, a wise parent would never favor one child over another." Moving to sit on the wing back chair, he said, "Emma has three older sisters, and I love them all," he paused, his left hand moved in an unconscious search for something.

Sam wondered—a cigar? cigarette?

Harry's hand came to rest on his knee, "Emma has a special place in my heart."

"I can appreciate that, sir," Sam said, wondering what was next.

Harry fell silent, resting his chin on steepled fingers.

Sam wrinkled his brow, hoping Harry would think him sincere not constipated.

"It seems I know all the men in the Freeman family except you."

Ah, that game. I'm to be dwarfed by my ancestors. With an appropriate hangdog look, Sam said, "I guess that's because I'm not distinguished." *Though the local constables know me,* he smiled inwardly. Then it occurred to Sam that Harry was an old hand at this suitor's game, practiced at culling the hounds sniffing around his daughters.

Sam watched as Harry stood again and moved back behind the chair. He wondered what the man, a father, was thinking. Finally, Harry said, "Well, you don't have to be distinguished, but it would help if you had an income before you and Emma start making plans."

Sam brought his hands together and placed them, fingers entwined, in his lap, *Now we're getting to it.*

"I understand you run a distributing business...any money in it?"

"You know, the name of the game these days—acquire low, sell if you can," Sam said.

Harry smiled at Sam's answer, "Especially in these times, when the entire country is in a state of economic depression. And, regardless of what you hear from the government, it will be no short term thing." Harry's eyes were hard when they locked on Sam's. He asked, "How do you define acquire?"

Sam didn't waver, he said, "These are hard times, you get what you can where you can. Sometimes you can pay, sometimes you can't. You survive." Sam worried, *What has he heard?* His eyes steady and voice level, Sam said, "We pay eventually. We just paid Wilbur's hospital bill in full."

Harry went to a window and stared out at the sparrows and dandelions on his lawn. Turning back to the room, he swung a hand in a gesture that included the furnishings and the thick carpet. Sam detected a note of embarrassment when he said, "I was caught up in the pervading euphoria too; buying stocks on margin as though the bubble would never burst. It was only by a great stroke of luck that I became more cautious toward the end. I was not totally destroyed like some others." He sighed heavily. He was obviously covering for the hundredth time familiar discouraging ground. "This house, for instance, is without mortgages."

He looked at Sam, and in a voice laden with irony, said, "But you can't eat buildings. These days you can't borrow on them either."

Sam, uncomfortable with Harry's disclosure, felt sorry for him. He wasn't surprised by the revelation. He didn't know anyone who had escaped the sudden downturn in fortune.

As they stood contemplating each other in the light of their discussion, Emma arrived bearing a steaming silver tea service. Sam caught the aroma of the dark tea as she set the scalloped tray on a high narrow library table behind the sofa. "Your pleasure, gentlemen," Emma announced softly, plainly enjoying the roll of hostess. There was a subtlety to the moment, the serving of tea, a silent communion, and a commonalty of experience that brought them all together for a peaceful instant.

Sam rose and walked, his borrowed shoes sliding over the thick pile, to the ornate display of tea and biscuits. He felt mesmerized and plodding like a bear approaching a honey tree. Discounting possible stings, he succumbed to Emma's sweet allure, as she gazed at him and offered a tentative smile. Cup and saucer balanced in his hand, he disdained caution, and feeling slightly foolish, braced himself and turned to Harry.

Standing statue-stiff, he asked formally, "Sir, I request permission to court your daughter."

There was a long pregnant pause, extended by the sound of Harry munching on a biscuit. He wiped his chin with a napkin, and pretending confusion, asked, "Which one?"

"Oh, thank you, Daddy," Emma cried. Leaving her cup and saucer on the tray, she embraced her father, who stood entrapped, his tea in one hand, his nose in Emma's hair.

The cup rattled in Sam's hand as he watched the emotional display.

As Emma disengaged, Harry said, the no-nonsense note back in his voice, "You have my permission to see each other and plan your futures. But, Sam and I agree," he looked to Sam with pleading eyes, "there'll be no serious steps taken until things are more stable, the future more predictable."

Sam listened to Harry's euphemisms and wondered, *When will that be?*

CHAPTER 11

June 1933

The assumed burden of oldest son and big brother weighed on Sam. He was in a constant stew, a swirling soup of scarcity, adversity and apprehension. He knew the dismal economic situation was not just a local phenomenon. Sam read the newspapers and listened to KDKA of Pittsburgh on the community crystal radio. Evenings, in the church hall, huddled around the crackling receiver, Sam and others listened to the news. Listeners fell deadly silent, hearing that in 1931 there were five million men jobless in America. Sam listened as President Hoover announced his plan to stem the run on banks, and frowned disbelief hearing that Detroit had produced five million automobiles. He cringed when Will Rogers quipped with dark humor, "We may be the only nation to go to the poorhouse in an automobile." Sam turned to the men around him and tried to gauge the depth of their sentiment when it was announced that the flow of immigrants had reversed, more people were leaving the country than entering. His stomach turned, those around him had the look of cattle in a holding pen awaiting slaughter.

So it was with exhausted patience, blatant disregard of the state of the union or the world, and reckless abandon that Emma and Sam yielded to the power of love and raging hormones and were married on the first Saturday in June 1933. In a small ceremony in the first Methodist Church attended by their weeping mothers, grinning siblings and a resigned but proud Harry Cooper, they were pronounced man and wife.

After the knot was privately tied, Emma floated lightly, resplendent in a white lace trimmed gown, carrying a spray of yellow sweetheart roses, tears of joy on her cheeks. Sam was a heavy contrast beside her, his black hair, thick brow and solemn dark dress relieved only by a yellow silk kerchief. He played a staunch support to Emma's blossoming, the grin of a conqueror across his face, as they moved to the adjacent church hall for an expected informal family send off.

"Surprise!" The hall vibrated from floor to vaulted ceiling with the trumpet sound of well- wishers as they entered. Loud and lengthy applause followed as the couple stood grinning and speechless before a throng of villagers and friends. There was no need for feigned surprise as they stood warmed by the goodwill evident in the faces and voices of the people gathered. They were buoyed by the realization that their union in such grim times infused those around them with renewed hope.

Sam recognized Moss Williams and his neighbors, Dan Owen with a group of miners, and Flanagan away from his den of inequity. That they had gathered on his account, left him with a feeling of warm wonder. Then he turned to Emma who was waving to coworkers and friends, and knew that they weren't gathered for him alone.

Emma tugged at Sam's sleeve. He bent to her, trying to hear over the applause. Her green eyes were bright and her breath warm on his cheek. Sam could see she was relieved of any doubts she'd harbored, Emma said, "Darling, we've done the right thing."

Sam nodded agreement. He hadn't been alone with his doubts. He turned to Josh, smartly attired in his Sunday best, and asked, "Are you responsible for this?"

"Partly," he chuckled, "but I can't take the credit. You can blame Harry Cooper."

Sam looked around the hall sorting through the myriad faces until he saw his new father-in-law standing with arms folded sporting the countenance of a new believer. He waved and Harry looked and responded with a smile and a thumb's-up. Sam leaned to Emma, and said, "Your father looks happy to be rid of you."

Emma responded to his jibe with full inviting eyes, "Not as happy as you'll soon be to have me."

Sam noted her moist lips and flushed cheeks. He believed her.

Lake Sheridan in the remote mountain setting was as serene as Sam remembered. The sheltered shore of the placid waters, and soothing sounds and smells of the surrounding pine forest provided a peaceful setting and promise of gentle relief at the culmination of their momentous day. Sitting beside Emma in the front seat of a borrowed Ford, Sam allowed himself to slow down. Comfortable at last in lightweight shirt and trousers, he let his hands drop from the steering wheel, took a deep breath and, with closed eyes, sorted through the piquant odors of hemlock, unseen creatures, a secret world. He was touched by a deep sense of the power of life and renewal.

Sam shook his head and smiled at himself; here he was, his new bride beside him and his mind wandering. He turned to Emma, sitting quietly studying him, and said, "Thank you."

She smiled, "You're welcome. You seem remarkably relaxed for a new groom." She leaned to Sam and he kissed her gently on the lips. "Are you man enough to carry me over the threshold?"

Inside the cottage with Emma in his arms, he assessed their home for a week. There was a collection of wicker chairs and casually pillowed settees among small tables supporting kerosene lanterns. Full bookcases flanked a narrow stone fireplace set in the center of the furthest knotty pine wall. There was a sense of disconnection, of remote ease about the setting. This was a place where you could gather yourself and contemplate your dreams. Someone had placed a sign on the fireplace mantle with an arrangement of daisies and lily-of-the-valley. It read, *Live Happily Ever After*. Emma sighed, "It's a fairy tale."

Sam was as pleased as Emma but didn't think he'd go that far. To bring her back down to earth, he said, "I'll get the luggage."

She laughed at his lightening of the moment and said, "I'll find us something to drink.."

Sam walked out into the waning twilight and inhaled again the heavy primal odors of the forest and lake. He looked up beyond the ensuing dusk into the vast open universe. There Venus shown brightly, a lonely hope rising. *It's not just me anymore. It's us.* He shivered, less in response to the cool evening than the impact of added responsibility.

He reentered the cottage. Emma stood holding a moisture-beaded Magnum of champagne in both hands. Sam took it from her and read the label. Shaking his head, he said, "Your father is an amazing man. I wonder where he found this."

"Open it. I want to drink with another amazing man."

There was a corkscrew set conveniently on a small side table. Sam carefully removed the cork, jumping slightly with the resounding, "Pop," and poured two glasses. Emma had moved to the window and was looking out over the black surface of the lake. Sam inched gingerly to her, wineglasses balanced in his hands. Arms entwined, they toasted, "To us." They stood in the magic of the moment, bubbles light in their noses. A climbing moon rising over the pine rim graced the lake with a shard of platinum brilliance. Sam set his glass on the windowsill and undid the top button on Emma's dress.

"Sam."

"Yes?"

"Do you remember a night at the hospital? A woman admiring her reflection?"

"How could I forget?"

"That was me," Emma confessed as his fingers undid her bra.

"I know."

"Did you know mine wasn't the only image in the glass? That I knew you were there?"

Sam revealed no surprise as he freed a final button. He moved the fabric from her shoulders and allowed the dress to fall. The soft down below her upswept hair brushed his nose as he bent and kissed her neck. Emma turned to him, her breasts bared. Sam took her in his mouth. She shivered and cradled his head, pressing him to her. Tears wet her cheek.

As the false dawn eased through the curtained window, Sam came awake slowly, a diver rising from the depths of slumber, body buoyant, and mind murky in the silt-clouded shallows of consciousness. He studied his wife languid at his side, her lips parted, her shallow breathing a faint flutter. Her head rested on one arm; the other arm and shoulder out from under the down comforter, an ivory breast with dark-disc areola revealed. The bed coverings followed the swell of her hip and flow of her legs. Sam was in an art gallery admiring the work of a master. He slipped quietly from the bed and, pants in hand, left the room.

Arriving at the edge of the lake, he stood and watched the mists floating off the placid surface. A short distance away, a shadow changed in response to a deft almost imperceptible movement. Something disturbed the fine line between flat lake and mounded shore. Watching, Sam saw that it was a small whitetail deer, a doe. She gave no indication that she was aware of his presence as she stepped daintily into the water. The deer drank, her tongue dipping into the cool aquifer, then walked out purposefully until she was swimming. He watched her disappear in the mist. There was something, otherworldly, mysterious, about the moment, perhaps a reminder that his wasn't the only journey beginning.

Sam turned and saw Emma pass the window of the illuminated kitchen. She was preparing breakfast. He smiled at how subtly she had emerged as lover, wife, and homemaker. He bent and found a flat stone. With a snap of his wrist, he sent it skipping over the still water. Seven skips, seven expanding rings. A harbinger of good luck?

Starting for the cottage and his new life, his heart was so full he could have floated into the rising sun. Sam was pleased to hear Emma humming and smell bacon frying. He had started a fire in the potbellied stove earlier and saw that she had replaced the round cover with a black cast iron frying pan. She was searching for something in the icebox.

He crossed the wooden floor, his steps light as laughter. "How are you?" he asked, concerned that he might have hurt her in their passionate mid night abandon.

She kissed him while juggling four brown eggs in her apron. "I'm fine."

"What's that you have on? You smell better than the bacon."

Smiling, she said, "Make yourself useful, set the table."

Later, walking a trail around the lake, enjoying the alternate shade and sun, Emma stopped to watch Sam. He had a stick with a gnarled end and, pretending it was a golf club, was knocking white caps off mushrooms. Taking giant enthusiastic swings, he would shout, "Fore"

"Did you see that? A hole in one," he said, turning to her.

She placed her arms akimbo. "I've married a little boy."

"Nonsense," Sam joked, taking another swing, powdering another mushroom, "you've married a tournament class golfer."

Emma's joy was complete as she watched his uninhibited movements.

Sam held the stick in both hands high over his head celebrating another perfect shot.

"You know, the last time I saw you prancing around like that, you were stark naked."

He looked at her, her sly smile, his mouth opened in disbelief.

"Except for your socks. You and your ape-like friend had just jumped in the lake."

"Ah," Sam remembered. "That was Lenny. I used to train with him when I was boxing. Here was where we did our road work, running around the lake." He cocked his head, puzzled, "Where were you?"

"Out from the cottage, picking flowers. I hid in the shadows when I heard you coming." She taunted him with a lascivious leer. "You were chilled and jumping to get warm. Your," she tilted her head and glanced below his waist, "was bouncing."

"Hussy," he accused, standing knees together, his hands over his crotch.

"That was the day I decided you were mine."

Sam said, "That was over two years ago." He roared and took her in his arms. They turned and turned until Emma's feet were off the ground. "Another innocent man trapped by a vixen."

They were both laughing loudly when they collapsed into the lush grasses at trailside. Overhead boughs shielded them from the climbing heat of the day.

Gasping for breath, she blurted, "Make love to me."

"Here?"

"Now."

"You don't hesitate when you receive an offer do you?"

They were lying side by side, naked in the greenery. Sam had a handful of small purple violets and was trailing them lightly over her flat belly. Around them, the grass was littered with articles of clothing. A red squirrel scolded from a high branch.

"No. I learned that at my grandfather's knee. I guess I was about six."

Emma closed her eyes and listened to Sam's low voice, memory-mellow.

"Old Jonathan took a coin out of his pocket—an event in itself. He had lots of pockets, mysterious folds full of watches, coins and a jack knife, He flipped the coin in the air. He asked me, 'Do you want a nickel, Sam?' I watched that coin tumbling, flashing promise in the air. I shrugged my shoulders and said, 'I don't care.'"

"Neither do I," he said, and put the nickel back in his pocket. "Since then, when somebody offers something, I take it."

"You really love him don't you?"

"He's been a father to me since my dad died." Sam sat up and looked around at the solemn stand of spruce, pine and hemlock and the beckoning solitude of the lake. He stood and gazed at Emma's nakedness.

Smiling broadly, he bent to take her hand. "We're Adam and Eve. It's the beginning of the world."

She gave her hand hesitantly, "What..."

He pulled her up off the forest carpet and into his arms. He was surprised that the body that pressed so purposefully upon his a short while ago was so light. She was weightless in his arms. He kissed her. "We're going to sanctify our new beginning," he said, as he started running toward the lake. He ran bent forward, knees high, gaining speed over the short distance, moving easily with his passenger. High-stepping and splashing until he was knee deep in the cold water, Sam leaped.

Emma screamed, "Noooo..."

Their entry into the water caused a great splash, expanding concentric circles, flying diamond-like beads of water, and a noise that resounded along the shore. The chatter of forest creatures and trill of surrounding birds stilled, until the playful couple burst from beneath the surface. Then, as if in congratulation, the cacophony resumed.

They left the wet warmth of the honeymoon basin and drove the winding roads back to reality. Sam drove by familiar white fences and neighborly greetings before easing the Ford to the side of the lane that breathed home. He flipped the ignition off, cramped the steering wheel to the right, and set the hand brake, action automatic in the hilly town. Emma rode beside him, the essence of shampoo and lakeside conifers surrounding her. She was wearing a yellow bonnet and a yellow rose above her ear. Sam thought she was beautiful. "You are the prettiest new bride in town," he said. Her eyes, emeralds in the late morning sun, sparkled, "The only new bride."

Sam looked at the rear seat crammed full of items from the cottage: an end table, a captain's chair, and other odd items. He knew if the vehicle were large enough, they'd have everything out of the cottage. Emma was looking at Jonathan Freeman's huge double house. They would occupy one side of the double residence, share the many-gabled roof and wandering porch. Sam bet she imagined herself inside rearranging the rooms.

Two flagstone walks left the roadside and led, in parallel, to the separate entrances. The wood siding was painted yellow and the trim, including the porch banisters, a somber dark brown. The contrast, strikingly effective, lent the home a bright but formal appearance. A plethora of blossoms and undisciplined bushes surrounded the porch, and encroached slightly on the wide stairs.

Sam was surprised that, on such a bright day and auspicious occasion, his grandfather was not seated in a rocking chair awaiting their return. He must know they were expected. Sam got out of the sedan and was immediately aware of the difference between the soot-laden air of the town and the fresh clean air at the cottage. *We're back,* he wrinkled his nose and opened the door for Emma. "You're home, Mrs. Freeman."

"I like the sound of that," she said, rising from her seat.

Feeling like a schoolboy, Sam took his bride's hand and started up the walk.

Screen door hinges creaked and his brother Ernie appeared on the porch. At eighteen, Ernie stood an inch shy of six feet, and at two hundred pounds was the answer to the dreams of the football coach. Not a quivering ounce of fat clung to his side-of-beef body. Sam saw that though under heavy brows his eyes were as flat as the lake, behind them thoughts darted quickly as minnows. He was as astute as he was shy.

Removing a wide hand from his coverall pocket, he grabbed Sam's arm and said, "Welcome home." But, there was in the greeting a thread of restraint, and Ernie shuffled his brogans in obvious discomfort while rubbing his neck with his free hand.

Thinking Ernie uncomfortable in the presence of Emma, conspicuously, fragrantly feminine, Sam ruffled his mop of hair and asked, "Where is everybody?"

As though revealing a secret, Ernie said, "Inside."

Sam searched his eyes, "On a day like this?"

Ernie stepped back, acting like he didn't know what to do with his hands. "Grandpa is dying," he revealed as though it were somehow his fault.

CHAPTER 12

June 1933

Standing at his grandfather's bedside, the corrosive lingering of carbolic acid disinfectant in his nostrils, Sam studied the outline of the frail body supported by numerous pillows. Was he always this small? Sam felt cheated somehow. This man he revered would scarcely make an armful. His variegated black-on-white beard proudly displayed atop the comforter seemed to be the greater part of him. One arm partially revealed was no more substantial than a chair spindle, an appendage of the clothed ghost hidden in the bed. The sunken eyes were closed, but Sam suspected his grandfather was awake.

"How was the honeymoon?" asked a remnant of the washboard voice that Sam knew so well.

Sam felt what he was asking, "She's a warm and loving woman, grandpa."

The old eyes opened. The left lid drooped, a reminder of his body's betrayal, of stroke—the cruel diminisher of men.

The eyes were open but Sam suspected thoughts were drifting.

"You'll have to collect the rents."

His grandfather was referring to the small rental houses he owned along Old Quarry road. Sam knew there wasn't a dollar among the tenants.

"All right, grandpa."

Sam stood in the dim light and dry air of the bedroom and considered the memories it contained. The mirror of the wide dark-cherry dresser had flattered both Jonathan's wives while they lived. Jonathan swore their images lingered there. The bulky armoire in the corner still closeted grandma Mame's petticoats and an astringent collection of mothballs. Sam remembered himself as a small boy peering out from under the bed, the dust ruffle over his ears, a lifetime ago.

"Raise the shade," Jonathan said, giving Sam a start. "I don't know why they think I have to die in the dark." Sam knew he meant the roll shade drawn down to the windowsill.

The room was gloomy in the faint light, the photograph of his grandfather's first freight wagon and team of mules barely discernible. Sam edged to the window and tugged on the shade until it rolled reluctantly upward. "You're not dying," he said as the light improved the room.

"Yes, I am. Something inside me has quit working. That's why my eyes are yellow."

Sam leaned over, his hand on the comforter, and observed the mealy eyes. He berated himself for not being more considerate of his grandfather at the wedding. *Could he fall this far in only a week?* There was a long silence as both men fondled reality.

"Mame was a loving woman too. Do you remember her Sam?"

Sam remembered Mame, straight-laced with her hair in a bun. Not his true grandma, but the only one to give him graham crackers and cleanse his boyhood wounds.

"I'm going to be with her," Jonathan said, his lip trembling. "Your father, too."

The old eyes flooded.

"Should I get the doctor?" Sam felt powerless and alone against the Reaper.

"I can die without that quack. All he does is feed me laudanum. I want to be awake for the passage." He laughed, "Know what he asked me? He asked me if I had any regrets. Thinks he's a priest. Hell, he isn't even a good doctor. I told him I regretted those times I didn't yield to temptation." He cackled, sounding like something was breaking in his chest. He paused wheezing heavily. "There weren't that many times…not enough." His head bobbed and his eyes closed remembering.

After a while, with one eye open, he asked, "Are you afraid, Sam?"

"Of what, grandpa?"

A trace of a smile formed on the dry lips behind the beard. "That's what I thought." The head of thin white hair turned and he struggled to hold both eyes open as he advised, "A little fear might be a good thing."

Jonathan Freeman died that night, his family gathered around him. There was no rending of cloth, no self-flagellation, no keening voices. Instead, a great emptiness settled upon the village and family. Jonathan Freeman, benefactor, provider, was truly gone. Every soul felt a bit more vulnerable, suddenly more alone, the hold on existence more tentative.

His casket was set open on a table in the living room. Draped in black and surrounded by candles, and specters on the wallpaper, it was the central attraction for two days. People appeared from the near hillsides and towns bearing casseroles and baked goods, wine and other spirits. Men with stern faces and teary women gathered on the porch, filed through the parlor, prayed over the wax-like countenance, and offered condolences. Low voices told of Jonathan's daring and his generosity as Death, the final equalizer, lingered in the hallway and drifted through chambers whispering to mourners of their common destiny.

In the unsettled rooms next door, Emma cradled Sam while he morosely considered the loss of his grandfather.

CHAPTER 13

June 1933

Sam watched as Ernie raised a spoonful of corn flakes and, with a broad thumb, squeezed the milk from the flakes. Milk dribbled back down into his white china bowl.

Alfred said, "He likes two bowls in the morning, but sometimes there's not enough milk to go around."

Sam looked around the table at his brothers, all quiet in their moment of mutual embarrassment. At his mother's house for the first time since his wedding, he pondered the length of his absence. How long has it been? he asked himself. His fingers moved counting unconsciously, the honeymoon, funeral, getting settled with Emma...three weeks...four? At least four, but it didn't seem that long in retrospect. Emma returned to her duties at the hospital, and it was past time for him to get back to business. He was determined to make something of what little they had—something out of nothing. He knew that with just Josh and the twins to make contacts, work had fallen off, especially the movement of bootleg where it was a matter of established trust.

Ernie, a giant in coveralls, filled the seat across from Sam and concentrated, eyes fixed on the spoon, eating the cereal. Alfred, beside him, was spreading fruit preserve on a thick slice of coarse-textured white bread. A viscous glob of the jam fell to rest on Alfred's clean blue work pants. "Damn," he said, "glad Lizzy didn't see that."

Sam caught the piquant odor of rhubarb and smiled. The morning light drifting past the curtains seemed to spotlight Ernie and his efforts.

Glancing at his twin, Alfred said, "A gallon of milk wouldn't satisfy him."

Ernie ignored him, but Josh, seated at the end of the table chuckled. Josh was slicing banana with a broad-blade bread knife and allowing the slices to plop into a bowl in front of Wilbur.

Wilbur's face held a look of peaceful concentration as he absorbed the heavy sound of the falling slices, the smell of oily-smooth banana, and his brother's good-natured gibes. Wilbur said, "Tell Sam about the walnuts."

Ernie's eyes shifted to catch Alfred's reaction to Wilbur's suggestion.

Alfred's hand paused, the jam-laden bread almost to his mouth.

Josh said to Sam, "You'll love this."

Alfred set his bread on the oil cloth table cover beside a steaming cup of tea. Looking at Sam he said, "I'm surprised you haven't heard this."

Josh and Wilbur displayed strikingly similar grins.

Ernie stared intently into his cereal bowl, as Alfred began the telling.

"You were still on your honeymoon," Alfred began. "I think it was a Thursday. We had the truck loaded with produce, some from the garden and some melons and bananas from the market. There always seems to be enough bananas. Then we," he circled his empty hand to include his brothers, "discovered we didn't have any eggs. The women in Scranton always want eggs. So, we decided to get a crate or two at Morgan's market on the way into the city.

"When we got to Morgan's, we ran the usual scam. Josh stayed at the front counter making eyes at Lucy, Morgan's daughter, Ernie and I walked in shouldering empty boxes like we were making a delivery. Back out of sight in the storage room, we each grabbed a crate and walked out of the store like it was routine. Josh bought a pack of gum."

"Spearmint," Josh added.

"To make matters worse, add insult to injury, a watermelon rolled off the back of the truck and smashed right in front of Morgan's. It made a mess. Looked like somebody had gutted a pig."

Ernie dropped some soggy flakes in Wilbur's open hand. He said, "Guts," and Wilbur withdrew his hand with a shudder.

Alfred went on, "Well, we got into Scranton, one of our regular neighborhoods, and were ready to start peddling house-to-house. We opened the crates."

"Walnut meats," Josh said.

"What?" Sam blinked.

'That's what they were," Alfred confirmed, "Two full crates of walnut meats, all nicely packaged."

Josh and Wilbur were laughing, a sad-but-true disbelieving snicker. "Can't tell eggs from walnuts," Wilbur chided his brothers.

"What did you do with them?" Sam asked.

"Well, we couldn't sell them in Scranton. Darn nuts are expensive, and Morgan had probably called the sheriff. We'd be waving a red flag. So, we drove to the Poconos and peddled them at the resorts and restaurants."

"Up where the rich bastards are partying while the country goes to hell," Josh spit, his lips curled in disdain.

Sam observed Josh's reaction, and wondered that such bitter feeling boiled in him and produced such venom.

"Got a good buck for them too," Alfred added. "Maybe we should be in the nut business full time."

"I wonder how much jail time you get for heisting nuts?" Wilbur asked as he wiped his hands with a dishtowel.

Ernie glanced at Wilbur, shook his head and reached for the box of cereal.

Sam ran a damp palm back over his hair thinking, *I'm back none too soon.*

That evening Sam sat with Emma on their front porch and watched the sun disappear behind West Mountain. "Past eight o'clock," he said, "days are long this time of year."

Emma had changed from her white nurse's uniform into a short-sleeved blouse and wide short pants that Sam jokingly called bloomers. "I had almost forgotten how long days could be at the hospital—maybe because it was my first day back."

Sam's chair creaked as he shifted his weight. He placed his hand on her arm, "Honeymoons can't last forever."

With a fingernail, she drew casual circles on the back of his hand. "Something else. It's the nature of the ailments we're seeing. The patients are malnourished, listless. They just lie around. Doesn't seem like there's much you can do for them. They don't seem to want anything done for them. Mostly older people and children. It's sad."

Sam considered the tone and substance of Emma's comments. Things were desperate for many. There was little work in the valley, and damn little money circulating. "I'm afraid things will be a lot worse this winter. At least now there are vegetables planted in every yard, and they can forage in the countryside."

Sam stroked his wife's shoulder and rubbed the back of her neck. He said, "Today I saw an old woman and a couple of kids in rags picking raspberries in the thorny shrubs by the old railroad tracks. Jesus, I've seen rabbits that couldn't get through there. And people after dandelion greens—sparse pickin's.

"I heard on the radio that there are thousands of veterans camped in Washington. Tents on the Capitol lawn. They call them the Bonus Army. They're World War One Vets from all over the country, and all unemployed. President Hoover is in a quandary. I'll bet he's sorry he was ever elected. He'll never have another term, probably doesn't want one."

Emma stared into the gathering twilight. Lights blinked on in surrounding houses as night slid into the valley. Shouts of boys playing chase, a game of fox and hounds where the pursued shouted "Hooper Hoy", punctured the evening veil. She sighed and turned to Sam, "I worry about you."

"Me?" Sam wasn't shocked. He sensed how his wife must feel regarding his dubious enterprises, but he opened his eyes wide and pressed his open hands to his chest in mock astonishment.

"The business," She leaned forward and took his hand. "I know you can't be legitimate and survive. Not here in the valley. Without the speakeasy trade, where would you be? I worry that one of these days you'll be caught..."

"Oh, honey. No, that's not going to happen.."

"Look what happened to Wilbur." Despite her effort at control, fear edged her words, and her lip trembled. "Sam, there has to be something better."

"Nuts," he said.

Emma sat rigidly upright, surprised at his response, at his evident lack of empathy. Sam reached into his pocket and withdrew two brown walnuts. He handed them to her and explained, "They were selling nuts."

Her expression turned quizzical, and as she listened to Sam's narrative she began to relax. As he finished, she was laughing so hard she had tears in her eyes.

Sam took her in his arms. He held her, smelling the day in her hair, and wished he could laugh about the situation. Emma didn't realize it, but he was more worried about things than she was. He was closer to the day-by-day stark reality of it all. Sam held a dreadful sense of walking on the edge of chaos. He feared the possibilities and felt there was a disaster in the offing. What had happened to Wilbur and Josh's accusation were stinging reminders. The things he was into and the business, weren't kid stuff anymore.

Sam took the nuts from her tightly clenched hand. He squeezed them in his fist until they cracked. He opened his hand and picked a large piece of nutmeat from amongst the shattered shells. "Here," he said, and placed it in her mouth open like a baby bird's. "Now, you are eating the same thing as those swells in the Pocono resorts."

He put his arm around Emma's shoulder and turned her to face the looming dark of the mountain. He pointed and said, "Someday, we're going over that mountain and crossing a fertile plain. We are going to live in a big house overlooking a clean green river. We'll sit in the evening and watch boats go by. Our servants will bring us fruit and wine and our children, a strong little boy and a pretty girl with your hair, will sit on our laps. A large boat loaded with ore will chug by, and the children will ask, 'Who owns that big boat?' and my eyes will light up and my chest will swell when I tell them, 'We do.'."

Emma trembled in his arms, and Sam trembled in his soul knowing that she trusted him to make it so.

CHAPTER 14

July 1933

Alfred was appraising the row of shoes displayed on a deep shelf in Miller's dry goods store. The light diffused by the dusty yellowed window glass did little to enhance the footwear, high stiff work-a-day brogans and shiny Sunday-go-to-meeting sandals monotonous in their black leather sameness. Alfred was interested in a pair of shoes cut lower than the heavy ankle-high brogans he was wearing. A childhood misadventure had left him with a nerve injury that caused his left foot to drop slightly when fatigued. He knew he would have less of a problem with a lightweight shoe. He imagined himself tripping lightly along under the shop awnings on Broad Street.

"Hello."

Alfred turned, startled by the young woman at his elbow. "Hello," he echoed her greeting while glancing about the confines of the store. Old Man Miller, engrossed moving boxes and rearranging dust behind a cluttered counter, was the only other soul in sight.

"You're Alfred Cordy."

He recognized her—Molly Walsh, a mystery to all men in the village. Unsubstantiated rumor hovered around her like butterflies around blossoms. She couldn't know, but he often watched her with concealed interest on Sunday mornings as she entered the Catholic Church. All Saints was separated from the Methodist church, attended dutifully by Alfred's clan, by a narrow street and wide differences of opinion.

"Yep," he said. Standing close, he was struck by the amusement in her eyes and a musky perfume smooth as butter in the popcorn-dry air. A hint of freckles graced her gently curved nose and danced on her cheeks adding a pleasant unassuming touch to her open manner. She had a habit of gently curling her lips that kept them dew-bright. Her left ear lobe was pierced and displayed a small gold earring, something Alfred had never seen before.

He'd heard the tales about Molly. Some said she was generous with her favors. He knew she was two or three years older than him, but he wouldn't have guessed it. She seemed so innocent, so…fresh.

"I know your brother Sam. We're friends." Her eyelashes fluttered.

Alfred, captivated, watched her hands toy with a small hand bag as she talked; his own pressed deeply into his pockets. Molly smoothed the collar of her blouse, then moved a wayward sprig of honey hair. She seemed to shift in a slow dance from foot to foot.

"Miller doesn't have the material I'm looking for." Shrugging, she rolled her shoulders. Her gaze drifted around the store, settling finally on a cracker barrel. "Are you with anyone?" she asked, arching her eyebrows.

Mesmerized by this woman of perpetual motion, Alfred stood quietly in thought.

"Oh," she blushed, her white-gloved hands pressed to her bosom. "I guess that's none of my business."

"No. No, it's all right," he rushed his words. He didn't know what to make of this girl-woman. She had him off balance. For something to say, he asked, "You know Sam?"

"Yes," she whispered, then added wistfully, "I lost him to Emma."

Alfred was astounded. Sam had never told of Molly. He blurted, "Sam never mentioned you."

She blinked. Her voice caught as she said, "No, he wouldn't. Sam's a gentleman."

There was a lengthy silence, while they both stood contemplating a threshold, before Alfred asked, as though compelled, "Can we walk?"

Molly laid her hand on his offered arm.

It had been a long day with Sam running, the wolf at his heels, looking for new business and trying to hold on to what they had. He was sitting at a table in a smoky corner of Flanagan's speakeasy. Above the odor of stale beer, he could smell himself, his sweaty damp shirt and grimy coat heavy with the day's worryin' and liftin' couched strangely in the now sickening smell of overripe pears.

At the wholesale produce market in Scranton that morning, Sam and Ernie had met a farmer anxious to be rid of a truckload of marginal pears. Inspecting the pears, Sam had appreciated the man's dilemma—the golden, brown-spotted fruit, some already soft as soup, would not likely last the day. The distraught farmer had nowhere to sell. Discerning wholesale buyers would not touch the far-gone load and he had no established retail customers.

Sam knew they could profit and had acted shrewdly and quickly. An opportunist, he had bartered sacks of coal, some on hand, some promised. The farmer had gladly forsaken the perishable pears for the durable coal.

With chunky Ernie, unsuited for running or selling, at his side Sam had used the steamy hours of the day to canvass the hot hilly neighborhoods. With bags, boxes, coal pails and other dubious containers laden with pears, they had lied, cajoled, threatened and charmed away the rotting load. They worked continuously except for ten minutes when they sat in sweat-soaked clothes and ate pears for lunch.

Now, the workday not over, he had business with Flanagan who, thin and pasty for an Irishman, sat on the edge of a chair across the plank table from him. Flanagan drew a bony hand over his bald pate and fished for reassurance. "No trouble now?" he asked.

Sam shook his head, "None." Flanagan needed the six barrels of beer Sam could deliver, but Sam knew he would worry the deal turning it with a stick, examine it until long after the deed was done, it was his nature. "Don't worry Flanagan, you're going to die rich."

"Och, Sam Freeman, not all that I have dealin's with are as honest as you. There's those make me wish I was back in County Donegal." He was long in the face.

Sam said, "Cheer up. Do something good for your soul, buy me a pint."

"Jesus, and you all think I'm filthy rich." Flanagan stood and waved one finger at Clarence the bartender. He offered Sam his hand. They shook and Flanagan said, "Tomorrow night, then."

"Don't worry, old man, nobody's worried about the beer. It's the hard stuff that brings the trouble."

Flanagan walked away mumbling, "It's all trouble."

As Flanagan crossed the room, Molly appeared out of a small room, a cave, that Flanagan had the nerve to call a kitchen. She took the pint from Clarence and, with the draught slopping foam, started across the room.

Sam watched her approach. He held many sweet memories of times spent with her. "Well," he said as she neared, "you're looking lovely."

"Sure, Sam. And, you've more blarney than himself." She turned her thumb toward Flanagan, and set Sam's beer on the table.

"Sit a minute." He turned a chair with his foot.

Molly placed a hand jauntily on her hip. "Is that what you want, to hold onto me? Are you not satisfied with your lily-white Protestant nurse? Do you think yourself man enough for us both?"

Sam was stung. Hurt. They were such good friends. Lovers. "You know me better than that."

"Yes," she slumped, "I do. I'm sorry, but I miss you."

Sam placed his hand lightly on her arm. "We made no promises." It sounded lame, but he didn't know what else to say. He cherished her as a friend. Still, what they had once was gone.

"Molly."

She looked back at Sam as he raised his glass to her. Sam winked.

She winked back, the devil again in her eyes. She said, "I met your brother Alfred today. Now, he's a gentleman."

"Yes, he is." *Alfred?* Sam was surprised.

"You know I don't like to sleep alone," walking away, she flounced her full skirt, "and every child needs a father."

Sam sat heavily in his chair, feeling like he'd taken a blow to the solar plexus. 'Every child needs a father'—Did she mean? When did I last lie with her? He counted the months. His brow became furrowed, It couldn't be me, could it?

CHAPTER 15

July 1933

Next morning, one of those sultry valley days, air spread thick and warm as honey, his mother appeared. Emma had gone to take day-shift duty at the hospital, and Sam was seated at the kitchen table with pencil and paper. He was scratching his head trying to determine how to make a dollar selling to a populace with no money.

Lizzy let the screen door slap closed, drew her rough hand across his shoulders and bent to kiss him on the forehead. Sam appraised her inscrutable poker face trying to judge her early morning mood. He saw that her walk through the village had started dark perspiration half-moon stains under her arms and lines down the center of her broad back. "Kettle's on," he said.

He watched as she placed her cup and saucer on the table cover and took a scone from a wide-mouth jar. She performed every movement authoritatively in the slow steady purposeful manner Sam admired. The kettle rose and tilted in her hand, water flowed spilling not a drop. When done, she considered her full cup a work of art.

"Bloody warm weather," she said.

"Didn't sleep last night?"

Lizzy answered by closing her eyes and rolling her gray head.

Sam hadn't slept either, lying beside Emma worrying about Molly.

The aroma of the dark tea hung over the table. The oblique rays of the bright morning light glanced off the heavy white china. She sighed. "It's not the heat that disturbs my mind. It's these awful times. I worry about what's to become of us."

"Us?"

Lizzy was seated now and soaking a scone in her tea. "Us. Everybody," she wiped her sweaty brow with a cloth napkin. She looked at Sam and he could see an unusual hurt in her. Her glance was unsteady; she appeared perturbed. "Yesterday children came to my door asking for food. Darlings' bellies was bloated. They hadn't eaten for days. Turned my heart. I gave them a loaf of bread and a jar of preserves. I recognized one as belonging to a miner's family of eight. Eight little beggars...Jesus."

Listening, visualizing the children, Sam unconsciously snapped his pencil giving Lizzy a start. He said, "Father's probably gone."

She looked at him, eyes questioning.

He added, "Men are out looking for work. There isn't any. They're too embarrassed to go home, so they're gone longer and longer each day until, finally, some don't come home at all. The women turn desperate." Sam looked away. "I hear there are women in the villages offering themselves for fifty cents."

"God help us."

Sam thought of the two quarters in his pocket, and was momentarily awed by his recognition of their power to corrupt. He shrugged, weighted by the seeming hopelessness of it all. "Hoover says that unemployment is the major reason for the depression." In a manner and voice divulging disgust, he went on, "He might have added that grass is green and water is wet."

Lizzy waited until Sam settled in his chair and she saw his inner stew had ceased to bubble before she pulled a crumpled white envelope from her dress pocket. "It's from your Uncle John Freeman in Niagara Falls," she said, sliding it across the table.

Sam stared at the stamped envelope addressed to Elizabeth Freeman in Palmer Method script. He'd seen the script before and immediately formed a mind picture of his Uncle John, a big gentle man with a hairy chest and a gruff voice. He'd been described as hard outside, but inside, "Soft as shit."

Sliding the two-page letter out of the envelope, Sam read the words written in the disciplined hand. John spoke of Jonathan Freeman. Of the time, as a child Jonathan had pulled him from a disturbed hide of buzzing bees. And, how, he'd watched, mesmerized, as Jonathan picked the bees out of his beard and placed them gently back in the upright hive. John said he'd never met a man of greater courage and offered condolences for his passing and apologies at not being present for the funeral.

The words stirred memories in Sam. Recollections of his uncle leaving for Niagara Falls years ago in a stake-body truck loaded with furniture. Sam read on. His uncle John told of his machine shop and of the piecework he was doing for various auto manufacturers. It seemed, John wrote, that there were still people in the country that could afford automobiles. Sam thought of Will Roger's comment about the country driving to the poorhouse. The bottom line, after John inquired about everyone's health, was that he needed to replace an employee who had died without asking permission. Sam smiled. Uncle John was offering employment to a member of the family.

Sam spread the two pages on the table. Niagara Falls. He'd been there once as a child. He remembered the long seemingly interminable days in an auto getting there and back. And, the frightening thunder of the falls as the green water spilled into the gorge. Green water...Sam gave a start, as the vision he'd related to Emma two nights before returned to him. Serendipity? Fate? Was this the green river he recalled? Sam lifted the letter off the table, and turned smiling to his mother.

Staring at the strange look on Sam's face, she said with a shrug, "It's a chance."

Sam didn't comment.

Lizzy rose from her chair and refreshed their cups of tea.

Sam stirred his tea spinning the tea leaves. Watching the leaves spin, he thought, Maybe our future is in the leaves. He shook his head, "We should send Josh." He was undecided, "Or one of the twins."

Lizzy stared at him. "No. He addressed this to me, but the opportunity is for you." She was emphatic, "If there is anything there, you are the one to make the most of it, You are the man in this family. Josh and the twins still think like boys. And my Robert," she looked away, "is Robert. He'll die at the mill. It's all he knows or wants to know," she sighed, "even though they shit on him."

Sam fixed on her words, thought she might cry and reached out to touch her.

She squared her shoulders. "No. In this, we must deal with our strength. This is for you. We can follow. This may be our only chance to escape this valley. Remember your promise to your grandfather, to take care of the family."

"By leaving?" Sam asked. He ran a hand through his damp hair. Considering her words, he stood and paced the floor. He was developing a headache. He ached to leave the valley, and felt guilty about it. What was the reality? Could he really do it? How long would it take? Could he make a home for him, Emma, and the family too? The headache was getting worse; he was sweating.

Lizzy's voice broke through to him, "We can scrape along here without you. We did over your honeymoon. Besides, with the duplex Jonathan left, we'll have a place to live and some rent coming in."

Dubious, Sam said, "If you can rent it. Selling it is out of the question. Harry Cooper says foreclosures are up. People are being put out on the street. Getting somebody in the place won't be a problem, collecting the rents might be another story." Sam moved to the window and stood judging the promise of the day. "It might rain," he said.

Lizzy moved the cups and saucers to the sink.

Sam was thinking, *What about Emma? How would she feel about leaving home.*

"Don't worry about Emma," Lizzy said, "she would follow you to the moon. She is a good Christian wife—whither thou goest, she will go, as it says in the Good Book."

Now she's reading my mind. "Sure, but she has family here. She works here. It's a hard thing.

Lizzy waved a hand at his concern. "Emma is a good strong woman. You are her family now. And, there are more hospitals in Niagara Falls than there are in this valley. That's one thing this damnable depression has accomplished—the hospitals are full."

Sam wondered if it was because of his vision of the river that he felt her argument taking hold. Didn't he really want it for himself? Then, he realized that Lizzy knew. She had come to him with the plan in her head. He studied her with increased understanding and respect. *She sure knows how to pull the strings.*

Lying in bed, Josh heard his mother leave. He scratched himself thinking, *she's probably left without me.* The twins, Alfred and Ernie, had taken the truck into Scranton to see what they could procure, legally or illegally, at the Farmer's Produce Market. Pop was at the mill diligently performing his thirty-dollar a month watchman job. Josh had resisted getting out of bed before sunrise and the twins had left without him.

It was daylight, he'd better get up. Alfred will be back demanding help shortly. He rolled to sit on the edge of the sagging mattress, pulled the chamber pot close and relieved himself. He wrinkled his nose over the reeking pot. Josh opted for nudity during the hot nights, and, the last drop of urine shaken into the pot, he searched for his pants. They were at the foot of the bed where he'd dropped them.

Walking to a small wooden dresser, his bare feet brushing the floor, he took a hair brush from the clutter on its surface, In an oval mirror fixed to the wall, he admired himself while running the brush through his hair. Pulling fingers over his cheek he decided he didn't need a shave. Unlike Sam who had to shave damn near every day, Josh could get by shaving once or twice a week. In the hall, he passed the other bedrooms on his way to the stairs. All empty, everyone gone to work. He snickered, "Things are so bad, even I have to work."

Lizzy had left the teapot under a cozy in the center of the kitchen table. He poured himself a cup of tepid tea. He looked in the icebox hoping for cream. None. "Shit," he said.

At the counter, he took the bread knife and cut a thick slice from a loaf. He was looking for jam when he heard a faint knock at the front door. "Who the hell..." he uttered aloud.

Swinging the front door open, he found a little girl standing there. She appeared terrified. She had a pale drawn face that accented her large brown eyes. Her hair was snarled and in disarray. Wearing a simple gray sheath that looked like a gunnysack, she looked pitiful.

Josh glanced up and down the lane that was deserted except for two stray dogs. For a moment, he watched with puerile interest, as one cur mounted the other.

The girl cringed. She looked ready to bolt.

"Well?"

Her eyes welled with tears. She was trembling but stood her ground.

Josh huffed in disgust, and started to close the door.

She mouthed quickly, "Please, sir, do you have any food?"

Josh was surprised by the question. "Don't you eat at home? Doesn't your mother feed you?" He waved her away. "Go home to your mother and father."

The girl sobbed, "My Da is gone. Ma is sick. We don't have any food at home."

Josh looked her over. She'd clean up all right. "How old are you?"

"Eleven."

"Eleven? You're small for eleven. Do you have any brothers?"

"Yes, sir. Four."

Four. "Do they sleep with you? Have they had you?" Josh saw she was puzzled by the question.

"What?"

Hmm. Josh scanned the lane. "Come in," he said, stepping aside. "I'll get you some bread."

The girl hesitated, then shuffled in on timid feet. Josh closed the door. "Stand there," he said.

She stood rigidly in place while he went to the kitchen. He returned with the brown-crusted loaf he'd been slicing. He broke a small morsel from the loaf and gave it to her. Her throat rippled as she wolfed it down.

"Easy," Josh said, "or you'll get cramps. Have you had cramps?"

The girl nodded, yes.

Josh set the loaf on a small table, and sat on the chair closest to her. "Come here," he said. The girl didn't move. "I won't hurt you," he assured her with a smile.

She slid a foot in his direction. He reached out and took her arm. She wasn't as thin as she looked. He laid a hand on her abdomen. She was bloated, in the earliest stage of starvation. Josh grasped the bread, and held it where she could smell it. "Would you like to take this bread home?"

She responded with a weak, "Yes," her eyes fixed on the loaf.

Josh lowered his voice, "You can have it all—if you do something for me."

Her eyes filled with tears; her tongue passed over dry lips.

Josh stood and unbuttoned his pants. They dropped to the floor. "Come here," he said.

The girl moved to him, staring at his tumescence.

"You can't tell anybody," he said, "if you do, you won't get any more bread."

She closed her eyes.

The evening arrived after a long day of Sam's mulling over Lizzy's plan. Finishing a light supper, he gave the letter to Emma who read it as he sat in his undershirt and poked at a bowl of green gelatin dessert. She unfolded and read through the pages deliberately. Sam watched her face, shaded in the weak light of the kitchen, for hint of reaction. Drawn after a long day at the hospital, and without makeup, she seemed ghostly serene. Spooning the melting gelatin, he wondered about this woman, who appeared so fragile yet was his strength.

"Niagara Falls," she said, lowering the letter to her lap. "That's about a day's drive, isn't it?"

"In good weather," Sam said, pushing away from the table.

"Do you want to take the job?"

Sam leaned forward. "I want to break the cycle, get away from this place and this life we're so worried about. This is a chance. It won't be easy, but what have we to lose?...For myself, I have no qualms, but it makes me sick to have to ask it of you..."

Emma went to him. She enclosed his head in her arms, and whispered in his ear, "I've always wanted to see Niagara Falls."

Unable to see her face, Sam wondered if she was crying. He swallowed hard, trying not to cry himself. He didn't know if he was terrified or relieved. "We'll make it a second honeymoon. Every gal should have a honeymoon at the Falls."

That night, Sam dreamed of the river in all its turquoise magnificence. He was piloting a launch filled with his family. Emma and his mother, seated along the gunwales, trailed their hands in the river. His brothers stood in the stern gazing at the sliding shore. Wilbur was fishing. Sam handled the wheel expertly, annoyed only by an increasing roar, and ahead a swirling mist. Emma turned to Lizzy and said, "We're going to see the falls." Her words floated to him slowly, and he nodded in pleasant agreement, He smiled, "The falls." With the last syllable, the smile left his face, and he screamed, "The FALLS!" As the scream lingered, the launch hit a rock and careened out of control, the wheel spinning wildly. Turning, bobbing, twisting in the rushing water, they sped toward the cataract. Sam turned to warn everybody, but they were gone. He was entering the mist alone, clenching his ears against the demonic roar. On the shore, Molly waved good-bye.

Sam woke suddenly, in a sweat.

Emma touched him and asked, sleep fondling her words, "You all right?"

CHAPTER 16

August 1933

The days following were saturated with purpose, as Sam toiled to solidify contacts that might prolong the business in his absence. He cajoled and bargained, raged and threatened, hoping he was making allies and not enemies. Some, like Flanagan, he could depend on to throw something to the boys. Others, he knew, would try to take whatever they could from them. He was apprehensive but determined; he had to go.

And all the while he moved making contacts, he looked for Molly. Flanagan said he hadn't seen her, and if Sam did, tell her she'd been replaced. She hadn't been to church and Alfred said he hadn't seen her. Her oldest brother Sean wouldn't talk to him, in fact threatened telling him to go away. Sam spoke to Sissy Malone, Molly's closest friend, who only smiled and said she'd let him know if she came around. Until, finally, Sam accepted that Molly was avoiding him. But, he didn't know why.

He'd thought about when he'd last been with Molly, and knew that if she was pregnant the child could be his. He also knew, Molly had intimated roguishly, that he wasn't her only male diversion. Though he wasn't married when last with Molly, he had asked for Emma's hand. Ironically, it was his raging need for Emma that had driven him, one last regretful time, to Molly's bed.

Now he was paying the price for his indiscretion, in the hardest coin: guilt, remorse, and fear. Fear that Emma would be hurt, and that he might lose her. There couldn't be a worse time to be away from her. What if someone, out of envy or cruelty, dropped a word in her ear? What if there was smoke, but no fire? What if Molly was taunting him out of her own sense of rejection? Christ! Sam decided to keep his mouth shut. Confession might be good for the soul, but he suspected it would be disastrous for his marriage. Especially if he were not around to tend to any wounds.

So, early one morning a week later, Sam nudged Harry Cooper's Chevy onto a bridge over the Lackawanna River, dark and slick as graphite. The hollow lament of a fog horn echoed his feeling, and was lost somewhere in the mists; one last mournful farewell, a reminder of Sam's painful good-bye with Emma's eyes and mouth wet on his neck.

"You be careful."

"I will," Sam said, hating to leave. "I'll be back in a couple of weeks, and if everything looks good, we'll both go."

Sam turned the Chevy northwest up the road to Clark's Summit. It hesitated on the incline, but didn't quit. When Harry offered it for the trip, Sam thought it looked tired but was assured it was in good condition. It was clean and had an extra wheel and tires in the trunk. Still, Sam worried it up every grade listening suspiciously to the complaining engine and wobbling drive shaft.

There was little traffic in the early hours and Sam made good time. He passed a stake-body truck laboring north. He waved, but the sour-faced driver and his bearded passenger only stared. Hopefully, Sam thought, he'd have no need of help from them. Maybe they had an illegal load under their canvas. Sam breathed easily realizing that, for once, he was completely legit.

Climbing, twisting, then descending the two-lane road, Sam wound his way to Factoryville, the first of many small towns. His first hint of the settlement was a white church spire thrust up through the dense forest canopy ahead. Except for a shopkeeper rolling the dew off his awning, the burg was asleep as he passed through.

The town faded from the rearview mirror as Sam approached the narrow bridge over the Tunkhannock. It seemed a miserable little trickle full of boulders and overhung with briars, hardly worthy of a bridge. Sam doubted that was the opinion of the local farmers, especially those with dairy herds. They probably thought it was God's gift. Sam wondered how the poor buggers could maintain a herd, since the bottom dropped out of the milk market. Farmers across the country, discouraged and desperate, were dumping milk in protest. It was insane, dumping milk with people starving.

Shadow-people, glimpses of occasional faces or movement, watched as Sam rolled through Hop Bottom. *Where do they get those names?* Just another steeple, a small tired place with fading paint and ridged pews. A place to gather neighbors on a Sunday to count heads and see how many are still hanging on, where they exchanged baked goods, and prayed with eyes downcast hiding their fears. The ringing steeple bell sent nervous vibrations through the trees and across the meadows. "We're still here, Lord," it rang, "We're still here."

Sam drove on anticipating the Susquehanna coiled near the New York State border. When, finally, he viewed the stream through a marsh-rotted stand of black tree trunks, he was disappointed. It bore no resemblance to the impressive roiling river he'd seen in the spring coursing through Harrisburg seeking the Chesapeake.

The sun was a burning disc rising over his left shoulder as Sam followed the meandering water. The countryside was awake. He had to take the center of the road to avoid a boy and a dog chasing a rolling hoop. Sam, seeing more cars and trucks, knew Binghamton was not far ahead. He planned to cross the river and search out the shoe factory west of the city, where it was rumored they were hiring. He had promised Emma that he would check all possibilities for employment, knowing she meant the closer to home the better.

It was midmorning, on what promised to be a steamy day, when Sam eased the Chevy to the side of the street a city block from the low jail-like silhouette of the factory. A silent crowd of sullen women, subdued as corralled cattle, was gathered along the cement sidewalk. There was no hum of conversation. They were hungry competitors, cowed look-alikes in their drab shapeless dresses, suspicious strangers, wary of the bent unknown souls at their elbows. Having little to carry, each held a small handbag close to her side. Trying for eye contact, Sam scanned the crowd, but they all looked away not wanting to acknowledge their need to be there.

Across the street near a sickly tree, yellowed leaves still in the thick air, a vendor stood beside a cart with large wooden-spoked wheels. His cart was raspberry red and supported a green canvas awning, useless against the slanted invasive rays of the sun. Block letters painted on the side of the cart advertised: Sandwiches 5 cents. Crossing the street, Sam saw that the Sandwiches consisted of sausages on a roll garnished with mustard, dill pickle or onion.

"Hot dogs?" Sam asked.

"If you want to call them that." The vendor tugged on a handlebar mustache.

"Some do." Sam replied casually, hoping to bypass his defensive manner.

Looking out from under his cap, Sam looked like a tough arriving to offer protection. "I'll take one. Driving makes you hungry." Pointing at the Chevy, he said, "I'm from Scranton, just passing through."

Seeing the Pennsylvania license plate, the vendor relaxed, tilted his straw hat, and asked, "What do you want on it?"

"Mustard and pickle." Sam looked across the street at the women enduring the rising sun. "How's business?"

The man gave Sam his sandwich. "Lousy, those gals got no money." He shrugged, "Sometimes the others, bosses maybe, they buy something as they come and go."

Sam flipped him a nickel.

He caught it. The mustache squirmed, "Thanks."

"They hiring?"

"Sure, 'cause most don't stay long," he said searching Sam's eyes. "Six dollars for six days." He spit in the direction of the factory. "Who can afford the shoes?"

"Mmm," a mouth full of sausage, Sam indicated his understanding. He wiped mustard off his chin. "Well, I'm headed to Niagara Falls to visit," he lied. "I hope you have a good day."

"Maybe."

Sam crossed the pavement shaking his head, *Why lie to him? He doesn't give a shit why you're going to the Falls. Is this where fear has brought you?* Squinting against the sun's glare, he opened the Chevy door.

The vendor shouted, "Take the road north out of Owego."

Settling on the car seat, he stared at the brown bag lunch Emma had packed. He regretted the nickel spent for conversation and heartburn. Now, he was left with eleven dollars and ninety-five cents. He turned the ignition switch and the engine responded. Avoiding contact with their empty eyes, Sam rolled past the throng of silently suffering women.

He reached Owego in twenty minutes and turned north. It was boiler-room hot. Windows open, the hot air sucked the perspiration from his shirt. The melting asphalt shimmered, and when he slowed for a turn or to read a sign, Sam felt he could grasp the August heat. Inspecting roadside foliage, he saw veined gray-tinted leaves with curled edges, sure evidence of drought. Local streams, rock-strewn gouges in the landscape, contained only small captured pools. Dry air abraded his nose and throat. Remembered reports of the weather drying the continent were suddenly real.

Arriving in Ithaca, on the curved south shore of Cayuga Lake, he spent a dollar and fifty cents for gasoline. Standing by as the attendant turned the gas pump handle, Sam studied a string of brick buildings fitted to a hillside south of town. He asked, "Cornell?"

"Nope," the red-faced mechanic turned his grease-blackened hand and wiped his forehead with the back of his wrist, "Cornell's up there." He pointed to the heights above the shimmering mists east of the lake. "Can't see it from here." He pulled at his coverall straps, "Oil's okay."

Sam experiencing a depressing flash of might-have-been thought, *I missed college.*

Fighting self-pity, he ascended the road north along Cayuga's western shore. He passed picnic areas where families in bathing suits carried wicker baskets and vied for tables in the shade. Pale women, skin the color of lard, and languid men, administrators and academics, watched their children tossing morsels of bread to screaming gulls. *God,* he envied them their leisure. *What a world, some folks playing others starving.*

The road rose gradually paralleling the lakeshore invisible beyond the thick deciduous growth. Narrow lanes, twin ruts in the tall weeds and heavy brush, branched off to hidden private cottage retreats. To his left, on the flanking slopes, signs appeared naming wineries awaiting the immature grapes suspended in leaf-shaded clusters. Sam passed a ragged tent encampment. 'Tent' was an exaggeration, the shelters were threadbare blankets and torn tarps draped over ropes. Stick figures in faded fabric moved in the brush—weather-darkened migrant workers. Sam bet they were having a slim season.

Just north of the camp, Sam swerved to avoid a small animal wobbling across the road. His light front tire rumbled along the rough pavement edge and, before he could ease back onto the road, it blew with a reverberating bang. Lifting his foot off the gas pedal, Sam steered the Chevy to a halt in the roadside dust, thinking, *Damn, I should have hit the varmint.*

Hot and disgusted, Sam got out of the car, opened the trunk, and gathered the mechanical jack and tire iron. Looking at the frayed rubber, he could see that the tire was shot. The sidewall was ripped, the bead broken, and the inner tube flayed. A truck swerved past leaving miniature tornadoes spinning in the dust. Sam sighed, glancing at the relentless fireball overhead. Tugging at his wet shirt, he removed it and bent to place the jack under the chassis.

Fortunately, the studs weren't rusted, and the wheel came off with little effort. The spare was in better shape than the shredded tire. Thankful for that, Sam gathered the tools from the roadside silt.

Starting for the rear of the Chevy, jack and tire iron in hand, Sam saw three men approaching from the direction of the migrant camp. They were small bent men, their heads bobbing as if in discussion as they shuffled nearer. They appeared unshaven and were roughly dressed. Pickers with nothing to pick, hungry and desperate, Sam judged. He dropped the jack in the trunk and slammed the lid.

"Afternoon, fellas," he said, balancing the tire iron in his hands. He appraised the three men. They wore sun-faded work shirts and baggy trousers bunched at the waist with hemp, ill fitting clothes, scavenged or stolen. Two wore wide brim hats. The other, older, had circled his head with a sweat-stained red bandanna knotted behind his head. They had the quick eyes of men living in a treacherous land where nothing was to be overlooked. Sam noted their prominent collarbones and pencil-thin wrists. Sam assumed a defensive posture as they neared, standing with his back to the car, feet spread and the tire iron obvious, presenting a mean facade.

He saw that the older hatless man moved with grim effort, arthritic pain in his eyes. The other two, perhaps his sons, moved with animal sureness, looking shifty and cruel. The older man stared at Sam with red-rimmed eyes, holding one hand behind his back. Earlier, Sam had caught the glint of sunlight on steel. The old man rolled his free hand, signaling, and the other two began to move, flanking, circling their prey. Moving, their breathing was labored, the long drawn breath of exhaustion. Mouths full of long green teeth hung slack in their grim faces. A feather of air carried their scent to Sam. It was the fruity odor of acidosis, the stench of starvation.

Sam slammed the tire iron against the chrome steel bumper. The three men jolted to a halt, startled by his loud command and the toothache scream of metal on metal. In a voice, sharp and as full of authority as he could manage, he said, "If you come at me, I will break your bones with this." He cut the air with the tire iron. "You will be useless, unable to work."

Please let them understand English. Sam was afraid. He felt the worms of fear loosening his bowels. He was afraid of being cut, of bleeding, losing his life here, his blood spilling onto this little dusty patch of nowhere. Not for himself, but for those who depended on him, Emma, his mother and brothers, if he should bleed and die. He would be lost to them; he was afraid of that. He felt the cold uselessness of it even on this blackened hearth of a day. Sam wondered if the three circling him could, like hunting animals, smell his fear.

The men saw that Sam had taken their measure, and stood dumb in agonizing silence. They couldn't know that this tall robust man with the singing weapon was afraid.

Sam noticed that the two closest weren't even sweating, and tensely awaited the old man's signal to attack. He sensed that the man crouched like a jackal to his right would come first, and try to grab the iron. Knives would follow.

Then, to Sam's astonishment, the old man sank to the earth and, hands covering his face, began to weep. Sam saw that the old man, long a farmer and not a bandit, was ashamed. The younger men backed away, their eyes fixed on Sam. They went to the old man's side. They knelt and crooned to him in a foreign tongue. Kneeling, their resolve broken, they were beaten sucked dry by misfortune and the cruel August sun.

Sam reached slowly into his pocket and withdrew two crumpled dollar bills. He threw them to the dirt in front of the old man. The three men stared in disbelief at the money. Sam said, "Take it and go."

The old man took the bills reverently, one at a time, from the earth. Two dollars, food for a week. The old eyes were swimming when he looked up to Sam. His joints stiff, he rose unfolding slowly. In a voice quavering and slow, he said, "Gracias. Gracias, y vaya con Dios."

Sam watched the trio retreat down the road, the younger men supporting the elder, his feet dragging in the dust. *Poor bastards. Two dollars is a flimsy safety net when you're teetering on the edge of extinction.* His guts unsettled, shaking from his close call and the realization that he had less than ten dollars to his name, Sam threw the iron to the floor by his seat and drove away.

CHAPTER 17

August 1933

The blinding sun was in his face when Sam passed through Waterloo on New York Route 5. A ribbon of blistered asphalt stretched due west, and his four tires played a sticky tune humming along. He kept an anxious eye on the temperature gauge, expecting a cloud of steam from under the hood. Passing shady glades, he was tempted to pull off and escape the heat of the sun.

As a diversion, he'd been trying to imagine the enormity of the ice cap that had plowed the furrows that became the Finger Lakes. He could use a chunk of that ice now, and sighed at the cool thought of it. Seneca, the deepest of the lakes, shimmered, a sausage-shaped mirage off to his left. Ahead, the brick buildings and narrow avenues of central Geneva appeared within strolling distance of the lakeshore. So few people moved in the heat of the day that the entire landscape seemed a lifeless museum model.

Sam's ears were ringing and fingers of fatigue clenched the back of his neck. He shrugged his shoulders rolling along an open stretch of road that offered only occasional farms and empty parched fields. Sam was considering a rest stop when he saw a man about his age sitting on a black suitcase beside the road. The guy looked as limp as his shapeless gray fedora, and as out-of-place as his white shirt and loose red necktie. Lonely, Sam pulled off the road sending coils of dust spinning into the weeds.

The stranger stood and approached through the settling dust, his suitcase bumping his leg with every step. Though obviously hot and fatigued, his eyes flicked with bright intelligence, and a hint of a smile turned his lips.

Sam figured he was as drained as he was, and asked, "Where you headed?"

"Buffalo. You?" he asked arching his back, revealing his fatigue.

"Niagara Falls," Sam said, appraising the stranger. "You don't look dressed for the road."

"Only clothes I have," he grinned exposing two rows of straight white teeth.

Sam liked his easy manner and, figuring he could use information and some distraction from the drone of the road, said, "Get in."

Sam noticed that the suitcase was handled with ease; it couldn't have much in it. The stranger sat with it between his knees. Sam pulled back out onto the roadway. The tires resumed their sticky tune.

"Lookin' for work?"

"Most are." He had removed his hat exposing a shock of blond hair and was mopping his brow with a white handkerchief that looked like fine linen.

Sam noted the crisp efficient speech and guessed, *Educated.*

"I'm going to a meeting." He fitted the handkerchief into a pocket and extended his right hand. "Name's Roger," he said, "Roger Morganstern."

Sam shook his hand, "Sam Freeman." There was gentility about the man that belied his hobo status, and Sam guessed, "Sales meeting?"

Roger smiled, "You could call it that."

"What would you call it?"

"I'd call it a rally," he said staring out the window at ragged fields of burdock, thistle and brown grasses, a scorched vista. At the edge of a field, a weathered smoke-gray farmhouse with a corrugated metal roof interrupted a row of columnar Lombard poplars. Roger asked, "See that farm house?"

Sam looked at the lonely house and wispy poplars. He nodded.

"Probably empty," Roger said, "in this country there were three hundred thousand foreclosures last year. That's likely one of them. A family broken and scattered. The government estimates a million foreclosures coming. Things are getting worse. Since the Bank of the United States failed in '30, the whole country has lost faith in the capitalist system."

Sam lowered the sun visor trying to block the intruding glare. "You a communist?"

Roger smiled, "If I said I was, would you kick me out?"

Sam studied the calm eyes set in the thin face. "Everyone's got a right to their opinion. Especially in these times."

Roger settled back in his seat. "I'm a socialist," he admitted, "but that's just a label. People who use labels tend to have their minds set in concrete. Democrat, that's a label. Democracy. Who can argue against pure democracy? But democracy's not what we have in this country now. What we have is oligarchy. All the money and power in the hands of a few industrialists. The poor farmer and working stiff has no say." He resumed mopping his brow as he spoke.

"Can't argue with you."

"Trouble is," Roger continued, "the majority of the people are so preoccupied with filling their bellies, they don't consider the real problem."

"That what you figure to do?"

"Try." He circled his hands in a motion that Sam took to indicate the enormity of the endeavor. "I guess that's what I'm about…trying to get people to think and act. People have to regain control of this country," Roger paused and stared at the fields sliding by, "I love this country as much as the next guy. I'm not interested in the brand of communism exported by the Soviets." He looked at Sam, "How about you?"

Sam grinned at him, "You should have been a preacher."

"Maybe so," Roger smiled back.

Sam said, "I believe in the commie motto—Don't starve. Fight! As long as they're just in the business of making mottoes, I don't worry about them." Roger took an open wrinkled pack of chewing gum from his pocket, and offered a stick to Sam. "You look like a fighter."

It was heavy dusk when Sam steered down Broadway Avenue into downtown Buffalo. A halo of bright light burst from the top of each pole lining the streets. They provided an artificial stage-like appearance to the first floor level of buildings along the sidewalks. Upper portions of the structures disappeared with the fading light, creating the illusion of a one-story town. An electric streetcar clanged through an intersection ahead as Sam pulled to a curb.

Three men pressed close to a marble edifice as they passed a paper-covered bottle. They stared with animal suspicion as the Chevy rolled to a stop.

Reading a sign that declared Lafayette Square, Sam asked, "This okay?"

"Fine," Roger replied, "that's the library." He pointed at an imposing huge flatiron of a building across the street. "I'll meet my friends there. Care to join us?"

"No, thanks. I've got a meeting of my own." Roger pushed his hat to the back of his head. He grabbed his suitcase and extended his right hand.

Sam shook his hand and said, "Good luck."

"You too, and thanks for the lift." He pointed ahead to the intersection of trolley tracks, "Just cross Main Street there. You'll find a traffic circle in front of the City Hall they call Niagara Square. From there, Niagara Street runs north following the river. The river will take you right to Niagara Falls. You know where you're going in the Falls?"

"I have an address, and that's all you need if you have an English tongue in your head."

Roger smiled, and unexpectedly threw a dollar bill onto the seat. "Put some gas in this thing." He spread his hand against any protest. "We'll meet again," he said.

Sam watched Roger cross the street then pulled out to follow a lonely auto. Crossing Main Street, Sam could see a marquee that read Palace Burlesque. Above it, a neon leg kicked at the dark sky.

Each city has a signature odor. Standing on the front porch of a frame house on 32nd Street in Niagara Falls, Sam smelled the boiled cabbage, sour, sharp as a stiletto, heavy as body odor, stench of the city. In the darkness thinned only by a street lamp thirty yards distant, Sam knew it was unlikely anyone was cooking at such a late hour. For the rest of his days, the smell of cabbage boiling would return him to Niagara Falls and that moment.

There was a light on in one of the back rooms. The sound of a man and a woman in jocular discussion peeled any apprehension from Sam. He took a deep breath and knocked on the screen door. The sound of voices faded to be replaced by the whisper of slippered feet on carpet. The door opened.

A big shirtless man with a hairy chest and broad face stood like a bear in the entranceway. In a deep gruff voice that insisted on an answer, he asked, "What do you want?"

Sam imagined that strangers at the door would be intimidated, but he was relieved knowing he'd reached his destination. "I'm Sam, Uncle John."

"So you are!" John roared pushing the door aside and capturing Sam in a bear hug. Sam swung, his feet off the floor, as his uncle called over his shoulder, "Come on in. Gerty, it's Sam."

Sam caught a whiff of armpits at the end of a hot day as John planted a wet kiss on his cheek.

"Son," John thumped Sam on the back, "we've been waiting for you."

Sam was studying John's wild gray hair and black eye brows as a short plump woman with blue saucer-size eyes appeared in a billowing dress. She took his hand and her red face beamed as she informed him, "I'm your aunt Gerty."

Her pudgy hand tugged at Sam's sleeve. "Come in, you must be starving. Where are your things? Come in. Sit down. Oh, John, isn't he handsome?"

Pressed between them, eyes wet and heart full, Sam knew he was in the right place. *These are my people*, he thought, wishing he could blow his nose.

CHAPTER 18

August 1933

At a baseball game, under a high midday sun that made fly balls damn near impossible to see, Josh leaned back on the rough bleacher plank and watched his brothers. He marveled as he considered the many ways he differed from them. He and Ernie and Alfred might occupy the same shaky seats but their interests and focus couldn't be further apart. Ernie's bulky shoulders hunched forward as he watched the pitcher massaging the ball and the runner edging a tantalizing distance off first base. He eyed the batter bent over home plate waving his bat before the nervous catcher. Alfred observed the runner's distance from the bag and wrinkled his nose in apparent disapproval.

Someone screamed, "Throw the damn ball."

The batter raised his elbows and leaned forward. The catcher, objecting to his crowding the plate, spit tobacco juice on his shoe.

Another scream, "Chuck it in there, Baby. He can't hit."

Alfred shifted in his seat and pushed his pork pie hat back on his head. His eyes were on the outfielders. Josh bet he was mentally repositioning them.

Uncoiling, the pitcher delivered a strike.

From the loud fan, a shriek of satisfaction, "Atta boy…Baybeee."

Josh, relaxed, scanned the assembled fans looking for a smooth nape of exposed neck, or a loose summer shift revealing a tender underarm or hint of milky white breast. While his brothers concentrated on the boys of summer and participated in the cheers and jeers, Josh appraised the girls of summer—their sighs and thighs. Loose garments provided real life reinforcement to the conjured images of his fantasy world.

Most nights, Josh dreamed with eyes open, creating for himself near-life images of the young flesh he coveted; white nudes, their anatomy detailed in Michelangelo perfection on the dark canvas of his psyche. No detail was lacking as naked children and nubile females bent to his every cerebral desire. Like a slave master wallowing in dark Nubians, he groaned and sweated, rolling and twisting in his bed. In his wild imagination, he dominated others, demanding unnatural services beyond the ken of rational men. In his semiconscious beast-like state, on the edge of madness, he fondled, tasted, penetrated, and, finally, oblivious to their cries, wasted the torn ethereal souls. Josh woke on those mornings after, satiated and smiling, his mind unable to differentiate between real and imagined experience.

Other nights, Josh closed the veil of imagination and ventured out to pilfer real visions in the dark well of night. He trembled at the thought of revealed flesh. A driven voyeur, he prized the sight of the absolutely forbidden: children naked in their beds, copulating couples, a brother's vulnerable young wife embracing a pillow surrogate in his absence. He coveted the inviting innocence on young faces, their tangible presence, lending reality to the film surface of his dreams.

On such a night, Josh lurked in a dungeon dark corner of Emma's bedroom. Sinewy and silent, he crouched, the black hollows and pronounced ridges of his face with eyes wild orbs aglow in the shallow shadows formed a repulsive nightmarish mask.

His flared nostrils gathered the dewy musk-laden scent of Emma sprawled before him in a lance of moonlight. The faint rise and fall of her breast, barely concealed by a sheer garment, lent life to her listless sleeping form. Lost in his private intimate exploration of the hills and valleys of Emma casually positioned, limbs spread and arms splayed, Josh, in a languorous stupor, massaged himself. *If Sam discovered me now, he'd kill me.* The dangerous prospect thrilled him. Excited by the confluence of the real moment and his erotic fantasies, Josh reached a sweaty pulsating orgasm. Empty, he slumped against the wall.

A migrating molecule and an involuntary gasp carried the sense of dark violation to Emma. She rolled and whimpered in her fading sleep. Her eyes opened. Exposed to the damp cover of heavy air, she shivered. Insomnia was foreign to her, but now she was suddenly awake in the deep reaches of the night. Something emerged from a corner of the room. Emma, her face pallid as raw clay, stared in muted horror at a malevolent shadow-form.

Josh tensed against the rhythm of his pounding pulse. Realizing Emma was awake he covered his face with a raised arm and retreated silently from the room on bare feet, his toes finding the way. A hinge creaked with a metal on metal whimper, and he was gone.

Emma, in the crevasse of confusion that borders sudden wakefulness, struggled to repel the realization of the terrifying invasion. Too late, she screamed, splitting the night with her ragged reverberating reaction. Neighborhood dogs joined in the wavering cry of one who'd seen a demon.

The telephone rang in the hospital office. One of few phones in the town, the ring was not to be ignored as it often signaled a mine or other emergency. Reaching it on the eighth ring, Shirley, a part time assistant, answered breathlessly, "Mid Valley Hospital."

"Hello, Emma Freeman please."

"Oh, I'm afraid Emma isn't here at the moment."

"Really? This is her husband, Sam. I thought she worked today."

"Sam, this is Shirley. You're right, she is on duty, but we discharged an old woman and Em volunteered to accompany her home. She'll be back soon. Care to leave a message?" Shirley searched the desk for a note pad.

"Sure...tell her I'll be home tomorrow night, and if she wants to see Niagara Falls, she should start packing."

Shirley heard the excitement in Sam's voice. "She'll be happy to hear it. Don't worry, Sam. I'll see that she gets the message."

"Thanks, Shirl. Say 'hi' to everybody." Sam hung up.

Shirley closed her eyes, *Niagara Falls*.

Emma was seated on the porch the next evening, a book—The Principles of Psychology by William James—on her lap open to a page she read several times without recalling a word. Each time she heard a motorcar, she leaned anxiously forward and looked up and down the lane, brushing a wisp of hair from her eyes. She was neatly dressed in a mint green welcome-home frock Sam favored, a touch of French perfume, a present from Sam, behind each ear. The sun had fallen below the mountain's hard silhouette and the soft breezes of evening were dying—moments Sam called the doldrums. *Where could he be?* She sagged in her chair.

The sound of a laboring engine disturbed the random sounds of cicada and crickets, and her father's Chevrolet appeared behind two dim-dirty headlights. *He's back*, she thought, her hands steepled. She mouthed a sincere, "Thank You, Lord." The book slid off her lap when she rose and ran with eager steps to the roadside.

Sam stepped stiffly from the Chevy as the clacking valves fell silent. He placed both hands in the small of his back, massaging miles from his spine. He was dusty and needed a shave, but he grinned and his eyes sparkled in the dusk. Falling into each other's arms, they embraced losing themselves in each other. Finally, Sam said, "It's only a bit more than a week, but it seemed forever."

"I know."

"You smell so good. I bet you're going to taste wonderful."

Emma struck his shoulder in mock surprise. "You," she said, "smell like a goat."

Sam laughed, "I've been baking in this car for hours." He opened a door and removed his bag from the car seat. Turning, he kissed Emma's neck. "You can give me a bath while I tell you all about it."

Sam leaned back in the white porcelain oval tub and observed his knees protruding above the surface of the tepid water. Water warming on the kitchen stove would provide the final rinse. Emma, wearing only cotton panties, was rubbing circles in his wiry black chest hair with a new block of yellow soap. Sam took her left nipple lightly in his fingers.

"I'll give you hours to stop that."

Sam kissed her soapy hand. "Em, we're going to love New York. Uncle John and Aunt Gert are wonderful. They'll find us a place to rent. His machine shop is working five days a week to fill orders. He says it's seasonal, but it looks real good. With me in the shop, he'll have more time to solicit work." He flexed his toes. "I guess that his is as stable as any business these days, machining small parts for Ford and others."

Emma dumped a pan of warmer water over his shoulders to rinse away the soap suds.

Sam closed his eyes in appreciation. "There are other big companies in the area. Shredded Wheat is there, Union Carbide too. There are rumors of an auto assembly plant coming to Buffalo. And, guess what…the steel mill that used to be on the river in Scranton is smoking away on the shore of Lake Erie." Sam sighed.

"What?" Emma asked, hearing some of the air escape from Sam's balloon.

Sam splashed his face. "I don't know," he said, "with all that industry, there's still a lot of unemployment. I met a guy, Roger, that says the end to the troubles is still a long way off. This guy was hitchhiking and I picked him up. He's a thinker, though a little too far left for me. Anyway, he thinks the economic depression is going to lead to worldwide struggle, maybe war." Sam glanced up at Emma, "I told him war might be good for business."

She scrunched her face, "What an awful thing to say."

"It's true."

Emma pulled the chain lifting the stopper out of the tub drain. The water began to spin out of the tub. She tossed Sam a huge bath towel. "I'll see you in bed," she whispered.

Sam kissed Emma's forehead, his lips brushing her hair. She was under him, her legs encircling, embracing him. He was motionless within her, as they clung to each other in a copulation of body and spirit.

"You okay?" he asked.

"I am now."

"You seem tired." His hand roamed her neck, his fingers in the fine downy hairs.

"Missed some sleep…woke one night with the terrors. I thought someone was in the bedroom. I think I screamed. It really spooked me. I haven't slept soundly since." She hesitated to tell Sam how truly frightened she'd been, and her suspicions about the intruder.

Sam began a slow rhythm. "I'm here now," he kissed her eyelids. Sam grew harder, his movement less controlled. "I love you," he said, "and you'll love Niagara, you'll see. We'll leave the local bogeyman behind."

With Sam moving reassuringly in her, Emma decided not to say any more about the phantom intruder. *It couldn't have been Josh, could it?*

Midmorning days later, Emma stood, in an old cotton house dress, a babushka containing her damp auburn hair, looking at the empty rooms, bare floors and walls of her home. The only detachable things remaining were the window shades, and there had been some discussion about whether or not to take them. All their worldly goods were loaded in a borrowed truck Josh and Alfred were driving to Niagara Falls. She was constantly, freshly amazed at Sam's resourcefulness. When she'd asked about the vehicle, Sam said it belonged to a guy that used to drive it to New Jersey.

Emma felt vaguely ill with a queasy stomach and general nervous unease. She realized it was a mixture of fear and anticipation, a natural reaction to change—exchanging the familiar for the unknown. A knock on the front door turned her from her musings. She walked to the door thinking, *Now what?*

Peering through the screen was a young woman with honey brown hair. Emma felt there was something familiar about her, she'd seen her someplace and thought she recognized her lightly freckled face and self-assured manner. She stood firmly but not stiffly erect, her chin high and her eyes fixed on Emma as she approached.

Emma saw that she clenched a black notebook in one hand. "Yes?"

In a habitual manner, the woman rolled her lips inward then smiled, a moist friendly smile, and said, in an unusual throaty voice, "I'm Molly…is Sam Freeman in?"

Molly Walsh, of course. From the Catholic Church. What could she want with Sam?

"Molly." Emma's hands smoothed her gray smock. For some reason she didn't comprehend, she wished she was more presentable, "I'm Emma, Sam's wife." Emma opened the screen door and stepped out onto the porch. She waved her hand at the door, and apologized, "I'd ask you in, but there isn't a stick of furniture in the house."

"Oh, I can't stay," Molly said. She extended her hand holding the notebook, "I've been sent by Mister Flanagan to give Sam this."

Emma took the black book. It was not as heavy as it appeared.

"And to give him a message." Molly tilted her head as though considering her words. "Tell Sam, Flanagan says all accounts are settled, and he wishes him the best of luck." She blinked.

Strange, Emma thought, *She seems ready to cry.* "I'll tell him," she said.

Molly cleared her throat, "That's all accounts, Flanagan says…business and personal."

"Personal?"

Molly nodded, "Yes. Tell Sam I brought the message, he'll understand." She turned to go, then turned and took Emma's free hand. She said, her throaty voice sincere, "Best of luck to you both." She punctuated her sentiment with a quick smile then moved hurriedly down the stairs and away.

Emma watched her go. She thought she understood the messenger. "I'll tell him," she said softly, "business and personal."

CHAPTER 19

September 1933

Christ, what a hole, Sam wiped his brow as his eyes swept the lower flat. To say it needed work would be the understatement of the year. There was crap everywhere. The previous tenants had skipped with anything of value, and what they left, worn clothes, old newspaper, broken end tables, and torn curtains, was scattered throughout the dingy rooms. There were holes in the plaster and the plumbing leaked. The toilet in the single bathroom was plugged with soggy paper and excrement. Depressed, Sam asked aloud, "How can people live like this?"

Uncle John had rented the flat within walking distance of his shop saying it had the three Cs—close, convenient and cheap. Sam added a fourth C—crappy. It was on the first floor of a two story frame house in a section of Niagara Falls occupied by struggling working class families with little work, families decent but desperate.

Sam was glad he'd left Emma with his Aunt Gert as he stood inspecting the pile of furniture and belongings piled in the living room where Josh and Alfred left them before turning back to Pennsylvania with the truck. His hands rested on the back of an upholstered chair as he examined the painted walls. He searched for a word to describe the color of the walls—sludge, cornhusk, piecrust—terms drab and uninspiring came to his mind. Under his feet, a nine by twelve threadbare carpet stretched to within a foot of each wall. Some form of linoleum was exposed around the perimeter; Sam wondered what horrors lay hidden underneath. Outdated magazines were everywhere. A lone floor lamp, plugged into the only electrical outlet, leaned as if about to fall. Thirty-five dollars a month for this! Inhaling, Sam caught the caustic odor of the ubiquitous factory smokestacks. *How wrong I was to think we could escape the stench of man at work.*

The ceiling, originally white, was soiled and yellowed by nicotine. Sam thought it inconceivable that anyone could smoke that much but the stains were there even in the dim light provided by a small chandelier of uncertain alloy and its four shaded bulbs. The three windows exposing the clutter of the street were flanked by brown drapes lined in a repetitive geometric design that reminded Sam of the three crosses on Calvary—Golgotha, the place of the skull, and he shuddered at the thought.

"Damn," he admonished himself, "I better clean up the worst of this before Emma gets here." He decided to start with the most disgusting. Where could he beg, borrow, or steal a toilet plunger?

Emma walked into the house and said, "You look dejected."

Sam wiped beads of perspiration from his eyes with the back of his wrist. He sighed at her observation. "I was comparing this shabby cave to the living room of your folk's home. I bet you're pleased I rescued you from that."

"I'd rather be in this room with you than lying with a Rajah in the Taj Mahal."

Sam smiled, and said, "You're nuts." He was uplifted. She never let him feel sorry for himself. "You look ready for some serious work," he observed her light cotton dress loose at the waist, flat-soled shoes, and headscarf.

"Well, we have to clean, and Gerty has some paint. This place needn't be dirty or dingy."

Sam took her arm and led her to a stuffed chair. Sitting with Emma on his lap, a coil spring threatening his back, he kissed her.

She straddled his lap with authority. 'We're going to be all right," she said.

"I know. I just wish it was better for you."

"It will be, I know it."

Sam held her and watched dust particles dance in a ray of sunlight. "You wearing anything under this?" He touched the light fabric of her dress.

"Why don't you find out?"

Sam ran his hand over her waist and felt a thin panty line. He slid a finger between the buttons on her bodice and slowly released them all. Pushing the fabric aside, he freed a pink nipple. He pursed his lips and blew gently.

She shivered, and nibbled on his ear.

Sam said, "I think I can find a mattress."

Emma kept a secret—in the thin dark hours of the morning, her protective shroud of domesticity shed, she often had a dream visitor. She was afraid to tell Sam that, when the phantom appeared, her soul turned in torturous approach-avoidance conflict. A construct of her own imagination, he was harbored in the deepest recesses of her mind and emerged, as she slumbered, with all the bell-shaped beauty and insidious threat of belladonna. Threatening and promising, he came in stealth.

Unconscious, Emma would stir in dark apprehension, as he loomed closer, his powerful nakedness assuming definition in the dissipating mists. In confusion and fear she would shudder and turn, her body wet and wanting, her mind engulfed in silent screams. His smooth, slippery, sliding, eel-like muscle would find her, caress her, dominate and enter her. Breathless, gasping, her fingers flailing his featureless face, her loins open to him, she'd struggle, strangling in a confused spinning vortex of carnal desire and moral anguish.

Soaked and weeping, she would wake in a moment of panic that quickly passed as Sam held her and she knew his soothing voice.

"You okay?"

The strength of Sam's arms became her strength and, her flesh inflamed, she'd turn seductress. With her frantic hands and mouth on him, Sam would succumb. But even as she knew her husband, Emma, thrusting in wanton abandon, her eyes closed, searched to confirm her suspicion, to know for certain the identity of her midnight torturer.

Sam, ignorant of the demon that inspired the bouts of abandonment, welcomed them. He attributed them to the newfound freedom and released inhibitions of a new bride. He also welcomed and was thankful for those nights that passed in peaceful slumber, mornings when he woke rested and relieved.

The night before Sam's first day of work at John's machine shop, Emma slept soundly, but he tossed in restless anticipation. He imagined all manner of difficulties with other resentful employees, broken down machinery, and his own broad ignorance. He envisioned himself, hot and sweaty, weary and sluggish, carelessly losing his fingers in the maw of an immense churning machine. *Ridiculous*, he chastised himself, but his imagination ground on.

In the morning, he rose reluctantly from bed trying not to disturb Emma. His eyes felt heavy and irritated, as though they held a beach full of sand. In the kitchen, he poured a glass of milk and sat rubbing his eyes. Their weekend efforts had left the smell of fresh paint to mask the noxious smell of the smoking stacks. Emma had made him promise they would move before even thinking about children. Sam thought that if she had lived closer to the smoldering dumps at home, she wouldn't be so offended. Still, he admitted, she was right. With thumb and finger he squeezed his nostrils closed. *For now we'll just have to hold our noses.*

After crunching through a bowl of Shredded Wheat and eating a banana, he dressed for the shop. He found the long sleeved shirt and dungarees Emma had left over the back of a chair. Passing the window, he saw the gray light of day easing between the crowded houses. He found his shoes beside the door. He felt the paper-thin soles and decided to cut cardboard inserts. *It'll have to do,* he figured, searching a drawer for scissors.

Closing the door soundlessly, Sam was surprised to hear the sound of birds in the damp morning mists. He planned to make the fifteen-minute walk to work on Buffalo Avenue where the shop was squeezed onto a property between two monster facilities with belching stacks. He wanted to be the first to arrive each day, feeling he owed it to John.

John's machine shop was in a one-story building with a flat roof supported by walls of unpainted concrete block. John said that when it rained, if the wind was right, it rained harder inside than out. He claimed that, most often, the wind blew from such a direction that inside they experienced only a light shower. Sam wondered. Thankfully, the high cirrus clouds lacked gray-black moisture laden bellies. There'd be no rain on his first day.

Sam found the door to the shop unlocked. Obviously, he wasn't the first to arrive. Inside, an eerie half-light played across the west wall. There was a bulb burning in the corner office, and Sam could see John at his desk. He was wearing a black Derby and chewing on an unlit cigar. His full face under the heavy curled eyebrows swelled with a sincere smile, "Come in, Sam, I've got the kettle on."

Sam wound his way across the shop floor of oil saturated wooden block. He stepped carefully in the dim light, weaving between machines and bins full of small parts. He'd had a tour of the shop the week before and had a good idea of what the enterprise was all about. Sam ran his fingers through his dry hair. There was an oily dampness in the air and the slick odor of machine coolant; he knew it would be his by the end of the day. He wondered which of the hulking machines would occupy him for the day.

"I'm going to start you on a drill press," John said, as though reading his thoughts.

Sam searched the floor trying to spot one, *Good, should be simple enough.*

The outer door banged open as another employee arrived.

Sunlight beamed horizontally through the west windows when Sam hit a red button causing the screaming drill chucks to slow to a halt. The noise of drive belts squealing and metal parts banging through the ten-hour day ended sporadically as the shop shut down. Sam had a headache. A persistent buzzing continued in his head even as the drone of machinery stopped, and he felt slightly sick to his stomach. He removed a leather glove and massaged a knot in his left shoulder. His fingers had little effect on the dull ache. He looked down at his dungarees and shoes saturated with oil.

A bin alongside the drill press was full of small square metal pieces, each with two holes near the center. Sam had lost count of the bins, but knew he'd earned his five dollars for the ten-hour day. He threw both gloves on the bench beside the press and walked to the office.

His Uncle John had just put the telephone earpiece back on the hook and was jotting numbers on a yellow pad. He turned to Sam, "Well, no overtime this week."

Rubbing a sore elbow, Sam didn't know if that was good news or bad. He turned and watched the other two machinists shutting down for the day. He'd been introduced to them the week before, and knew their names were Earl and Jack, but they'd alternated lunch breaks and had no conversation during the day. He watched as they gathered their lunch buckets and walked quietly out the door. "They don't say much, do they?"

John chuckled, "They're afraid you'll take their jobs. I told them not to worry about it. They'll come around." He put his foot up on a cast iron radiator and asked, "How'd it go?"

"No problems, just sore muscles."

"You'll get used to it. I'd give you a lift home, but I'm going to be awhile."

Sam said, "That's okay, it's a short walk." He pushed his pork pie hat to the back of his head, "Maybe my ears will quit ringing before I get home."

John said, "Goodnight," and turned to the papers on his desk.

Outside the building, Sam looked at his oil-soaked shoes. He wondered if they would survive the walk home. He was going to have to buy work shoes. Damn, he hated to spend the money.

Trudging along, barely conscious of looming factories and streets lined with tired frame houses, Sam considered his situation. His full day of honest labor had impressed upon him the full realization of the task before him. How was he going to help his family back home, when he was exhausted providing for himself and Emma? Sam had the sick suspicion that he'd bitten off more than he could chew. He saw himself as a discredited knight, horseless, facing the dragon of despair.

A small house converted to a Mom-and-Pop store occupied one corner of the intersection of two neighborhood streets. Its' wooden siding was a dingy gray from the soot belched routinely out of local smokestacks. An old man was cleaning a plate glass window using a long handled squeegee. Sam's attention was drawn by the strong biting odor of ammonia, and he waved to the man as he passed.

Across the intersection, Sam turned abruptly when the old man shouted, "Stop! Come back here."

He was yelling at two urchins running from the store. Sam stood and watched them disappear down an alley. The old man threw his squeegee to the sidewalk. He put both hands to his head in a gesture of futility. Staring at Sam, he pleaded, "What can I do? I know they're hungry, but I can't feed everybody." He dropped his hands in defeat.

Sam sighed, "I know just how you feel."

CHAPTER 20

September 1933

Ernie shrugged, autumn was here and winter was coming. He looked at the eastern slope of West Mountain as he walked along. He'd be spending less time there on the wooded slope, where he often wandered feeling he belonged amongst the giant trees. On the mountain alone, his size didn't matter. Ernie bent his arm at the elbow drawing his hand up to his face. He looked at it, wide as a ham with sausage-like fingers. *Why are they so big? Alfred's aren't big with knobby joints.* Alfred could make a silver dollar dance across his knuckles. Ernie, envious, tried it once when no one was around. The coin kept falling until, in frustration, he threw it at the wall.

He looked down at his thick legs and huge feet, looking gigantic in galoshes. His mother hadn't cut his hair in weeks and brown curls flared out from under his woolen cap topping the collar of his bulky coat. With his size and striding in galoshes, he resembled the Norse God Thor emerging from a fjord…*Why am I so big?* His brothers weren't like him. He was different from everybody. He hated his body—it was different. He felt people looked at him and laughed behind his back. *Maybe I should work in a freak show.*

Lisa scolded him when he spoke disparagingly about himself. She made him feel good, almost normal. It was why he so enjoyed her company. She was his only true friend, and he would soon see her. Swinging heavily from his gloved hand was the basket for the minister's household, his mother's weekly down payment on a resting-place in heaven.

Despite his heavy clothing, Ernie felt the dampness and chill left by the brazen wind and recent downpour. The sky was gunmetal blue overhead and the lane muddy brown under his feet. Maybe Mrs. Christer would offer him a cup of tea.

He sloshed along Martin Street, his boot prints filling quickly, forming puddles. He could see the picket fence that delineated the church property and the sprawling Victorian house that sheltered Reverend Christer and his cluster of females, wife and daughters and Lisa. Ernie treasured Lisa's friendship, and he missed her. She wasn't home when he made his last delivery and he hadn't seen her around school all week. He missed her bright innocence and pretty face.

It was depressing to see the gnarled trumpet vine devoid of blossoms and surrendering its slippery wet leaves to autumn. Across the front of the house, where flowers had bloomed all summer, there were mounds of mulch. A ground squirrel eyed Ernie's approach before scurrying under the porch.

On the porch, Ernie knocked on the wide door, rattling the leaded glass window. Waiting for a response, he stared at the ceiling hooks for the porch swing, now stored for the season, and remembered swinging with Lisa, counting their bare toes. He sighed, *If you bared your toes out here now, they'd freeze and fall off.*

The door opened to reveal Lisa's sister Sarah, standing with a heavy knit shawl over her shoulders. She had all the sympathetic, warm beauty of a Madonna. A young woman in the full blooming flower of her youth, she had the large blue dancing eyes of a temptress. Her musky fragrance, borne on escaping warm air, reached Ernie and he looked away. He was uneasy, confronted with Sarah so established in her womanhood, but comfortable with Lisa, not yet a woman.

"Oh, Ernest, it's you." Her lashes fluttered and her blond curls bounced, as she looked down at his muddy galoshes. "Take your boots off and come in out of the damp."

"I just came by to bring this," Ernie gave her the covered basket, "but I will step in for a minute. It is cold out here." He bent to release the metal buckles. "Is Lisa home?"

Sarah stood a moment, her mouth agape. "Oh, Ernest," she said, her bright face yielding to a cloudy sadness, "you mean you don't know?"

Ernie asked, "Know what?" his fingers fumbling with the buckles.

"Lisa went to stay with our aunt in Syracuse. She's gone."

He straightened, his galoshes half-undone, bewilderment evident on his open face, confusion and questions clouding his eyes. Ernie asked, "For how long?" He couldn't believe it. They were friends, best friends. *She didn't say good-bye.* "When will she be back?"

Sarah watched Ernie's reaction to her news. She adjusted her shawl, held it closed at her throat and said, "I don't know."

Ernie turned silently away; the disappointment evident in his bowed head was punctuated by the clack of overshoe buckles as he shuffled down the walk.

Sarah watched him go, tears in her eyes. "Not so long," she whispered, closing the door.

Returning home in a funk as gray as the day, Ernie found Alfred and Josh lugging bushels of apples from the huckster truck to the chill of the root cellar. He stood quietly watching their grunting efforts, as they slid the loaded bushel baskets off the rear of the vehicle and wrestled them with short wide steps into the cool of the crypt-like storage room.

In halting words abbreviated by exertion, Josh huffed, "Don't hesitate to pitch in."

Alfred said, "Leave him alone. He looks like he's been rode hard and put away wet."

"You've been reading too many dime westerns." Josh sat heavily on the lowered tailgate.

Alfred stood, apparently trying to guess the cause of Ernie's mood. Finally, he asked, "What's wrong?"

Ernie rolled his head and, in a tone that reflected his disbelief, said, "Lisa's gone." Alfred looked puzzled.

"That's it? Josh snorted, "You're depressed about a twat?"

The words were still in the air when the back of Ernie's open hand caught Josh on the neck just under his ear and sent him sprawling on the wet ground.

Ernie turned and slouched slowly toward the house.

Josh growled, "Goddamn!" He struggled in an effort to rise.

Alfred, watching, said, "I'd let him go if I were you."

Staring at Ernie's receding backside, Josh let the tension flow out of him and began to chortle.

What?" Alfred asked.

"Nothing…nothing," Josh said. Rubbing the knot rising below his ear, he remembered the sweet yielding innocence of Lisa. He smiled at the lascivious recollection, and said, "I forgive him."

Alfred stroked his chin, "I guess I'm missing something here."

Josh closed his eyes, and recalled the pungent smell of Lisa as she received him.

CHAPTER 21

October 1933

Walking across waxed floors buffed to a liquid sheen, Emma moved uncertainly in the halls of Memorial Hospital. With mincing steps, she passed before a line of wall plaques, images of stern men, founders, doctors, priests and healers whose dreams and efforts built the institution in which she wandered. Like any person of responsibility in a new situation, she felt inadequate, exposed. *Who is reliable?...What do I do if?...What are the policies?...Where is the proper place for this?...Am I handling it correctly?* It was all so intimidating, not at all like Mid Valley Hospital where everything was so familiar, where she knew all the staff and most of the patients. She wished she were back there. *No you don't.* Get a hold of yourself everything will be all right.

She took a slow calming breath and straightened the white cap perched like a gull on her brushed, fifty-strokes-per-side, auburn hair. After a lonely claustrophobic ride in a stark metal-sided elevator smelling of disinfectant, she stepped out into a long ill lit hallway. She approached a Nursing Station, an island of light, where a large older nurse bent over a desk. Emma stiffened her back, took a deep breath and exhaled, "Hi."

Startled, the dowdy nurse turned and stared, her eyes surveying the newcomer.

She nodded, "Hi, yourself...You my relief?"

"If this is Two North, I am."

"Where's Her Eminence?"

"Who?"

The nurse chuckled, causing her broad body to shake, "You must be new. Mrs. Stoddard, the head nurse. She usually introduces you new gals."

"Oh," Emma smiled, understanding, "she told me to come up and introduce myself. Said she'd be along later. Apparently she has a problem. There were a lot of people milling around near her office. She said you were very good, an old hand, and could get me started," Emma thought a little flattery might help, "she'll be up as soon she can."

The older nurse brushed a gray hair off her brow. Her white uniform was spotted and stretched tightly over her prominent bosom, abdomen, and broad hips. "Well," she said, "Stoddard was right about me being an old hand, anyway. My name is Louise, Louise Nelson, everyone calls me Lou." She smiled and placed her hand heavily on Emma's arm.

"I'm Emma Freeman," Emma responded, "pleased to meet you."

"Likewise...your friends call you Emma?"

Emma nodded, "Emma or just Em."

"Come on, Em, let me show you around." They toured the floor. Lou slowly paced her practiced way, her broad hips shifting inside her dress like amateur actors behind a curtain. Emma followed, asking questions and adding comments as they nodded past patient rooms, rest rooms, housekeeping and linen closets. She sniffed. The smells were familiar—foul odors of incontinence and putrefaction thinly disguised by sharp antiseptic and cleaning agents. Funny, everything is different but familiar. Emma was in her element.

Back at the Nurse's Station, Lou looked at her. "You'll be okay. None of this is really new to you, is it?" Appraising Emma's bright youthful face and attractive figure, she said, "The only problem you'll have will be hands."

"Hands?" Emma's eyebrows formed in a quizzical expression.

"Doctor's hands," Lou said, flexing her own pudgy fingers. She clenched her jaw, and shook her head. "They'll be all over a sweet thing like you. The older incorrigible ones will be worse than the interns. They've had more time to develop their God complexes." She watched Emma as she spoke. "But I have a feeling you can handle them."

Despite a rising feeling of unease, Emma said, "I'm sure I can."

CHAPTER 22

March 1934

Due to her part time status, Emma worked weekends. Sam had weekends off as the need for overtime at the shop was infrequent. Saturdays he scoured the Help Wanted columns in the morning paper seeking additional work for himself and possibilities for his brothers. The thought of them, their situation and expectations, ate at him. Advertised opportunities were rare and the process discouraging. He often walked the downtown streets looking for help wanted signs in storefront windows. The signs weren't there but the street people were and they begged Sam for help he couldn't give. Sometimes he grabbed a pole, pushed the burden of guilt aside and went fishing, just to escape the frustration.

On one such Saturday, he stood wearing a sweater beneath his heavy coat and a black watch cap pulled down over his ears. It was impossible to determine where the black cap ended and his thick black sideburns and eyebrows began. He stared at the cold green water and sliding ice of the lower Niagara. With experience gained on previous Saturdays, he tossed his lure into the swirling waters between the bobbing ice flows.

He was just upriver from the town of Lewiston and, from his position on a patch of rocky shore, he could view the sheer bluffs and trees of the Canadian shore. Everything, rocks, trees, and scrub brush, was covered with frost that glittered when occasionally the sun broke free of the scudding dirty-gray clouds. The intermittent sun did nothing to lessen the cutting effect of the cruel wind. The frigid fingers of the wind slid up his sleeves and down beneath his collar where they felt dry and dangerous as dry ice. The cold dried the hairs in his nose and he brushed it ineffectively with the back of his glove. Sam closed his eyes and imagined he could hear the crash of water as it fell in torrents over the Falls and roared through the deep gorge scant miles upstream. Amazingly, he felt inflated rather than diminished by the realization he was taking from the waters of one of the wonders of the world.

At the end of his stringer, jerking in the sweeping water, a large blue pike twisted its life away. The fish had enough size to provide an ample meal for him and Emma, but he wanted another for John and Gerty. The cutting cold had him ready to quit. He looked down at his empty thermos bottle—no comfort there. He was about to retrieve his line when the rod bent sending flecks of frost into the air. Sam set the hook; he had John's dinner. There was more than one way to put food on the table. Someone said, "You'd have to be stupid to starve living by the ocean." Sam figured that applied to lakes and rivers too.

He took the fish, another blue pike, off the hook and tossed it up on the rocks where it flopped around, gills opening and closing as it drowned in the air. Sam knew just how he felt. He pulled his stringer and the first fish from the water and placed it on a flat rock. With his thin filleting knife, he slit it from gills to vent then shook the entrails into the river. Gulls overhead squawked their disapproval and dove frantically to pluck the guts from the racing river surface.

Sam stopped at John's on the way home. His uncle wasn't there but Gerty asked him in. "My word, you look frozen. You'd better have some hot tea." Her face was flushed, and flesh, perspiration damp from the humid air in the overheated kitchen, swung beneath her arms. Her wet gray hair covered her scalp like a helmet.

Warm air laden with cinnamon and ginger enveloped Sam. "No, thanks, Aunt Gert, I just stopped by to leave you this." He placed the fish, wrapped in newspaper, on the kitchen table.

Gerty rolled the package opening the damp newspaper, and looked at the sightless eyes and silver-blue scales. "Oh, Sam, he's a beauty. Thanks." She moved the fish to the sink. "Here, take one of these." She pulled a squat quart Mason jar full of yellow-orange peach halves from her cupboard. It was one of many amid canned tomatoes, beans, and bread and butter pickles.

"Aunt Gert, these look great."

"Your Uncle John picked them in an orchard up by Lake Ontario. They might need a little sugar."

Sam took the peaches and kissed Gerty on a chubby cheek. "Have a good weekend," he said opening the door and stepping out into the welcome crisp air.

It was dark when Emma came through the doorway at the end of the day. She was moving slowly, and her shoulders slumped as she fell into a chair and tugged at her white shoes.

"Tough one?"

"Mmm," she moaned, draping her coat over a chair. Using both hands, she began to knead the muscles of her shoulders and neck.

"Here," Sam said, "let me do that."

She leaned forward. Sam kissed the top of her head and began to massage her neck.

"Better," she sighed, "I smell you were successful today."

"Sorry," Sam smelled the fish on his hands.

"Don't stop. This uniform is going into the laundry anyway At least you haven't had your hands in the egg wash." She rolled her shoulders, rose and looked at the fillets in the kitchen sink. "Blue pike."

"Yep, I caught a couple. Gave one to John and Gerty. She gave us that jar of peaches for dessert. Why don't you take a bath while I fry the fish?" Sam lifted a fillet by the narrow end and swung it into a pan.

Emma smiled, "You're spoiling me."

Though the kitchen smelled of cooking oil, the supper went well. Sam presented the fillets with carrot buttons and diced potatoes and onions. He set the table and didn't forget the napkins. Emma, scrubbed pink, was pleased.

After supper, they stood at the sink. Emma washed the dishes and, towel in hand, Sam dried. As he toweled, he described the river, "It's swirling green water filled with bobbing chunks of ice. Gulls, resting on the ice, float by or swoop overhead. You'd love it. Maybe we could walk there tomorrow, if it's not too cold."

Emma tugged on a chain and a rubber stopper came loose. Dish water spun slowly out of the sink. She turned to Sam. "Honey, I'd like to rest tomorrow. I'm tired. I don't know if it's the long work day, or because I'm pregnant."

It was like a blow to the solar plexus, but Sam recovered quickly holding tightly to a dinner plate.

"Pregnant?" he said, thinking, *What a heavy word.*

She smiled, almost laughed, at his wide-eyed surprise.

"Oh, Em," Sam took her in his arms, the dinner plate waving in the air, "That's wonderful."

Emma could feel his heart thumping. She asked, "You're not upset?"

"Upset?…no, flabbergasted?…yes," He held her at arms length, "and happy. But, if somebody asked me to recite the ABCs, I couldn't—my mind's a whirl." He hugged her again. "I love you. I'm happy for you, for us."

"I'm relieved," she said, "I was a little worried. I know the timing's not right."

"Oh hell," Sam grinned, "is the timing ever right? I feel like I've been struck by lightning. We're blessed, let's celebrate. Break out the Jello!"

Emma laughed at that, and in a moment they were both laughing hysterically.

Sam was at the river watching the swift water above the falls. He could see the rapids, saw the green water churn and splash, heard the roar beyond the rocks. The water was full of ice floes, large and small pieces racing in the current. There were babies on the ice, little tykes in diapers. They were all smiling! He could hear them cooing. God, he had to save them.

Sam was horrified. They must be freezing. They're headed for the Falls. Why are they smiling. They're waving at me. "I'm coming," he screamed. He was shaking so badly that he couldn't get his shoes off. His fingers were cold and stiff, he couldn't get them off! No matter—they had holes in the soles. Sam plunged into the dark water, his arms thrashing against the power of the river. He was freezing, his arms were too heavy and he struggled to reach the surface. Something bumped him.—a giant fish. There were bloody entrails in the water. Are they mine? Sam was terrified. Out of air and kicking at the water, he tried to stay alive: drowning, gasping like a fish, he swallowed cold water. Finally, his head broke the surface. There was nothing but water and ice—the babies were gone.

"Sam, Sam, wake up." Emma stroked his shoulder. His nightshirt was soaking wet.

His eyes, open wide, were clouded with confusion. His ears rumbled with the roar of the falls. Sam shuddered, The babies were gone. He couldn't save them.

"Sam, it's all right. It was only a dream."

"Was it? "he cried, "all of it?"

CHAPTER 23

November 1934

In the impoverished mining town, small clapboard houses stood side by side separated by patches of weeds and joined by dilapidated, bleached picket fences. Too small for families with too many children, the average being six, they were dismally inadequate. Brothers and sisters shared bedrooms until split by mother's recognition of puberty. Then, the boys would be assigned to a loft already crowded. The very youngest often shared the bed of mother and father comfortably sleeping in the presence of expended passion. In a sparsely furnished bedroom corner in one of the dingy houses, Josh stood quietly observing two children asleep on a dirty mattress. One was a cherubic six-year-old lost in the deep sleep of the innocent, resting peacefully unaware of the evil lurking in her bedchamber. Curls, undisturbed by warm furnace air, circled her face. Naked, but for a loose diaper that masked her loins, her pale skin was exposed, her button-like nipples exposed in the shallow night. Beside her, a ten-year-old sister was sprawled face down sharing the twisted blankets.

Standing darkly silent beside their bed, a sinister blackness in the small cube of a room, Josh allowed his mind to feed on the two morsels. Considering the tender thighs below the diaper, his mind seethed, embroiled in recurrent fantasy. Slowly, his steady hand slid forward, a serpent nearing, olfactory senses heightened, sensing prey. His warm fingers settled on smooth, soft flesh. Held in placid slumber, the child smiled in misguided comfort at his touch, and her arm moved suddenly touching her sister.

Nudged alert, her sister's eyes opened, white and wide. Jolted awake, by her sister's screams, the younger girl sobbed - convulsively, then began to cry. Josh, his unnatural presence discovered and no longer needing the cover of stealth, recoiled and leaped through the chamber doorway, and bounded down a narrow passageway. He hit the front door with athletic force and burst out onto a wooden platform that served poorly as a porch. Flushed with adrenaline, moving with speed but no control, he ran forcefully into a man standing, mouth open, on the stairs. Josh's momentum carried them down the stairs and spilled them on the ground. Another man, companion to the first, stood transfixed watching the figures entwined in the clarity of moonlight.

Scrambling frantically to free himself, Josh clawed at the terrified man. The man, smelling of whiskey, flailed insanely, his arms and legs entangling Josh. Finally able to free himself, Josh jerked upright and stood, in a brief moment of indecision, staring at the frightened, confused, gaping men. Then, as suddenly as he had collided, he escaped into the night.

"Who the fock was that?" the fallen man blurted.
"That," his companion replied, "was crazy Josh Cordy."

The next day, the day before Thanksgiving, was marked by the first snow fall of the season in Niagara Falls, and the birth of Josh's niece.

In Memorial Hospital, attended by an obstetrician and her friend, Louise, Emma gave birth to a squalling six pound eight ounce baby girl. Pacing nervously in a waiting room, away from the pulsing pain, sweat, strain and miracle of the delivery room, Sam recalled, with wonderment, that it would have been another of Jonathan Freeman's birthdays.

When presented with his daughter, and informed that Emma was fine, he bit his lip to keep from weeping. Feeling as punchy as a heavy bag, he took the baby from a smiling Louise. "Thank you…thank you," he said, looking at the pink face of his bundled daughter.

"She looks like a healthy monkey with my hair," he grinned.

"Yes," Louise said, "she does look like you, poor thing."

Sam laughed, handling the baby nervously. He was afraid to hold her too tightly, and afraid not to. He handed the bundle to Louise. "Can I see Emma?"

"Yes. Go down the hall," Louise pointed, "first room on the left."

Emma, in a simple white hospital gown, her face drawn by her recent exertion, and her damp hair combed straight back, looked as lovely as the first time he'd seen her. Sam stood beside the single bed and took her hand, "You do good work," he said, and kissed her lightly on the forehead.

Emma, obviously limp from her labor, looked up at Sam. "Isn't she beautiful?"

"Yes, like her mother."

She smiled, her eyes drooping.

"Today would have been my grandfather's birthday." He hesitated, letting Emma consider the coincidence. "Maybe we should name her Johnny."

Emma said, her voice drawn and lazy, "Her name is Mary," and fell asleep.

"Mary," Sam mouthed the words of the song, "it's a grand old name."

CHAPTER 24

December 1934

Aunt Gerty became a bustling presence during the weeks following Emma's return home with the baby, Mary. The mailman brought cards and letters postmarked in Pennsylvania, along with packages of pink frilly clothes and knit booties. Emma and Gerty, "Oohed and Aahed," over the gifts. Sam contemplated the challenge of another soul to provide for, while reading the congratulatory mail. Letters from both grandmothers expressed regrets over their absence, and promised to visit soon. Sam was privately pleased they were not in the house; gurgling Gerty was quite enough. He hoped the grandparents, should they invade, would not all arrive at the same time. He dreaded the sugary madness that could result—Grandpa Harry, beaming, leaving Sam to referee the tug of war between competing grandmothers.

Chilly Canadian air sliding out of the northwest gathered moisture over the Great Lakes and released it as snow over Western New York and Northern Pennsylvania. The cutting winds and shifting snows discouraged motor travel through the month of December. Good sense prevailed, and when Sam announced that he, Emma and the baby would visit soon after the weather cleared, the frustrated grandparents decided to wait.

Emma gradually returned to her household duties, Gerty retreated, a subdued Christmas passed, and Sam settled into a stressful routine of insufficient work and debilitating worry. The city of Niagara Falls was held graveyard quiet under a heavy shroud of ice. An ice bridge formed beneath the Falls, downtown storefronts were glazed by ice crystals, and motorist and pedestrian alike navigated at their own risk. Work at the drafty machine shop became spotty as winter took its toll on automobile sales. By February, Sam was working only three-day weeks, and he suspected his Uncle John was exaggerating the demand even then.

As the workload lightened, Sam's worries increased. Carefully trudging the icy rutted walk home at work day's end, he dreaded the moments ahead, the suppressed evidence of disappointment on Emma's face when he announced, "No work tomorrow." He became desperate for spring, the release of winter's effect on the markets and his malaise.

So, at the end of one such disappointingly light workday, when Sam returned home to find his brother Alfred standing with arms wide at his door, he was flooded with emotion. Alfred's grinning countenance brought instant overpowering memories of home and family. Sam bit his tongue to prevent a sob. Throwing his arms around his brother, he squeezed to prevent his speaking, fearing the sound of his voice would sever what little control he had remaining. Finally, Sam asked with a slight catch in his voice, "What are you doing here?"

Breathless, Alfred thumped Sam on the back and gasped, "I'm here to see my niece," he pushed Sam to arms length, "not to have my ribs cracked."

Sam stood appraising him; the months had taken their toll, Alfred had lost weight, Sam could see it in his drawn face, and his hair had thinned. Wearing a long black overcoat, gloves and galoshes, Alfred was hatless. Sam was pleased to see that there still remained an energetic glint in his brother's eyes. "Well, we're sure glad to see you, aren't we, Em?"

Standing in the doorway, Alfred's hat in hand, she said, "We certainly are." She was grinning. Sam knew she was relieved to see him happy, knew she'd been worrying about his depressed state. Emma had always expressed her fondness for Alfred, his positive attitude and quick subtle wit. Of all his brother's, Sam thought Alfred was her favorite. She'd been unable to relate to Wilbur—his blindness got in the way. And, Ernie, the strong silent type, always fell uneasily mute when she tried to communicate. Josh? Sam was unsure about Josh. When he was around, Emma fell unnaturally quiet. Something seemed to make her wary of him. She denied it, wouldn't talk about it, but Sam sensed a change in her when Josh was near.

Releasing Alfred, and kissing Emma, Sam said, "Let's get out of the cold. This calls for a drink."

After dinner, Emma kicked them out of the house. "Go get the stink blown off you," she said, knowing they wanted to talk, needed to talk.

Out the door, Sam said, "We can walk to Crowley's. It's a gin mill around the corner." He grabbed a fistful of Alfred's coat sleeve, "Careful on this ice, it's slicker than shit. Walk with your feet spread wide, and shuffle along or you'll end up on your ass."

As they edged carefully along, Alfred blurted, "I've got a girl."

Sam smiled at the suddenness of the declaration. It was obvious that Alfred needed to get it out. "I should hope so, you'd make a lousy fag."

Turning a comer, the wind-driven sleet stinging their faces now fell on their shoulders. They looked cautiously up and down the street before crossing to a narrow building. Above the door of the windowless front, a sign swinging in the wind read, "Crowley's Pub."

Sam drew the heavy door open and they entered a long barroom full of hazy cigarette smoke, low growling conversation, the clink of glassware, amid the smell of stale beer. Conversation that halted upon their entrance resumed as they settled on a pair of bar stools, overcoats clutched tightly around them. The bitter cold that had tweaked their noses settled in their bones. Looking at Alfred, Sam noted ice crystals in his thinning hair.

Sam placed his hat on the bar. "Where's your hat?" He shook his head, "You'll learn to wear one up here. Sometimes the mist blown from the Falls covers the city and everything in it. Like the top of your head."

Alfred drew his long fingers back over his hair, then wiped the moisture on his coat. His hair was lighter and thinner than Sam's black bush, just as his frame was smaller and lighter. Still, he moved with an evident confidence that belied his size. Alfred shuddered in delayed response to the evening chill. "Buy me a drink," he said.

"Crowley," Sam called to the bartender-owner, "two boilermakers."

Crowley, a huge pock-faced man with a torso like a beer barrel, drew two mugs of draft beer and placed them on the bar. Into each he poured a shot of amber whiskey.

Sam explained, "This is my brother Alfred, just up from Pennsylvania. He hasn't had a drink since the start of prohibition."

Crowley laughed, his big belly shaking, "When they started the foolishness, he was too young to drink." He said to Alfred, "Now that they've repealed it, I'll wager you can drink your share like any fool."

Sam dropped a few coins on the bar. As Crowley selected two, Sam said, "Take a little, leave a little."

Pointing to a wooden bowl on the bar, Alfred said, "Pass the pretzels."

Sam slid the bowl across the polished surface. "So," he took a twisted pretzel, and responded to the earlier revelation, "you fancy this girl?" He watched Alfred's face, reflected in the back-bar mirror, for a reaction.

"I do." Alfred cast his glance self-consciously around the tap room, and added, "She's Catholic." Silence, then, "She's a good woman."

"There's good and bad in all," Sam said, tipping his mug searching for the hint of coarse whiskey.

"She's a good lass, comely and warm."

"Willing, you mean?"

Alfred avoided Sam's glance, his face flushed.

"No offense," Sam added quickly, "it's no sin to seek whatever comfort you can in this life"

Alfred was quiet, toying with his drink, forming interlocking wet circles on the bar. His head came up sharply with the sounds of an altercation, raised voices from the end of the bar.

Crowley, his huge mitt swinging with the force of a heavyweight, brought his bar rag down on the flat bar surface with a resounding slap. "Gentlemen," he admonished with a roar, and the row was immediately silenced.

Obviously, the regulars knew when Crowley meant business. Crowley adjusted the apron that covered his ample belly and announced, "Last call."

"Want another?" Sam asked.

"You know her," Alfred searched Sam's face for a reaction, "Molly Walsh."

Anticipating the news, Sam was able to retain a poker face. "Yes, I do," he said.

"she is a fine lass, honest, full of fun."

"She has a child, a baby," Alfred said, his low voice full of anguish.

"Ah," Sam uttered, as though all of life's mysteries were suddenly cleared.

"Not mine," Alfred said, now in real pain.

"The father?" Sam asked, expecting the worst.

"She won't say."

"Ah," Sam repeated, life full of mystery again. He sipped his drink, *She is a good lass.* He said to Alfred, "Have another." They settled into contemplative silence. Sam thought of the old retort, *What? You buy the cow, you don't get the calf?* and was immediately penitent. He turned to his brother, sitting with his head down. "You love her?"

Alfred's head came up, "I do."

"Then marry her. To hell with the clucking tongues."

Alfred managed a crooked smile, "Thanks, Sam."

Sam waved his hand and, to change the subject, asked, "How're things at home?"

"Desperate. There's little or no work. Most families are on relief—fifteen dollars a week. Christ, I don't know how they do it. There's eight million on relief in this country. If something doesn't change, there's going to be a revolution."

Listening, Sam suspected he was right. "Maybe Roosevelt can set it straight."

"He's just another rich bastard. I doubt he gives a shit about the workin' man."

Sam speculated, "All the little guy can do is hope everything will eventually be all right." He asked, "How's the family? You're not on relief?"

"No. Pop does maintenance work at the mill. Sometimes he even gets paid." He shook his head at that. "We keep the huckster truck going. Of course, now that booze is legal again, that part of the business is dead. Mom canned an awful lot of fruit and beans. If people around town knew how much she's got stashed, we'd have to stand guard. So, we've got a warm place to sleep and enough to eat, more than most folks."

Sam felt a small amount of relief from the burden of his unfulfilled promise to move the family out of the valley. He placed his hand on Alfred's shoulder and said, "I haven't forgotten my promise." He saw that Alfred believed him. "I'll know when the time is right."

Alfred said, "Don't fret. Time's the same for all of us. We know how the desperate days crawl, and the months fly by. We each handle it in our own way. Wilbur, for instance, is always on his crystal set listening to the news from everywhere. He says he can get London. A friend of his, Alvin Roberts, I don't think you know him, comes around. Alvin goes to some technical school in Scranton and he passes everything on to Wilbur. It's amazing what he can do, not being able to see much."

"Ernie's a real bear; a girlfriend of his left town. His mood swings from solemn brooding to angry outbursts." Alfred shifted his weight on the stool while taking a swallow from his mug. He looked at Sam for a drawn out moment. "Josh is the problem."

"Why?" Sam asked, his interest piqued, *Am I about to hear the real reason for this visit?*

"He does strange things. He was seen coming out of a neighbor's house in the middle of the night."

"Whose house?"

"You remember Miller? He worked in number seven mine. The family with all the daughters, uphill on the other side of the road."

"Jesus, did he take anything?"

Alfred shook his head, "No. The constable wanted to charge him with trespassing, but Miller wouldn't press charges. They just gave him a warning. Lizzy was really upset, if he wasn't so big, she would have beaten the hell out of him. As it was, she just looked puzzled and sad. She threw up her arms, like she's given up on him."

"He didn't take anything?" Sam asked again, mystified.

Alfred rolled his eyes, "Nothing he could carry out."

"Damn," Sam said, catching his meaning, "he's not a kid anymore."

"Closing time," Crowley shouted.

Sam looked around the barroom—empty. He grabbed his hat. "He must mean us."

CHAPTER 25

March 1936

With the coming of spring 1936, it looked like more than the ice in the Niagara gorge was thawing. The climate seemed to have changed—the damning droughts and dust storms plaguing the country gave way to blessed rain. To Sam, it seemed the country had finally been absolved for the excesses of the Twenties. New Deal programs: the formation of the Works Progress Administration, the Civilian Conservation Corps, and the signing of the Social Securities Act had given him reason to hope.

But, Sam was thinking, *You can't eat hope,* when he rapped softly, a tentative tattoo with one knuckle, on his Uncle John's office doorjamb.

Behind a desk covered with invoices and statements, John sat shuffling papers under insufficient light. Beside him, a black telephone was ringing. John threw an invoice aside, and seemed about to reach for the phone when it stopped ringing. "Another impatient creditor," he mumbled. He turned in his seat and saw Sam at the door. He rolled his unlit cigar to the corner of his mouth and said, "Come in, Sam."

Stepping into the office, Sam noted the chair in front of a small desk in a corner was vacant. "Ellen off today?" Ellen was an older no-nonsense woman John had hired to bring order to the paper shuffle of his business.

"She's off...only working a couple days a week now," John sighed. Sam noted the bags under John's eyes were the same shade of umber as the polluted sky visible through the dirty office window. He saw how years of fatigue from fighting the exasperating commercial battles, of trying to gain business that simply wasn't there, had taken their toll. Like many of the machines on the shop floor, John was wearing out. For the first time, it occurred to Sam that this hulking man he'd always viewed as indestructible, was not. John should have been a minister, a politician, a teacher, anything but a businessman-industrialist in the early Thirties. The thought, an unexpected jab, gave Sam pause, and he hesitated, thinking that what he had come to say might prove to be the proverbial last straw.

Seeing Sam's hesitancy, John said, "Have a seat."

Sam removed his pork pie cap, held it in two hands before him like a penitent youngster, and sat on one of the two gray metal chairs. Being a day with no production scheduled, the shop was oily quiet. Sam licked his lips nervously, not knowing how to begin.

He twisted his cap, *Shit, here goes. Might as well just spit it out.* "Uncle John, the new automobile factory coming to Buffalo is taking applications." Sam looked at cobwebs in a ceiling corner, avoiding John's eyes. "They're looking for machine operators."

John slumped almost imperceptibly in his chair.

Though unsettled by John's reaction, Sam went on. "I figure I can work there until things get rolling here. You really don't need me now. Besides, I could still come in part time if you need me. And, if things really pick up for you, I could always come back."

John straightened, arched his back, turned in the chair, but didn't speak.

"Don't think I'm not appreciative of all you've done for us," Sam said, anxious to bolster his uncle. "Emma and I think you and Gerty are the best people in the world." Sam hurried on, his hands in motion, "I think that my leaving will cut you a little slack, give you some breathing room. You'll be able to give the other guys a few more hours. It'll be good for everybody."

John rose from his chair and began to pace in a small circle. Sam watched him with increasing nervousness, stroking his rudimentary mustache, a recent growth that caused Emma to roll her eyes, and, now, added to Sam's discomfort. *I should have been more subtle.*

John stopped pacing and said, "I guess you're right, Sam…damn, I hate to lose you."

The tension drained from Sam. He leaned forward on his chair, forearms on his thighs. "Actually, I'm glad you have the opportunity," John put his hand on Sam's shoulder. "You're a racehorse, Sam. You weren't here long before I realized that you shouldn't be hitched to this little wagon. There's a time for everything. Maybe this is your chance…I hope so."

Sam stood and they embraced, Sam being careful not to get John's cigar in his eye. John smelled of sweat and coarse laundry soap. He considered his uncles face, as John held him at arm's length, trying to judge the sincerity of his last remarks.

Grinning, John said, "If you're going to apply for a job, get rid of the mustache, it makes you look like a gangster."

Sam felt the patch of hair under his nose and agreed, "Emma will thank you for the advice."

The new motor plant rose from the clay soil in Tonawanda, Buffalo's northern suburb, to stand beside the Niagara River near the point where the river divides to surround Grand Island. Sam stood admiring the yellow brick of the administration building from his place in a long line of men strung along a ten foot high chain-link fence. He was reminded of the throng of women at the shoe factory.

The early morning sky was streaked with a soft fleshy pink in the east, but was dish- water gray overhead. A soft persistent rain was falling and Sam hunched his shoulders against the wet that had found its way under his turned up collar. He moved his feet out of a shallow puddle. *Dismal,* he thought, pulling his cap down closer to his eyebrows.

"How long we been here?" It was a voice cowed by the damp chill and fear of rejection.

Sam turned to a knotted little man behind him. "You speaking to me?" The man was shivering and his arms were folded across his concave chest in a feeble attempt to steel himself against the insidious blowing moisture. He was wearing a light threadbare jacket that was soaked through, and a wool cap equally saturated. "Y-yeah," his dentures clattered behind his sunken cheeks.

"Too long for you," Sam said. He pointed ahead at the line of men leading to the guard shack. "At the rate we're moving, you'll have pneumonia before you have a job."

"I g-g-gotta get a job," the man stammered, his eyes flooding.

"Good luck," was all Sam could say. He turned away from the depressing sight of him. They were within hearing range of the gate, and Sam wanted to catch what was being asked that caused some men to be turned away and others admitted.

"Name?" Sam heard the big uniformed guard ask the first man in line. He couldn't understand the muted reply, and winced slightly when the man was turned away. The man looked like a potential suicide as he left. The little man swore, "S-s-son of a bitch."

"Name?" the guard asked the next man, a ghost in ragged clothes.

"Ronald…"

Sam couldn't hear the last name.

"From around here?"

A tentative nod.

"Skilled?" the guard asked, his voice carrying an underlying sneer.

The man shook his ragged head slowly, side to side.

"Sorry, we ain't hiring no laborers." He waved him away.

Sam stepped aside, surprised when the man in front of him left with the rejected man.

"Name?"

Sam looked from the man's badge to his red bulb of a nose, "Sam Freeman."

"You lookin' for work?"

Stupid question. Sam pushed his hat back on his head, "Yes, sir."

"You from around here? We don't want no migrants."

"Niagara Falls," Sam envisioned a left hook to his nose, "just over the bridge."

"Skills?"

"I'm a machinist," Sam exaggerated.

The guard spit on the wet concrete walk. His eyes fixed on Sam, he rolled his massive shoulders, "We got enough machinists."

Sure you do. Sam held his hand open to the guard, exposing a ten- dollar bill. "I'm a good machinist."

"That's different," the guard said, "step in here, I'll sign you in."

Two weeks later, Sam stood in the center of the motor plant and looked at battleship gray machines and row upon row of conveyors. Brand new equipment. He couldn't imagine the amount of investment capital it represented. He drew a deep breath and smelled the machine oil, coolant, and fresh paint. He could smell the distinct newness of it all. There were other odors that would eventually overpower those, odors that indicated the price he'd have to pay: exhaust fumes, sweat, and his own dirty oozing pores.

But, this was it. This was the opportunity he'd been searching for since rising out of the valley. He felt his scrotum tighten with the challenge and the fear. He ground his teeth and vowed, *I'm going to work the ass off every son-of-a-bitch in the place.* Sam knew he would be able to honor his promise, spread before him were the means Lizzy would say the Lord had provided.

He was convinced he was looking at his future, and the future of his family: Emma, Mary, his mother and brothers.

The haunting vision of the big house on the river returned to Sam. He saw a family get together; everyone looked healthy and prosperous, the men in suits and the women in sweeping skirts and parasols. A banquet table was laid on the wide green lawn; everyone was eating. There were mounds of food and casks of drink, more than enough for all. Party boats floated by, white paint and polished brass flashed in the summer sun. Affluent people on the boats waved in recognition.

Sam captured the images. He played them over and over again in the theater of his mind.

Back to reality, Sam looked around. The means were at hand, all that was required was work, and he was no stranger to that. He looked around and found a steel bar. He swung the bar striking an empty metal bin. It made a noise like a church bell gone flat. Sam grinned, *I'm going to be somebody!*

CHAPTER 26

April 1936

Emma got off the bus and opened her umbrella. It was a short walk from the bus stop to the hospital doors, but the driving rain fell in sheets heavy enough to dampen her uniform and drown her spirits. She looked up at the looming stone building where she would spend the next ten hours tending to patients and avoiding, as much as possible, doctors that acted like they self-administered testosterone. Emma remembered what Louise said that first day about the doctor's hands, and she was right. Some were incorrigible.

Her first few months had passed without serious incident because she was pregnant. Glances, and innuendo she had countered with pretended unconsciousness. But, now there was one doctor, a Doctor Reading, who persisted, had actually had his hands on her. Though she had moved and evaded him as much as possible, she knew she was fighting a losing battle. It was simple economics—doctors admitted patients, patients paid the bills, hospitals cowed to doctors. It was that simple. And nurses? Nurses were servants, inferior beings to be tolerated for their utility, cursed for their stupidity, and used by physicians to satisfy their needs. Older established physicians, having convinced the hospital board of their indispensability, were free to lord it over the staff. Resistance, Emma knew, meant dismissal.

She also knew that taking her complaints to Stoddard the head nurse would not ease her situation. Stoddard, Lou had informed her, had employed the oldest of strategies, *if you can't beat' em, join' em.* Stoddard was the evening companion, to put it kindly, of Doctor Jamison, Chief of Staff, who had a wife and family in Lewiston, down river a comfortable distance away.

So, there it was—surrender or leave. Emma felt the situation would collapse over her like the umbrella she had lowered. She took a deep breath and pushed through the heavy doors, entering the hospital universe of peculiar smells, a mixture of disease and detergent. She hoped to get through another night, another week before facing the inevitable. Whatever happened, she had to keep Sam out of it.

"Good afternoon, Em," Louise greeted her. Louise looked like the end of a shift had settled over her, leaving her in disarray. Her uniform was wrinkled, soiled, and had perspiration rings at the armpits.

Emma glanced around. A pair of civilians huddled in the hallway, an elderly man with his arm around the narrow shoulders of a sobbing slip of a woman. No employees in sight. "You alone?"

"No," Louise said, slumping in a chair that barely contained her bulk. "Karen, the redhead from Three North was here all shift. She just left. I sent the aide down to Housekeeping for more linen, but she'll be back shortly." Emma knew the short linen supply was Louise's pet peeve.

"Tough day?"

"Not unless you consider wrestling Smythe in 202 on and off the bed pan every hour on the hour, and arguing with the sputum suckers from the lab. Oh, 206 is empty, patient went home. Sign the sheet and it's all yours, honey."

Emma read the log entries and signed it accepting the evening duty. It had all the appearances of a quiet night. "Off tomorrow?"

"Yep, a whole day away from this zoo. Take care." Louise waved and swayed down the hall toward the elevators.

"See you Thursday," Louise said, breathing heavily from the effort of getting out of the chair

Emma watched her ungainly progress and thought, One of these days, you poor soul, you're not going to make it. Sighing, she turned and looked for the Meds chart.

Halfway through the shift, a doctor appeared at the Nursing Station. Emma knew him, had been trying to avoid him, Doctor Reading, a psychiatrist member of the medical staff. He was an imposing figure, about fifty with gray sideburns and thick salted eyebrows. He had a deep voice, a commanding presence enforced by a sturdy physique, and a wide reputation. Emma had encountered him on two separate occasions while in the performance of her duties. The first time, she'd turned to leave a patient's room and found him blocking the doorway. "You're new, aren't you?" he'd asked, his eyes blatantly undressing her. On the second occasion, she had been alone at a Nursing Station, and he had put his hand on her hip and called her, "Emma." She had flushed and withdrawn from his possessive touch. Now, he was back.

"Well," he said, his manner disdainful, establishing dominance, "it's Mrs. Freeman."

Emma shrunk internally, but stood erect facing him. He moved to sit on a corner of a desk. He unbuttoned his coat. Emma guessed that his three-piece suit cost more than a month of Sam's wages. Hands folded, he asked, "Have you been instructed regarding your duties in this hospital?"

Emma swallowed, her mouth suddenly dry, and her insides loose. She clenched her hands into fists to keep them from trembling. "I believe so."

"Splendid," he said, standing. He seemed to tower over her. "Keep them in mind. Especially," he smiled, his eyes on hers, "the extracurricular ones." He walked to the chart rack and pulled a patient's record. "I'm going to look around," he said, "there have been some irregularities."

Emma reached for the words, "Is there something you want me to do?"

He waved a hand, "Not at the moment, see to your charges."

Emma left the station and walked to a patient room at the end of the hall, relieved at the opportunity to put some distance between her and Reading. In the room, the patient an elderly woman wasted by malnutrition and emphysema, smiled a ghastly toothless smile upon seeing her. Emma took her bony hand, and murmured wordless consolation, She caught the wet earthy smell of pseudomonas bacteria—the woman was prayer-time ill. Emma filled the bedside water pitcher, adjusted the window blinds and left the room.

Out in the hall, she looked for Reading, but he was nowhere in sight. Assuming he had left, she felt a surge of relief. She was not so naive as to believe she had seen the last of him, knowing he saw her as a challenge, an eventual conquest. She moved to the next patient.

"Oh, Mister Wheeler, what have you done?" Wheeler, a consumptive man of eighty, smiled a guileless apology. A vile puddle of vomit, a mixture of digestive juices and what looked like dog food covered the front of his gown. Emma, trying not to inhale, shook her head and placed a towel over the mess. "You hold still," she said, "I'll get you another gown." She left the embarrassed old man and walked to a supply room where extra linen occupied the shelves along with an eclectic assemblage of other items. The room, too small for the contents, was cluttered. Emma flipped through a stack of gowns thinking, *I hope Reading wasn't in here, it's a mess.*

Behind her, hinges complained. Alerted by the noise, Emma turned to see Doctor Reading, suit coat removed, standing there. Startled, Emma stood, instincts heightened., assessing the situation. Reading's eyes held an unmistakable leer as he loomed between Emma and the closed door. At that moment, she almost fainted. He seemed the beast in her recurring dream.

She moaned, "Please."

Reading snorted, "You don't have to beg."

He moved quickly and placed both hands on a counter trapping Emma between his arms. He leaned against her, pressing with his flat abdomen and eager loins.

Emma knew she was in the grasp of an animal. She could feel his body heat and sense the ungoverned lust in him—knew she was to be ravaged. She struggled, squirming, trying to free herself, but he was too strong and held the advantage. There was panic behind her eyes and high in her throat. She was dizzy, afraid. Emma feared that if she closed her eyes she would sink as if in her dream, and all would be lost. In command, he would devour her body and destroy her soul. She screamed.

"Don't struggle," he said, placing one hand over her mouth and one on her breast, "you might as well enjoy this, it comes with the job."

Emma, weak at the knees, fought to regain herself. She willed herself to relax. With her free hand, she searched the counter where she had noticed boxes of syringes. Her hand moved frantically amongst the boxes.

"That's better," Reading said, feeling her relax. His fingers moved over the buttons on her bodice and he bent to kiss her neck.

Emma felt a package of hypodermic syringes. *Too small,* she pushed it aside. She groped for the box next to it, hoping they were larger. Reading's breathing was heavier; he had forced a finger under her bra and was tweaking her nipple. *You Bastard!* She bit her lip. Desperately, she moved her hand, feeling for something, anything. Her fingers found a glass cylinder. What was it? She knew—a large aspiration syringe, the type used to suck fluids from a joint or body cavity. It was heavy duty, with a one-inch tube and a needle that could be substituted for a one eighth inch pipe. She grasped it, and when her thumb felt the plunger, she knew she had it in the correct position.

Reading was panting and mumbling things unintelligible. Grunting like an animal, his hands were under her dress and he was pressing hot against her. He had forced his fingers between her legs.

She took a deep breath, and with a swift sure stroke she drove the thick needle into his thrusting buttocks.

Reading reacted with a sudden jerk and a gripping scream. "Bitch!" he shouted. Releasing her, he reached for whatever was tearing at his rear end.

Scurrying from the room, one eye on Reading, she could see the instrument of her salvation hanging from his hip. She hoped it broke off in there.

Emma was trembling, *Oh Lord, what now?* She sat in the darkness of 206, the vacated patient room. The staccato beat of Reading's footsteps fell around her as he passed bellowing down the hall. The sound of his fury rang, receded and was gone. He was gone. She shuddered; *had she put an end to his advances or thrown down the gauntlet turning him on? What will he do? Do I still have a job?*

She took a folded blanket off the foot of the bed and wrapped herself in it. In her improvised pod, she wept while waiting for her soul to quiet. Mister Wheeler would have to wait.

Emma wanted Sam, needed his strength. *Could she tell him? No, he would kill Reading.* She hugged herself, swaying in her cocoon. Her head spun with the recognition of their desperate vulnerability.

"Are you all right?"

"What?" Emma could see Sam seated on the edge of the bed, could smell his early morning perspiration. Her mouth tasted like an old sock. Vague morning light sifted into the bedroom around the drawn shades. She focused on the hands of the alarm clock—five o'clock.

Sam reached and pushed the small lever on the device, preempting its disturbing clatter. He placed a hand on her hip. "You tossed and turned all night. You okay?"

She looked at him, her eyes full of distress, "Cramps."

He arched an eyebrow, "I didn't think it was that time of the month." He put an arm over Emma's shoulder and kissed her ear. "You sure that's all?"

Her eyes were leaden in her pale face, she pretended offense, "What do you mean, that all? You ever have menstrual cramps?"

Sam smiled defenselessly, "You know what I mean. You okay?"

She closed her eyes, "I won't be going to work today." *Even if I have a job.*

Sam's face clouded with concern.

"Don't worry, Gerty will be here to care for Mary." She watched him as he prepared to leave. "Sam, don't worry, it's nothing." *Just assault. Unless you find out, then it will be murder.*

He waved good bye.

CHAPTER 27

April 1936

At seventeen months, Mary had lost her baby fat. She was walking and looked like a small cookie-cutter version of Sam bumping around the house. She had his dark hair, eyes and try-anything-once attitude. Sam in pajama bottoms and undershirt, was watching her sway energetically back and forth in her highchair seat.

He was afraid she might tip over. "No, no," he said, pulling the highchair closer to the table. "Eat your cereal like a good girl." With her baby spoon, he stirred the lumpy mush in the small, bunny-embossed bowl. He passed the bowl under his nose and smelled the warm oatmeal. "Yummy," he said. Carefully, Sam teased her with a spoonful until she opened her mouth. He inserted the spoonful. Mary clamped her lips together, and he gently removed the spoon. "Umm," he said. Mary smiled.

"Big girl," Sam said pushing the bowl closer to her. He placed the handle of the spoon in her chubby fist. "Mary's a big girl. Big girls feed themselves," he cooed. He hoped he sounded convincing, imagining how wonderful it would be if she could feed herself.

Mary dropped the spoon, then clutched the bowl with both hands, and before Sam could react she turned it upside down on her head. The gooey mixture of cereal and milk ran down over her forehead and around her ears. She gave her daddy a big grin.

Emma entered the kitchen. "Ah, you're making progress."

"Yes, she's discovered how to empty the bowl without using the spoon."

Emma gave Sam a towel, "Mop it up with this."

He kissed the back of Emma's hand while searching her face. He said, "Good morning. You're looking chipper. Feel okay?"

She kissed him on the nose, "Yes."

Sam took the bowl from Mary and draped the towel over her head. Mary laughed at the wonderful game, and seized the messy fabric.

"Are you going to be okay today?" Emma asked.

"Sure, how about you?"

"Oh, it's just routine. I have to see the doctor before I can return to work. It's policy."

There was a knock at the door, as Uncle John pushed it open. His broad face was flushed: he looked overheated in his bib coveralls and jacket. Seeing him, Mary squealed with delight and resumed bouncing in her chair.

"Good morning, all," he said, making a face at Mary. He held a brown paper sack. "A few things from Gerty," he explained, setting it on the counter. Sam and Emma watched as he smooched Mary.

"Careful," Emma said, "she's a mess."

John removed the bib from Mary and wiped her face with it. Lifting her from the high chair, he held her, his thick arm under her bottom. He began to waltz around the kitchen table while singing the family nonsense song:

> "There was Buffalo Joe
> the New York crow,
> Teddy the rough old rover,
> Cleveland Bill
> from over the hill,
> and the baldheaded man
> from Dover.
>
> Seldom seen, often heard,
> Jack the Gaiety Kid,
> Bull Throwin' Ned
> the old red head,
> and Miss Mary
> Pee-the-Bed."

There was a lump in Sam's throat as he watched his daughter and uncle whirl around the room. Their dance was in the present, but the song was from his past. Though John was singing, Sam was hearing the voices of his father and grandfather. He choked inwardly on the sharp bittersweet remembrance.

Emma laughed watching them. She cautioned John, "You better hope she doesn't spit up."

Sam rose to take Mary from John as he huffed to recover his breath. Clutching Mary, he wondered why John was visiting so early. "You're out and about early this morning," he said.

John took a seat, his chest swelling with deep breathing. "I didn't know what your schedule was, and I didn't want to miss you." He paused. "We got a phone call last night," he looked at Sam, "from your mother. She wants you to call this number." He handed a slip of paper to Sam. "She said she'd be there at noon."

Sam knew Lizzy had no phone. He looked at the number on the paper. "This is the church telephone. Did she say what it was about?"

John raised an eyebrow, "You better hear it from her."

Emma's eyes were dancing.

Sam knew her mind was racing.

She said, "I'll be home by eleven, you can call from Uncle John's."

Sitting in the Pastor's office, Elizabeth Freeman watched a collection of dust particles lift from the valance atop the faded draperies and drift lackadaisically to the carpet.

How like ourselves, she thought, *falling, drifting, lost.* Her gaze fell on the bookshelves in the office that obviously served as a study. There was one framed photograph of a group of miners, men as hard and linear as slate. She considered their dirty faces and barren lives. The books explained the meaning of it all, she guessed. *Perhaps the Pastor, having studied all the books, understood what life was all about. She sure as hell didn't.*

How could one woman bear sons so unlike each other? She considered Sam—he was his father—strong, resourceful, a rock. And Josh, so strange, conniving, pleasure seeking, lecherous, directionless. Lizzy sighed. Of course, they had different fathers, but God had never put a more gentle, honest soul on this earth than Robert, her present husband, Josh's father. Josh was an errant bastard; she had to get him out of town before outraged fathers took the law into their own hands.

She brushed gray hairs off her brow. It was Josh and his predicament that had her sitting in the borrowed office waiting for the phone to ring. Lizzy looked at the upright black instrument standing in the center of the cluttered desk. It was but one outlet on a party line, and she knew that every word would find more listeners than just Sam and her. Oh well, it couldn't be helped. I have to talk to Sam and quickly, she thought, glancing at the loudly ticking clock across the room.

She was a bit early. She closed her eyes and asked herself, her lips barely moving, 'Is it fair to ask this of Sam? Emma?" It was her last thought before she slipped into a shallow troubled snooze, her head nodding erratically.

The tearing jangle of the telephone jarred her awake. Shaken and a bit fuzzy, Lizzy lifted the receiver off the hook and pressed it to her ear, "Hello."

"Mom, it's Sam." He sounded like he was speaking from beneath an iron bridge, his voice muffled by flowing water. Still, she thought it a miracle, hearing his unmistakable voice from so far away.

"Sam, darlin', how are you?"

"I'm fine, Mom. We're fine. What's going on? What's wrong?" Sam's concerns filled her ear.

"Settle down, Sam," she said, "everyone's healthy," she straightened in her chair, "but, we have a problem." Lizzy lowered her voice, prayed there were no other listeners, and explained the difficulties caused by Josh's mid night excursions. "He's been seen coming out of houses in the middle of the night. Frightened children swear he was in their bedrooms. Scares the poor little darling's to death. If the fathers weren't so dull, they'd had him tarred and feathered and out of town by now."

Sam listened, and when she had finished her tale, she heard him exclaim, "Damn him!"

"We'll not be damning anyone," she bristled. She was quiet for a moment, collecting herself. "We do have to get him out of town before he's arrested or worse. Some outraged father is going to shoot him. That's why I'm calling." She stopped talking and allowed the water-flowing sound to fill the void.

Sam spoke, breaking the uncomfortable silence, "I have an idea."

"Good," Lizzy said, willing to listen to anything.

"The CCC, Civilian Conservation Corps. They're taking men his age. It will get him out of town. Get him doing some hard constructive work. Hopefully give him a chance to work things out for the better."

"Oh," she replied, her voice tinged with disappointment, "we looked into that. They only accept boys from families on Relief. But, you're right it would be good for him." She imagined the scowl on Sam's face, the curling of the dark eyebrows, as he puzzled over the situation. She knew the look, he'd had it as a boy chewing on a problem until he had an answer. There was no quit in him, never had been.

"Has Uncle John offered him my old job?"

"Yes," she said. Closing her eyes, she squeezed the bridge of her nose, *You always were a quick one.* "And, now he needs a place to stay."

"Yes," Sam sighed, "I'd say he's welcome here, but I'll have to speak to Emma, for some reason I don't quite understand, she's uncomfortable around Josh."

Lizzy shook her head thinking, *What don't you understand?*

"In any case, we'll arrange something. You better send Alfred with him, he'll get into mischief by himself."

"That he would."

"And, Mom, I'm sorry I haven't been able to keep my promise. It's taking longer than I thought. Things haven't been much better here than in the valley."

Lizzy heard the anguish in his apology. "Don't you worry, we're getting by. We know you haven't forgotten."

"Thanks...there is some good news. I'm feeling really good about my job at the auto plant. I believe I'll be able to get the boys in with me before too long." Sam had his fingers crossed.

"Sure. We know you're doing all you can. Don't worry, nothing changes much. It seems but yesterday that you left us." There was a silence between mother and son during which nothing was said but everything was understood. "God bless," Lizzy said, and placed the earpiece back in the cradle.

CHAPTER 28

April 1936

Emma sat, eyes closed, arms folded, a wool sweater pulled tightly around her. She was filled with dread. Sam had told her Josh was coming. It had been decided. There was nothing more to say. He was coming. Feeling sick, her heart pounding, her feet were like ice, and her hands were clammy. She recognized the symptoms; she was having an anxiety attack. She shuddered. Her head was spinning at the thought of Josh in her house, near her, near Mary. She didn't know why she felt as strongly opposed to Josh's coming as she did. There were tales of his escapades, of course. But why did she have such a personal sense of revulsion when she thought of him? What had he ever done to her? Was his the face of the satyr in her dreams? Were they dreams?

Sam watched tears seep from under Emma's eyelids, clamped shut against the world. "Em," he spoke words of comfort softly, "it will be all right."

"Oh," she gasped. Trembling, she rose from her place on the sofa and walked unsteadily into Mary's bedroom.

Sam followed her. Entering the bedroom, Sam stood and watched Emma, ghostly detached, frighteningly pale, their child in her arms, trance-like, swaying and moaning. She was responding to a dirge only she could hear, a dirge that could echo only in the soul of a woman aware of the monsters that inhabit some men, men who could threaten her and her daughter. Threatened at work and now at home, she had no safe haven.

Emma felt Sam's hand on her shoulder. She knew he was bewildered. Everyone he loved was in trouble, and she sensed his feeling of helplessness.

"Em, it will be all right."

She knew that he could think of nothing else to do or say, and she responded with a wild keening causing Mary to utter a gasping cry of sympathy. Further shaken, having frightened her daughter, Emma sank to sit on the edge of the bed, where she sat rocking herself and Mary into numb silence.

Sam looking transfixed, a fighter with no recognizable opponent, stood helpless, until, finally, Emma turned to him and asked with trembling lips, "Sam, how could you?"

He crumpled, as though absorbing a body blow. "He's my brother. How could I not?"

Emma, armed with a letter from her physician, returned to the hospital after her time off. She wished she could just stay at home and be housekeeper and mother, but they needed the money. She floated in a dream world full of uncertainties since saying her good-byes to Mary and Gerty. She plodded with tiresome discipline through the practiced motions of her life. Her argument and rift with Sam left her feeling detached and vulnerable. Emma pondered the situation at work. *Did she still have a job? Could she hang on for more than one day? If she was terminated, how could she explain it to Sam?*

Upset, she had been unable to eat and felt nauseous, her empty stomach grumbled and acid rose high in her throat. On the ride to work, the pervasive stench of diesel exhaust pushed her to the edge of a migraine headache. There was a dull pain behind her eyes, a dark omen of the day ahead.

Her card was still in a slot beside the time clock, and on the floor Louise greeted her with a hug, but no sympathy. "Hope you had a restful time off, 'cause we got a house full."

Emma accepted the news and damp embrace with a weak smile.

Later, Stoddard appeared on her usual round and, outside of routine, nothing was said. Mystified, Emma pushed ahead with the routine of patient care. The work involvement took her out of herself, gradually easing her physical distress. Still, like a student at exams, she tirelessly considered the possibilities. *Was Reading sick? Were there contaminants in that syringe? Was he plotting some other more devious revenge? Was he able to work?* She checked the staffing schedules. There was his name. He was on duty, due to perform surgery. He must be okay. Maybe he would forget the incident. Fat chance. *God, she needed somebody to talk to.*

"Mrs. Freeman?" There was that deep pressing voice.

She was startled out of her reverie. Emma turned to face Doctor Reading standing in the somewhat dimmer light just outside the Nurse's Station. She was speechless, her mind fearfully racing.

"Please," he said, "I'm here to apologize," his eyes pleading, he stammered, "my actions that day, ah, night, were inexcusable."

Emma stood dumb with astonishment. *What was his game? Could this apologist be the same person who had assaulted her that night?* She studied him. He was wearing a standard white thigh-length hospital lab coat. His manner was uncertain, not like the bully in the three-piece suit.

Shifting nervously, from foot to foot, he awaited her reply, seemed to be judging her mood.

Then, Emma understood—he was more afraid of her than she was of him. Could she be the only one who had resisted him? That must be it. She had shown her audacity, and he was probably afraid she would speak out, point a finger at him threatening his reputation, his position. He had more to lose than she did.

The insight enabled her to relax. Firmly, she said, "Yes, they were inexcusable." She saw Reading had affected a cringing hound dog look.

"I'm really sorry. I've been under a lot of pressure; I don't know what got into me. I only hope you can forgive me."

His impression was less imperial than before, Emma thought. Maybe he was sincere. She remembered him as almost statuesque with a dark imposing face of classic chiseled features. This scare, and she was sure now that's what it was, had softened him. On the chance that he was not a chameleon, Emma decided to compromise, "I'll try to forgive you. I'll keep my letter to the board in a safe place," she ad-libbed, "my lips are sealed."

Reading sighed, and the long signs of distress melted from his face. "Thank you," he said, starting to turn away. He paused, folding his hands as if in contemplation, "Perhaps we could have coffee…"

Emma stared at him, not answering. *Some nerve.*

She watched him walk away. He strode with a slight limp, favoring one side. Was this it then? Were her tormentors going to fade away? She didn't believe it. Limp, she wished she was fat and ugly; maybe the lechers would leave her alone. She knew Reading would be back, pressing her with a more subtle insidious approach.

Then it hit her, and a wave of anxiety returned the acidic gorge to her throat; she knew for certain—so would Josh. He would be back in her nightmares and her life.

That night, Emma arrived home shortly before midnight. She checked on Mary then threw a sheet over the couch in the living room. She feared her nightmares would be back, and she didn't want to disturb Sam. As tired as she was, she tossed in an agitated state, unable to sleep. She was tired, nearing exhaustion, evading sleep. Emma began to cry, a soft lost-puppy whimper. She cried until even her fears couldn't keep her awake, and she slipped into a clammy, damp deep death-like repose.

It was not until the first light slipped through the window and Mary began to wail that Emma bolted awake and sat, terrified and soaking wet, wondering where she was and who was after her daughter.

CHAPTER 29

May 1936

It was a brisk unseasonably cool May day that Sam stood in his living room appraising Josh. Over two years had passed since he'd last seen him and he was no longer a boy, but a man standing with easy self-assurance. In his dark pants and sweater, Josh looked taller and slimmer than Sam remembered, but with his fedora tipped back on his head, he was the same jaunty pleasure-seeking Josh. His quick eyes and half smile told Sam that Josh knew life was just a game made up of losers and winners, and that he was amused by both. The same Josh, looking to bend the rules.

Sam threw his arms around his brother, "Damn, you're looking good."

Josh's hardboard suitcase fell to the floor making a slapping sound. He grinned, "You don't look so bad yourself, Sam. Lost a little weight?"

Sam shrugged, "A little, but I'm doing okay." He took Josh's arm, "How was the bus ride?"

"Long, we stopped in every jerkwater town. Then there was Alfred going on about his love life…"

"Where is Alfred?"

"Coming. He's talking to a neighbor he met on his last visit. He'll stop and talk to anyone, and he isn't satisfied until he knows their life history. Drives me nuts."

"Well, come on in. Sit down. I'll get us a beer."

Josh sauntered into the room, eyes ticking.

As Sam headed for the kitchen, he had the notion that Josh was taking inventory. Carrying two brown bottles into the living room, Sam studied Josh. Now that he had matured, the features he had inherited from Pop were more evident. He had his long face and receding hairline. "You're looking more and more like Pop."

"That's what they say," he said, taking one of the long necked bottles. His head tilting back, he asked, "What's that smell?"

Sam chuckled, "Our fair city, you'll get used to it." He reached out with his beer, "Here's to home."

The bottles clinked. Josh countered sardonically, "Wherever that is."

Sam ignored the comment, not quite ready to argue about Josh's relocation. "How are things at home?"

Josh set his beer on an end table, and picked up a magazine lying there. "The truth? We're wasting away in that hole." His eyes locked on Sam's, "Waiting for you to get us out of there."

Like an unexpected left hook under the ribs, his jibe landed where it hurt the most, leaving Sam momentarily speechless. He recovered quickly and sharply, "I haven't forgotten my promise." He blurted, "It's said, 'God helps those that help themselves.'" Sam bit his tongue. *Damn, where did that come from?*

Josh took a long pull on his beer, and opened the magazine, a sly smile touching his face.

Sam pressed the cold beer bottle to his forehead. Reasons and excuses banged around in his skull: *there's been no full time work, no solid jobs open, we have a baby. Excuses, excuses.* He said, "I'm close. I finally got a good job with a big company, and things in general are looking up." Sam ground his teeth, *Why am I so defensive?* "It's been a ditch-digging bitch just keeping a roof over the three of us."

Josh softened, flipping through the magazine, he said, "No, I know you'll keep your promise. Fact is, it's been the hope that you'll come through that's kept us going." He smiled his crooked smile, "Anyway, we're making progress, I'm here."

Sam studied Josh's face, trying to find in it some trace of the threat everyone felt. "Yes," he said, "you're here. You want to tell me what went on that got everyone's ass in such an uproar?"

"Well," Josh tossed the magazine onto the sofa and slouched back, his eyes focused on some distant spot, "It's all my fault, I had too much to drink and got horny. I went looking for a gal I knew that could ease my condition and got into the wrong house. I was stumbling around and scared some kids." He looked at Sam, "That's all there was to it."

Sam wanted to believe him. He said, "I heard it happened more than once."

"No, it was just that one time, I swear. It was just that once, and I had the bad luck to run into some guys that recognized me. There was some other trouble around the village, but it wasn't me." He hung his head, "Jesus, I'm only here five minutes and we're already into this shit."

Sam got up and paced the floor. "Unfortunately, we are, but you've been preceded by your reputation, deserved or not, and pretty much, your acceptance will depend on how everyone reacts to your explanation and behavior." He flipped his hand in a that's-the-bottom-line gesture.

"Emma, you mean," Josh said.

Why Emma? Sam asked himself. *Why would Josh think that?* "Not just Emma," he said.

"She's never liked me. I can feel it."

"Emma likes everybody."

Josh said, "I've never done anything to upset her. Ask her." He crossed his legs, sat back, and tipped his bottle drinking the last of his beer.

"She's not here. She took Mary out to do some shopping. She's going to join us later for supper at Uncle John's"

"Good," Josh shifted in his seat.

Sam broke the news, "We're going over there to get you settled in." He watched for Josh's reaction.

Josh raised his eyebrows, "I'm not living here?"

Sam hated to say it, "John and Gerty have more room. Besides, it's only a few blocks from here."

Josh sighed. Uncrossing his long legs, he sat upright.

Sam rationalized, "It's more convenient. You can ride to the shop with Uncle John." He watched as Josh's face went expressionless, and offered some consolation, "You'll be spending a lot of time here."

"Sure," Josh said, "a lot of time here."

As she climbed into bed that night, Emma asked, "How did he take it?"

Sam pressed his head into the pillow and stared at the ceiling. "Take what?"

"You know, finding out he'd be at Uncle John's instead of here."

"You saw him at supper. He was comfortable with everyone…relaxed."

She squirmed, settling under the blanket, she faced Sam.

He looked at her "What?"

She blinked, "It's me, I guess. What you see as relaxed, I see as cool and calculating."

"Em, that's not fair. You're not giving him a chance." He cupped her cheek in his palm. "Everything will be fine, you'll see. Once John gets Josh into the shop, he won't have the time or energy for mischief."

She kissed his hand, a soft considered touch, "I pray you're right."

Sam said, "Good night, I love you."

"Love you too," she said.

Lying in the dark, Sam asked, "What happened to the wailing woman of a week ago?"

"I apologize for that. I've resolved to become the calm observant professional."

"Thank you."

"I hope the thanks are deserved. I hope I never have to say, 'I told you so'."

There was a creak of bedsprings as Sam moved and took her hand. In a short time he heard the soft flutter of her breathing. She was asleep. He wondered at the ease with which she succumbed to the balm of night. He wished he could too, but he was bothered by doubt. Sam thought back over his talk with Josh, over his performance, and Sam feared that's what it was. How amiable and innocent Josh had seemed. Sam wondered if it was just a facade. Did the real Josh lie hidden deep inside? He'd caught flashes of inappropriate condescending smiles. There was more than a little con in Josh.

Sam agreed with Emma. It would pay to be patient and observant while getting to know this older troubling version of his brother.

He slipped into a shallow sleep filled with shifting formless shadows. In a heavy swirling mist, the shadows drifted and took shape, Sam recognized Alfred standing arm-in-arm with Molly. Smiling, Molly handed Sam a blanketed bundle. He could hear a baby whimpering inside. Sam opened the blanket; it was Mary. "Don't cry, honey," he said. He stroked her cheek, and she wailed louder. Sam didn't know what to do. He asked, "How can I make her stop crying?"

Hands appeared, and Josh said, "Let me take her, I'll make her stop."

From out of the mists, Emma appeared running, screaming, "Leave her alone, leave her alone!" She drew a long knife and plunged it into Josh.

Josh leered lasciviously. "You missed," he said, as the blood ran down over his shoes.

Ernie came with a towel. He said to Josh, "You're making a mess. I'll wipe it up."

Emma smiled, "Thanks, Ernie."

Sam was confused. He apologized to Josh, "Sorry. I don't know why she did that."

Wilbur wandered in, his hands swimming in the mist. "What's going on?" he asked, "I can't see."

Sam shook awake, terrified, not knowing where he was. He sat on the edge of the bed, confused and shaking.

In her sleep, Emma drawled, "Is it time to get up?"

CHAPTER 30

March 1937

The fickle weeks of late winter whirled into March of 1937. It was a time of uncertainty, of uneasy truces, and made for interesting reading. There always seemed to be a number of discarded newspapers in the plant cafeteria, and Sam fell into the habit of catching up on the news during lunch. In Europe, well-intentioned but misguided diplomats attempted to quell the ambitions of the fascists leading the frustrated masses in Germany and Italy. In the United States, workers smarting from the deprivations of the lingering economic depression were gaining a sense of their own power. In Michigan, major automobile manufacturers were suffering the effects of widespread sit-down strikes organized by leaders of emerging labor unions.

Sam had only a passing interest in the situation across the Atlantic, but the labor strife in Michigan was cutting into his hours worked and putting an unwelcome dent in his paycheck. He had no inkling that it would be the response to international events that would most effect his situation.

With the compliance of the Roosevelt administration, Britain and Canada began to contract with American manufacturers for production of the tools of war. Orders were being received for the manufacture of airplane engines that would fly through the Battle of Britain and beyond. American companies began to search for facilities and men equal to the task.

Sam found his way down a tiled hall and rapped lightly on one of the many office doors, the one with the sign reading, General Foreman.

A strong voice responded, "Come in."

Sam ran his hands over his dirty pants and sweat-stained shirt, brushed damp hair back out of his eyes, and crossed the threshold.

"Sit down, Sam."

Sam glanced around in the quivering fluorescent light. It was the first time he'd ever been in the General Foreman's office and thought it was rather small—smaller than he'd imagined. There was just enough room for two file cabinets, a blue-gray metal desk and two matching chairs, Harold Mason, the General Foreman, was seated behind the desk. He indicated the other chair in front of the desk and motioned for Sam to sit.

Sam sat and tried not to stare at Mason's bald head. He watched his liver-spotted hand twist a cigarette to extinction in a small metal ashtray. As the cigarette crumpled, the only sound, aside from the omnipresent hum from the production floor, was the spatter of light rain on the metal framed, pebble glass window. Sam knew Mason only as the gaunt power striding down the greasy aisles of the production floor; always thought he looked like an anxious farmer trying to get the hay in before the rain.

Sam could think of no reason why he'd be summoned to Mason's office except to be fired. He'd only spoken to the man once before. The assumption by Sam that he was to be terminated had him suppressing a growing anger, and it showed.

Mason smiled, his moon face full of creases. "Relax, Sam. You're not in any trouble," he chuckled, "unless you accept my offer."

Sam was breathing through his mouth trying to minimize the irritation to his nose and throat caused by the combined cigarette smoke and pervasive plant fumes. Also, he felt uncomfortable sitting in front of Mason, in white shirt and tie, in his oil stained pants and open blue-collared damp shirt. He tugged at his dirty shirt and wondered, *What offer?*

"Homer says you're the hardest working man on the floor."

Homer was Sam's foreman, and had never told him that.

"More than that, he says you are the smartest guy out there." Mason sat back in his chair.

Sam stroked his chin—*Come to think of it, I haven't seen Homer. Maybe he got fired.* "I appreciate that," he said.

"Sam," Mason stood and leaned forward, both hands on the desk, "there's going to be a lot of changes coming in the near future. There will be plenty of opportunity for good dedicated men. Homer is working with me on a special project, and we need a man to take his place. Homer says you are the best qualified for the job." Mason paused to let his words sink in. "What do you say?"

I say I'm damn glad I'm not being fired. Sam had to contain his excitement, "Are you asking me if I'll take the foreman job?"

"That's right," Mason nodded.

At that moment, Sam had an instant vivid memory of his grandfather asking if he wanted the shiny coin turning in the air. Struggling to maintain a poker face, he said, "I'm your man."

Mason reached across the desk, offering his hand. "I know you are," he said.

Sam pumped Mason's hand. He wished he could leave immediately. He couldn't wait to tell Emma.

"Oh, Sam that's wonderful," Emma exclaimed, looking at him standing like a schoolboy with a good report card.

Sam grinned, he was so happy, he felt like he might piss his pants.

Emma, wiping her hands on her apron, came to stand beside Mary hanging on his pant leg. "Tell me about it."

Sam leaned and put his nose in Emma's hair. She smelled wonderfully like onion soup.

Little Mary, her dark curls bouncing, was repeating, "Up, up, up," as she clung to his leg.

Sam had both hands behind Emma's hips.

Emma said, "I suppose it can only be told horizontally."

"Well, it's a long story, best told in bed."

"Hmm," she shoved him to arm's length. "Just give me the short version while I fix supper. You can give me the long slow comfortable details later."

Sam watched as she swayed seductively back into the kitchen. He lifted his bubbling daughter and followed.

Mary, a bright bouncing toddler, seemed to sense the extraordinary excitement in her parents. There was an uncharacteristic vibrancy in their conversation, and when she spilled her soup there'd been no harsh, "No, no, no!" When daddy played with her after supper, he was more animated and loving.

It took an extra long time to get her to sleep. But now she was curled in peaceful slumber in her bedroom down the hall.

Emma, naked in the pale moonlight, had her leg over Sam and was fingering his dense black chest hair as he talked.

Sam rambled on, as though inspired by the glow of the full moon. His enthusiasm had fired their lovemaking and now, temporarily physically depleted but in high spirits, he talked on about promise and possibilities. "and, we can move out of here, out of the smell and this drafty little flat. Maybe we can buy a car, a used one."

She rolled her eyes at that.

"I'll be able to get Alfred and Ernie jobs in the plant. Mom and Pop, and the boys can move up here. We can find them someplace to live. You can have that dress you were looking at, and we can get Mary a bed." He paused, then added, "maybe a puppy."

Emma moved her hand between his legs.

"And an eye doctor…what do you call them?"

"Ophthalmologist."

"Yes…for Wilbur," he sighed. Overwhelmed by the possibilities, Sam returned, enlarged by Emma's massage, to the present, the flush and readiness of her. He tasted the dew covering her breasts, took a rigid engorged nipple between his teeth and applied a firm urgent pressure.

She moaned and opened to him.

He was home.

CHAPTER 31

June 1937

Josh had never been confined before. Working with his brothers on the huckster truck or doing odd jobs, he was always outdoors. Walking through the double doors of his Uncle John's machine shop, into the dark interior, Josh felt he was entering a prison for the day. In his mind, the heavy metal doors slid shut behind and dead bolts slammed home. As the musty shop odors of rust, mildew and lubricants filled his nostrils and filtered down into his lungs, a steel hand gripped his guts, and he shuddered over his prospects. To make it worse, the stink of the place never left him. It permeated his clothing, hair and skin, so that at night, even after a scalding shower, it never left him, never set him free.

This day was no different. He entered the cavernous dim interior long after starting time, made late by his reluctant dragging feet. The drone of spinning armatures and drive belts, the slam of hydraulic hammers filled his ears. His eyes automatically searched out the coworkers he privately cataloged as Easy Earl and Black Jack. Earl, short but broad and sturdy as an oil drum, was wrestling with a wooden pallet. He acknowledged Josh with a curt nod, his greasy engineer's hat tight over his ears. Black Jack, his mood generally as dark as his Mediterranean skin, stood at a drill press and stared at Josh, flashing the whites of his distrustful eyes.

Fuck you, Josh thought, walking toward the office cubicle pressed into the recesses of the furthest corner. He knew his uncle saw him coming though seemingly captivated by the papers on his desk. Josh also knew uncle John wished he was more like Sam with his attitude, drive, and temperament. He smiled, knowing John had given up on efforts to change him.

John leaned back in his chair. "Good afternoon, Josh," he greeted sarcastically.

Josh glanced at the dusty clock high on the cinder block wall. The hands were perpendicular at nine o'clock. "Morning," he contradicted. John pushed a black derby up off his forehead and flicked ashes off a cigar stub.

"I'd like you back on the grinder where you were yesterday."

The day before, Josh was at the grinder for eight hours knocking burrs off iron castings. There were bins and rusty bins of castings to be put through the tedious process.

"Sure," Josh said. Without further comment, he took leather gloves and safety glasses off a shelf and headed listlessly for the familiar workstation.

John, watching him, shrugged his obvious disappointment. He clamped his teeth on his soggy cigar.

Flipping a switch on a gray wall-mounted electrical box, Josh powered the hulking machine. As the abrasive wheels settled into a steady whine, he pulled the safety glasses on and tugged into the pair of leather gloves. He spit, *another inspiring goddamn day.* He jerked a rusty red casting from a bin.

After an hour of dry metal dust that settled in the rear of his throat, flailing sparks, and repetitive motions, Josh stepped away from the grinder, arched his back and stretched his neck. The incessant clamor had given him a droning headache and he was thinking, *I've got to get out of here!* Turning, he pushed the glasses up on his forehead and saw Black Jack staring at him. Josh stared back. He knew the other men resented his presence. Since he was hired, there had been no overtime. Plus, they knew if they had his work habits, they'd be gone. *Tough shit,* Josh thought, scratching his crotch, *nepotism is the way of the world.* "What are you looking at?" he growled.

"Not much," Jack said.

"I don't like you staring at my back all goddamn day."

Jack spread his hands in a 'so-what' gesture.

"If you don't knock it off, I'm going to kick your ass," Josh said.

Jack said, "If you feel froggy, jump."

Weeks of pending rebellion driving him, Josh grabbed a casting and threw it at Black Jack.

Jack stepped deftly aside, and the casting crashed into the wall behind him. He backed away from his machine and braced himself. Josh clutched an iron bar and rushed at him. The quick thin smile on Jack's face said he welcomed the opportunity to put Josh, the unwelcome pain-in-the-ass, in his place.

Josh swung the bar at Jack's head, missing him. Jack stood feet planted and, with an efficient uncoiling of his upper body, drove his gloved fist into Josh's abdomen. Josh dropped to his knees and threw up. Convulsed, he dropped the bar.

Jack kicked it ringing under a workbench and stood back, an observer, as John stepped out of the office and asked, "What's going on?"

Black Jack stood, both thumbs hooked in his belt, his face blank.

Josh rose slowly. He wiped his mouth and chin with the back of a glove. The other hand pressed to the hurt in his guts, he gasped, "I slipped on some oil."

John looked at Josh and Jack, sliding innocently to the side. He shook his head, and containing a smile, said, "Back to work."

That night, Josh eased himself into bed. He'd been unable to eat all that Gerty had put in front of him. With careful fingers he explored the area Black Jack had hammered, nothing was busted. He smiled at himself as he laid back and stared, trying to discern cracks in the plaster ceiling in the waning light. "Well, Josh," he admonished himself, "you're not a fighter, so you must be a lover." His thoughts drifted to other bedrooms, other excursions, other gratifications. He recalled innocents vulnerable in their beds. He savored the recollections, especially that of his sister-in-law Emma sprawled invitingly in a pool of moonlight. Josh wondered if she was now alone in bed a short distance away. And, the child, Mary, he thought of as little Emma, where was she?

Josh touched himself, "Yes," he muttered, "other diversions."

A rainy spring gave way to a lush humid summer. In most areas of the Niagara Frontier, Mother Nature had spread blessed greenery and exploding blossoms. There was a profusion of trees, a green canopy spread over Niagara Falls' Hyde Park, partly shading the walk-laced lawn underneath. Emma began taking Mary for long strolls on the afternoon she was free. There were more of those now that she had changed from full to part-time employment at the hospital. Sam's increased income made that possible and she was very grateful. Her time spent with Mary was the most precious of her days.

She enjoyed dressing Mary in frilly dresses and bonnets, and treading the park behind her stroller. She smiled inwardly when other mothers and young couples under wide hats and vanilla suits complimented her daughter. Emma swelled with pride and nodded her appreciation.

Passing flowerbeds heaped with blossoms, Emma passed close to ponds full of ducks, occasional swans and multitudinous gulls. She always brought a few slices of stale bread so that Mary could feed the birds.

"Birdy, birdy," Mary cried, pointing to gulls sweeping low over Gill creek.

"Yes," Emma said, halting the stroller.

The gray and white gulls circled and swooped around a man tossing bits of bread out over the silver slick water. In her portable seat, Mary jiggled with delight.

Emma looked to the south where winds off the southernmost tip of Ontario swept yellow and dirty-brown smoke from towering chimneys. *Sad,* she mused, that such a beautiful summer sky should be tainted. She sniffed and reaffirmed Sam's opinion that the city smelled like boiled cabbage. Soon, Sam assured her, they would move south along the river to Buffalo and cleaner air. He would be closer to work too, and maybe she would see more of him.

Emma turned the stroller and began the slow walk home. She dawdled a bit. There was time to spare. A crock pot at home held their prepared supper, and there was little else to do. Along Pine Avenue she indulged in an hour of window shopping, noting that there were fewer empty stores. Some had regained faith in the economy.

Arriving home, Emma left the stroller on the front porch and ushered Mary through the front door. Inside, she stood chin raised and plied her senses. She felt another presence. Squeezing Mary's hand, she called, "Hello." Silence. Mary tugged to be free. "Hello!" No answer. Emma shivered involuntarily. *What was bothering her?* She lifted her daughter and backed out onto the porch. *Was she being silly?*

Outside in warm comforting sunlight, she stood wondering what to do.

"Hi."

Emma jumped. She turned to see Jim, the mailman, coming up the walk. "Oh, I'm sorry, but you startled me."

"Gosh, Mrs. Freeman, I didn't mean to."

Emma looked at the rangy mail carrier. She thought his blue uniform and full leather bag a most welcome sight. "That's all right," she said, "it's not your fault." She hesitated, watching him as he sorted through his bag. *Should she get him involved?* As he handed her an envelope, she asked, "Jim, could you do me a favor?"

"Sure," he shrugged, "I guess so."

"I," Emma felt silly asking, "I just got home, and I have the strangest feeling that there may be someone in the house."

Jim stared at her. He knew she was a nurse and a stable no-nonsense person.

"Could you, I mean would you walk through with me?"

Jim raised his hat and ran a hand through his hair. "Sure, I can spare a minute." He set his bag on the porch deck beside a pot of daffodils.

Emma surmised he was thinking, *this is one for the guys back at the post office*. But, to her he looked lean and mean like Doc Holiday at the OK Corral.

Preceded by the curious mailman, and carrying Mary, she walked through all the rooms and peeked in closets and drawers. Finally, back in the living room, she said, "Well, thanks. I guess my woman's intuition failed this time."

"That's okay, Mrs. Freeman. You can't be too careful." He retrieved his bag from the porch and waved as he left.

Mary cried, "Bye bye."

I'll bet he could write a book. Emma didn't say anything to him, but someone had been in the house. There were things slightly out of place: a picture, small things, items ruffled in her lingerie drawer. And, frightening, someone had passed his hand over their beds. Something else she couldn't quite capture, a scent? Something nudged her subconscious. Something whispered to her, something threatening. *Nonsense, I'm just letting my imagination run away.* She locked the doors.

That night, lying beside Sam, she massaged his shoulders, and debated with herself regarding her experience and suspicions. She hated to burden him with her troubled thoughts. His new responsibilities had him drawing on all his wit and energy. He was exhausted at the end of each day. She really had nothing substantial; nothing was missing, no harm had been done. Someone had intruded, had disturbed private things, but she had only her own observations and suspicions.

She made a decision, her next walk would be to visit Aunt Gerty. She would find out when Josh was at work and when he was not. She couldn't imagine that their visitor had been anyone but him, but she couldn't explain why.

"Sam."

"Hmm?" he rolled his shoulder.

"I want to go to Buffalo on Sunday, to look for a place. I want to move."

Sam replied with a drowsy, "Okay."

Emma slipped her hand over his hip and into his patch of pubic hair. Her fingers wandered through the wiry hair and surrounds. Sam began to snore. *My, you are tired.* She kissed his ear and said, "Good night, Lover." Pressing close, feeling safer with him beside her. Full of trepidation, she fell into a shallow sleep.

She was wandering naked through a house with many closets, desperate for something to wear. Exposed and cold, she trembled. Emma was ready to cry; there was a faceless man watching her, beckoning to her. In each closet, there was a gown, and seeing it, she would be greatly relieved, but when she tried to grasp it, it would vanish. And, the faceless man moved a step closer.

Who is he? What does he want? Her arms crossed over her bosom, she scurried from closet to closet. She was crying. She knew what he wanted, and he was closing on her. "Sam," she screamed in her sleep, "help me."

Sam, sunk in slumber, murmured, "Yes, dear," without stirring.

Emma woke shaking, in a panic, scrambling to cover herself, her tears wetting the pillow. She was breathing deeply, trembling, wanting to scream.

CHAPTER 32

June 1937

Emma couldn't recall ever entering Gerty's kitchen when she wasn't preparing a meal or preserving something for future meals, and today was no exception. At first glance, she was amazed at the number of jars, pans, spoons and various utensils everywhere. *Is it possible this mess can be cleaned up in less than a week?* Of course it could. It was hard to recognize, but Gerty was well organized; there was method to her display, and no one worked harder with the intoxicating ingredients: tomatoes, vegetables, garlic, vinegar, and love.

"Good mornin', Dears," Gerty bubbled, holding the handle of the wooden screen door. "How wonderful to see you two."

Emma steered Mary around Gerty standing, cheeks flushed and damp with perspiration, in her domain. Emma pecked a kiss on Gerty's rosy cheek as she passed into the room. Mary dashed ahead. She was very fond of Gerty and had expressed concern over her weight.

"Don't worry about me," Gerty would reply, "I'm here until the Lord calls, and until then I'll not miss a meal." The excess flesh swaying beneath her arms attested to that. Still, Emma had not ceased trying to influence her.

"Aren't you the sweet one in your little blue jumper?" Gerty patted Mary on the head as she scooted across the linoleum making for the cupboard doors and the extensive collection of pots and pans. The large assortment of metal pans was a child's dream. It was possible to create all kinds of havoc with them. Mary loved to drag them all out onto the kitchen floor where they became drums, big girl's possessions, and instruments of destruction. They could be banged and clanged, arranged and rearranged. They were surely the most marvelous of things. She placed them in specific order, but not before she banged each one to hear it ring.

The process was not a quiet one, and Emma said, "Mary, get away from there," knowing Gerty would allow the child any liberty.

"Tush, let her be," Gerty said, a holiday-ribbon smile gracing her face.

Emma raised her hands in surrender. As Mary found the first saucepan, Emma turned her attention to a huge pan on the gas stove. She wrinkled her nose. Testing an odor predominantly of vinegar, she asked, "Pickles?"

"Bread and butter," Gerty confirmed.

"Umm."

"Umm," echoed Mary, imitating her mother.

Gerty returned to the sink where she had been cleaning pickles with a vegetable brush and dumping them in an ascetic solution. "You're out and about early today," she observed.

"Yes," Emma said, settling on a wooden chair, the spindles against her back. She bent to Mary and removed her bonnet. "I have to work this afternoon, so I thought I would finish my errands early in the day. Before Mary's nap."

"Ah, is this an errand then?"

"Well," Emma brushed a wisp of hair from her eyes. "I wanted to ask how you are getting along with Josh."

Gerty halted her scrubbing. "We'd best have a cup of tea."

When the tea had been poured, and Mary's play had settled down to an occasional clank, Gerty settled onto a chair and asked, "What is it, Darlin'?"

"I was wondering if Josh was a bother. Does he work every day?"

"Ah, Josh…well he is a quiet one. Keeps to himself mostly. John says he does his job, but he doesn't like it. But, he's there everyday. Well, except some days. Like yesterday when they didn't work, there being some problem with supplies."

"What did he do all day?"

Gerty had poured her tea into a saucer that she had balanced in her fingers. She slurped from it noisily before answering, "Well, I don't know, do I? Like I said, he's quiet, comes and goes with hardly a word. Gives me a shrug if I ask. So I quit askin'."

"You don't know where he was yesterday afternoon?"

Gerty looked away. "I thought maybe he was at your house."

Emma wondered if Gerty suspected something. She took a drop of tea from her lip with a napkin, *I think so too.* She said, "Not at our house. We weren't home." She looked at Mary sorting the pans. "Maybe he was fishing," she offered.

"I don't think so. It's impossible to know what he's thinking about, but I don't believe it's fishing. He's a deep one. When you try to get close and personal, he pulls shades down over those window-eyes of his…spooky the way he does, becomes inscrutable. Is that the word?"

Emma nodded then asked, "He's made no friends?"

Gerty stirred her tea. "None I know of. John says he doesn't get along well with the fellas at the shop. I'd be surprised if he has a friend in the world." She watched Emma's face as she spoke.

Emma took a heavy cast iron frying pan from Mary and set it on the table out of reach. She didn't want to upset Gerty with what were really only suspicions. After all, Josh was family.

Gerty said, "Something I have noticed though."

Emma raising the tepid tea to her lips asked, "What's that?"

"There's been a morning or two when I've gone to make his bed, that it's as neat as a pin, as though he hasn't been in it. Makes me wonder what he does the whole night long."

Blocks of wood-frame houses in Niagara Falls, like most cities of the era, were divided by a service alley. At daybreak, horse-drawn wagons delivered clanking bottles of milk to closed and silent back doors. As the night lifted and the occupants stirred, the doors opened a crack and the dairy products were spirited inside. In the winter, frozen cream rose from the necks of the bottles of pasteurized but not homogenized milk. Summer brought various peddlers, hucksters, and dripping wagons of block ice for the icebox often placed on the back stoop.

The rear of each house offered a kitchen window, a shaded narrow stoop, and a patch of ground containing a mud hole, a vegetable garden, a variety of weeds, or urchins at play, depending on the season. Some plots sported a makeshift doghouse and a surly mongrel snapping at visitors and passersby.

With the passing years, the advent of motorized delivery trucks and emerging Mom and Pop corner stores, the alleys fell into disuse. They became neighborhood catchalls, the resting-place of battered trashcans, discarded rusty bedsprings and three legged chairs. In areas where residents cared, it was a challenge to the spring cleanup committee.

Each morning on his way to work Josh would walk the alleys noting children and dogs. He found the alleys, with their pockets of dark shadow, ideal for his nocturnal wanderings. On the blackest nights, he shared the urban canyons with cats, rodents and an occasional soul stumbling in the dark.

One summer night with only a sliver of moon and peeking persistent stars, Josh in clothes as black as death slipped along a board fence in an alley he had recently scouted. This was his first night in this neighborhood, and he moved cautiously, stopping frequently to listen for sounds other than the buzzing of cicadas.

Voices signaled other wanderers in the vicinity. Josh stood quietly, calmly in place assessing them. His ears told him there were two men, walking slowly and erratically, bumping into things, some distance away but approaching. Josh stepped out of the lane and placed his back tightly against the rough siding of a small shed. One of the men was trying to explain something, and his partner kept repeating, "Yah, yah." It was obvious to Josh that they had been drinking. He saw them. One of them stumbled and the other brayed like a distressed mule.

Josh, in black, was invisible to the men as they passed close enough to be touched. He smiled. When they were gone, he studied carefully each of the houses nearby. His night vision enabled him to assess the major features of each. Josh was looking for the house where he viewed two young girls at play as he passed during the days. It was a sultry night, and he wiped perspiration from his face as he explored.

Across the alley, a light came on illuminating a bright yellow rectangle, an open second story window. He closed one eye against the light, to preserve his night vision, and waited to observe any activity beyond the window frame. Josh watched as a burly man in a sleeveless undershirt shuffled past the window. The man was coughing, a hacking cigarette cough. Josh waited.

Josh listened to the whistle of a far off train as the minutes passed. The man reappeared. He bent over and appeared to be shaking someone. Josh caught a feminine voice whimpering, "Don't, don't." The man began swinging his thick arm, and a woman began to cry. The light went out. A hacking cough and the low moan of someone suffering escaped through the window. Josh wished they were on the first floor so he could watch. He sighed, *ah, the pleasure gleaned while unseen.*

Stepping carefully, Josh moved along the black alley as his imagination created scenarios based on the bedroom sounds and slim sights: a large horny brute, a reluctant cowering woman, forcible sex. *Too bad he hadn't had a better view.*

He came abreast of the house and yard where the girls had been playing. He recognized the wire fence with the center sagging gate. Placing each foot carefully as he moved, Josh reached the gate. He removed a small flat can of oil from his rear pocket and squirted a few drops on the gate latch and hinges. He lifted the hatch gingerly and pushed the gate. It swung silently open, and Josh stepped into the narrow yard.

Entering, he heard a throaty growl. Josh froze, fully alert, his nerves as taut as piano wire. *What lurked in the night?* His answer came as a snarl increasing in conviction and volume. A big dog, Josh realized. Reacting instinctively, he back peddled out into the alley pulling the gate shut behind him. He heard the large animal bound heavily into the gate. Dark in color, the dog was nearly as invisible as Josh, but he could see that it was huge. And snarling. This animal didn't bark—it didn't have to!

Josh moved away. He was trembling. *Jesus, that was close.* He was soon out of the alley and on a sidewalk. To his right, a corner street lamp beamed. He stepped into long shadows cast by trees lining the street. Calmer, he remembered the two girls at play, their laughter fresh and uninhibited. They were deliciously innocent.

He would have to walk the street and check the house from the front. *Yes,* he envisioned a frontal approach, dangerous and thrilling. He began to walk with a quick purposeful step as he mouthed the words of a popular advertising jingle.

> "Plunk down a nickel,
> say,'Here I come,'
> for Ziggy's Activated
> Charcoal Gum."

Josh hummed, "Here I come."

CHAPTER 33

July 1937

1937 was a gut-wrenching year for the auto industry and Sam. After months of labor unrest, the United Auto Workers and the Corporations signed a pact. When the terms were revealed and things had settled, Sam wondered what the workers had won. Management retained authority over production line speed, and the work force couldn't strike without approval of the Union's national officers. He knew there would be more anguish down the road, but at least the men were back to work, though only a few hours a week.

Sam figured somebody was convinced there would be an increasing demand for manufactured goods. He scratched his head as the facility expanded and supervisors and managers spent as much time in the classrooms, storage space pressed into service, as they did on the production floor.

He found himself in class most afternoons and Saturday mornings. On an unforgiving metal folding chair, in a white shirt with a seventeen-inch neck, Sam listened and scribbled notes. He was exposed to new ground., the idiosyncrasies of helical gears, relevant math, and the newly published ideas of Dale Carnegie. His mind spun with new insights and, more than once, caught himself chewing on fingernails underlain with grease.

He rediscovered books and libraries, and kicked himself for ever allowing those interests to fade. Learning, he decided, was like mining—you keep picking away until you are rewarded with valuable nuggets. Sam put on a half smile, impressed by all that mankind had achieved without him, Sam Freeman, and vowed to somehow leave his mark on the world.

Emma hummed as he studied. Evenings after Mary had been put to bed, they sat at the kitchen table, and she would hum her tune of the day. It would be some song she'd heard on the radio or from a passing neighbor. Her notes filled Sam with a peculiar peace and he did his homework while she sewed or read. Their reading materials couldn't have been more different: as Sam struggled with algebra and geometry, Emma read sociology and psychology. Sometime during the course of the evening, Emma would bring tea and gingersnaps.

Some nights, she would go into the living room and listen to a favorite radio program, Fibber McGee and Molly or Amos and Andy. Returning, she often found Sam head down on the table, asleep. Massaging his temples and shoulders, she would wake him gently, "Hey, professor, time for bed." The next sound Sam would hear would be the alarm clock, and it would all begin again.

One night Sam rebelled. He went to Emma and buried his face in her intoxicating bosom. They went to bed and fell into slow easy lovemaking. Their mutual pleasure was intense and prolonged as they clung to each other afraid to let go, afraid to lose the moment.

Finally, drained and damp. they lay beside each other for a long time not wanting to break the spell. They held hands and listened to each other breathe.

Sam sighed, "Thanks, I needed that."

Emma poked him in the ribs. She curled her finger in the damp hair on his brow. "Don't forget, this Sunday, it's back to Buffalo to look at that house again."

I arranged to borrow a car for the day. One of the guys has a '34 Chevy he wants to sell, so he's agreed to let me drive it."

"No strings?"

Sam said, 'We'll see."

"A place to live comes first," she reminded him.

"Yes," Sam said, "but we'll be renting for some time...we may be able to swing both."

"You're an optimist."

"Always have been." He kissed her lips and let his hand slide over her hip. "Speaking of the weekend, don't forget you promised to cut my hair Saturday."

"Yes, Master," she said, placing her leg over his.

"And trim my eyebrows."

Her lips were on his chest; she couldn't answer.

Emma was relieved; things were finally working out. She was buoyant over the way Sam had clamped onto the job at the motor plant, his acceptance of responsibility, and renewed thirst for learning. She'd always recognized the thirst in him; his need to persist and prevail. There was a down side, she'd noted, when she mentioned his family in Pennsylvania, he became quiet. Emma feared they could be the obligation, the straw that would break her camel's back.

Perhaps when they moved to their flat in Buffalo, left this depressing place, they could bring Sam's family north. She prayed the locale would help. Sam would need less travel time, and, though only twenty some miles south, there was no eye-stinging chemical stink in the air.

Also, Emma thanked God, they'd be further from Josh. Though she had told Sam someone had been in the house, she had not mentioned her suspicions about Josh. It was a weakness of Sam's, he wouldn't believe anything negative about his brothers, so she kept her thoughts to herself. Emma felt uneasy about her aversion to her brother-in-law. Josh had never done her any harm, had he? What was it about him? Was she being unjust? Well, she'd feel better being unjust at a distance.

Another bright spot—when the hospital was informed of her leaving, they offered her a part time job at a Buffalo affiliate. Everything was working out. Well, not everything. Sam had been put on second shift, three to eleven and usually later. But, he said it was a special project and only temporary. Over all, they were lucky. If only the weather would improve, the nights were so darn warm.

The night was slow-down hot. The mosquito visiting his ear seemed lethargic, and the singing of crickets and cicadas had fallen off lazily. Shiny jade-green leaves of the ungainly lilac bushes hung heavily in the humid air. Josh standing in the foliage in Sam's side yard was invisible in dark clothing. He had been standing in the same spot nightly, in a near trance, since learning Emma and Mary were leaving Niagara Falls, depriving him of a favorite fantasy.

He had been standing motionless, his breathing shallow, for half an hour. This was the night of fulfillment. He'd seen Emma turn her radio off at what he guessed was ten thirty. A switch had clicked before the ensuing silence. She had left a small lamp burning in the living room, then gone, click into the kitchen, click into the bathroom. Lights off, lights on, lights off as she worked her way through the house, Mary's bedroom, and into her's.

Emma's window was fully shaded, and Josh used his imagination as she dressed for bed. In his mind, Emma's lingerie floated to the floor and she stood naked and vulnerable. She extinguished her lamp before raising the window shade. There was a hint of filmy gown, and she was gone from sight. Josh started his mental clock. Confident in his ability to estimate accurately the passing minutes, he gave Emma fifteen before he'd enter through a screened window. He was only seconds away from living his fantasy. Josh stood thinking, Sam could never know the pleasures of the night as he did. How the sights smells and caresses could bring the consuming thrill and release. Sam could never know how composed and complete he became experiencing the forbidden, the taboo. And he could never explain.

Over the windowsill and inside, Josh became just another shadow. He willed himself another persona, cold-blooded, metabolism slowed, lizard-like, at one with his surroundings. From previous intrusions, he knew the location of every piece of furniture; the child-size bed in the corner., the chest four drawers high, the toy box, and the diminutive desk and chair. He listened to Mary's gentle breathing. He closed his eyes and examined other sounds and vibrations, the tics and creaks of the household. Satisfied that his was the only body stirring, he moved on nimble feet to stand beside the innocent, deep in slumber.

Scarce light flitted through the sodden air, the child form and bed sheet melded in a montage of tender flesh on pristine background. Mary's lips fluttered a subtle exhalation. Josh was quivering with anticipation. He placed his hand lightly on Mary's leg. She smiled. Josh knew she dreamed of a loving touch, protective, devoid of lust. He gently slid the bedclothes from her, pushing them to the foot of the crib. Uncovered, she was clad only in pale blue panties. He slipped a practiced finger under the elastic waistband. She stirred in her sleep. Coiled on her forehead, a moist black curl trembled. Josh waited patiently, then began to slide her panties down.

A beam of light shot through the room. Josh froze, startled, his mind racing—*Headlights! Was Sam home early?* He straightened in the dim light, and turned to face the blank doorway. If it was Sam, he'd have to slip out the window as Sam came in the front door. He'd be gone, just another shadow in the night. Turning, his foot caught the cord of the bedside lamp. The lamp teetered. Josh whirled to catch it, but missed.

The lamp hit the floor, shade askew, bulb popping to create a loud violation in the otherwise silent night.

Sam stood motionless at the front door, his entry halted by the noise.

From her bedroom, Emma called, "Sam?"

Mary, startled awake, began to cry. Cursing, Josh slid through the window opening, dashed across the back yard, and was gone.

"Sam, is that you?" Emma asked in a tremulous voice.

"Yes, I'm home...what was that noise?" he asked pulling a lamp chain and flooding the living room with light, adrenaline firing his body.

Emma appeared in the hallway donning a dressing gown. Puzzled, she gave Sam a questioning look as she strode toward the back bedroom and her crying daughter.

Sam listened as Emma consoled Mary.

"Mary, it's okay, Mommy's here. Hush, hush don't cry. That's a big girl."

Sam followed the soothing words into his daughter's room. The only light was that sneaking in from the hall. He looked for Mary's bedside lamp and discovered it on the floor, bulb broken. "Watch your step, there's glass on the floor."

With Mary crooning in her arms, Emma stepped back gingerly away from the bed. She looked across the room and saw that the window screen was missing. "My God," she moaned with the realization, "someone was here."

Sam responded to the fear in her words with a loud, "What?"

"Look," Emma pointed at the gaping window, "the screen." Her eyes widened, visual evidence mounting as she stared at the fallen lamp. She shuddered. "He was by the bed. He knocked the lamp over. My God." Her eyes sought Sam's.

He saw the torment in them.

"He's after our baby."

Sam's forehead creased, his black brows curled. The scar in his left eyebrow turned an angry white. Realization filled his face as he absorbed the obvious truth. He enclosed Emma and the baby in his arms and they stood swaying, contemplating the situation. "Don't worry," Sam said, fearfully biting his lip.

They were in bed clinging to each other. Sam had found the window screen and brought it into the house, and had closed and locked Mary's bedroom window. He could hear the gentle whisper of Mary's breathing as she slept.

Sam said, "You're the aspiring psychologist, why would anyone sneak into a child's room?"

Emma remained quiet for a long moment, then breathed softly, "You know why."

Sam said, "It's hard to believe." He stroked Emma's shoulder. "Whoever it is must be sick."

"Yes."

"Maybe seeking help."

"I don't think so."

In a thick troubled tone, perplexed, Sam asked, "You don't think so?"

Emma found his cheek in the dark. Her hand gentle on his face, in a voice full of sorrow and dread, she said, "Sam...I think its Josh."

Sam stiffened beside her.

Emma was holding her breath. She exhaled consciously, "I think so...I think it was him in the house."

"Why do you think that?"

She was restless, she moved her fingers through her hair. Damp, she rolled to stare into darkness. "I know there's no absolute proof, just his history, circumstantial evidence, and the probability. I've been thinking it for some time; it's Occam's razor: explanations of the unknown should be sought in terms of known qualities, and intuition...I know it's him."

Sam swallowed hard, "Josh has had some problems, but...no, not Josh."

Emma turned to hold Sam as he considered the painful possibility. She blinked away tears. Josh's escapades had fallen on Sam with a cumulative burden.

He didn't want to believe it, but began to agonize over it all. There was harbored in him, the sickening suspicion that Emma was right.

Sam sat on the edge of the bed on a morning as hot and heavy as his heart. His head was full of vague clutter, the legacy of a fitful night. He'd been tempted during the spirit draining hours to rise and question Josh, but couldn't bring himself to disturb John and Gerty. He turned and stared out a window at muted sunlight dispersed by low-hanging clouds. He felt the weight of the humid polluted air. He closed his eyes and wished for a cool forest and a cold rippling stream. He rubbed his eyelids trying to erase an ache.

Today. The thought made him sick. Today there would be Josh and a long overdue confrontation. Sam had a rule: tackle the day's most difficult task first. Today would be no exception. He would find his brother first thing.

As he sat there, pulling his trousers on, he could hear Emma and Mary in the kitchen. Listening to their spontaneous uninhibited interplay, he swore they would be safe in their home. *If not, what good am I?* he asked himself.

The house smelled of freshly brewed coffee and something from the oven. There were sweet rolls on the corner of the table. "Ah, coffee and rolls, and two beautiful ladies..Who could ask for anything more?" he forced a light tone.

Emma turned to him with a thin-lipped, "Good morning."

In a light house dress and white apron, her auburn hair perfect, she looked fresh and organized. Sam wondered how she did it. Then he wondered why she did it. Did she want a formal start this morning? Was this how you start a no-nonsense day? He turned his attention to Mary grinning in her highchair, one fist in her cereal. "I don't know which beauty to kiss first."

"Me," Emma instructed, "you'll be a mess after smooching our little piggy."

Sam kissed her on the cheek then held her at arm's length, and searched her eyes. "How are you?"

"I'll be a lot better after you get something settled today."

He reached for the coffeepot. "Don't worry, my only problem today will be avoiding manslaughter."

"Good morning, Niagara Machine."

"Good morning, Ellen," Sam pictured the efficient little bird of a woman that ran John's office, "it's Sam Freeman. Is my Uncle John available?"

"Oh, it's you Sam," she answered in a voice she usually reserved for Sunday choir. "He's out in the shop. I'll call him for you."

"Thanks," Sam heard the noise level rise when she opened the door.

"He says he'll be right with you. How are Emma and Mary?"

"Fine. How's John treating you?"

"Here he comes," she said, "tell him I deserve a raise."

Sam smiled. He knew John considered her indispensable and paid her what he was able.

"Sam, how are you?" Uncle John boomed.

Sam held the phone away from his ear. Uncle John was bellowing like he was still in the noisy shop. It was probable that years around noisy machinery had destroyed his hearing. "I'm okay. How about you and Aunt Gerty?"

"We must be okay," he laughed, "we haven't lost an ounce of fat. What can I do for you?"

"I need to find Josh. What's his schedule today?"

There was a pause. Sam knew he was checking a production schedule. "Today," he said, "is not a full day. He'll be through at noon."

"Thanks, Uncle John."

"You want me to tell him you're coming over?"

"No," Sam swallowed; his stomach had turned sour, "it's a surprise."

It was just before noon when Sam pulled the black Chevy sedan into the lot beside John's shop, Niagara Machine. It was developing into a blistering day; there were no gulls hovering around the parking lot, and the only stray dog to be seen was lying, tongue-out under the sole tree in the vicinity. Sam heard machines winding down; the half-shift was over.

Since he'd last seen it, the concrete block walls had been painted green and a sign with yellow letters indicated you had found Niagara Machine. There was a black-rimmed roofing kettle parked along a rear wall. John must have contracted to do a hot- roll roof. As Sam recalled, it needed it. Things must be going okay. He was pleased.

A door opened and an employee walked out of the building shading his eyes against the white sunlight. Sam recognized him and waved. The man raised a hand in recognition and walked on.

A few minutes passed before the door opened again and Josh appeared. Seeing Sam leaning against the Chevy, he strolled over to him. "Hey, Sam, I didn't expect you. What's the occasion?"

Sam hadn't seen Josh since dinner at Gerty's weeks ago, and was surprised at how much slimmer he looked. Maybe it was the dark work clothes and pork pie hat. He looked like a young water front tough, mean and whip-lean. Sam said, "We've got to talk." He touched a black enameled fender gleaming like a blister under the sun. "Get in the car, we'll find some shade."

In the car, Josh asked, "Is there a problem?"

Sam turned the ignition, *goddamn right there is.* "Maybe," he said. He looked at Josh's poker face. "You getting enough sleep these nights?"

Josh looked away, "Yeah, why?"

"You sure you're not getting all sweaty crawling in and out of windows?"

Expressionless, Josh looked at Sam, "What are you talking about?"

Sam steered into an empty lot partly shaded by a three-story windowless brick building. He turned the engine off and rolled to a crunching stop on the cinders and dry weeds. "What I'm talking about," Sam said, controlling his mounting anger, "is we had an intruder in the house last night, and think it was you."

Josh flushed involuntarily, his eyes turned from shallow pools to deep unfathomable wells. Both his hands were in the air. "What?" he exclaimed, "Me?"

"And, we don't think it was the first time either. Someone uninvited has been there before." Sam's words were sharp and hard, there was no mistaking his inner furor.

Afraid, Josh opened the car door. "This is bullshit. I don't have to listen to this."

Sam grabbed him by the shirt with both hands. Snarling, he said, "Sit where you are, I'll let you know when you can leave."

Josh's face was blotchy with fear, he was starting to shake. "Sam, you've got to believe me. I wasn't in your house last night. I'm your brother, for Christ's sake." He removed his hat and wiped his brow with it. He was sweating profusely. "You said, 'we'. You mean Emma, don't you? You don't believe it, do you?"

Sam looked at him, remembering the many times Josh had stepped out of line. He heard the guilty whine in his words. Sam pinched the muscles at the back of his neck. This was difficult. *What a sorry shit.* "Yeah, I've come to believe it," he said. He slapped the cap from Josh's hand. It was a poor substitute for punching him silly. Exasperated, Sam asked, "What the hell's wrong with you?"

"It wasn't me, Sam," Josh cried.

"Liar," Sam said, and added sorrowfully, his stomach turning, "there was a time when I would have believed that. But now, you're like a dog that's rolled in something obscene, the stink is all over you."

"It's Emma, she hates me," Josh sobbed.. He wrung his hands and stared at his cap on the floor. "She's just a nurse, not a doctor. She doesn't understand me. She can't know how I hurt. How empty I am."

"No, Josh. Emma doesn't hate anybody. And, she doesn't hate you. She understands you. She thinks you're sick...I think you're sick. You've got to get help."

Suffering, his face twisted in anguish, Josh pleaded, whined, "I didn't hurt anybody. I didn't hurt Mary. I love little Mary. I love you." His voice flew to a higher whine, an operatic pleading. "Why doesn't anybody care about me? What about me? I deserve to be loved, same as you."

"Then, you've got to get help. You've got to see a doctor." Sam was sweating.

"No," Josh stared at Sam, defiance rampant in his eyes. "I'm not going to see any quack!"

Sam sighed and started the car.

Josh looked at Sam. He was bewildered and fearful. "I can't go home to Pennsylvania." There was the strain of panic, hysteria, in his statement.

"Relax," Sam said, "you're going to be okay. We're taking a ride."

Josh was shaking, "Are you locking me up? Where are we going?"

Sam looked at him, *pitiful.* He shook his head and answered, "A U.S. Army recruiting station."

CHAPTER 34

June 1938

By June of 1938, Harold Mason had moved up in the world. He was now General Superintendent of Production for the manufacturing complex, and the size and furnishing of his office reflected his rise. Sam recalled his first meeting with him in his General Foreman's office with no elbowroom and only one pebble-glass window. This office in the administrative building had windows and an impressive view of the Niagara River and Canadian shore. One thing hadn't changed, Mason was still an inveterate cigarette smoker, judging by the full ashtray on the corner of his broad oak desk.

"Good Morning, Sam," Mason greeted. He stood to shake his hand and simultaneously dismissed his personal secretary who stood beside the open office door. Mason pointed to one of the captain's chairs situated in front of his desk.

"Thanks," Sam said, moving to sit. Sam's mind was racing wondering what changes in his life this meeting might introduce. In the past months, he'd gone from no work at times to working all the time. He was beginning to think the job was his life, and was undecided how he felt about it. He was at the point where he could fulfill his goal and bring his mother and brothers out of the village, but he was seeing less and less of Emma and Mary.

The plant was rife with rumors in response to world events of the past months. The Japanese had bombed a U.S. gunboat on the Yangtze in December, and America was providing the Chinese Nationalists with arms. In March, Hitler had invaded Austria, demonstrating the value of his promises, shaking European alliances and causing many Americans to reassess their isolationist views. In America, it was the ninth year of the Great Economic Depression, and there were still ten million unemployed. In response, Congress passed a minimum wage law setting the minimum at twenty-five cents an hour and limiting the workweek to forty-four hours. These were turbulent times.

Harold Mason unconsciously drew his hand from his forehead to the nape of his neck as he relocated a chair and sat in front of the desk facing Sam. "I would like to blame my bald head on the changes of the past year," he chuckled, "but, as you know, I've been naked on top longer than that."

Sam smiled and relaxed in his chair. He knew Mason's success was largely a result of his talent at people handling—his ability to cajole and influence.

"I guess you've been a foreman for more than a year now, haven't you?"

Sam assumed he rarely guessed. "Yes, sir."

Edgar Hulse

"Well, I hear nothing but good things about you. Seems you thrive on responsibility." Mason adjusted his trouser legs and leaned forward with his hands on his knees. "How would you like more of it?"

Sam recalled the old adage, 'Be careful what you wish for, you might get it.' He swallowed hard and replied, "I believe I'm ready."

"I believe you are too," Mason said, then uncharacteristically rubbed his temples and added, "though I wonder if we as a people are." He lapsed into silence as Sam wondered where this conversation was headed.

Mason left his chair and paced the room, stopping at times to stare across the river at the Canadian shore. Sam looked at the American flag on a stand in the corner and at the large framed picture of the President, Franklin Roosevelt, on the wall behind the desk. There was no mistaking F.D.R. the aristocrat. Sam smiled inwardly thinking, *This is the same decor as the recruiting office*. He pondered Mason's words and waited for him to continue.

"Sam, there are men in high positions in government and industry, realists, who think it's past time to gear up for the job ahead. Men who foresee a worldwide conflict between ideologies, a conflict that has already begun." Mason continuing to pace made a huge circular motion with his arms as he added, "A world war." He stopped pacing and said, "This country, industries like ours, will be the providers of the materials of war."

Sam listened to Mason's hyperbole. He shifted in his chair, *The smell of hot money was in the air.* He knew money was flowing from England by way of Canada.

Mason turned, his eyes on fire, and pointed a crooked index finger, "It will be guys like you running the engines of production." He had Sam in spite of his suspicions and skepticism.

Sam was shrinking in his clothes, Mason was describing a formidable task.

"Believe it or not, the greatest shortage is not in money or raw materials, but in talented men." He sat again, directly in front of Sam. "We've been watching you, myself, your foreman Homer, and others. We feel you've got the stuff for the job ahead: intelligence, guts. and more important, a can-do attitude."

Sam was hanging on Mason's words thinking, *Why the big build-up? What is it they want me to do?*

Mason leaned back in his chair and studied Sam. Finally, he said, "What does all this mean for you? Here it is. We've been directed to convert the Delevan Avenue plant from auto to aircraft engine production."

He stopped, Sam supposed, to let the enormity of the task sink in.

Then, he continued, "We need a ramrod for the job, and we want you."

Sam's mind was in overdrive. His gut feeling was, *This is too big for me.*

Mason interrupted, "I know it's scary, a big job, but you can do it. The way you handled the breakdown on the water pump line last week, saved us days of down time. It's that kind of thinking that got you here."

Sam was excited and apprehensive, pleased to be chosen and leery of the unknown. *Am I being hung out to dry? Will I have to live at the plant, spend less time with the family? What will Em think? How long will it last? Can I handle it?* His thoughts whirled. He became aware of Mason staring at him, waiting for a response. Sam put aside his concerns, *wasn't this what he'd been working for?* In a steady voice, he stated with conviction, "I'm your man."

Mason stood and offered his hand. "Congratulations, General Foreman."

A month of seven-day work weeks later, Sam stood and surveyed what was destined to be the production floor. *What a goddamn mess.* He adjusted his safety glasses. From his position on a catwalk around a gigantic hydraulic press, he could see from one end of the cavernous sprawling plant to the other, from the receiving dock to the front offices almost a quarter mile away. It looked like mass confusion with men and machines, bulldozers and high lifts in motion everywhere, but Sam knew there was method to the madness. *There better be, or my ass will be in a sling.*

He wondered what the men below thought about him, the guy in the white shirt and tie. Under him a millwright driving a bulldozer with padded treads was nudging a smaller piece of machinery, a kitchen-stove size yellow grinder, into place. Watching the activity involved in the metamorphosis of the Delevan Avenue facility Sam was beginning to think of as his plant, he was oblivious to the din created by motors running, tools banging, sheet metal tearing, and men cursing.

He saw Bill Ness, an engineer in the Standards Department, striding his way, his arms swinging. Bill never moved slowly. He had someone with him, and whoever it was jogged to keep up.

Sam climbed the circular metal steps down off the mountainous press. Reaching the floor of wood blocks set on concrete, he turned and called, "Over here, Bill," knowing he was on the opposite side of the press looking for him.

Bill came around the press and waved. Bill supervised the plant layout section in Standards. Sam wondered about the nature of his problem, assuming there must be one. "What's the matter, Bill? Something in the wrong place?"

Bill Ness grinned flashing a row of white teeth under a blond mustache. "I'm sure there is but I haven't found it yet. No," he turned and looked for the man following him, and as he appeared, said, "I've been asked to introduce you to a new man in Personnel."

Sam considered the new man as he approached. There was something familiar about him. His walk? His gangling frame? The fact that he looked comfortable in shirt and tie? He smiled, "Roger." His face had lost its' gaunt appearance, and he'd misplaced the aura of youth, but it was him. "It's been a while."

Obviously astounded, Roger uttered, "Well, I'll be...hello, Sam."

Bill watched them shake hands and shrugged, "Looks like you don't need any introduction, so I'll get back to work."

Sam said, 'Thanks," as he departed. He turned to Roger, and with a grin said, "Let's hitchhike up to my office where we can talk."

In his office, a ten foot square cubical, sparsely furnished with a desk, metal file cabinet and four chairs, Roger stood looking at a framed photograph of Emma and Mary as he closed the door.

'Wife and daughter?"

"Yes," Sam said, sitting on the corner of his desk. "My wife Emma, and our daughter, Mary."

"Well, it's obvious you've been busy the past few years—a beautiful wife, a pretty little girl, and a white collar job." Roger observed standing with his hands on his hips. "Yes, very impressive for a guy who barely had enough money for gas."

Sam nodded. "It seems like a long time." His sweeping hand offered a chair. "Have a seat...what have you been doing with yourself? I see you're still a white-collar guy." Sam spoke louder to overcome the resonating buzz of activity outside.

"I have two neckties now. That about sums up my material gain, though I have learned a lot." Sitting, he said, "I spent a couple of years trying to organize my fellow socialists and got my skull cracked as a reward. It's amazing how fast comrades disappear when the shit hits the fan. So, I decided rather than promote socialism, I'd fight fascism."

Roger raised his hands in a believe-it-or-not gesture, "I went to Spain and joined the Abe Lincoln Brigade fighting that bastard Franco." He shifted on the seat, rolling from hip to hip. "I got a rear end full of shrapnel for my efforts. It wasn't like the literature; no nurse fell in love with me. Lying in a hospital bed, it occurred to me that the outcome of the coming global contest was going to be decided in favor of the firstest with the mostest. Besides," he chuckled," it's safer in here." He stopped and added apologetically, "Well, you asked."

Sam snorted, "I remember you as a speech maker, and you haven't changed. Also, I think you're right. More importantly, the people that call the shots think you're right."

Roger sighed, "Roosevelt was right when he said, 'war is contagious'. Isolationism will be short lived, and the coming years will bring cataclysmic changes. I only hope we'll be around to witness them."

Amen," Sam said. For a few moments, they both sat without speaking. Sam rose and placed his hand on Roger's shoulder, "Well, philosopher, glad to have you aboard," Sam squinted, "That is if you're not a union organizer."

Roger grinned ear-to-ear, "Damn, it's easy to see how you got where you are. You've got eyes in your ass." He stood, "No, I promise. It's not the time for that."

Sam said, "Good. If it turns out that you are, we'll still be friends, but you'll be out on the street." Sam let that settle in. "I have a meeting in five minutes, but if you're around when I finish up this evening, I'll let you buy me a beer."

"You're on," Roger said," and, Sam I want you to know I think they have the right man for the job."

Sam opened the door. "Thanks," he said.

CHAPTER 35

July 1938

It was a rare cool Sunday morning in late July. Sam was still in bed. He had decided not to go into the plant. He'd been working seven days a week and decided Emma needed a break, even more than he did. When he left the plant Saturday he told his foremen, "If you call me tomorrow, this place better be on fire!"

The wrangling of blue jays and a chorus of mocking birds and robins filled his ears. He was wide awake, but not because of the raucous birds. Habit opened his eyes at 5:30, but he'd rolled over. Now, as displayed by the Big Ben alarm clock ticking on the bedside table, it was 8:15.

He could hear Mary talking, a low continuous monologue. Sam imagined Emma nodding and mumbling agreement as she moved about the kitchen. He could smell bread toasting and the aroma of freshly brewed coffee blessed the air. He looked around the bedroom at the newly papered walls, and the polished surfaces of recently acquired furniture. It was a great improvement over the ratty downstairs flat they'd left in Niagara Falls. *Yep,* he scratched himself, *we're getting up in the world.* He knew this new place wasn't the Taj Mahal. "But then," he said, with a chuckle, "I'm not a Hindu."

Feeling relaxed and loose, Sam laughed at himself. Throwing the sheet aside, he sat on the edge of the bed. He stretched and yawned like the Cheshire Cat. He was in a remarkably good mood. The uplifting chime of church bells sounded through the open window. He listened and responded in a low plea, "Pray for me."

Emma turned to look at him as he entered the kitchen. "Well, good morning, Lazy Bones," she said.

Mary, in bare feet, bobbed hair, and bib, echoed, "Lazy Bones, Lazy Bones."

Sam lifted her out of her chair, placed his lips on her neck and blew forcibly. She screamed with delight and grabbed a fistful of his tousled hair. "Let go, Honey," Sam pleaded as he returned her to her seat.

"Leggo," she mimicked, releasing him.

Moving to Emma, he asked, "How's my big girl?" and kissed her.

Emma in a ruffled apron and waving a spatula, said, "I love this kitchen." The spatula indicated the white and black enameled gas range, and maple table and chairs.

"Good," Sam smiled, feeling appreciated. "What's for breakfast? I could eat a bear."

"Naturally," Emma shrugged her shoulders, "pancakes, eggs and bacon."

"My favorite," he said, taking a seat next to Mary, who studied him with wide eyes.

"Everything is your favorite."

"Lucky for you," Sam said. "As a lifetime tea drinker, I appreciate this coffee habit you brought home from the hospital. It gets me kick started in the mornings."

Emma nodded, "I know. The hospital runs on coffee."

Sam took a bite out of a slice of warm buttered toast.

"Me," Mary screeched, both hands grasping.

Sam withheld the toast. He wrinkled his nose, "Say please."

"Pease."

He took another bite out of the slice and surrendered the rest. He watched as Emma poured a measured amount of batter into a skillet. "We should get out of here after breakfast—go to the zoo or something, before the plant calls." He knew ten to one, something would come up, and there'd be a call. Because of his new responsibilities, they had a brand new black telephone on a table in the living room. It was the only one on the city block.

Emma flipped a pancake. "On a sunny day like this, the animals will be out. We can buy Mary a balloon."

Sam raised his cup and, as if on cue, the telephone rang.

Sam and Emma looked at each other. Emma, biting her lip, looked dejected. Sam's stomach dropped, his spirits deflated. He rose to answer the jangling instrument.

"Sit still, I'll get it." Wiping her hands on her apron, she left the room.

His appetite gone, he heard her say, "Hello."

There was a long silence with Emma obviously listening. He heard her say, "Just a minute."

Then she stood in the doorway, a sad look over her face. "It's not the plant, it's your mother...I'm sorry, Sam," she hesitated, her eyes moist, "Pop died."

He exhaled slowly, *Why is it always bad news?* He crossed the room to his wife and placed his palm gently on her cheek. "Don't cry, Honey," he said fighting to contain his own tears.

In the living room, he lifted the phone. "Hi, Mom. Sorry...how you holding up? Uh-huh, good. How did he die? Oh, his heart. Yes. When is the funeral? Sure, of course I'll be down, but only for a day or so. I know, but every day at the plant is crucial now. Yes, I will be there. Again, I'm sorry...let me talk to Alfred."

Trees lining the cemetery lanes were throwing long midmorning shadows. People were milling about in silence, trying to discern their place on the grassy stage in the final scene of Pop's life. The air was stable and there were few clouds. The hillsides looked soft, quiet and serene, pastoral. Holding his mother's arm, Sam moved with a slow resignation. He considered every funeral a dress rehearsal for his own. He watched as six pallbearers in their best leather soled shoes, Sunday suits, and black derbys walked with timid steps over the slippery grass. Ernie and Alfred, long-faced and somber, were the two lead bearers. Sam recognized one of the other four as Pop's cousin. The other three, he assumed were friends, or coworkers of Pop's he'd never met.

The number of people at the gravesite had swollen by the time Reverend Christer arrived, and the ceremony began. As the affair dragged on, he reminded himself to leave instructions to keep his funeral short and sweet. There were many nods of recognition for Sam, but also eye contact with no sign of acquaintance. Slowly settling on him was a realization of how long he'd been gone. The surrounding hills, winding roads, aging structures, and weary people were no longer dear to him. Too long out in the world, this was no longer his home. He shuddered, wishing it was windy enough to blow his mountain of sorrow away.

He wondered how Wilbur, standing beside him holding his sleeve, dressed like his brothers, was perceiving the event in his sightless world. *How did it sound? What did he hear? Was he aware of spirits invisible to everyone else? Were there more souls present than Sam could see?* Sam felt a soul-wrenching sadness, and an acute longing for the balm of Emma's touch.

Pop was beyond all this. Sam tried to recall the wisp of a man that gave him his first jack knife, that told him to piss on his finger when he burned it, that seemed content with his back-up roll in the family. Trying to remember his own father, Sam failed. The shadows of his life were growing longer.

With the funeral over and Pop finally at rest, people gathered at the family home. It was an amorphous crowd of milling souls coming and going; muttering heartfelt condolences then departing after an offered bite or drink of Pop's White Lightning, getting back to their lives quickly, as though loss might be contagious. Sam moved through the rooms shaking hands and kissing cheeks. He experienced a lingering deja vu as vaguely remembered faces passed.

"We're so sorry," whispered Mrs. Miller.

"He will be missed," declared George Lowery, owner of the silk mill.

"Our condolences." Sam had no idea who he was.

Then as tentatively as they came, they were gone and only the family remained. They assembled out of habit in the kitchen but decided to move, each with a cup of tea, to the living room on the cooler north side of the house. Sam studied his mother. With her broad black veiled funeral hat removed, he could see that her hair was totally gray, and that she seemed smaller, less commanding, than he remembered. Another husband gone, she was a survivor resigned to remaining shallow days full of remembrances and sighs, contemplating the certain perhaps-welcome end.

Sam's gaze drifted across the faces of the sons, his brothers, Alfred, Ernie, and Wilbur who surrounded her.

Ernie, his stiff collar still buttoned around his thick neck, hair the color of his tea, and his mournful countenance, sat in seeming contemplation, his broad hands folded on his lap.

Alfred, his twin, sat more relaxed, typically resigned to the inexorable press of events. Leaning back in an upholstered chair, his collar undone and shoes off, his lean face inscrutable, he caught Sam's eye and shrugged.

Wilbur sat on the piano bench, his back to the upright box, straining like a fledgling sparrow unable to see beyond the boundaries of the nest. Then, to Sam's surprise, Wilbur turned to the black and white keys and began to play, slightly off key, Rock of Ages. Sam knew he felt the need to make a sound in his fearful darkness. The notes filled the room raising sinking spirits, and they all began to sing the old hymn. Singing, Sam realized—he was now their rock.

The music ended, the resonating piano stilled, as Sam cleared his throat and wiped his eyes. He pushed the handkerchief into his hip pocket and placed his hand on Lizzy's shoulder. He felt the need for contrition. He said, "Some years back, when I left here, the plan and hope was that I could establish a foothold and you would all follow. Well, the road's been longer and the promise slimmer than we'd hoped." He looked guiltily from face to face. He shrugged, "I feel I should apologize, I" Words failed him. He couldn't admit what they must know—that embroiled in his own struggle, he'd forgotten them.

Lizzy put her hand on his, "It's all right, Sam."

The boys looked away.

"But now is the time. I'm finally in a position to get, Ernie and Alfred into permanent jobs. There's opportunity. Things are moving. With Pop gone, there's nothing to hold you here."

Alfred breathed, "Amen."

The last day of August, Sam steered his Chevy sedan down Richmond Avenue in Buffalo. Overhead, a canopy formed by arching branches of the towering Elms and Maples lining the roadway shaded their passage. It was raining, a reluctant late-summer patter, but the pavement was dry. "What do you think of this?" he asked Lizzy seated beside him.

"It's glorious," she said, opening her dress at the throat, "but muggy."

"Yes," he turned to Wilbur seated on the rear seat by an open window, luggage piled beside him. "It's raining, but the trees are so tall and thickly leafed that no rain is reaching the ground."

"I can smell the rain," Wilbur said, pushing his hand palm up out the opening.

"Will we live near here?" Lizzy asked.

"No, this area is near the center of the city. You'll be in Riverside, a neighborhood on the north side near the Niagara River. It's just as pretty. There's a park there, and you'll be just a short walk away. Ernie and Alfred will be able to walk to their jobs at the plant."

"When can we move in?" Wilbur asked.

"Saturday, Alfred and Ernie should have the furniture here Friday noon."

"It was good of Al to let us borrow a truck for the move."

"Well, Mom, grandpa Freeman started that company, you know."

She stared at Sam, her shrouded eyes and slack jaws reflecting her long-term resignation, "How well I know," she said.

Sam turned onto a residential street lined with well-kept homes. Boxes filled with blooms of every description adorned the front porches. "We're the red geraniums" he said.

CHAPTER 36

August 1938

Eleven hundred miles south of Buffalo, in a one street Georgia town miles from the army base, Josh, careful of slivers from the sun-dried siding, leaned into the shade of a frame building, removed his uniform cap, and watched the bus disappear like a mirage. He was soaked; his slick-sleeved khaki shirt had dark perspiration stains under his arms and a snake-like streak meandered down the center of his back. The humidity inside the bus was bad enough, he had trouble breathing, but this was worse. *Who would live in this forgotten hell?* There was a slim movement of air close to the ground, and a wide expanse of angry clouds off to the west that hinted of improvement. With luck, the much needed rain lay just over the shimmering horizon. *Almost too hot for sex.* Josh rubbed himself, remembering why he was there.

Josh needed a cold drink, soda, iced tea, something. He doubted he could buy a beer in this bible-thumping town, and this was no day for moonshine. He knew this town rarely saw a soldier on leave—they all headed for the bright lights. Josh wasn't interested in bright lights. He searched for desperation, for vulnerability, for those barely clinging to existence and willing to sell themselves or others for the price of a few slices of bread.

He looked along the road, asphalt streaks of black in the milling dust, past a one door ramshackle garage where a shirtless bucolic youth in grimy overalls struggled to remove an obstinate tire from a rusty wheel. There were two women engaged in conversation under the faded awning of the general store, and across the road a man entered the Center cafe. Josh draped his service cap over his web belt. *Center of what?*

That was it, only four souls on the main road through town. About the same as it was four weeks ago when he'd had his last twenty-four hour pass. "Good."

Treading the sometimes sidewalk on the north side of the road, taking advantage of the little shade provided, Josh moved past the general store. He saw that the women had moved inside. Past a cinder block building that looked deserted, he turned down an alley that stretched toward two houses sharing a barren field. The houses, little more than shacks sided with gray barn wood, had tarpapered roofs. They were two stories tall with long narrow windows gaping at the wasteland. Curtains thin as mist hung unmoving behind the upper windows. Stirring blistered ochre dust as he walked, Josh reached the easternmost structure and stepped up onto a banisterless porch. He was sweating profusely, but not from the sun. It was the beast within.

He rapped on a frail torn screen door. The woman that appeared was likely in her thirties but looked a sickly fifty. Her skin was tight as paper and her sad eyes mousey gray. Her faded shift dress hung off ridge-like clavicles and concealed her protruding rib and pelvic bones. Her arms reminded Josh of turkey bones picked clean, a Georgia Peach stone.

"Y'all came back," she said.

Josh stared past her at vultures circling on the horizon. In a flush of despair and disgust, he almost turned and ran. Bile rose in his throat, and pain swelled behind his eyes. Weakened, he swayed and shook his shoulders like throwing off a cape, and as quickly as the brief fugue came it was gone.

No longer shaken, he stepped through the doorway. "I told you I would. I paid you the dollar."

"Upstairs," she turned to wooden stairs that clung tenuously to the wall.

Josh watched her bare feet and dirty ankles as she moved sluggishly up, one stair at a time.

The steep narrow stairs led to the second floor, and Josh climbed them gingerly trusting they would not collapse. He followed the slight woman across the tinder-dry creaking floor and into a bedroom off the head of the stairs. A metal bed frame supported a cupped mattress covered by a frayed yellowing sheet. Black wire hooks on the wall held articles of clothing, a belt and a pair of work pants. In a corner was a wooden chair with a spindle missing. Hanging from the ceiling was a shuttle-like fan, a strange contrivance Josh considered rather clever. *All the features of a five-star hotel.* A cord led from the contraption down the wall to a cam on a shaft that could be turned by a descending weight, a bucket full of pebbles.

Josh threw his cap on the chair and looked at the makeshift fan, knowing it would do little to relieve his discomfort. He turned to the woman standing by the door, "Where's the girl?"

The woman raised the bucket of pebbles to start the fan. The blades overhead began to sway back and forth as the bucket slowly descended. She moved hurriedly to the bed and sat on the mattress. "Y' don' need her," she said pulling the dress over her head. As the flimsy dress settled on the sheet, she laid back. Naked, she raised her knees and spread her bony thighs.

Josh stared in disbelief at her crotch. There was a white patch of skin where black hair had covered her mons.

"See, ah shaved. Y'all don' need the chile." She pleaded, "Do me."

"You stupid bitch, it would take more than a shave to make me do you." He stepped closer to her and raised his fist. "Go get the girl," he said, his patience draining away. Josh reached in his pocket and produced a crumpled five-dollar bill. He dropped it on her flat belly.

Grasping the money and her dress, she scurried from the room.

Josh, hearing her pause in the hallway, assumed she was donning the dress. He heard the stairs groan as she went down. He paced the room in an agitated state, realizing the woman could disappear with the money and he would be screwed. "Stupid," he exclaimed slamming the wall with a hammer fist. Pain grasped his wrist. "Damn." Beads of sweat ran down the side of his face; his clothes were soaked.

Moments passed, and he considering his vulnerability, considered leaving. *What if she returns with a posse of rednecks?* He started for the door. He stopped. There were footsteps on the stairs. Bare feet, more than one pair. He moved to the window and looked down. He could jump.

As he vacillated, the woman appeared in the doorway. She had a child by the hand, a girl, Josh judged to be eight years old. There was some color to her skin, and her bones were straight, but the woman had her and in twenty years she would be an empty soul. Tension left Josh as he studied the fearful wide-eyed girl. *Eight, no older.*

The child stared past him with round empty eyes in the detached manner of the abused and unloved.

"Y'll not hurt her will you sojer?"

"No."

The woman walked the girl to the bed where, releasing her hand, she looked away. From a pocket, she took a small jar of petroleum jelly and handed it to Josh. Before she left the girl, she placed her fingers alongside her cheek and said. "Y' do as the nice man say." Then she turned and, dragging her feet, left the room.

When the woman had left her, the silent girl settled on the thin bed sheet. She'd been there before, staring at the rustic fan moving hypnotically without effect in the heavy air.

The sun was an inverted bowl resting on the western horizon when Josh stepped off the plank porch. A lone hawk soared high overhead searching the dry landscape for a morsel. Josh, his predatory appetite satisfied, was headed away from the house, back the way he came. He walked with his feet swinging wide like a saddle-sore rider. Every few steps, his fingers flicked at the front of his khaki pants. *Sore, wet, and abraded, but it was worth it.* Josh wished he had more time, but couldn't risk missing the bus back to the base. The last time he did, he spent a week cleaning garbage cans. *There'll be other afternoons, maybe cooler.* He smiled, in his pocket was a souvenir- the top off the jelly jar.

It was early twilight, darkness was sifting into the alleys of the town and the shallow gullies of the fields. The air had stilled again, it was time for the night foragers to stretch and consider the dusk. There was a strange quiet, no scavenging dogs, birds or insects to be heard. A sly gray cat watched from under a small woodpile, his tail twitching. The people of the afternoon were gone.

Josh stepped out into the deserted street; he was thinking he had plenty of time before the bus passed this way. He knew the town had closed. There was no place to get anything to wet your throat. He pulled at the fabric between his legs and looked for a place to sit and wait.

There was the determined shuffle of shoes on hardpan.. Josh reacted viscerally. He whirled, only to catch a peripheral glimpse of darting bodies. He was not quick enough. A vicious blow to the side of his head, dropped him instantly to the ground.

The leather-faced, long-boned kid slashed the tire iron through the air. "Shit," he said, "he fell like a hog."

"Well, he be a pig," a bent older man said, nudging Josh's leg with his boot.

"You got the pictures?" The kid asked, his eyes jumping, excited.

"Yeah." The old man, wheezing, reached into a hip pocket of his coveralls.

"We should kill 'im, Paw."

Pushing several pornographic pictures into Josh's pocket, the old man said, "No. We git the police." He pronounced it, 'Po-leec'. "He goin' to the stockade where he wish he was dead."

CHAPTER 37

August 1938

Elizabeth Freeman-Cordy was uncomfortable in Buffalo. Motoring about, with Alfred at the wheel and Emma serving as tour guide, she discovered that the Niagara Frontier was flat and ugly. She missed the rolling hills of Pennsylvania and the aura of seclusion and privacy they rendered. Alfred assured her that away from the lakes the terrain began to roll.

"But we're not livin' away from the lakes, are we?"

The streets of Buffalo ran for miles with hardly a dip, and she found that disconcerting. She saw that Buffalo, Niagara Falls and adjacent communities owed their existence to lakes Erie and Ontario and the swift, thundering Niagara River that joined them. Sucklings, they drew from the life-giving waters, while giving back nothing she could see.

Moving into Buffalo's Riverside district, she found her neighbors to be a hearty, industrious, mixed lot, full of hope, sensing the stirring of industries along the water's edge. The steel mills, manufacturing, and assembly plants were beginning to show the signs of revitalization: repaired fences, wide expanses of wet paint, puffs of hope from stacks long dormant. Of her generation, the people tempered by the bitter lean years of the depression were cautiously appraising the scent of change. They were leery of the Bankers and Industrialists, but with a growing trust in the administration of Franklin Roosevelt, they were ready, needed, to go to work. And there was a swelling sense of freedom in the easy way they came and went, in their hearty hellos, and the increasing vigor of the children climbing fences and playing stickball in the street. Lizzy sighed, maybe she could be happy here.

Her two story, three bedroom house, she thought adequate. The neighbors, ten feet away on each side, were amiable. They waved and exchanged gossip and recipes as they edged closer hoping to be friends. In her bedroom on the first floor, down the paneled hall from the kitchen, she arranged personal belongings: garments, shoes, a parasol and purses; the accouterments of her days, mementos and photos to help hold on to the past.

Framed photographs of both husbands rested on her dresser between the hairbrush and the wooden jewelry box. She felt their eyes on her as she prepared her face each morning, as she examined the wrinkles and sagging chin. She closed her eyes, "Good morning, my darling." And, depending on her mood, she would reminisce with one of them. "Elizabeth," she reminded herself, "you've had a full life."

She allowed herself only brief moments of sadness when considering Wilbur's blindness or wondering about Josh. *Why doesn't he write?* When she prayed, it was for them. But moments of prayer and sadness were short. Years of running a household, and work habits ingrained, stirred her as she rallied to take on each day.

Upstairs, Ernie and Alfred shared a room with two windows and one closet. On one end of the closet, Ernie's clothes hung neatly arranged on hangers, his second pair of shoes, toes aligned, underneath. Next to them a shoe box held a few personal belongings: a jackknife, pocket watch, and, in an envelope, a photo of the Christer family posed in front of the Methodist church. There was a circle drawn around Lisa smiling in the front row.

At the other end of the closet, were Alfred's clothes, some on wall hooks, some on hangers, most in a pile on the floor. It was a typical morning. Ernie, dressed for work, sat on the edge of his bed, already made with pillows fluffed and blanket taut, and watched Alfred search.

"You seen my blue work shirt?" A small lamp atop the chest of drawers at the far end of the room threw Alfred's scurrying shadow on the wall.

"The one on the floor by the radiator?"

"That's it," Alfred grabbed the shirt, "come on, we're going to be late."

Ernie shook his big head and followed his brother down the stairs.

In his bed across the hall, Wilbur, dressed in a white undershirt, slacks, and socks, snored. Following his routine, he had been awake until three o'clock, sitting at his receiver, head set on, monitoring international short wave traffic. In his twilight world, radio and its mysteries broadened his horizons. He heard and experienced what his brothers could not see.

A door slammed behind the twins leaving for work. Lizzy sat with a cup of tea, children passed on their way to school, a dog barked to be let in, the mailman passed with a wave but no mail.

Next door, Mrs. Kingsbury opened her rear door and sloshed a bucket-full of soapy water into her yard; another day began.

Nestled in the womb of the waking city, Emma had a day off. Sam had risen and left for work, adhering to his six ten-hour-day schedule. She could hear Mary wondrously asleep, breathing contentedly in her bed. Emma stretched, contented, she lazily contemplated the opportunities open to her. *Should she clean the bathroom or scrub the kitchen floor?* The walls in the stair well needed washing.

She sipped her coffee. She wanted to attend college part time; maybe she should fill out the application. Reading said he would sponsor her, give her a letter of recommendation, help her overcome the handicap of womanhood. She never knew if he was serious or jibing, but she knew he now respected her, and recognized her desire to study psychology.

Emma could clean the china cabinet. There was work to do outside. "Hmm," she slumped, "maybe I won't do anything." She had to move, her cup was empty. As she rose from her seat the phone rang. "Now what did you forget, Sam Freeman?" She scratched her scalp as she walked to the phone.

"Hello."

"Good Morning," a woman's voice greeted, "this is your long distance operator. I have a collect call from Josh Cordy. Will you accept the charges?"

Shocked, her stomach flopped and her free hand fled to her breast. She stood silent as a guillotine.

"Hello?"

"Um...no, operator. If it is an emergency, have him call C02323." She gave Sam's work number.

"Thank you," the operator said, and disconnected.

Emma sank into an upholstered chair, her easy day gone, her face buried in her hands, "Oh God, what now?"

That evening, Sam turned into the driveway and pulled into the garage at seven o'clock, one half hour earlier than usual. He entered the house and removed his shoes in the rear entrance hall. As he entered the kitchen, Emma stood staring at him. He was drained, the worries of the world seemingly all with him. His burdens lent him an exhausted melancholy air that Emma seemed to mirror. Sam put his arms around her and they stood entrapped in a copulation of their spirits, fearing to speak, not daring to acknowledge what threatened them.

Sam kissed her closed eyes then held her at arm's length. He said, "The Army Provost Marshall's Office called about Josh."

Emma shivered.

"He's going to be imprisoned then eventually discharged for 'the good of the service."

Emma pushed away from Sam. She crossed her arms and retreated into what he recognized as her inner stronghold. In a steady imperturbable manner, she asked, "What has he done?"

The white scar in Sam's eyebrow twitched. He massaged it for a moment, then, avoiding her question, he continued, "Josh has two options—the stockade or release on parole. It's not that simple, but basically that's it. If local authorities cooperate, for parole he needs a place to live, a job, and someone to accept responsibility for him."

Emma reacted as though Sam had slapped her face. Jolted, she snarled, her eyes fiercely defiant, "He's not coming here."

"No," Sam concurred as calmly and as firmly as he could, "he's not coming here." Emma slumped in a chair, her head in her hands, fingers twisted in her hair.

Speechless, Sam watched her. He was torn between his need to do his best for Josh, and concern for Emma and Mary. Watching his wife, his heart bled. He knew he only partly appreciated the depth of her fear and pain. *What was it that he didn't know?*

He sat on a chair beside her and placed his hand on her shoulder.

With a twitch she recoiled.

Sam paled, she couldn't have hurt him more. He moaned, "Oh, Em."

Emma stood and started to pace the room. "You don't understand, do you?" She looked at him, dismayed. "You think he's a bad boy, a pickpocket, a petty thief. Slap him on the wrist, put him in jail overnight and he'll be okay...well he won't!" Afraid and angry, her hands white and trembling, she screamed, "He's sick, obsessed, unstable, a pedophile. Sick. Sick. Sick!" She pounded on an end table with both hands. A lamp fell to the floor.

Sam sat, overwhelmed. He'd never seen her like this. She glared at him. Rigid, her eyes devoid of tears, her voice filled with resolve, she said, "If Josh comes anywhere near here, I'll take Mary and leave. I will not live behind locked doors."

Troubled, Sam considered the enormity of his dilemma. Standing, he vowed, "If they let him out on parole, I swear he'll come nowhere near us."

Emma placed her hand on his arm. She nodded as though accepting the inevitability of it all.

Sam doubted she believed him.

Sam paced the carpeted floor in the living room of his mother's house. Night had settled outside the triple set of mullioned windows and sheer drapes. Wet leaves fallen from towering elms covered the sidewalks. Summer was readying a farewell. Street lamps provided separate pools of light for children playing against the end of the day. He could hear their parents calling.

Alfred, sprawled in an armchair watching Sam pace, asked, "Why a family meeting?"

Sam didn't answer. He could see his mother in the kitchen passing from stove to sink, then to the refrigerator, then back to the sink. Lizzy couldn't know why he had come, but it appeared, intuitively, she suspected.

Ernie had gone upstairs to coax Wilbur away from his radio. Sam tried to recall what he looked like without a headset. Wilbur lived on the airways, in an audio world beyond his dimmed eyes. Sam caught a few notes of 'Harbor Lights' before they started down the narrow stairs.

China rattled and they all responded to an ingrained call to order. Every family crisis was discussed around the kitchen table. A lodestone, it pulled them together. Alfred stood, in a short-sleeved shirt draped loosely over his trousers, and shuffled to the table. Sam followed him into the bright room that smelled of supper's chicken and dumplings. Ernie, in freshly laundered shirt and pants and thick hair combed, held a chair for Wilbur.

Wilbur sat, confident that Ernie and the chair were there. Somewhat chagrined at being interrupted, he said, "I was talking to London. It was afternoon there. Boy, have they got problems. There's going to be a war."

Sam stood at the head of the table. He was drained, emotionally and physically; he had the dark-rimmed eyes of a coal miner. He said, "Well, if there is a war, I know one soldier who won't be in it."

Ernie looked to Alfred. Alfred shrugged.

Lizzy distributed clinking china and poured tea. Anticipating bad news, she sought solace in routine.

Wilbur sat, waiting.

Sam hesitated then said, "It's Josh. He's being thrown out of the army, discharged."

"Son-of-a-bitch," Alfred exclaimed, the reason for the meeting suddenly clear.

"Now, now," Lizzy warned, "no profanity."

There was an extended moment of silence as the news settled upon them and they gathered their questions.

Sam was visited by the recollection of Josh spread on the bed with his back flayed, another lesson unlearned. He was incorrigible. Not waiting for their many questions, he said, "Josh has two options if we offer our support. Without us," he looked into Lizzy's long-suffering eyes, "he has only one—the stockade."

"What the hell did he do?" Ernie wanted to know.

Sam said, looking to Ernie, "He was found beaten in an alley. The Captain I spoke with assumes he was worked over with a tire iron or something...anyway, he was in a town off limits and out of uniform. Whoever beat him took his shoes." He waved at Alfred, "Josh had photographs," he cleared his throat and added, "sex pictures." In a whisper, he said, "Of kids."

Everyone stirred uncomfortably.

"To make matters worse, the army has a witness, someone in the town that says he's been there before, for...ah, dubious purposes. He's in trouble up to his eye balls."

"His two balls, more like it," Alfred said.

Lizzy, teetering on an emotional edge, glared at him.

Wilbur, his face expressionless, asked, "What's the other option?"

Sam massaged his neck, *One Emma refuses to discuss.* He said, "The army will consider a discharge if...a lot of ifs actually; if local authorities will assign him a parole officer, if we provide him with a job and a place to live, if we agree to supervise his activities."

Alfred sat with his head down pondering the ifs.

Ernie, cracking his knuckles, seemed to be studying the wallpaper.

Lizzy poured tea.

Wilbur said, "We can put twin beds in my room."

Sam said, "There's something else you should know."

Alfred's head came up sharply, "What?"

"Emma is against my getting involved. She says Josh is dangerous and will never change. She swears that if he shows up anywhere near our home, she will take Mary and leave. She's adamant."

Alfred murmured, "Emma's a smart gal."

Lizzy placed both hands on the table. "There's good in Josh. He can change; he will change. He needs our love and support."

There was an uncomfortable silence that lingered until Wilbur spoke, "We have no choice. You take care of me; we have to care for Josh." His voice rose with emotion, as though he might cry. "He's our brother and he's in trouble, we have no choice."

Sam knew he was right. He turned to the practical aspects of the situation. "I'll speak to Peterson, the plant manager. I don't think getting Josh a job will be a problem."

"No," Alfred said, "getting him to keep it will be the problem. That and keeping him out of jail."

Sam thought he was undoubtedly right. He signaled agreement with his hand, and went on, "Another thing, we don't know if the local police authorities will go along with this arrangement. But, there's a lieutenant from Station Sixteen that moonlights on plant security along with some of his regular cops—maybe he can help. To make this work at all, I think we'll need support from Congressman Kern, and I don't know him. So, that's a gray area." He sighed and rolled his shoulders, "Who knows? Maybe we can swing it."

Ernie rose slowly to stand with his fists clenched. His six feet plus, three hundred pound body filled the end of the room. His eyes, set in stone, flashed his bone-solid determination around the room. "You get it done," he said, "and I'll see that he toes the line."

Sam believed him. He reached to console his mother.

CHAPTER 38

August 1938

On the drive home after the family meeting, Sam's thoughts were of Emma and Mary, and the home they'd made. Oblivious to the city streets, his head was full of the sight, sound and smell of them. As real as if she were there, he felt Mary's stubby fingers in his hair and heard her squeal with delight as he held her at arms length high in the air. Her scrubbed-pink smell of Ivory soap and talc rode with him.

Emma's piercing green eyes hovered beyond the windshield searching his face for reasons why Josh must be in their lives. He saw her soft bare arms, auburn fuzz aglow, under each street lamp. There was the promise of her comforting breast, that comforting place so near to her heart, where he longed to retreat, to lie, to rest.

In the confines of his dark garage, sitting with the headlights extinguished, listening to the tic tic of the cooling engine and exhaust pipes, he recalled walking in the predawn shadows of village streets. He thought of himself and Josh sliding past looming shapes as still as death as they climbed a conveyor, the belts rumbling like the gut of a giant praying mantis. He felt again Josh's small hand in his and heard the fearful pleading of his tremulous voice, "Don't leave me, Sam," and his answer, "Don't worry, I won't."

Encompassing it all were his mother's words echoing down the years, "Take care of your brothers."

He had almost failed them, taking too long to bring them hope. He would not fail Josh.

He pulled the heavy wooden garage door closed and walked to the house that stood with one eye, the back-lit kitchen window, open awaiting his return.

Emma stood, ending her vigil, as he entered.

Shoes off, he moved to her on silent feet. He needed to explain, needed her to understand. He reached for her, and she turned away.

"So," she asked, "what's the verdict?"

Sam sank onto a chair and sat stroking his brow with trembling fingers. This was his critical moment. He spoke to her alien posture, her expressionless back, "We can not turn our backs on him."

Emma wheeled, her eyes fiercely defiant. "Don't say 'we'. Say 'I'. They can't do a damn thing without you."

"Okay," he conceded, his throat dry. "'I'. I can't leave him out there. I can't desert him, not help Mom."

Emma sagged, palms up in surrender. "I know you can't."

He rose and took her in his arms. His lips brushed her hair and he promised, "You and Mary are my life. You'll never see him, I swear." Emma began to cry softly. Her tears fell on his shirt, already dampened by his trials. With her limp in his arms, he vowed, *One last chance, Josh. One last chance.*

That night, after a long hiatus, her night visitor came again. Out of a dream cavern, where secret fears dwell, animal-naked, he came. Upon his appearance, she wilted. She ran, her gorge rising. Slowed by the fingers of clinging terror, straining against the inevitable, her clothes falling away, slower and slower and slower until she fell exhausted, weeping, and, God forgive her, embracing the fornicator.

When, for the first time, she saw his face, the lean leering face of Josh, she howled. She clawed at his face, flaying the flesh of his cheeks and jaws. From the core of her being issued the growl of a she-wolf and she sank her teeth into his pulsing throat.

Her quavering high-pitched scream roused Sam. He turned fearfully alert, rattled and wide-eyed in bed. Emma's contorted face and flying hands shocked him into action. He slapped her hands aside and clutched her to his chest. Her warm, soaked body shook convulsively as she moaned and wept, resisting consolation.

Sam held her, soothed her, saying, "Emma, Em...Baby, it's okay. I'm here."

Emma shuddered, "So is he."

The next day, in an industrial complex where Sam spent his time in a daily struggle conning, coaxing, cajoling, and cursing men to maintain an impossible schedule, he stood before a small group in coveralls smiling at their expressions of disbelief.

One of the men, a burly Irishman with graying red hair, spit a stream of tobacco juice into an empty fifty-five gallon drum. He smiled at Sam. "Sure," he said, "and you're jokin' now. There's no way we can double the speed of this line. For one thing, there's coolin' time to contend with."

A smaller man in greasy coveralls and engineer's hat, said, "Mick's right. This is bullshit, Sam. Another wet dream out of Engineering. No way!"

Sam said, "it ain't bullshit, Steve, and there is a way," he placed a hand on his shoulder, "and you're just the man to find it." Stepping away, and staring into the distance, Sam snapped his fingers as if an idea had just come to him. "How about a cooling tank?"

"Jesus, a swimmin' pool, he says." The Irishman shook his head.

An older man, slim with receding hair, said, "It might work."

Steve wiped his eyes, "Shit."

Behind Sam, a short distance away, a man in the uniform of a police lieutenant, stood and watched as the men dispersed shaking their heads. It was unlikely he'd heard any of Sam's discussion due to the high noise level in the plant. Ten feet from where he stood, a barrel of a man slammed at the base of a reluctant machine with a sledge hammer, and there was an unworldly screech of tearing metal echoing off the structural steel overhead.

Sam saw the tall policeman in blue uniform and shining badge, his hat tilted back on his narrow head. He stuck out like a ballet dancer on a bulldozer. Sam waved for him to follow as he headed to his office. Marching down an aisle with the lieutenant taking long strides to keep up, he said, "They're going to give me an ulcer, Lieutenant Hull."

They turned off the aisle and passed through a doorway. As the door closed behind them, the noise dropped to a low persistent rumble that complimented the faint tremor of the surrounding partitions and furniture.

Entering Sam's office, the lieutenant automatically ducked his head as he passed through the doorway. He said, "There's only two kinds of men in this world, those that get ulcers and those that give' em, and you strike me as a giver."

Sam nodded agreement. He said, "They're good men, all they need is a suggestion and some encouragement, and they get the job done." He pointed to one of four chairs. "Have a seat." As the lieutenant got settled, Sam said, "Thanks for coming over." He sat on the corner of his gray metal desk, one foot dangling over the floor, his hands together, fingers interlaced. "I've got a problem," he began, "and thought maybe you could help."

"Hey, anything I can do." Producing a pack of Camel cigarettes, he offered one to Sam. "You've been good about throwing us extra security work." He winked, "One hand washes the other. I appreciate it; the whole precinct benefits."

"I appreciate that," Sam said, refusing the cigarette. "Actually, this may require the attention of some other department. It may be out of your sphere of influence."

The lieutenant lit up and blew smoke at the ceiling, "Try me."

Sam shrugged. "This has to do with arranging parole for someone being discharged from the military."

"Hmm, that is a new one." He placed his hat on the desk and rubbed his chin. "Sounds like it would require a transfer of responsibility. Interesting." He stood and peered at the pebbled reinforced glass of a shoulder-high window. "About as cloudy as your window," he grinned, "there is someone in that sphere of influence, my brother-in-law."

Sam was puzzled by the grin, until he added, "I love dumping on him."

They stood silently thinking until the policeman asked, "Who is this someone?"

Sam sighed and confessed painfully, "My brother, half-brother really, the black sheep of the family...I can get him into the River Road plant. They don't want him here distracting me. He'll be living at my mother's place in Riverside with his three brothers. They shouldn't have a problem keeping an eye on him. He'll eat, sleep and work with them. If he strays, my brother Ernie will kick his ass."

Listening to Sam, the lieutenant extinguished his cigarette in a piston serving as an ashtray. He said, "Sounds like a tight arrangement, I'll see what I can do," he paused, picked up his hat and turned it in his hands. He looked sideways at Sam. "You know you're going to have to pull some political strings."

"I know, that's my biggest problem."

"Well, good luck."

They shook hands. Sam said, "Thanks."

"Hey, I pat your back, you pat mine. It's what makes the world go 'round."

Later the same day, Sam was engrossed in a progress report when someone knocked on his door.

"Come in," he said, undecided whether he was annoyed or relieved at the interruption.

Roger stuck his head into the room, "You alone?"

Sam dropped his pencil. "More and more."

"I know what you mean." Roger was a mess, he had a three- corner tear in his pants and his sleeves, rolled to his elbows, were grease stained. But, he was smiling and his eyes were dancing. He looked like he'd just stepped out of a greasy amusement park.

"What the hell have you been doing?"

He grinned, "Chasing some characters that think they don't have to talk to me, the god of paper work."

"Have a seat." Sam studied him, rubbing his jaw. *We're both busy, what does he want?*

Roger said, "I'm here to offer my help."

"Help?"

Roger shifted in his seat; he gestured with his dirty hands. "With your brother."

Sam's jaw dropped. "Jesus, word travels fast."

Roger nodded "Guys in here gossip more than old women in an Arab market place."

Sam fell quiet for a while, thinking. Finally, he asked, "What makes you think you can help?"

"Well, for one thing, my father and your congressman Kern are law partners." He coupled his hands, "They share considerable interests."

Sam looked at his friend in amazement. "Goddamn, you're one of those Morgansterns?"

Looking like he wanted to apologize, Roger said, "Yes, one of those."

In the plant north of the city, Ernie sat at a table in the second floor cafeteria where hundreds of men sat with brown bags and metal lunch buckets. Across the steel benches and tables, engulfed in the smells of lubricant, perspiration and coffee, the male voices undulated. Unmindful of his fellow workers, Ernie gazed out the window across the manicured green lawn at the tireless emerald river. Half his work day behind, he was relaxed. Though vaguely aware of the men uniformly dressed in blue or gray, he pondered the nature of Josh's behavior. *He must be sick like Emma says.*

At his table, men came and went, sat and rose to leave, milled in conversation, or sat with lunch pails open and jaws rolling. His own bucket sat open on the shining surface. Inside were three ham and cheese sandwiches wrapped in wax paper, dill pickles, an apple and a banana. His open thermos stood beside it smelling of hot tea.

"Ernie Cordy, right?"

Ernie turned and looked at the man addressing him. He was wearing a green shirt, pants and unkempt hair. His smile revealed a mouth full of green-tinged broken teeth. He had dark bags under blood-shot eyes. Ernie tried to guess his age; looks like a rough life but about the same age as me, he decided. Short and wiry, Ernie thought he looked vaguely familiar. "I know you?"

"Well, we was neighbors, practically. I'm from Dunmore. You played us in football my last year there." His smile widened, "Thumped us," he said.

Dunmore, another village further up the valley, Ernie knew. Still, he couldn't quite place the guy.

"Name's Ronny Lester, mind if I sit here?" He placed his brown bag on the table, not waiting for an answer. He straddled the bench. "I got thrown out of that game for hitting the referee."

"Of course, that's where I know you from," Ernie said, "you had all your teeth then."

Lester chortled, "How long you been working here?"

"A few months. My brother Alfred's here too. How about you?"

Lester opened his brown bag and produced a sandwich and an apple. He unwrapped the sandwich of thick brown bread. "Still working on my first pay check," he grinned.

Ernie caught a whiff of something unpleasant. *Limburger cheese or Lester?* He drowned the smell with a swallow of tea.

"Anybody else from home around here?" Lester asked between bites.

"No," Ernie shook his blond head. His shoulders rippled with the effort. "You with anybody I'd know?"

"Nah, the last familiar face I saw was in Binghamton. I stopped on the way up. Got relatives there. They dragged me to church, and there was that Reverend Christer from the Methodist church at home."

Ernie's eyes danced as he turned fully attentive. "Really? His family there?"

Lester grinned lasciviously, "You know his daughters? Beauts, ain't they?"

Ernie ran a hand through his hair, *How would you like to lose more teeth?* "Yes," he said, "all three. Were they around?"

"Sure were—six fine tits in a row. I didn't take my eyes off them, missed the whole sermon," Lester grinned and rolled his eyes. He took another bite of his Limburger cheese sandwich.

You stink worse than the cheese, Ernie decided, flexing his fingers. "Was the whole family there?"

"Mother, three daughters and the kid. All listening to the Rev."

Ernie moved his thermos, "What kid?"

Lester removed his apple from the bag, then crushed it into a ball. "A little boy. My cousin says he belongs to the youngest daughter. Hell, she ain't but a kid herself. He says it's the talk of the whole congregation." Lester looked at Ernie's lunch bucket. "Ain't you going to eat your lunch?"

Ernie slammed his lunch bucket shut. "None of your goddamn business," he growled, his thick features suddenly menacing, "Get lost."

Lester left the crumpled bag on the table, got up and walked away. He looked back over his shoulder at Ernie staring out the windows. He asked aloud, "What the hell did I say?"

CHAPTER 39

March 1939

On the first day of March, Josh arrived in Buffalo's Central Station accompanied by an imposing Military Policeman dressed in civilian clothes and a late winter snow fall. In response to the intervention of Congressman Kern, the Army had agreed to his discharge and release to the family under the supervision of a parole officer. But, only after weeks during which they extracted their pound of flesh.

Sam stood with Alfred on the trembling floor of the immense terminal building and watched as people exited huffing trains, iron behemoths, lined up on the several parallel tracks. High overhead, roosting pigeons cooed unheard.

Alfred nudged Sam and pointed to Josh stepping carefully down the narrow metal steps of a passenger car, his balance impeded by manacles partly concealed by his brown overcoat. The M.P., a tall broad man looking disgruntled and suspicious, followed closely behind. Sam glanced around nervously for the parole officer who had agreed to meet them at the station, and was now late. Alfred waved.

Josh saw him, said something to his warder, and they marched toward them.

They saw immediately that the Army had taken youth from Josh. He looked older than his years, and in spite of his exposure to the southern sun, was pale and gaunt. His hair, thinner and graying, had recently been cut badly. He walked with mincing steps, flinching almost imperceptibly, bothered by an injury. Overall, he looked like an abused turkey; his excess skin hanging on atrophied muscle.

It was not until he closed and made eye contact with Josh and saw his crooked smile that Sam felt certain it was his brother. He embraced him under the disapproving eye of the Military Policeman.

"Don't worry, ah...?" Sam said to the M.P., raising his voice to be heard over the sound of people prating and grunt of engines reverberating in the cavernous building.

"Sergeant Olson," the big soldier replied, "and he's my worry until signed for."

Sam nodded. Olson was all trooper; he'd have to be to make rank in the peacetime army. "Don't worry, Sergeant, a police officer will be here shortly to sign your papers."

Alfred embraced Josh. With a tremulous voice he managed, "Good to have you back."

Josh shuddered, looking for an instant like he was going to break down, but he contained himself. Sam watched him draw himself together and go calm. Standing handcuffed and at the disposition of others, Josh watched and waited like a caged animal anticipating a long awaited release.

Sam, getting edgy, spoke up, "Station Security said we can use one of their offices." He pointed to a row of doors, "I suggest we wait in there. It will be quieter."

Sergeant Olson nodded agreement, and they headed through the milling crowd toward the doors. As they moved, a tall man in a gray raincoat and hat carrying a thin black attaché case approached, waving to get Sam's attention.

Sam saw him, "Hey, Stan, you had me worried."

"Stan Mitchell with the Office of Parole," he introduced himself, his quick dark eyes surveying the small group. "Sorry I'm late, but the streets are all slush." He brushed wet snow from his shoulders and shook his hat adding droplets of water to the already slick floor tile.

"We're heading for the office."

"Good," Stan said, "lead on."

Sam went to a door marked Conference Room. He held it open as the party filed in.

From the ceiling, ten feet above, fluorescent lights illuminated a room sparsely but adequately furnished with a large folding table and a stack of folding metal chairs. It was stark but utilitarian. Sergeant Olson grabbed two chairs, one in each hand, and placed them at tableside, his nearest the door. Nobody was leaving the room without passing him. After removing Josh's coat, he placed him on a chair then settled heavily on his own. The tiled room, suddenly filled with the rattle of metal chairs, smelled of stale air and dirty ashtrays.

Stan Mitchell, assuming his role as Parole Officer, was the first to speak; "You know why we're here." He opened his case and produced a sheaf of papers. He selected a few and replaced the rest. "Fortunately, we only need these," he said, passing them to the Sergeant.

Sergeant Olson reached inside his vest and withdrew a folded manila envelope. He pushed it across the table to Stan. Stan flipped through the documents, signed a pair and passed them back along with his pen. The M.P. signed copies and passed them back to Stan.

Sam sat stoically watching the paper shuffling, realizing that Josh's status change, his freedom, was bound up in the mundane action.

Josh sat without movement, his manacled hands on his lap, his breathing shallow, and his eyes following the drifting papers.

Done, Stan Mitchell placed the papers neatly in his case. He stood and stated formally, "I accept responsibility for the prisoner."

Sam watched a fear form in Josh's eyes.

Sergeant Olson moved to Josh and removed his handcuffs, saying, "He's all yours." There was a hint of resignation in his voice.

Josh rubbed his wrist and said, "Thanks, Sarg. No hard feelings."

Sergeant Olson looked disdainfully at Josh. Turning to Sam, he said, "I hope you know what you're doing." He folded his documents, pushed them into a pocket and stalked from the room.

Sam stood and took Josh's hand. "Welcome home," he said as Alfred joined them, arms on shoulders, in a quiet embrace.

Stan allowed them their moment then said, "Sam, if you and Alfred will excuse us, I have some things to tell Josh. Just the two of us," he shrugged, "it's policy."

'We'll wait outside."

Stan left after conferring with Josh, and Sam, motioning with his hands, said, "Mom will be waiting; we can talk in the car."

Free of the army and with Stan Mitchell gone, Josh's demeanor changed. No longer the quiet, apologetic, remorseful prisoner, he became talkative, almost buoyant. Rubbing his wrists where the handcuffs had rubbed, he said, "Boy, am I glad to see you guys." His voice was pitched with excitement and he rambled on, "I thought I'd never get out of the goddamn army. What a bunch of rednecks. You wouldn't believe it, talk about tight-ass. This is great."

Seated alone in the rear seat, Josh spread his arms expansively. "Let's stop for a beer," he said, pointing to a corner bar with a flashing neon sign. As an after thought, he asked, "Where's Ernie?"

Alfred stated flatly, "He's working."

Somehow, Sam wasn't surprised by Josh's abrupt change in behavior. To remind him of his status, he asked, "Didn't Stan say no drinking?"

"Well, sure, but he's gotta say that."

Sam shook his head at the response. "I notice you're walking kind of gingerly. You injured?"

Reminded of his pain and recalling the source, Josh said, "Zoo keepers at the stockade are pretty clever with a night stick," his cheek twitched as he remembered. "They work you over without leaving any marks. They didn't approve of my 'alleged proclivities'. So, I've got some hurting inside. The army doctor said it was all my imagination, but he couldn't explain this." Josh held his hand over the rim of the front seat.

They looked at his hand. The back of it was concave, and the knuckles were popped out of normal alignment.

"One of the guards stomped on it," Josh explained, "they claimed I caught it in a cell door." He fell back on his seat. "If you didn't get me out of there, they'd have busted every bone in my body, one by one."

At that moment, Sam felt confident that he'd done the right thing, and hoped that Emma would understand. He said, "Unless you want to end up back in the zoo, I suggest you play by Stan's rules. No booze." The neon sign faded in the rear window as he maneuvered through the slush. "And I mean it!"

Alfred lit a cigarette and offered one to Josh.

"No thanks," Josh said, "they didn't allow smoking, and I got out of the habit."

Alfred put the pack back in his pocket, and said, "Notice you don't have any luggage."

Josh snorted, "Just a toothbrush. Olson kept the safety razor. Prisoners travel light."

Sam decided there would be no better time to explain Emma's conditions. Alfred had a right to sit in, as he had agreed to be Josh's shadow. He pulled the car to a curb on a residential street lined with the wet black trunks of leafless trees. He left the engine running and the heater blowing warm air.

Alfred said, "Crack the windows. It smells like a wet dog in here."

Sam turned, placing his arm on the seat back. He wanted to be in Josh's face. He looked in Josh's eyes and at his prematurely graying hair and drawn face. He had obviously been through hell. Sam studied his questioning eyes.

"What?" Josh asked.

He spoke frankly, "Stan's aren't the only rules. We have some others. First, Ernie and Alfred have agreed to keep you straight. You'll be living, traveling, working together. They'll keep you out of trouble. Second, and this is my personal rule, you are to stay away from my house, my wife and daughter. And, until I say otherwise, everyone else's wives and kids." Sam paused for emphasis, and took Josh's broken hand in his. He lowered his voice and, in an ominous tone, said, "If you break my rules, I will break your bones." Sam squeezed his hand until Josh's eyes teared and his arm trembled.

Josh cried, "Don't worry, Sam, don't worry." He was shaking in his seat.

Sam released his hand.

"I'm thankful for what you've done. I know you stuck your necks out. I'm okay with this; you won't be sorry."

Relieved by Josh's apparent acceptance, Sam said, "Good." At the same time, he asked himself, *Why do I feel so uneasy about this?*

Alfred, watching Josh, blew smoke out the open window.

CHAPTER 40

April 1939

Josh settled into the routine. Waking every morning Monday through Friday in response to Ernie and Alfred grumbling across the hall, he threw the bed covers off and planted both feet on a small throw rug. I can do this, he told himself. Four feet away, Wilbur slept, his breathing slow and rhythmic. Grabbing his pants and shirt, he dressed as if in a bad dream. Once downstairs, he jostled his brothers for five minutes in the bathroom.

Invariably, Alfred said, "This house needs another can."

Lizzy watched her three sons move resolutely through their morning routine. She saw them moving around, dressing, and eating, allowing each other space, as though the wrong move could tip the entire day into a malignant spin. Up and dressed for hours, she had breakfast prepared and three lunch buckets standing ready. On the table she placed two mugs of amber tea for Alfred and Ernie, and a cup of coffee for Josh.

"Just one of the bad habits I picked up in the army," he said.

Army coffee served in stainless steel bowls was vile, but his mother's was worse. Decades of brewing tea had ruined her for any other beverage. Disguising the impact of the syrupy coffee with scones smothered in jam, Josh got it down and the caffeine dragged him into the day.

From the back seat of Alfred's black 1935 Ford, Josh watched houses slide by. It was a short drive to the factory where at 7 AM his mind-numbing shift began. Walking past the security shack with two company guards watching, Josh felt a chill and the short hairs on his neck stiffen. He fought the sensation that he was entering a stockade as the gates closed behind him. *What if they won't let us out?* He was near panic; his stomach soured.

The engine assembly area of the plant was housed under a roof covering almost ten acres. Naked steel bar joist supported by 'I' beams ran in parallel rows sliding off to the horizon, an endless cage. Trapped under the roof hung a yellow-gray cloud of polluted mist. The effect was surreal. Feeling confined, Josh pulled at his clothes, loosened the crotch of his pants, swung his arms, shrugged his shoulders. Anything to feel loose.

The noise level was so high that after a short numbing period, Josh didn't hear it. The clanging of metal on metal, the tearing of sheet metal, grinding of spinning abrasive wheels on bearing surfaces, the high pitched whine of electric motors, all combined to desensitize his auditory nerves. Men in clouded safety glasses moved about, deaf to their torturous surroundings.

Josh could scream and no one would hear. The prospect of facing eight hours performing a repetitive task, breathing foul air, bombarded by continuous noise, challenged his resolve. In his gut, Josh knew he couldn't continue to do it.

But he tried. Josh stood his place beside the assembly line running one hundred and twenty pieces per hour and tried to ignore the buzzing in his head. Across from him, a small man with a foul mouth, he knew only as Al, mirrored his actions—gathering four hex nuts from a long metal tray and starting them on four threaded studs protruding from the engine block, fifteen times an hour. The line kept running, engines kept coming, and the men scurried to keep up. Down the line, men with air-powered wrenches drove the nuts with a searing rat-a-tat-tat.

Josh was sweating; he had a sinus headache. He felt an annoying trickle down his back. He wiped the sweat from his brow with a shirtsleeve. Flicking four nuts from the tray he was about to start them when Al gave a bone-shaking scream. Josh stood amazed as the little man, his eyes wild, gathered nuts from the tray and flung them high into the air. Al shouted obscenities, "Fuck, shit, damn," while flinging the eight-cornered missiles. Some nuts bounced with a ringing noise off the steel bar joist overhead, others caromed off machines. Josh and the men around him jumped away from the assembly line and out from under the raining nuts.

Josh smiled as a man beside him swore, "Ouch, goddamn it."

Al screamed and scattered more nuts. When he'd emptied the tray, Al dropped his weary arms and looked around at coworkers staring at him. Emptied, his face vacuous, he slumped against a machine and started to weep.

Someone punched the ALL STOP button causing an abrupt unaccustomed quiet.

Josh stared, entranced, "Guess you never know what the other guy's thinking."

"Jesus Christ," someone sympathized.

Josh waved his arm signaling the foreman for relief. He watched as two men pulled a sobbing Al from the area. When the relief man arrived, Josh headed for the rest room.

In a toilet stall, he removed a silver pint flask from inside his shirt and took a long pull of the throat-searing vodka. Sucking stale air, he felt an instant burning relief. He sighed and took another pull. Josh raised the flask in a salute to his supplier. Sinking to the seat, he took another swallow and sat reading the graffiti scratched into the gray metal partitions. He pressed a thumb and knuckle against his eyelids. "One life to live, and I ain't going to spend it here."

Al wasn't missed. The assembly line ran as persistently as the April rain. Josh swore each day would be his last. He was mulling over his options, thinking about quitting when Bullach, his foreman, appeared with a relief man. He tapped Josh on the shoulder and said, "Come with me."

Now what? Josh trailed after Bullach.

George 'Spider' Bullach was a large framed man with a huge bald head, thick heavy features, long hairy arms and distance-eating stride. Josh had to jog to keep up. They left the assembly line and headed for an area choked with machinery. The air got oily-dense. Josh felt he could part it like sodden draperies, as they moved among the low gray broaches boring cylinder blocks, and precision grinders processing crankshaft bearings. Men tending the machines were deeply engrossed and Josh and Bullach passed unnoticed.

They turned into a cul de sac and Bullach said, "Here we are."

Josh looked into a U-shaped area closed on three sides by identical machines. Metal castings were entering the U hanging on the hooks of a chain conveyor about six feet high. A separate conveyor at shoulder level ran below the other. Arriving empty and leaving with finished pieces, the conveyor was within arm's length of the operator. In the center of the U stood a man in knee-high rubber boots and a yellow rubber apron. Josh wondered about the need for the rubber until the operator unlocked one of the machines and a greenish fluid coolant splashed the surroundings.

Josh watched in amazement as the operator, an automaton in yellow, removed a finished part from an opening machine and hung it on the lower, exiting conveyor. He then took an unfinished part from the upper conveyor and, flipping a lever, locked it into place. This caused the synchronized machine to the operator's right to unlock and open with a finished piece. Turning to the machine to his right, he repeated the process and the third machine opened. As he turned, his boots squished on the floor soaked in coolant, and lubricant. The lime-green machines shined in the dampness and whined as they ground on. Smog filled the air, and the operator turned and turned.

Bullach stood behind Josh as they watched the operation. He said to Josh, 'We'll get you a pair of boots and an apron and get you started."

Josh said, "Fuck that."

Bullach pivoted, his big nose pointed between Josh's eyebrows. 'What did you say?"

Josh said, "I ain't doing that. Get yourself a trained monkey, one that breathes green air."

Bullach sighed, his shoulders slumped. "Tell it to the General Foreman."

Josh shrugged, "Lead on. I'll tell it to a four-star general. I ain't doin' that shit."

Bullach said, "Wait here," and entered the General Foreman's office.

Left standing, Josh slumped against the wall. He considered the irony of the situation, they probably thought they were doing him a favor, taking him off the line. He sighed and brushed his lips, thinking of the flask resting in his locker. He'd never been in the office area before. He looked down the empty hall. The floor tile gleamed like the surface of a pool. He guessed it must be how the upper crust lived—nice and clean, and no noise. He turned a shoe on its side and made a black mark on the tile. Maybe I should write, 'Josh got his ass chewed here.'

The door opened and Builach said, "Come in."

Josh was sprawled on the living room couch gazing out the window at the street lamp when Sam eased his Chevy to the curb. Sam guessed Josh was thinking, 'Here's Sam with his speech.' Two days had passed since Josh's suspension, and now it was the weekend. Josh was probably wondering why he hadn't appeared before this. As Sam thumped across the porch, he saw Josh sit rigidly upright on the couch.

Sam was in slacks, wrinkled white shirt and loose tie. It had been another ten-hour day. He moved like he was carrying a heavy weight and looking for a place to set it down.

In a jocular tone, Josh said, "You look like shit. You've got bags under your eyes, and, maybe it's the light, I think I see some gray. You better sit down and take a load off."

Sam looked down the hall past Josh, and asked, "Where is everybody?"

"Good evening to you too," he tossed a Life magazine onto an end table jostling a lamp.

Sam looked at him and shrugged, "Sorry, long day…where's Mom?"

"She's in the cellar sorting laundry or something. She'll be up in a minute. Sit down." Josh pointed to a stuffed chair. "The twins have gone to the corner store, Wilbur is upstairs on the short wave listening to some native jabber on Timbuktu."

Sam sat, took his shoes off and began to massage his toes. "Amazing how your toes are connected to your ass," he said, causing Josh to smile crookedly. "Rub your feet and your ass feels lighter."

Josh leaned forwards, his forearms on his knees. "How come your ass is so heavy?"

"Well, for one thing, I spent most of yesterday on the road from Hartford Connecticut with a carload of guys. And, today was another ten hour routine grind."

"Connecticut? What the hell you doing there?"

Sam unbuttoned his shirt sleeves and rolled them to his elbows. "The company sent us there to study the Pratt and Whitney aircraft engine." Sam laughed, "Can you imagine, a Pennsylvania stump-jumper building aircraft engines?"

Josh studied him sitting dog-tired. He observed, "Tired as you are, your back is straight and you seem full of energy. I envy you your life and your sense of purpose. I don't know how you do it."

"God damn it, Josh," Sam lost it. He slammed his open hand on the arm of the chair. He stood and huffed pacing the room. "There are still ten million men out of work in this country, Hitler is in Austria, the world is about to go to war. We are about to jump aircraft production from one to one hundred fifty per hour...how can you not do it?" Sam threw his hands in the air, "and, you refuse a job." His face flushed with exasperation. He stared at Josh, "I should break your other goddamn hand."

Josh folded his hands in his lap.

Sam watched as Josh withdrew into himself. He stopped pacing and pointed his finger at his solar plexus, "You know you don't have any choice...No job, no parole. You're walking a very thin line. If you weren't my brother, you'd be in custody right now." He looked at Josh's expressionless face. "Christ," he said, "I'm talking to a wall."

Lizzy appeared, a shadow in the doorway.

Sam put his hand on Josh's shoulder. "Monday," he said deliberately, "you are going back to work, wherever they need you. Monday evening you can tell Stan that you're holding down a job."

Sam ran his fingers through Josh's hair damp with perspiration. "You've got to stand up and do this. If you don't, instead of eating one of Mom's meals here with the family, you'll be in a cell gagging on shit-on-a-shingle."

Josh closed his eyes and nodded compliance.

Sam crossed the room to his mother. He embraced her as she mouthed a silent prayer. When she was still, he held her and said, "Talk to him. He must get back to work, all our promises depend on it. Talk to him."

"I'll do my best," she said, dabbing a corner of her eye with her apron.

Sam clenched his jaw, and sighed, "I know. Mom, I've got to go. Emma and I are meeting friends for dinner. I've got to get the baby-sitter."

"Go," she said, "we'll be all right."

Sam paused a moment and placed his hand on Josh. When he walked out the front door, his step was uncertain.

Sam parked in front of the house, got out, walked around and opened the passenger door. A blond girl of about fourteen years looked up at him wide-eyed. "Thank you," she said while struggling out of the front seat with an arm load of books. Sue explained, "I do my home work while Mary is sleeping."

He nodded his understanding. He thought she was cute, a little pudgy and self-conscious about her budding body. Sam wondered if she had grown since he'd last seen her or if it was his imagination. *Probably me,* he pushed his hat back, *half the time I don't know what's going on around me.* He closed the car door. *No wonder, chauffeur, disciplinarian, father, husband, engine-builder, lover I hope*, he chuckled at himself.

Declining his offer to help with her textbooks, Sue climbed the stairs. Sam watched her calves flex above her short stockings, and her hips shift and sway. *Did girls have legs like that when I was in school?*

A second thought rocked him as he reached the door, *What right had he to judge Josh?* His hand shook on the doorknob. Lust, how thin the line between thought and action.

"Hello, Sue," Emma said as they entered. She was dressed for the evening in a blue skirt that stopped just below her knees, a matching jacket and a small white hat with an accenting blue feather.

"Hi, Mrs. Freeman. You look nice."

"Thanks, Sue. Is that lipstick you're wearing?" Her gaze shifted to Sam. She noted his abstraction. His mind was elsewhere. "You still at work?" she asked.

He shook his head and kissed her on the cheek, "Sorry, just thinking. I'm home now." He looked into the dining room at Mary sitting alone at the table. He made a face, "Now what?"

"She's pouting," Emma said, using the low voice of a conspirator, "She doesn't want us to go out. She's not being a big girl."

Sam crossed the floor to Mary, and turned her in her chair. "My, you're a big girl. How old are you?"

She didn't speak but held up four little fingers.

"Oh, you are big," he said, "pretty soon you'll be five. Look who's come to see you."

On cue, Sue said, "Hi, Mary."

Mary whispered, "Hi."

Sam looked at Emma. "Give me a minute. I've got to freshen up." He kissed her, allowing his hand to drift low on her back. "You look lovely."

She looked at him. "Would you rather stay home?"

"Nonsense," he said, "It's Saturday night, we're going out."

In the car, Sam looked at his watch, it's face dim in the early evening light, "Eight o'clock, right on time." He looked through the windshield at familiar surroundings now mysterious in the changing light.

Emma smiled, "Only because everybody else is always late." She was studying his profile. "You're more handsome than ever. At the pace you keep, you should look thinner, ragged, disheveled. I don't know how you do it." Wrinkling her nose, she said, "I love that after shave."

The lights from passing cars crossed his face creating an unusual alternate shadow effect. He said, "You gave it to me."

Emma moved to the center of the front seat. She put her hand on his thigh. She asked, "Want to tell me about it?"

There was silence as Sam turned the windshield wipers on in response to a light mist.

Emma said, "Your day, I mean."

"I know what you mean."

"It's all right if you don't."

Sam rolled his window halfway down. 'It's starting to rain. I love the clean smell of it."

"It's just a shower."

"Yes…it's Josh." Sam answered the question hanging heavily between them. "He was suspended for refusing a job assignment."

"Oh," Emma cringed, her face paled.

Sam hurried to calm her, "It doesn't mean anything. I talked to him, he's going back to work Monday."

"It's started," she said, subdued. "He'll soon be out of his cage."

"When he's been back a week, I'll try to get him into Maintenance."

Emma stared out the window at the increasing rain. She whispered, "You didn't hear me." A droplet insinuated itself inside the rubber windshield molding, a slippery intruder hinting of more to follow. She heard the song of rubber on wet pavement. She pressed back into the seat. After a time, she said, "This evening, I think I'll have the lamb."

Sam thought her voice strangely distant. He placed his hand on her arm, and was alarmed at the urgency with which she withdrew.

Still brooding over Emma's response the night before, Sam opened the door to Mason's office. There was a musty odor. Sam wondered, *Doesn't he ever open a window?* He could use a breath of air, it had been a rough morning.

From behind his desk, Mason grunted, "Sam, sit down."

The greeting was perfunctory, unlike Mason who was a people-person by nature and training. Alarm bells sounded as Sam took a seat in front of the wide oak desk. He sat watching the General Superintendent's bald head bob almost imperceptibly as he scanned the papers spread before him.

Mason pushed the paperwork aside, looked at Sam and said, "I see the changeover has fallen behind schedule by almost a week."

No, "How's the family" or "Nice weather." Sam felt his throat go dry, and the worm of insecurity squirming in his guts. He had to swallow hard and moisten his throat before replying, "Four days, as of this morning." He knew better than to offer excuses, though he could think of a few.

"When I gave you this job, I expected one hundred per cent from you. Is that what I'm getting?" Mason settled back in his chair, his cold steel eyes on Sam.

Sam knew there could be only one answer, "Yes, Sir."

Mason leaned forward, slipping one thumb under a suspender, the other under his chin. "Homer says you requested a job in Maintenance for your brother."

Ah, that's it. His stomach sank. "Yes."

"You know, Sam, it's always a mistake to let personal problems interfere with your job." Mason drew a hand over his pate. "Because he's your brother, what's his name, Josh, I approved it. But, let me tell you, he better settle down. Any more crap from him and he's out the door...and, Sam, if you don't keep your personal life outside the plant, I can't guarantee your job either."

"Jesus Christ," Sam jumped to his feet, startling Mason. He paced, waving his arms, "I've busted my ass for you people, and this is the thanks I get." He put both hands on Mason's desk and leaned over him. "Don't worry about a couple goddamn days. We'll be ready when you are. And, as for my brother, the only thing you'll hear about him is that I'm kicking his ass."

Mason grinned. He stepped from behind the desk and put his hand on Sam's shoulder. "That's what I wanted to hear." He walked to the window and looked out at the river. "When Central Office calls, they want to know what we've done for them today. They don't give a shit about yesterday. Today's how they measure us, and that's why we have to stay on top of our game."

Sam couldn't stay silent. He blurted, "I'm on top of my goddamn game."

Mason turned from the window. "You'd better be."

He saw that as controlled as Mason was, the demands and stresses of the job were getting to him too. Feeling a sudden empathy, Sam said, "I'll get it done."

"I believe you," Mason started to his desk, then turned to Sam headed for the door, "Sam, on your way back across town stop at a cemetery. Let me know how many indispensable people you find there."

Damn, I better stop worrying about Josh and cover my own ass. He allowed the heavy door to drift closed behind him. Listening to the hiss of the pneumatic closer, he bit his lip.

CHAPTER 41

April 1939

Ernie stared out the road-dirty bus window at a green sign with gold lettering; it read, Binghamton. He had begun to believe he'd never reach the unassuming crossroad town. Then the lumbering bus slid through Endicott and Johnson City the shoe-leather towns to the west. He stood in the narrow aisle and flexed his knees to relieve the bunched muscles of his legs and lower back. It was a long ride from Buffalo, and it seemed they'd stopped in every one of New York State's four-corner villages, some with only a post lamp, a bench, and no visible rest facilities. It had been a long night of dark anonymous countryside, rumbling tires, and diesel exhaust. A clock on the station wall read 9:12 AM.

Moving slowly, shuffling behind a bent woman and a palsied old man, he exited the bus. In the east, the morning sun had climbed over the rooftops, and chattering whirling sparrows promised a warm spring day. The smell of breakfast cookery rode on bacon fumes and coffee vapors over the morning air. Ernie felt his stomach begging. Careful to avoid the green remnants of a broken bottle and a small puddle of sticky liquid swarming with flies, he stepped along a concrete sidewalk. A large plate glass window spotted with community posters exposed an eatery with a long narrow counter and small wooden tables. Behind a counter lined with three-legged stools, a crab-like man with a sunken chest and narrow shoulders hunched over an oily black grill half hidden by a steaming mountain of home fried potatoes. He was flipping eggs with casual ease and singing, "You cry, I fry; you ring, I bring."

The smell of warm toast and underlying tone of easy morning conversation lent Ernie a relaxed homey feeling as he filled an empty counter seat between two disinterested diners, and watched the short-order cook. He dropped his small overnight bag to his feet. To a waitress with dark hair and darker eyes standing with a raised eyebrow, he said, "Four eggs scrambled, home fries, double order toast, and coffee."

She studied his thick neck and broad shoulders, noting he filled the space between the two customers, and said, "You're a big one, ain't ya?" To the cook's bent back, she called, "Double with fries, scrambled"

Ernie devoured the food, relishing the down-home flavor. He downed his third cup of coffee while watching the large-framed hard-edged waitress at work as she skirted around the diner serving food and retrieving china. He waited for her to stride in his direction, wiped his mouth with a paper napkin and asked, "Where's the Methodist church in town?"

She stopped bustling and looked inquiringly at Ernie, surprised by the question. "You a minister?" she asked with a grin.

Ernie, relaxed on his seat, remained dead pan.

Seeing he wasn't amused, she lost her grin and said, "There are two: one in a neighborhood with a little money that thinks they're Presbyterian, and one in a poorer section that acts like Baptists. Which one you lookin' for?" She pressed her jelly-spotted apron to the counter.

"Not sure."

"Well, if you go stand on the corner to the right of the door, you can see the poorer one. The other is a pretty good hike from here on the far west side of town." She removed his empty plate and utensils.

"Thanks," Ernie handed her a dollar, "keep the change."

"Thank you." She appraised him as he stood. "if you don't find what you're looking for, stop back. I'll be here." She swung her hips walking away.

Ernie walked to an old stone building with a corner tower topped by a cross made of thick wooden timbers. The sun, now in the south-southeast, sent glancing rays off a large stained glass window high over the front door. The building was like a proud woman long past her prime but strong. He found a wiry little man in paint-spotted work clothes scraping old blistered varnish off the imposing front door. His tool squeaked as he forced it along the visible grain. As he worked, he hummed a tune Ernie didn't recognize.

"If you put anything on that, it won't be dry for tomorrow's service."

The man turned with arthritic languor. He stopped humming. He looked at Ernie's wide shadow on the curved stone steps. "Just going to prime the bare spots," he drawled, "finish the whole door on Monday." He craned his neck to stare up at Ernie. "You here to help?"

Ernie chuckled, "Sorry. I'm looking for the Reverend Christer."

The old man nodded, "Well, you won't find him here. He's the minister on the west side. It's about ten miles." He looked at Ernie's overnight bag. "Walking or riding?"

Ernie shrugged as if to say, *what do you think?*

Waving his scraping tool in understanding, he said, "Just walk over a block to the main drag westbound and stick out your thumb. Not far. Big red brick church on the north side of the road."

"Thanks."

"You going to the wedding?"

They were good directions. Ernie thanked the young driver of the pickup truck that carried him to the edge of town. The church loomed in the center of two acres of fine-trimmed lawn, a stones throw off the highway. It was twice the size of the old church in town and, with its' clean lines, bright trim and landscaping, bore a fresh modern air. There were two large open-sided white canvas tents pitched in the center of the expanse of green. The reflected rays of the sun on canvas bothered his eyes and he looked away to the stone-surfaced parking lot behind the church. It held fifteen vehicles and more were entering off the road.

Self-consciously, Ernie brushed his rough shirt and trousers. "Right on time," he said. The painter had said one of the minister's daughters was getting married. He decided to wait until the pews were filled with invited guests, then slip into a seat in the back.

He stood in the shade of a silver maple and watched cars arrive and people file into the church. Wishing he had a watch, he looked up at the sun alone in a pale blue cloudless sky. *What's the difference,* he thought waving his hand at an annoying fly. When it appeared that the last guest had entered, he crossed the lawn and quietly crept through the front door. He edged his way to a seat at the far end of the last row.

He smiled at a primly dressed grim-faced woman that stared suspiciously at him. "Grounds keeper," he explained.

She twitched her nose and turned away.

An organist was playing a medley of like-sounding compositions waiting for the crowd to settle. An older, thinner Reverend Christer stood behind the altar. A tow-headed boy in a white robe was lighting candles. He saw Mrs. Christer seated in the front row. He wondered where the daughters were, then realized they must be in the wedding party. Ernie looked up at the high-vaulted ceiling. Slowly rotating fans were pushing the spring air that entered through narrow open windows.

The organist stopped playing and, for a moment, silence fell over the congregation. Ernie was giddily returned to the Sunday mornings of his youth. He listened dreamily until a reverberating note issued from the pipes. The crowd rustled, skirts and frock coats stirred, and the familiar notes of the wedding march took hold as necks craned and everyone turned in building expectation to watch for the bride.

Two young men unrolled a satin fabric down the aisle with practiced motion. A slender maid, right out of King Arthur's court, casting rose petals followed them. Behind her inched a timid young boy, a ring bearer, who turned his head in wonder at the people on both sides of the promenade.

Ernie's knees weakened, he grasped the knurled end of the pew; the boy was a miniature Josh! *Another Josh—from a smaller cookie cutter.* He slipped into a sweaty disassociated state. The organ sounds thumped in his head. Bride's maids and maids-of-honor passed vaguely noticed by Ernie in his confusion and disbelief. He felt ill. He turned to a portly gentleman in a coat and vest and asked, "Who is the little boy?"

"The bride's son," he nodded, "she's a grass widow."

As if summoned by a magic wand, the bride appeared in a cloud of lavender organdy. Ernie studied the remembered face. Surrounded by lace, she was prettier, serene. Lisa was a strikingly beautiful woman. Eyes bright, chin high, she floated confidently forward.

Ernie slumped, giving in to a tidal wave of emotion. Eyes closed, he sat swinging, watching hummingbirds, sniffing perfume, a bare-foot innocent. Opening his eyes, he bowed his head and tried to remember how old Lisa was when he'd last seen her. *How old when Josh last saw her?* He shook, filled with loathing for his brother. Tendons drew tight in his thick neck, his shoulder muscles cramped, and his head throbbed..

The man beside him asked, "You all right, son?"

Ernie rose and walked slowly out of the church, blood thundering in his ears. Reaching a shade tree, he sank to the grass and sat holding his head waiting for his rage to subside. As his pulse slowed, he realized he needed to talk to Lisa. There was something he had to know. Walking to the parking lot behind the church, Ernie lingered, waiting for someone, anyone he could question about the newlyweds.

Saturday and Sunday nights, Ernie lodged at the YMCA. Other men, strangers, noted his physical size and brooding disposition and gave him a wide berth. Mornings, before others stirred, Ernie walked the streets and streams, gazed at the river, and, counting clouds, wondered at the vast sky. Deeply troubled by the appearance of the boy, a young Josh, he was inconsolable, restless and impatient.

In the parking lot, milling among strangers, he had learned that Lisa and her husband didn't plan a honeymoon. He was an engineer working for a firm in town and couldn't take the time. They were building a new home in Endicott, but until it was ready, they were staying with her parents, the Reverend and Mrs. Christer.

Monday morning, beads of dew lingering on the grass, Ernie stood examining the parsonage situated on a hillside street a mile removed from the church. It was an expansive home two stories high with a central tower embraced by gabled wings and wide porches. The tower resembled a steeple and lent the house a church-like appearance. Two porches, partially hidden by heavy growth of mock orange and lilac bushes, were well supplied with furniture, white wicker tables and chairs, settees and chaise lounges. It was a setting designed for Sunday fresh air bible reading.

On the lawn, a robin cocked his head listening for tunneling worms. Ernie watched it as he tried to decide how best to approach the bride of only two days, especially as she was surrounded by family. He thought he'd simply walk up and say hello. Standing on the porch near the front door, he could hear intermittent conversation and the random noise of people moving about in the house. His eyes were drawn to a white wooden swing swaying with the morning breeze, The sight evoked such unsettling memories that he struggled to maintain his resolve. He exhaled, drew himself together, set his jaw and knocked on the screen door. For a moment, the inhabitants fell silent, then there was the sound of purposeful footsteps on hardwood and conversation resumed.

Lisa's sister Sarah appeared and stood wide-eyed at the door. "My word, Ernest, is it you?"

Her eyes were the same disturbing blue he remembered. He moved uneasily, "It's me."

Sarah was suddenly, obviously suspicious. "What are you doing here?"

"I work here in town," he lied, "and heard about the wedding. I just want to congratulate Lisa."

Sarah stood with the door closed considering him. He had assumed she was going to dismiss him when she said, "Wait here." She faded into the house leaving the screen door closed. There was a sudden flurry of words inside followed by a long silence.

Ernie endured the painful lull imagining the family's confusion and uncertainty. He regretted coming. Despairing, intimidated by the whispered past, he turned to go.

"Don't leave."

At the sound of Lisa's voice, Ernie paused on the top step. He stared out over the wide lawn, afraid to turn. The creak of door hinges sent a shiver through him. He turned and looked at the woman he'd watched walk down the aisle such a short time ago. Her eyes were moist. Fearing his voice would fail him, he whispered, "Hello, Lisa."

"Ernie" Lisa raised a hand and reached for him.

He fought the subtle summons of her perfume. He took her hand and, without thinking, uttered, "You never said good-bye."

She paled, a hand pressed to her breast. "I couldn't, I just couldn't. I'm so sorry." She placed her hand briefly on his cheek before turning to a white settee. "Let's sit over here."

Seated, they were quiet, each at a loss as to how to understand or explain the lapse of time and turn of events. He studied Lisa's face, her high cheekbones and flawless skin, features as delicate as dew, with wide compassionate eyes set like jewels. It was the face he remembered, that disturbed his dreams, more mature but the same. "I was at the wedding," he said.

"Oh," she turned away.

He saw that she understood. "I saw your little boy." He refrained from adding cruelly, my nephew.

Lisa's eyes were closed, her head bowed. "I was so young. I couldn't resist him. Josh was so smooth, so persuasive. He gave me things; I let him…it was so innocent at first," she sobbed, "I let him go too far."

He absorbed the pain of her words. He placed his hand on hers and felt the clammy accumulation of embarrassment and self-loathing. Ernie wished he could ease her suffering.

She shrugged, stating the obvious, "I got pregnant." Lisa straightened, sifting erect on the wicker seat. She looked away. In a voice draped with anguish, she said, "Josh laughed at me."

Lisa's pain, echoing in the corners of his mind, left Ernie feeling tainted, shamed by his brother. Lacing his fingers to steady them, he thought, *if Josh was here, I'd kill him.*

Lisa sighed, and in a manner tempered by time and contemplation, said, "I was bitter for a long time, but I've forgiven him." Sensing the depth of Ernie's seething emotions, she said, "You must, too."

He was stunned by the total disregard for others, Lisa, himself, families, evident in Josh's actions. Ernie thought, as he rose to pace the deck, *He should burn in hell.*

She watched him. She said, "Jon is a wonderful boy, and Davis loves him as I do. He'll be a good husband and father…Ernie, look at me!" When he turned to her, she said, "I'm going to be all right. Ernie, you have to forgive and forget."

Looking at her with swimming eyes, he saw the innocent, unassuming girl on the swing, his girl friend of summers gone by. He slumped, burdened by great sadness.

Lisa looked surprised to see him shudder as he said, "I'm not that big."

CHAPTER 42

May 1939

Sam knew when he entered the kitchen that Emma was gone. The room was spotless. There were no dishes in the sink, no pots simmering on the stove, and it was quiet, cat's breath quiet. No radio playing, no screaming or giggling. No welcome arms to envelope, welcome and comfort him. He'd entered a house not a home. Sam dropped his coat on a chair and suppressed a deep sigh. He was deflated. Emma had lost faith in him, in his ability to protect her and Mary. Her absence said *you care more about Josh than Mary and me.*

Propped on edge in the center of the table was a white envelope. It seemed more threatening than a bloodied ax. Sam raised the unsealed flap and removed the note.

Dear Sam,

I love you. You must believe that. But, I fear for us, Mary and me. We've gone home. Come for us when it's safe.

Love, Em

Sam's hand was shaking as he dropped the note to the table. Feeling dizzy, he walked to the sink and held on. When he opened his eyes, he stood staring out the window into dark emptiness. With thumb and forefinger, he squeezed the bridge of his nose. "Safe? Where in this world was it safe?" He had to bring them back; he needed them here. Without them his life was empty, pointless. "Damn." When he could least afford to be away from the plant, he needed time off. He turned the cold water faucet on. Cupping his hands, he captured the running water and brought it to his face.

It never changes, Sam thought, steering the Chevy down into the valley. A vague mist drifted at chimney height, though as far as he could see, there wasn't an active stack. Strange, for a spring cleaning Saturday in May, something should be burning even though no one was working. He shrugged, thinking he must be too accustomed to the constant activity around the plant.

There were four men tossing horseshoes under the canopy of two ancient willow trees, and women and children at a picnic table as he turned a corner. The sight was enough to stir pleasant memories of his carefree youth in the valley: picnics and parties in paradise, *now, look at it,* The combined effect of reminiscence and anticipation had increased his concern about Emma's departure. *Would he be able to convince her of his intent and abilities when it came to Josh?*

What if Emma decided she was better off without him? The idea made him sick. He hadn't seen them for a week, a week of self-doubt, of haggling for time off, of relentless job pressure. Inward and outward pressures tore at him, boiled in him like magma ready to boil over. He knew that without Emma he would soon burst. Recently, he'd been spitting blood. "Ulcers," the plant doctor said, "bleeding ulcers." *Some get 'em, and some give 'em, he remembered with a sardonic chuckle.*

"Daddy, daddy."

Sam stood by the parked car and looked up the sloping walk. Mary ran towards him, her strawberry blond curls billowed in the wind. He dropped to one knee; joy welled in him as he swept her up and swung her around, her frilly blue dress alive in the spin.

Sam admired her, thinking, *You're as pretty as your mother.* He gave her a wet smooch on the neck and turned to see Emma watching.

With Mary alive and bouncing in his arms, he steadied his gaze on his wife. Emma was in a gray dress, white apron, and her hand, hanging at her side, held a wooden spoon. She was pale, without makeup, and wearing her hair drawn back in a disciplined bun. With a bonnet, she could pose for a stark charcoal sketch of an Amish mother. Sam lowered Mary slowly to the sidewalk.

"I must look awful...I haven't slept."

Was there ever a woman that didn't proclaim that? But, Sam was shaken; *where was the strong vivacious woman that was his wife? Where was the Emma he knew?* He was shocked. He'd failed to realize the reality, the depth of her fear. He'd failed her.

He folded her in his arms feeling for the spark of forgiveness. They stood gauging each other's resolve, as Mary tugged on Sam's pant leg and chanted, "I want to go home."

He studied Emma's face, searched her eyes, wondering what price she meant to extract.

She asked a question as if knowing the answer, "Has something changed?"

Sam pointed to the porch and said, "Let's talk in the shade." He took Mary's hand and they strolled up the walk. When they'd settled on the porch, Sam and Emma in separate chairs, Mary on his lap, he said, "One thing hasn't changed—I can't function without you."

Emma stared out over the lawn, a green carpet spread over the hill. She said, "It's strange, there are no dandelions. Where do you suppose they've gone?"

Perplexed, he asked, "What?"

"The dandelions are gone...Is Josh gone?"

What could he say? Sam stumbled, "No...I did get him a better job. One where he has to think, where he's not as confined. Where he's stimulated. And, Alfred says Josh is settling down, says he is crazy about a girl at the bank where they cash their checks." Sam quietly kicked himself for using the word crazy. "Emma, Honey, Josh is growing into a healthy routine, he's okay. Besides, everyone is on him like a new suit: me Alfred, Ernie, his parole officer, everyone.

"Em, you have to believe me. Josh is no danger to anyone. not you, Mary, anyone. Please, I guarantee it. It's safe, please come home." He set Mary aside, and knelt beside his wife, his hands on her arms. The familiar dusky perfume of her, the butter on warm bread smell of her, the bedroom and dining room sense of her, his deep visceral need of her crushed him, and he begged, "Baby, please, please come home."

She folded against him. She whispered, "They'll come back...the dandelions. They always come back. Bad seed always comes back."

He shuddered, afraid she hadn't heard, or didn't believe a word he said. He was frightened, *had fear driven her over the edge?* They swayed, embraced in dubious harmony.

Finally, Emma took his hand and pressed it to her breast. Her eyes were cold, removed. In a sharp tone that would permit no misunderstanding, she said, "You must swear on our daughter, that you will kill him if he touches us...say it," there were tears on her cheeks that belied her deep resolve, "say it, even if you don't mean it."

Sam's mouth was dry when he uttered, "He won't touch you."

"Say it."

He felt transparent and that she was looking through him. He began to sweat.

"Say it."

He had to, she required it. In a voice he didn't recognize, Sam said, "If my brother touches you, I will kill him. I swear it."

Her shoulders fell and she moaned. He saw that she didn't believe him, but had surrendered. *Had he won or lost?*

Mary jumped up on him, her small hands clenched behind his neck, "Home," she cried, "I want to go home."

CHAPTER 43

May 1939

The Monday morning in late May that Josh returned to work was sodden. The heavy moist air clung to every surface, grounding even the swirling clouds of sand flies. The rooftops damp and dripping, sidewalks and streets wet and treacherous for the unwary, and Josh's spirit was soaked. He had slipped into a dark spiritual pit and was treading water listlessly, not caring if he drowned. Detached, he wasn't sure he was sitting in the rear seat of Alfred's car staring at the back of Ernie's head, or that Alfred was dutifully driving. He pulled at his crotch, *Yeah, they're real, as real as my jewels.*

Josh knew something was wrong. Alfred mumbled to him every morning and answered if Josh addressed him, but Ernie was ominously quiet, never looked him in the eye. Ernie had a bug up his ass. Josh was puzzled. *Were they pissed because he was suspended and was returning to a cushy job? That's it, I embarrass them.* He didn't care.

Was there something else? Ernie had been a dark mystery since his long weekend. *What the hell is his problem?* Josh rubbed his eyes. He said, "Good thing Mom and Wilbur don't work with us, I'd have nobody to talk to."

He stared out a window and thought, *Screw it, I don't care.*

Who and what he did care about was Ivan and his endless supply of vodka. Ivan, nobody knew his real name, held the supply most critical to plant operations. Ivan was never around until you had the need and the money, then, like a genie, he appeared.

Josh reported to Bullach as instructed. The foreman's bald head gleamed after an hour in the plant's oily atmosphere. Bullach passed a shop towel over his pate and glared at Josh standing with his thumbs in his pockets.

"Cordy," the big man thundered, "they tell me you're too fragile for production." He spit a stream of tobacco juice into an inverted piston. "Bullshit."

Josh studied Bullach's strawberry nose. He smiled inwardly at the foreman's frustration at being unable to condemn this one man to an endless redundant hell. "Let it all out, Stan, I know how you feel."

"You have no idea how I feel, you son-of-a-bitch," he spat, "come with me." Stan Bullach took off at a half trot, like a man with his guts in an uproar, and Josh followed, lagging farther and farther behind.

"Wait for me," Josh called. Ahead, Bullach stood between two thumping hydraulic Goliaths, eyes bulging in his red face.

Bullach left him with Fred Wilson, millwright, who claimed he could repair anything. Flipping his thumb at Josh, Bullach said, "See if you can fix this," as he left.

Fred Wilson was a docile patient man with a moonlike face and a low center of gravity that had served him well on the lake boats where he had honed his skills. Between lakes Superior and Ontario, Duluth and Montreal on the St. Lawrence, he had kept propellers moving mountains of ore and grain, until his nagging wife brought him ashore—on shore to a power plant full of compressors and steam boilers on a ship that never strayed.

Now, Fred had a helper. He slipped a twelve inch crescent wrench into a back pocket of his blue coveralls and used a shop towel to clean his hands before offering one to Josh, "Mornin', son."

Josh took the offered hand and appraised Fred Wilson. He recognized him as belonging to that breed of men domesticated by women and work. Josh relaxed, he could suck up to Fred. "Mornin'."

Fred leaned against the bulk of a machine-green air compressor the size of a locomotive. He had steady honest eyes that fixed on Josh. "You're Sam Freeman's brother."

Josh wasn't sure whether it was a question or an observation, but he suspected Fred might not be as dull as he looked. "Half brother," he said.

Fred nodded. "Well, Josh, while you're working with me, it don't matter whose brother you are as long as you hand me the proper wrench when I call for one, or when I send you for something you come back with it. Pay attention to what I'm doing, keep your hands off all switches, and at the end of the day we can go home with all our fingers. Got it?"

"I got it."

For days, Josh thought he had it. *Had it,* he asked himself. *Had what?* The life of a drone, that's what he had. Fred Wilson was a nice guy, but, Jesus Christ, was he boring. And silent. Hours crept by as Fred fucked with a machine without a word, as though Josh wasn't there, didn't exist. Josh's skin crawled with tedium bugs. The incessant combined hum of pistons pushing, motors spinning, flow meters inching long minutes away, pressed at the base of his skull causing it to vibrate in sync with the quivering floor. He fought continually to suppress the screams that welled within him. His only release was in the vodka and day dreams and fantasies the genie brought.

Josh removed the padlock and slid the catch silently upward. The locker opened. He reached with a trembling hand for the flask of clear liquid. "God, I love potato juice." He twitched and looked around. *Had he spoken out loud?* He wasn't sure. It didn't matter, no one was in the locker room. It was the middle of a shift. Josh took a long pull on the flask and welcomed the burn in his throat. He pressed his forehead to the relative cool of the gray metal locker. He took another pull.

Ignoring altered photos of a nude Shirley Temple taped inside the locker door, Josh turned and leaned against the metal. It pressed torturously on his shoulder blades as he reached inside his pants. Curling his fingers around his scrotum, he admonished himself, "If you had any real balls, you'd get the hell out of here." He slid down the enameled surface of the locker and sat on a wooden bench. Struggling with his fragmented thoughts, he knew one thing for sure—Fred would be looking for him. "Get off your ass," he told himself.

"Took long enough."

Josh forced a serious expression and tried not to slur his words, "Supply didn't have any. I had to go to the Maintenance shop. They didn't want to give me any without a requisition slip." Josh gave Fred a box of brass shim stock.

"Sounds like those pricks." Fred shrugged his round shoulders as he opened the box.

Doesn't take much to make you happy, Josh mused while finding a seat to watch Fred piss endlessly with the shim stock. Josh snickered to himself, wondering if Fred fucked his wife as meticulously; contemplating, measuring, fitting, lubricating, inserting, never reaching a climax.

All the weeks dragged tediously on, but Josh thought this goddamn day would never end. Hours and hours he looked over Fred's shoulder as he disassembled and reassembled a compressor shaft. Over and over, it was maddening. The workweek was five days long, sometimes six for everybody in Maintenance and that included the Power Plant personnel. Maintenance droned on seven days a week, twenty-four hours a day, independent of production. The only time Josh envied anyone working production was when they ran a three-day week.

At the end of his shift, alone on the abandoned production floor he headed for the main gate. Walking along rows of machines and conveyors, Josh stepped with exaggerated care in the sly manner of the slightly drunk, a fearful trespasser in an iron graveyard.

He was headed for the main exit and the rows of time cards that lined the final passageway. Once there, he had to squint to find his card in the dim light, but he knew it was there, a blotchy record of his miserable wasted days. He knew other men feared the grim lottery, not knowing if at week's end the card would produce a paycheck with a pink slip. Josh didn't give a shit, though he assumed a check would be there and he could look forward to another shit week. That was how he thought of it, *Life's a shit sandwich. Every day, I wake up and take another bite.* He smirked, thinking he and Ivan could handle it. *Like hell he could.* He'd had it.

Josh held his lunch bucket open for the guard's inspection. *Think I've got a motor in there?* Everyone knew the story of the guy who smuggled a Cadillac out the door, piece by piece. *Bullshit.* He stepped out into the slashing glare of the afternoon sun and onto the parking lot simmering like a black cauldron. "Whew," cruel white light flashed off his retinas, and he rocked on his heals temporarily blinded. Fighting nausea, he heard Alfred call his name. Alfred—dependable as an oasis, as suffocating as a sand storm.

"Josh, over here! What took you so long."

Josh cautiously raised an eyelid. Alfred was leaning against the family sedan, a toothpick bouncing on his lower lip. Heat waves rose around his shoes; he looked like he was hovering.

Josh asked. "Wadda you mean?"

Alfred flicked the toothpick onto the gooey asphalt. "I been here since 3:15, it's after 3:30."

"Hey, you want to walk back to the Power Plant?" Josh tripped and almost fell but caught himself with a hurried step.

Alfred watched with jaundiced eye as Josh stumbled and recovered. "You been drinking?"

"I wish. It's the bright sun after working in the dungeon all day."

Alfred scoffed, "It's your life, but if you don't straighten up, your ass will be in a sling."

Josh fought the fire in his gut, "Don't worry about it."

Alfred slid into the dry heat of the car's interior. "I'm not worried, but you should be. If Sam saw you now, he'd beat the shit out of you."

Josh tossed his lunch bucket onto the cloth-covered rear seat causing dust particles to dance in the heat. "Sam ain't here. Take me to the bank." He slouched in the passenger seat as Alfred steered out of the parking lot. "The same weekend routine. Christ, I'm too bored to even pull my pud."

Tonawanda Street, the focus of Riverside activities on a Friday afternoon, was crowded with busses, cars, and delivery vans. The sidewalks squirmed with people gathered at week's end, shopping, banking, and strolling listlessly. Mothers tugged at youngsters, couples strolled hand in hand, men stopped to count the bills and change in slim white envelopes. A boisterous group of young men in baseball uniforms and tossing a softball was heading for the park and a hard-pan baseball diamond.

Josh scanned the vehicles lined at the curb. There were no open parking spots. Good. "Drop me off, and circle the block. I won't be long."

Alfred eased the car to a halt in front of the bank.

Josh opened the passenger door.

"Got your check?"

"Yes, Mom." Josh barked. He was out of the car standing in the heat of the sun. "Don't worry, if the bank has sufficient funds," he added sarcastically, "I'll cash this and be right out." He waved his paycheck at Alfred. "Be here."

A truck horn sounded a sharp blast behind the double-parked car.

"Yeah, yeah," Alfred grumbled as he watched Josh disappear into the bank. He put the car in gear and rolled slowly down the block and around the corner.

Ceiling fans turned ineffectually as Josh chose the shortest line in front of the four bank tellers. Stifling air hung unmoved at floor level. He ran his fingers inside his collar and looked at a sign on the rear wall. Emergency Exit. "I've got an emergency," he said.

"What?" A thin old man behind Josh asked with a worried frown, "What did you say?"

"I said, I hope there isn't another bank emergency." Josh smiled to himself. The old man looked like he was going to cry. Apparently he'd endured his share of bank failures."

"Next," a teller summoned Josh.

Alfred was on his third turn around the block. "What the hell is taking him so long?" he asked aloud. He slowed as a couple stepped off the curb and into the street. He continued driving after they'd passed. He thumped the steering wheel with the heel of his hand, "Ah." He slid into an open parking space two storefronts from the bank. The engine smelled like it was going to boil over. Alfred killed it and stepped carefully into the street.

Hurrying, Alfred looked into the Drug Store and the Hardware Store as, leaning with purpose, he strode to the bank. He scanned the surroundings in all directions. Josh was nowhere in sight. He opened the heavy door and surveyed the bank interior. There were few customers remaining. The black-spider hands of the round clock high on the wall were approaching closing time. Josh was not to be seen. Gone! Alfred looked at the door in the back wall and the Emergency Exit sign above.

"Shit."

Two blocks away, Josh entered a liquor store. A small bell attached to the door emitted a tinny sound. He stood looking down the lines of shelves stacked with bottles. He admired the diverse colorful labels.

The clerk, a thin middle-aged man, watched with obvious anticipation, as Josh said, "Who needs Ivan?" and pulled a thin white envelope from his pocket.

CHAPTER 44

May 1939

"Emma, please, we're going to be late." Sam stood watching her, his hand on the front door knob. He was dressed for the evening, a suit coat casually draped over his arm, his shoes a shining ebony.

Emma, wearing silk stockings and heels and a stylish green cocktail dress Sam had never seen before, gave Mary a stuffed garish looking clown. Bobo was Mary's bedtime companion. Emma's head bobbed as she gave the baby-sitter, Sue, last minute instructions. Mary, in flannel pajamas with attached feet, listened, her face pressed into Bobo's middle.

Sam heard Emma say, "We won't be late." He hoped she was wrong, they needed a good relaxing night on the town.

"That's okay, Mrs. Freeman. We'll be fine; you have a good time." Sam thought Sue sounded more mature than she looked. She affected a self-assured manner in her speech and attitude that sometimes required a double take on the part of the listener. Often an adult would question, did that youngster say that?

If Sam didn't know her, he would guess her age at twelve or thirteen. On the other hand, he observed silently, there are those legs. Girls or women, to Sam they were all a mystery.

"I'm coming," Emma smiled at Sam's exasperation.

"Wonderful," he noticed she faltered slightly. "Gin?"

"And tonic," she said, "it's been a long day."

Sam took her elbow as they moved down the steps to the car. The sunlight was lasting longer each day as June approached. Sam could see the blue chicory blossoms scattered amongst the burdock in a vacant lot across the street.

He opened the car door for Emma and, as if on cue, the street lamps turned on to replace the fading sun. In the car, he turned to her, "We don't do this often enough."

"True." She tugged her skirt down over her knees.

Sam kissed her cheek and breathed her perfume. "Ravishing," he said.

"That wasn't much of a kiss."

He kissed her on the neck, and ran his tongue over her earlobe avoiding her tiny diamond earring. "I don't want to spoil your makeup."

Emma feigned a sigh filled with longing, "We should have showered together."

He turned the ignition switch and the engine spun into life. "You're kidding. We wouldn't be dressed yet. Besides," he smirked, "we can shower later."

Emma slid closer on the seat as the car counted street lamps. She tossed her perfumed hair.

"What is that wonderful smell?"

"Chanel Number Five, from last Christmas. You gave it to me."

After a lengthy contemplative silence, Sam said, "I don't want to jinx the evening, but you seem to have let it go." He knew he didn't have to explain what 'it' was.

Emma settled back in her seat. "I spoke to your mother today."

Sam turned to her, trying to see beyond the placid eyes.

"Josh has settled down. She says he comes home from work limp as a rag. Wilbur has him interested in amateur radio. Apparently, he sleeps like the dead; they have to drag him out to work mornings." Emma opened a small silver handbag.

Gripping the steering wheel, Sam inhaled a silent, *Thank you Lord.*

"Anyway, I guess you're right though I still have trouble believing it. If they keep a tight rein, we can hope he'll be all right." She lit a cigarette.

He crinkled his nose, "I wish you wouldn't smoke those things."

Ignoring his wish, Emma turned a crank lowering the window an inch. Smoke slipped serpent-like into the night and sounds of the city slipped in, a horn sounded and a siren moaned over a distant tragedy. She said, "I'd have more confidence if he got some professional help."

"Who? A doctor? Minister? Stan keeps him straight."

"Stan's not enough. He's a baby-sitter." She studied Sam's face as he maneuvered in traffic. "There's a doctor at the hospital, a Doctor Reading. He's certified in Psychiatry. I think he'd do us a favor. It would be confidential."

Sam imagined she smiled at that. "Let's think about it."

She flipped the glowing cigarette out over the street. "Tonight I don't want to think about it. I want to pay too much for dinner, drink too much wine, and dance too long to music too loud. Tomorrow is Saturday and I'm off."

Sam nudged the Chevy into an open slot along the curb, and killed the engine. He turned to her and said, "And shower too long." He opened the door.

CHAPTER 45

May 1939

From the break wall along the Buffalo shore of the Niagara river, on a clear night, Josh could count the lights on the Canadian side, could see them spattered amongst the trees, the homes of the more affluent and occasional street lamps where the road met the river. He could see fishing boats trolling against the swift current and watch pleasure craft meander in midstream on a stream as black as the river Styx. He knew if injured stumbling along the wall he could slip into the cold water and die slowly, to be found bloated days later miles downstream.

A toothless man with the emaciated look of a career alcoholic sneaked a look at Josh nodding on the rock beside him. He took a long pull from Josh's second bottle. He kicked the first, now empty, into the black water and giggled as it bobbed away.

Thinking Josh was still conscious, he continued his story, his spongy lips slurring the words, "We wuz all working. A dollar if you stayed the whole day. It wuz dang hot, and we wuz in the open, no shade. Sun overhead, blazin' hot. Like the desert."

"I looked at my partner. He wuz soakin' wet. Damn, I said, Jeb, your cock is stickin' out. It wuz too. Like a tube of fresh ground sausage."

"Jeb sez, 'No it ain't.'"

The man wiped his nose on his sleeve and took another slug from the bottle.

I said, "It is stickin' out."

"Jeb sez, 'No it ain't.' You got to know Jeb, he's thicker'n any mule."

"I sez, Jeb, dang it, it's stickin' out."

"Jeb sez, 'Ain't stickin' out. I'm too tired. It's hangin' out.'"

"Hee, hee," the toothless vagrant giggled insanely and slapped Josh on the shoulder. Josh toppled over, face down in the rock and gravel.

"Goddamn," the old man said, and staggered off with the bottle.

Josh had passed the point where he could differentiate between the sliding surface of the river and the slippery facets of his mind. Anesthetized, he waded through conjured horrors. He was twelve and alone in the dark on a long dirt road. Behind him, a coal breaker four stories tall loomed against the night sky. He heard quick footsteps on the dirt and thrashing in the undergrowth. They were coming for him. He knew he was going to die on the breaker with the coal dust in his eyes and throat, suffocating him. Stone flew in his face, tearing at his flesh. *Where was Sam?*

Josh screamed, a lonely desperate howl, "Sam! Sam! Where are you, Sam?"

From the dark bank close to the water, a fisherman shouted, "Quiet, asshole, you'll scare the fish."

Josh tried to stand. He managed to get to one knee, then slipped and fell hard against the rocks. He felt moisture on his face. Something was in his eyes. Blood. He moaned as the pain rattled around in him. "Sam," he screamed, "why did you desert me? Why did Emma take you away?"

"Shut up!"

"Sam's my brother," he whined, "and she took him away."

Josh stared through blood-smeared eyes at the rocks of the break wall, but saw the tangled black beams of the breaker. He felt it shudder beneath him as he frantically began to climb. He slipped, cutting his hands and skinning his knees, but the new abrasions were lost on his muddled mind.

The sound of his suffering faded as he lay exhausted on the top of the wall.

Below, near the water, someone breathed, "He's gone."

"Good riddance," another said. "Hey, I think I got a bite."

The subtle sounds of water lapping the shore and fishermen moving on loose detritus were interrupted by the coughing of an engine. The engine coughed again, then started.

"Earl, hear that? Sounds like your truck." Tires crunching on gravel sounded along the top of the wall, then faded as they rolled onto the roadway.

"Jesus, the bastard took your truck!"

"Son-of-a-bitch," Earl kicked a bait bucket.

Josh drove the truck unconsciously, lost in tortured thought. Sam had to keep him off the breaker. Emma couldn't keep him from that. *Didn't the bitch know he'd die up there?* She must know that. He'd teach her, he'd teach her that.

The weaving truck careened off a parked car with a shriek of torn fenders.

"Yes, scream. Scream you bitch. I'll make you scream."

"I've got to go, someone's at the door." Sue placed the phone back, on the hook. She'd have to call him back.

"I want a drink of water."

Surprised by the soft request, Sue looked at Mary standing in the hall doorway. Mary swung her clown Bobo by his red nose as she moved into the room.

"Mary," Sue admonished, "you're supposed to be sleeping."

There was another knock on the door, louder this time.

Sue looked at the door, then at Mary.

"I want a drink of water."

"Just one minute. Someone's at the door." Sue straightened her blouse and tugged at her skirt. Patting her hair, she checked her reflection in a wall mirror as she crossed the living room carpet to open the door.

Josh lurched into the room and collapsed on the carpet.

Mary cried out. Sue gasped and scrambled away from the dirty bleeding man struggling to his feet. Sue's breath caught in her throat, her eyes were wide, frightened.

Mary's rising scream tore around the room and caused a chill to vibrate up Sue's spine.

Josh managed to get disjointedly to his feet. He swayed a moment, then shuffled across the room and slapped Mary, knocking her to the floor. "Shut up, Emma, shut up."

Frightened and confused, Sue looked at the horrible man in wet torn clothes and said, "She's not Emma."

Josh, staggered unsteadily, turned and looked at Sue, now cringing behind a couch. Her face was flushed and she was fighting tears. Sue shrunk from his piercing gaze.

His face twisted in an evil smirk as his bloody hands took her.

Sue howled and jerked spasmodically as Josh tore her dress away. As his hands moved over her and his fingers probed, she scratched and spat, punched his horrific face and, finally, in her last effort at defiance, bit his ear as hard as she could.

In a corner, behind an end table, clutching Bobo, Mary closed her eyes tightly and sobbed, "Mommy."

CHAPTER 46

May 1939

Sam stared through the windshield at trees and parked cars as he flashed by them. He was driving, but his mind was fixed at home as he tried to will himself there. On the seat beside him, Emma sat, her face bleached of all color, a papier-mâché tragedy mask. It was painful knowing that, only minutes before, she'd been gaily floating across a dance floor. The phone call had ended that.

He was startled when she asked again, "What did the policeman say?"

He took a corner too fast and almost lost control. Sam clung to the wheel, his knuckles white. "Someone broke into the house. Mary's all right."

Sam could feel her studying his profile.

"Someone?" she asked with cutting sarcasm, then, "How's Sue?"

"He didn't say," Sam lied.

"Mary's okay, but he didn't mention Sue? I don't believe you."

Her words cut him. If he wasn't hurtling down a dark street, Sam would have hung his head. He'd never lied to her before. He turned a corner and saw the flashing red lights of a police cruiser in front of their house. Sam sucked air through pursed lips, and exhaling caught the bitter taste of bile.

Emma moaned, "What has he done?"

They slid to a halt, and before Sam could get out and around the car, Emma had started up the front stairs leaving behind a broken heel.

He leaped to catch her.

"Get your hands off me!"

Her words laid on him like a whip. He was thrown back breathing his hurt, "Em."

Emma's broken shoe beat an irregular tattoo up the stairs. She jerked the door wide open.

A uniformed policeman filled the foyer. "Whoa," he said, his arms wide, "who are you?"

Surprised by the challenge in her own home, Emma lost momentum and stuttered "Mrs. Freeman...the mother." Quickly regaining her composure, she asked, "What's happened? Where's my little girl? Where's Mary?"

The officer looked back over his shoulder seeking support. "Sergeant?"

A tall gray-haired man with a sad heavily jowled face appeared and stood behind the policeman. "Sergeant Barker," he said, pushing a crumpled gray hat back on his head, "thirty-third precinct...Mrs. Freeman?" He offered both hands, "Come in, your daughter is all right. Just frightened."

Emma was listening very closely. "Let me see her. Where is she?" She cast her glance everywhere; into corners and behind furniture, at the walls and floor. She saw a dark stain on the carpet. "My God," she pointed, "is that blood?"

The Sergeant hesitated, "...Yes, but not your daughter's."

"Maryyyy!" Emma wailed.

Her scream shook both officers. Sergeant Barker took her arm. "Mary is in her bedroom. She's all right, your neighbor's with her."

Through Emma's ordeal, Sam stood mute, needing to know everything, but afraid to ask. He was shaking, feeling sick, regretting the highballs, the heavy meal, and the wine. Sam steadied himself and asked, "How's Sue, the baby sitter?"

The Sergeant removed his hat and ran his knobby fingers through his hair. Sam saw that he was touched by the violence, by another incident, the down side of a policeman's lot, and was struggling to maintain a professional distance. He started to explain, as though disbelieving, "Your daughter is okay. She was struck, slapped I think...but she's okay."

Sam wanted to sit, but he was too nervous. His eyebrow was twitching, and there was the copper taste of blood in his throat. *Goddamn ulcer...not now.* He paced the room. "The girl, Sue?"

Sergeant Barker couldn't keep the disgust from his voice, "He hurt her, probably trying to rape her, but, I doubt there was penetration. I think he was too drunk. You can smell the alcohol vomit by the door." He paused and looked away. "He beat her though, beat her bad...must have been in a helluva rage. We've notified her parents, they're on the way to the hospital." He swivelled his head, stretching his neck, obviously attempting to ease the stress. "Christ, she's just a kid."

"My God, her parents! What can I say to them?"

The Sergeant looked at Sam standing in the center of the room, shoulders rounded, swaying, clenching and unclenching his fists. Observing him, intuitively, he guessed, "You know who did this."

"I've got to see my daughter." Sam started for Mary's room, moving heavily, burdened. He turned to the Sergeant, and, choking on the words, begging his understanding, he said, "It was my brother."

Mouth slack, the Sergeant watched him leave the room.

In the shallow light provided by a small lamp, he saw Emma sitting on the edge of the bed, surrounded by stuffed animals, cooing, rocking their daughter, trying in the timeless manner of all mothers to erase the trauma of the evening.

Sam placed his hand on her shoulder and felt her shrink away. He engaged his daughter's eyes, but they were empty, unseeing. He was frozen out. He was torn, weakened, by his failure as a husband and a father, a man. The two souls that he lived for were within arm's reach, but distant. Words were of no use.

Fingers tight on the back of his neck, Sam wondered, *Will she ever forgive me??* He turned, intending to leave the room.

Emma's voice, flat and funeral-cold, stopped him, "Remember your promise."

He walked away, knowing it was a promise he couldn't keep. She wanted Josh dead.

Sam needed to make a phone call; he had to find Josh. Painfully, he realized too late that Emma was right. Josh belonged in a cage.

In the living room, Sam went to the phone resting on an end table. As he reached for the black instrument, the Sergeant grasped his wrist.

"Who we calling, Mister Freeman?"

"My mother's house. They'll know where he is."

Sergeant Barker studied Sam for a long moment before releasing his grip. "Lieutenant Hull called. He said we should cut you some slack." he nodded, "Go ahead, make your call."

Sam's finger was stiff and cold on the dial.

"Hello?"

"Wilbur," Sam recognized the relaxed, unbound tone of his youngest brother's voice, "it's Sam."

"Oh. Hi, Sam, what's wrong?" Wilbur was a professional listener.

"Wilbur, is Mom there?"

"Not on Friday, there's church choir practice. She never misses."

"Is Alfred there?"

"No. He's out looking for Josh. Seems he took off at the bank. Ernie's here. What's wrong?"

"Put Ernie on." Sam waited, figuring Ernie might know something about Josh. Alfred might have told him something he would keep from Wilbur. It was their habit, protecting Wilbur.

"Sam?" It was Ernie's low steady voice.

Ernie, do you know what's going on with Alfred and Josh?"

With a visceral grunt that Sam took to mean 'I told you so', Ernie said, "Josh left Alfred standing at the bank. Just cashed his check and took off. Alfred's really pissed. He's out looking for him. You know where he is?"

Sam was in a quandary. What if he was wrong? What if the intruder wasn't Josh? What were the chances of that? None, he admitted to himself—it was Josh.

He could feel the Sergeant's presence, his interest in every word. "No, I don't know where he is, but," he sighed, "I know where he was." He pressed fingers to his temple, trying to subdue a growing headache. *How much should he say?* "Someone broke into my home tonight and assaulted Mary and the baby-sitter. It may have been Josh."

Silence, except for Ernie huffing like a bear. After a painful moment, he asked, "Is Mary okay?"

"She'll be all right, but," he hesitated, "he took advantage of the sitter."

"Took advantage? What does that mean?"

Sam felt the need to protect Ernie, and not prejudge Josh, "Sexually. He tried to take advantage of her sexually."

"You're talking about Sue?"

Sam was starting to sweat. His vision was starting to blur. He knew the early symptoms of migraine. "Ernie, did you hear what I said? You wait there. If Alfred comes in, have him wait. We've got to find Josh. And, Ernie, if Mom comes in before I get there, don't say anything."

"Sue's just a kid."

Sam could hear the anger mounting in his brother.

"He likes kids." Ernie hung up.

Sam stared at the telephone. The Sergeant was staring at him, unsure of the conversation just ended. "Do they know where he is?"

"No," Sam rubbed his eyes, "but we'll find him. He's got nowhere to go."

"You've got to turn him in." There was a compassionate understanding in the order. Sergeant Barker knew what he was asking; he'd asked it of families before. "Where will you look?"

"The bars. He'll be sloppy drunk in some gin mill." Sam turned his hands in a gesture of assumed certainty, "If he's really out of it, he might show up at home. Who knows?" Dejected, he started for the door.

"Sam."

He turned to face the Sergeant, expecting instructions.

Sergeant Barker crushed his fedora in his hands, "Sorry," he said.

Sam nodded, managing a sick smile, knowing he meant it. "Look after my wife. Tell her I'll be back."

CHAPTER 47

May 1939

Ernie roamed the room, a restless bear. Wilbur listened as he paced and talked to himself. Wilbur had a trained ear; he could pick five-letter Morse code groups off the short wave radio unerringly. Ernie was agitated and seemed confused, not making any sense. He kept repeating girl's names: Lisa, Mary, Sue. He paced, cracked his knuckles and mumbled. He was sweating, great blotches of perspiration spread on his shirt. Wilbur studied the great roving shadow that was his brother. He could barely discern the dark expanding spots as he sat and pondered the situation. It was useless to ask questions—Ernie only grumbled.

Wilbur heard a car pull to the curb in front of the house, and said, "I think Alfred's here."

Ernie ceased his pacing while they both listened to the thud of hurried footsteps on the porch. The door opened and Alfred, obviously exasperated, stomped into the room. He threw a rolled newspaper onto a chair, saw the questions on his brother's faces and said, "Damned if I know where he is."

Ernie studied Alfred, saw the turmoil in his eyes, and said, "Sam called, the price of poker has gone up."

Alfred dropped heavily onto a chair, and, looking at Ernie all in a sweat, asked, "What do you mean?"

Ernie dropped his hands with the weight of frustration, "Josh has violated more than his parole."

Alfred leaned forward, teeth clenched, anticipating the worst, "What has he done?"

"Josh, drunk as a Roman God, broke into Sam's place while he and Emma were out and assaulted the girls."

"Jesus Christ," Alfred said, expressing disbelief, "Are you sure?"

Ernie stared at him and asked, "Do you doubt it? Sam didn't say he was drunk, but this is beyond even Josh. He must have been."

Wilbur, his hands searching for a seat, asked, "How are the girls?"

Ernie shook his burly head, "Mary's all right. Sam was vague about the sitter, Sue." Alfred rested his head in his hands, "Is mom home? Has she heard any of this?"

"She's still at church."

Wilbur cocked his head. "I hear Sam now."

His brothers were standing when he burst into the room. Sam knew by their faces that Josh wasn't there. He asked, "Is mom home?"

Alfred said, "Not yet. You heard anything more?"

Sam's reply was cut off by the squeal of brakes and a resounding crash followed by dead silence. Exchanging glances, all but Wilbur headed for the door.

Sam said, "I think our search is over."

Sam, Alfred and Ernie pushed through the front entrance out onto the porch. They saw that a battered red pickup truck had smashed into Sam's parked Chevy, and that Josh had spilled out of it to lie on the pavement. Sam and Alfred ran to Josh sprawled in the street. Ernie watched from the porch as they helped him to his feet.

"I'm awright," Josh slurred as he attempted to pull from their grasp.

They looked at him, standing rubbery in the knees. Josh had his evening misadventures written all over him. His trousers were torn and wet from the knees down. There was a spot dark as ink around his crotch. Josh had pissed his pants. The smell of urine was barely discernible above the stench of vomit and alcohol. His shirt was fetid and had a bloodied sleeve.

"Christ," Alfred exclaimed his face twisted in disbelief, "the dumb bastard shit his pants."

Sam glanced at his parked car. Damage seemed to be limited to a crumpled rear fender. "C'mon, let's get off the street." Sam gave Josh a sudden strong vindictive jerk and, with Alfred's help, muscled Josh to the house.

"Hey, eeezy," Josh complained.

Alfred shuffled to keep pace. Ernie stepped aside knowing it was no time to get in Sam's way.

On the porch, Sam ordered, "Get your shoes off."

Josh fumbled with one hand as they supported him. He succeeded in throwing both shoes aside.

Ernie said, "You should drag him into the back yard and hose him down."

"Stand him on the throw rug."

Sam pulled Josh into the living room before releasing him.

Wilbur asked, "What's that stench?"

Josh stood on a braided throw rug, pinned by his brother's eyes. He looked first at Alfred, then turned to Sam. He shrugged his shoulders as if to ask, 'What did you expect?' He studied Ernie standing ominously by the door. "Wha, what? Can't a guy have a drink?" The question slithered off his lips.

Sam consciously restraining his urge to cause Josh severe knee-bending, bowel- emptying, teeth-shattering pain, hit him full in the face with his open hand. Josh dropped to the floor.

Alfred jumped back, startled by the brutality of Sam's action.

A foreign silence hung in the room. Wilbur asked, "What happened?"

Ernie told him, "Sam's explaining things," and watched, his hands balled into fists, as Josh rose slowly to his knees.

Josh sobbed, "What was that for? I didn't do nothin'."

"Where have you been?" Sam grabbed his collar and pulled him to his feet.

"Drinkin," Josh cried, "down by the river, drinkin'."

Sam had him by the shoulders, shaking him wildly. Spittle flew as Josh's head flopped side to side. "You didn't stop by my house?"

"Your house? Never been your house. Emma won't let me." His hand fell on Sam's chest. He was sobbing, "Why does she hate me?"

Sam asked him again, his voice like a razor, "Were you at my house tonight?"

Josh blubbered, his hands spread in a believe-me gesture. "No, honest, Sam, I didn't touch those girls."

Sam knew then, and his shoulders sagged. His sad eyes fixed on Josh. Sam didn't want to believe what he was witnessing.

From across the room, in the tone of an Inquisitor, Ernie probed, "I don't suppose you touched Lisa either?"

Puzzled, Sam looked at Alfred, "Lisa?"

Alfred seemed confused. He shrugged an I-don't-know.

There was a tidal change in Josh. His limp defenselessness drained away. A rigid defiance emerged as his natural arrogance returned. A lascivious sneer creased his face. He pointed at Ernie and laughed, "I suppose you mean, you thick shit, the preacher's daughter.?" He licked his lips deliberately, "Now, there was a tight piece."

Ernie felt the rage swell within him. He recalled the hurt in Lisa's eyes as her quavering voice revealed, "He laughed at me." His brother Josh mocking the end of innocence ignited Ernie's soul. He was launched uncontrollably at Josh by an implosion of long suppressed emotions. Yielding to the seething emotional vortex, Ernie sprang for Josh's throat.

Surprised, Sam jerked when Ernie leaped.

Frozen, Alfred gaped.

Wilbur listened without comprehension or reaction.

They all stood immobile as Ernie closed the distance between himself and Josh in a few quick steps. Ernie's massive hands and arms encircled Josh's head and shoulders. Efficiently as a hangman, he snapped Josh's neck.

A dislocated vertebra severed Josh's spinal cord, and he hung limp in Ernie's crushing embrace.

Stunned, Sam stared into Ernie's eyes. Sam moved solemnly, slowly, recognizing Ernie's trance-like state. Sam slipped his hands under Josh's arms. In a voice strained by the sudden turn of events he said, "Ernie, let go. Give him to me."

Ernie frowned. His viselike grip softened as he released Josh to Sam. His voice echoed strangely when he said, "Josh is gone now."

"Yes," Sam said, and took the full weight of his dead brother. Sam had never before felt so helpless, so powerless in the face of events. He suppressed an urge to cry out.

Ernie slumped to the couch and began to sob. Realization pierced him and he cried out, "God, what have I done?" He looked at Josh, slumped in Sam's grip. He twisted his thick fingers in anguish, and asked Alfred, "Didn't he deserve to die?"

Christ, things have turned from bad to worse, Sam thought, *from one brother in trouble, to one dead and another in worse trouble.* Overwhelmed, he asked, "What can we do?"

Alfred stood stiffly watching. Partly to himself, in an effort to soften the impact of the event, he said, "It was an accident."

Sam looked at Alfred. He understood Alfred's need to rationalize, to partly dispel the shock, and caught the idea. "Yes," he said, "an accident."

"He fell down the stairs."

They all turned to Wilbur, standing pale and slim, his face calm and certain. He said, "I heard him stumble and fall down the stairs. He cried out."

"Yes, that's it," Sam said, quickly thinking. "We'll need his shoes."

Wilbur said, "The cellar stairs."

Alfred stepped to Josh, bent and lifted his feet, now shod. They began to carry Josh, struggling with the dead weight, to the cellar doorway. With the door open, they stood Josh at the head of the stairs. Sam looked into Alfred's eyes and grimly tipped his head. They carried Josh down the stairs and placed him on the cold cement floor.

Sam swallowed, there was the taste of blood in his throat. Placing his hand gently on Alfred, he said, "Don't take it too hard, Josh fell a long time ago."

CHAPTER 48

May 1939

Lizzy, taking measured steps, moved through the small front foyer gripping her black handbag in both hands. Deep creases on her brow signaled confusion and concern. "What's happened?"

Sam was struck, somehow suddenly appreciating the change in her. *Was this the same woman who descended the creaking stairs that morning on the threshold of Wilbur's darkness?* Of course, it was. But, what changes the years and events had wrought. The robust embodiment of that dominant woman in his past had eroded. Now, she stood, smaller, grayer, confused, under a silly pillbox hat, a folded church bulletin in her trembling hand. Her eyes were troubled as she glanced about the room taking in the unusual circumstances. She blinked at the spinning blue ambulance light flashing redundantly through the room.

Sam's heart cried for her, for all the family, as he crossed the room to intercept her. He took her hand and led her to a chair.

He tried to gently break the news, "There's been an accident."

"Wilbur?" her voice cracked. She looked at Alfred and Ernie sitting on the edge of the couch.

"No, Mom," Sam bent closer and spoke gently in her ear, his hand brushing her hair, "it's Josh."

"Josh? In the power plant?"

"No," he placed his hand on her shoulder, "here." He looked to his brothers, afraid his voice would betray them. He said, "Josh fell down the cellar stairs."

She frowned. "He fell?"

"Yes, Mom," Sam studied her puzzled expression, and added, "he'd been drinking."

Lizzy shook her head. "He's not supposed to drink; he knows that!" Squinting against the disconcerting blue light, she asked, "How bad is he hurt?"

Sam took a deep breath and dropped to one knee. He took both of his mother's hands in his, and said, as easily as he could, "Mom, Josh is dead."

The blood drained from her face, her hands trembled, "Dead?"

Sam felt her stiffen, stifling a cry. Her English toughness emerged. Staunchly, she proclaimed, "He never listened to me, never. I asked him not to drink. He became a different person when he drank. But, he never listened."

Alfred watched, listening in silence. Sam glanced at Ernie, sitting quietly, his eyes closed. Sam wondered if he was praying.

A tall figure appeared in the hallway. It was Lieutenant Hull, in civilian clothes, accompanied by a uniformed officer.

Sam looked up; a spider of dread skittered across his mind, "Lieutenant?"

The Lieutenant pushed a folded sheet of paper into his inner suit coat pocket and beckoned to Sam.

Lizzy grabbed Sam's sleeve. Concerned, she asked, "Police?"

"Procedure, Mom," Sam assured her, and crossed the room to the Lieutenant.

Lieutenant Hull took Sam by an elbow and steered him down the hallway away from his mother and brothers. He screwed the top on a silver fountain pen and clipped it in his shirt pocket. Tilting his head toward the cellar door, he said, "The Medical Examiner is finished." He looked at Alfred, Ernie and their mother seated apprehensively in the front room, then back to Sam. "It's officially an accident."

Nodding his understanding and relief, Sam prayed silently, *Thank You.*

The Policeman pinned Sam with his cobalt blue eyes. "Nasty fall," he said.

Without a blink, Sam agreed, "Yes, nasty."

Sam was in a funk, feeling disassociated, living the wrong life, existing in a different time and place. Spending the greater portion of his waking hours embroiled in punishing efforts that demanded everything of him, he'd slipped out of his self, lost sight of what was important. He had become a slave to the tasks at work and, partially because of Josh, allowed his own life and loves to be subordinated.

He needed to regain his sense of self; he needed Emma and Mary back. He felt he had a good shot at it if Emma could forgive him the latitude he'd allowed Josh, and the pain he'd caused.

Should he tell her the truth?

When he returned to her, Emma was sitting wrapped in a heavy knitted sweater beside Mary asleep in bed. He'd been gone for hours, had tried fruitlessly to call. She appeared catatonic after sitting cold and afraid all that time. Sam stood in the doorway, emotionally exhausted, limp after the evening's bizarre trials. Afraid he might say the wrong thing, he hesitated to speak and bare his emotions. The moment was so tenuous, the stakes so high, that he shuddered and turned to leave.

"What if he comes back?" she asked, her fear palpable.

Quivering, stung by the hurt Josh had caused, Sam turned. "He's not coming back, ever." And he said the words, still strange to him, "Josh is dead."

He saw that she was dubious as she studied him.

Sam sighed and knelt beside her to relate the fabrication. "Josh was drunk when he showed up at Mom's house. Raving…we tried to grab him. He ran from us into the hallway to the kitchen. The door to the cellar was open halfway and

Josh ran into it. He fell backwards down the stairs and broke his neck. Josh was dead when we got to him. It was an accident."

Her hooded eyes searched his face.

Sam pleaded silently, as her eyes moved on him, *Believe me, please believe me.*

Weather through the days of mourning and the funeral was more suited to a wedding. The only clouds were mere wisps high in a pale blue sky. The only breeze, just enough to keep the warm late spring air moving, and black dresses and veils stirring.

Inside the funeral parlor, on the soft carpet, under the muted light, breathing the stale musty air, wandering amongst the spirits of the long dead, suffering the hours and condolences, the family drew together. The first day Josh was shown, Sam and Emma were the first to arrive. Both in somber black, they were escorted to the assigned room by an assistant in an ill-fitting suit. They stood hand-in-hand looking into the open casket. On his back, eyes closed in his powdered face, Josh lay dead, unaware of the heavy velour draperies, floral wall paper, empty chairs lining the walls, or Emma and Sam.

Sam prayed that Josh's soul, so disturbed in life, be at peace. Emma pressed Sam's hand and leaned consolingly against him. Hearing Alfred's voice, Sam turned to see him with his mother and Ernie moving slowly into the room. As they approached, Emma left Sam's side. After briefly embracing Lizzy, and pecking Alfred on the cheek, she took Ernie's hand and whispered, "Thank you."

Sam stood wondering, his hands steepled under his chin. An observer would think he was praying, but he was asking himself, *Why, thank you? Does she know?*

Lizzy moved to Sam, a hint of consternation on her brow. She asked, "Why is Emma thanking Ernest?"

Sam placed his hand protectively on her's. "For the flowers, Mom," he said, and embraced her.

Time is elastic, some days pass quickly to be forgotten, others drag interminably, unpleasantly, seemingly without end as did those at the mortuary. That first day particularly, Sam itched as the minutes dried his senses. He hovered near Emma, needing to know what she knew, to know how she felt. He was beginning to feel, as the hours oozed by, that he would never, ever, have her alone, never know where he stood.

But, all days end and night falls.

Sam rolled under a crisp cool sheet to face Emma in the bedroom's half-light. He placed his hand on her bare arm. He had to ask. "How did you know?"

When she turned to him, he saw she'd been crying. Emma's eyes were red and her face slightly puffed.

"You've been crying."

"Yes, for Ernie. For all of us. Life is hard for the evil and the innocent."

Sam repeated his question. "How did you know?"

She wiped her eyes. "Ernie told me. He wanted me to know because Josh hurt Mary. And he told me about Lisa, how the thought of Josh with her smoldered in him. I think telling me eased the pain, and guilt he feels.

Sam's head shook slightly. He exhaled an "I'm sorry," a weak, "I couldn't..."

"It's all right," her palm covered his cheek, "Very noble of you, protecting Ernie...my noble knight." Emma kissed him.

"I'm afraid my armor has lost some of its' luster."

"Nonsense."

Sam read that psychologists think we cling more desperately to each other, the intensity of the sex act is heightened, orgasms more numerous and stronger when there's been a death in the immediate family. They believe it has something to do with our ignorance regarding life's end, the great mystery, our own historicity, and the sharp reminder that we are mortal.

Since that night coiled in Emma's arms, Sam believed them right.

Despite how Hollywood portrays them, it doesn't always rain at funerals. The morning was bright and dry, the tarp covering the mound of dirt at graveside superfluous. It was a dry event, no water, no mud, no moisture at all, except for the tears. Everyone was in black dress, purchased for the occasion. Sam knew that if Josh was alive, vertical and conscious, he would be amused, tickled by their conformity.

Inside the casket, a clay-Josh lay silent.

Sam watched as the wide woven web belts inched over the rollers and the coffin lowered. It suddenly came to him—what he worked for had been realized. At last, the family was secure at home, if home is where secrets and kin are buried.

Edgar Hulse

ABOUT THE AUTHOR

Edgar Hulse came screaming into this world during the Great Depression. In Throop, a mining town set precariously atop the idle anthracite field just north of Scranton, Pennsylvania, he was another mouth to feed.

Over subsequent decades, serving in the Marines, graduating from the University of Buffalo, and raising a family, there grew an appreciation of his parents' struggle.

A desire to tell their story gave rise to the turbulent settings and indelible characters found in his earthy novel, *Brother's Keeper*.

Printed in the United States
4071